Praise

The Wattle

'Written with warmth, humour and sincerity, offering appealing characters and an engaging story, *The Wattle Seed Inn* is a lovely read, sure to satisfy fans of the genre.' **Book'd Out**

'Léonie Kelsall makes a welcome return that offers plenty of happiness, fun and heartbreak . . . With a wonderful message about letting go, seizing the day and embracing all experiences on offer, *The Wattle Seed Inn* is an encouraging read I highly recommend.' **Mrs B's Book Reviews**

'Heart-warming.' *Family Circle*

'Endearing and full of possibilities.' *Country Style*

'[*The Wattle Seed Inn*] is a meditation on the city/country divide, as well as a salutary tale about the importance of finding community. It's also a rollicking good read.' *Australian Country*

Praise for
The Farm at Peppertree Crossing

'Kelsall is a bold and fearless writer who is unafraid of presenting her readership with a plethora of darker style themes . . . authentic, insightful and sensitive in the right places.' **Mrs B's Book Reviews**

'Léonie Kelsall's skilful portrayal of life on the land and the people who live it comes alive. An absolute gem of a book!' **Blue Wolf Reviews**

'. . . moves from foreboding, funny, breath-holding, sad and sweet. I loved the way Kelsall unwrapped the secrets slowly throughout the story—little teasers that kept me glued to the pages.' **The Burgeoning Bookshelf Blogspot**

'It's a mark of Kelsall's unique storytelling ability that she is able to combine both the dark and light elements of this story to create something so appealing.' **Jackie Smith Writes**

'A fantastic tale with relatable and loveable characters.' **Happy Valley BooksRead**

' . . . told with plenty of heart and humour . . . a charming book full of strong, unforgettable characters you'll fall in love with.' *Glam Adelaide Magazine*

'A thoroughly delightful read that had me thinking of the characters long after I'd finished the book.' **Claudine Tinellis,** *Talking Aussie Books*

Raised initially in a tiny, no-horse town on South Australia's Fleurieu coast, then in the slightly more populated wheat and sheep farming land at Pallamana, Léonie is a country girl through and through. Growing up without a television, she developed a love of reading before she reached primary school, swiftly followed by a desire to write. Pity the poor teachers who received chapters of creative writing instead of a single page!

Léonie entertained a brief fantasy of moving to the big city (well, Adelaide), but within months the lure of the open spaces and big sky country summoned her home. Now she splits her time between the stark, arid beauty of the family farm at Pallamana and her home and counselling practice in the lush Adelaide Hills.

Catch up with her on Facebook, Instagram or at www.leoniekelsall.com.

ALSO BY LÉONIE KELSALL

The Farm at Peppertree Crossing
The Wattle Seed Inn

LÉONIE
KELSALL

The River Gum Cottage

ALLEN&UNWIN
SYDNEY·MELBOURNE·AUCKLAND·LONDON

First published in 2022

Allen & Unwin
83 Alexander Street
Crows Nest NSW 2065
Australia
Phone: (61 2) 8425 0100
Email: info@allenandunwin.com
Web: www.allenandunwin.com

 A catalogue record for this book is available from the National Library of Australia

ISBN 978 1 76106 608 5

Set in 12.4/18.2 pt Sabon LT Pro by Bookhouse, Sydney
Printed in Australia by McPherson's Printing Group

10 9 8 7 6 5 4 3 2 1

The paper in this book is FSC® certified. FSC® promotes environmentally responsible, socially beneficial and economically viable management of the world's forests.

*Taylor—thanks for allowing me occasional
full use of our shared brain so I could finish this one.
Back to you now. But you're on a time limit. x*

1

Lucie

Sometimes, she wished him dead.

It usually only happened in those hazy, sleep-drugged moments between dragging herself from her dreams and the start of her day, though. Once she was awake, her emotions were generally more rational.

But awake or asleep, there was no arguing that if he was dead, she would hurt less.

Lucie squeezed the crystal pendant strung on a leather thong around her neck. The quartz—for destroying negative energy while storing positive intentions—would need cleansing next full moon: it got a pretty hard workout whenever she thought of her father.

She eased out of the back door of the two-storey townhouse, letting it close quietly behind her so as not to wake the sleeping household. The tiny courtyard was bathed in a peachy ruddiness she told herself was sunrise, though she knew it was more an ambient glow from the Melbourne city lights.

As the ivy swallowing the garage rustled, she flinched, then hissed, 'Scat, cat.' Her neighbour defended, with a wooden spoon, a lot of gesticulating and what were very probably Italian curses, the black tom's right to roam the entire suburb, so Lucie kept the four-year war strictly between her and the cat.

The tom shot straight up the smooth bark of the magnolia and sat on a naked branch, glaring balefully down, his tail swishing.

'Don't jump onto the road, stupid,' Lucie muttered, moving away so the cat wouldn't dash onto the street. She drifted her hand across the potted lavender to release the early morning scent. Nearby, the fruit on the mandarin tree glowed like Chinese lanterns, so small that, with a bit of a stretch, she could fit three in one hand. Which meant the tree would yield only six handfuls of citrus-flavoured nostalgia, Lucie decided with a quick count. She couldn't expect a three-year-old potted tree to do much better, even though she moved it around the courtyard with the rickety trolley purchased online, finding shelter from the worst of the frosts. Not that Melbourne frosts were anything compared to those back home on the farm nestled in the Adelaide Hills. There, the birdbath tucked beneath the skeletal winter fingers of the cherry tree along-side Dad's favourite mandarin regularly froze over until after midday.

Lucie hesitated. Would visiting this memory be a pathway to old hurts? Tentatively, she allowed the images to trickle in: her breath steaming the air through mitten-wrapped hands as Mum lifted her up to check whether the slivers of pale, buttercream sun threading through the branches had melted the ice in the stone bowl, releasing the flowers and fruit they had arranged in it the night before.

The reminiscence was sweet, safe. Yet, like pressing on a bruise, she couldn't control the urge to push further, to rummage around in memory until she made herself hurt. She found a wound instantly: her feet sliding back and forth in wellington boots and her hand in his, skipping beside Dad as he strode across the dirt yard surrounding the neat double-brick house. Beyond the corrugated iron sheds, row upon row of identical mounds stretched across hectares of paddock. As they reached the nearest furrow, Dad thrust strong fingers into the dark loam, checking whether the soil was warm enough to nurture his precious strawberry seedlings. Then, his work-roughened hands cupped around hers, they would bed a tiny, three-leaved plant in the mound of crumbly earth, chanting a silly rhyme Dad had made up.

Snug tight little plant.
God the rain and light will grant.
Sun will shine, you'll grow fine,
And one day you'll be mine.

Tucking the plant in a nest of hay, they moved thirty centimetres along the row that stretched up a rolling hill to a horizon hazed with the shadowy giants of silver gums. Dad's hands guiding her, they eased the next plant into place. Sang the song. Then onto the next. And the next. Countless hours spent together in the ice-tipped sunshine, working the rows until an entire field of small, lime-coloured leaves waved in the chill breeze.

The memory itself didn't hurt: the pain lay in the contrast to the betrayal that came later. Though they had grown apart, Lucie had never expected her father to turn his back on her.

She dug a thumb into one of the tiny mandarins, then smoothly shucked the fruit. She crushed the fragrant, dimpled peel and inhaled deeply. The tangy scent wasn't the only reason for the film of tears that blurred her view of the courtyard: even after more than four years, home-sickness snuck up on her sometimes. Rural South Australia and suburban Melbourne had few similarities, but shared fragrances often evoked her unwanted memories.

The crescent moon of fruit puckered her lips as it exploded in her mouth. She grimaced, swallowed the excess saliva, and then squashed another segment against her teeth. There was a perverse pleasure to be found in mixing the sour juice with the false sweetness of her childhood memories.

She tossed the peel into the terracotta pots of oregano, basil and chocolate mint—which never tasted any different to regular mint, but she lived in hope—near the back door. The smell of citrus was supposed to keep the cat from spraying the herbs. Feline pee wasn't the kind of organic she coveted, and it would be nice to use her produce without imagining a hint of ammonia in everything she plated.

An egg-shaped patio chair swung from a bracket on the wall, the wicker spangled with dew crystals suspended on delicate webs. She edged onto the seat, careful not to destroy the spider's work. From here her tiny garden seemed a little larger, her boundaries less constrained. The watery sun peeking between the magnolia branches held a promise of the summer still months distant, although Melbourne never seemed to match the unrelenting dry heat of Adelaide. At Blue Flag Strawberries, in the hills to the east of the city, spring sunshine would herald an early ripening of the berries, along with the anticipation of an extended cropping season.

Lucie gave a sharp grunt, annoyed with herself for letting her mind wander there again. Even after all these years, she related every quirk of the weather to what would be happening on the farm. She piled the three mandarins in her lap and reached into the pocket of her dressing-gown. The powder-blue velour hung in a loose flap where the stitching had torn free. She had been using the same robe for more than a decade, addicted to the soft, slightly threadbare reassurance of the well-washed material. A few years back there had even been a stage when she had practically lived in it, adding trackpants and a long-sleeved t-shirt in the depths of winter. The oversized pockets were always stuffed with her life and had, over time, housed everything from uni textbooks and late-night study snacks to baby bottles and tiny, powder-fragranced nappies.

She flinched as her fingertips brushed crumbs hiding along the lower seam, before locating an envelope. She pulled it out, scanning the familiar handwriting. No return address. That always hit her hard, as though the deliberate omission somehow voided not only the letter's right to return but her own.

The letter would be nothing but a dry recount of local events, a journal of minor happenings in her hometown over the past month. The fact that the lifeless depiction came from someone who professed to have a love of the written word made it seem more of a betrayal, as though Mum was determined to make home less inviting. The charitable part of Lucie wanted to think this was a deliberate strategy so she wouldn't miss Chesterton so much.

The realistic part of her had other explanations.

Lucie flicked her thumb and forefinger against the envelope, punishing its existence. Collecting the mail from the doormat was one of Keeley's favourite jobs, but the almost four-year-old hadn't mentioned the arrival of the letter yesterday. Lucie had found it this morning among the sneakers and dirty socks in the entry hall when she came down to make her first cup of tea of the day. Saturday morning tea was a ritual. With a long commute to the office, weekdays were too rushed to relax and enjoy the steaming vapours from the herbs she had dried the previous year. She always brewed the tea as soon as she woke, leaving it to steep on the kitchen bench while she took a few precious moments to centre herself in her small garden.

The roller door on the neighbour's garage, which shared a rendered-cement wall with her garden, rattled and laboriously ground open. Seconds later, Mrs A revved the life out of her old Volvo. The ghost departed in a cloud of blue smoke that drifted across the courtyard, and Lucie waved aside the burning oil, returning her attention to the envelope.

As always, it was postmarked from Settlers Bridge. Mum chose to bypass a half-dozen villages, most with their own postal agency, to drive more than forty kilometres to send her mail from a town so tiny that the post office doubled as a general store, tripled as a lottery outlet and quadrupled as a dry-cleaning agency. Lucie suspected only letters to her were dispatched from Settlers Bridge. No one there knew Mum: they wouldn't ask where Lucie was or what she was doing these days.

She had only been to Settlers Bridge a handful of times—for the district agricultural show held in a paddock on the outskirts—and could barely remember the place beyond the smell of fried donuts, battered hot dogs, fairy floss and overheating grease from the labouring fairground rides. She would have forgotten the riverside town entirely except that Jeremy had said he had lived there for a while. She remembered everything he had ever told her: of course, she'd had more than four years to relive each of their conversations, dissecting what was said . . . and what had been left unsaid.

As always, she pushed thoughts of him from her mind. It was enough to have lost Dad; she didn't need to dwell on Jeremy.

Noise blared from inside the townhouse, scaring a tiny grey fantail from the potted echinacea she was coaxing along so she could harvest it before next winter's colds and sniffles set in. Lucie groaned at the inevitability of her weekend. It was time for the battle over the Saturday morning cartoon volume and, as always, there would be only one acceptable solution according to Keeley: pancakes traded for volume moderation.

No matter how light and fluffy, pancakes left a bitter taste in Lucie's mouth—because they should be served with strawberries and vanilla-bean cream.

But she hadn't touched a strawberry in years.

The last vestige of morning tranquillity vanquished, Lucie heaved a sigh and slit the envelope with her thumbnail. She slowly stood up from the swinging chair, skimming the words that marched across the page with a decisive, spiky abruptness.

The paper trembled from her suddenly numb fingers. Drifted to the ground like a leaf, the grace at odds with the panicked hammering of her heart.

All oxygen abruptly sucked from the air, the blood thundered in her ears.

Her legs gave out.

Her lips moved wordlessly. *No.*

Frozen fingers inching back towards the letter, she crept up on the news, rather than confronting it.

Her mother's impersonal writing wavered before her eyes. Disjointed sentences with large areas blacked out, although

Lucie couldn't tell whether that was in her head or on the page: . . . *heart failure . . . instantly fatal . . . funeral . . .*

No. No one sent this kind of news in a letter.

Mum was lying.

Had to be.

Because Lucie wasn't one of those girls who fled the farm, vowing never to return once she'd had a taste of city living. No, Lucie had always promised herself she would go back.

One day.

As soon as Dad forgave her.

2
Jack

'Hey, Tay. Your uni friend not around anymore?' Jack asked, leaning across Taylor to grab his helmet from the kitchen bench. His cousin had done a heck of a job whipping the hundred-and-fifty-year-old farmhouse into shape, seamlessly blending mod cons with the stone-walled cottage. Sleek steel appliances and polished-granite benches somehow fit perfectly with the original small-paned window above the sink and the aged floorboards. Instead of recipe books, the open shelves above the microwave were packed with Taylor's medical tomes, and Luke's *AgJournal* and *Ingrain* magazines teetered in a high pile on one end of the comfortably cluttered counter. Taylor would be the first to admit she didn't need the kitchen space for baking.

Taylor glanced up from the cream and jam-stuffed cake she was hacking into wedges. 'You keep your eyes to yourself, Jack Schenscher. Her partner flew back from the mines yesterday, so she headed home. In any case, she's not technically a uni friend—I was med, she was law. Just a pal from back in the day.'

Jack shrugged, trying to seem nonchalant. 'P-p-potatoes, pohtartoes.' His shoulders tensed in habitual anticipation of the blow that would fail to correct his stutter. 'Anyway, I tuned out as soon as you said *partner*. Though you can't blame a guy for looking: you've no idea what it's like to spot a girl around here that I didn't know in high school.'

'More like one who you didn't *do* in high school, from what I hear,' Taylor smirked, licking the finger she'd swiped along the side of the knife blade.

'Hey, fair go,' he protested. 'I'm related to most of them.'

'Mm-hmm.' Taylor lifted one eyebrow. 'Thought I heard the sound of banjos in the distance.'

'Harsh,' Luke said, shaking an empty Cheezels box as he wandered into the room. He dropped the box onto the counter and rooted through the bag of groceries spilling across the table. 'But true enough. There's a distinct lack of fresh blood in this area. That's why I picked me a city gal,' he drawled, laying on an American twang. 'Don't got me no taste for string music.' He pulled open a bag of corn chips, offering them to Taylor, then Jack. 'Anyway, who are we gossiping about like we're at a Cranky Women's Association get-together?'

'Death wish, cuz,' Jack warned.

'Slip of the tongue. I meant Chicks With Attitude, obviously,' Luke grinned.

Taylor butted him with her hip, though the shove failed to move her husband an inch. 'Nice save, except that was from a decade ago. We're Chicks With Agency now. You guys like to rag on the CWA for being a bunch of gossipy cooks—and I'm not going to pretend we don't have a good old yak—but there's a lot more to it than that. You can thank the CWA for seatbelt laws, flashing school lights and free mobile breast-screening units. Maybe instead of teaching food tech, schools should be empowering students by showing them that it's possible to bake the best scones *and* change the world.'

'Take it easy there, hon. Let's not completely abolish the cooking lessons,' Luke said, then yelped as Taylor flicked him with a tea towel.

Jack chuckled. 'I was chasing down intel on Tay's friend,' he said, hoping to spark a bit of bro-based sympathy in his cousin. Short of *Farmer Wants a Wife* coming to town to shoot a season, there was a fair chance half the local guys were going into the next decade still solo. 'She's the first new girl I've seen round here since Roni turned up.' He tilted his head towards the lounge room, where laughter from a handful of their friends drowned out the dying moments of the footy on TV. As usual, Taylor had mother-henned them all together. Not because today's game was anything special but because she kept a close eye on the outliers— the guys who, isolated by hard work and the rural lifestyle, tended to shut down tighter than a diesel storage tank. He knew Taylor's initiative was partly because, as the local GP, she blamed herself for what had happened with Simon

Krueger a few years back. Not that anyone else did; they might not talk about the black dog much, but there weren't many locals who hadn't heard his growl.

With her trademark mix of nagging and professional insistence, every few weeks Taylor made them all get together for a couple of beers and a barbie. A yarn about stock, crops, the weather, the footy. Whatever. There were only so many conversations that could be had with your dog, and sometimes a guy just needed some semi-articulate company to not share his feelings with. Not that any of them ever got a chance to sit around dwelling: even in the down season there was equipment to fix, fencing to maintain, projects to start. And the paperwork. He hated the damn stuff. Numbers were not his thing.

'Speaking of Roni,' Taylor said. 'She made this sponge, so you'll be safe eating it.'

Jack shook his head. 'I'll take a raincheck. The pump at The Twenty is giving me grief, so I'd best go sort it out.'

'You've persuaded your partner on that new set-up?' Luke said.

'Nope. Can lead a horse to water, but that's about it.'

'What is it you want to do?' Taylor asked.

She had managed to smear cream across her cheek and Jack let his gaze wander the room, so he wouldn't laugh. 'I'm trying to talk Gus into putting the pump on solar.'

'You pump straight from the river?'

He waited for the fridge to stop beeping as Luke held the door open, checking out the contents. 'I wish. But The Twenty doesn't have a water licence.' With the coveted licences hard to come by, for years he'd been jonesing for a piece of the three-kilometre river flat nestled between fossil-studded, orangey-yellow sandstone buttresses. But until the nine-hectare property came on the market, it had been nothing more than a dream. Actually, if the block had ever officially made it to market, the organic dairy next door would have snapped it up. Luckily, he'd had an inside edge—plus a priceless introduction to his business partner, Gus. 'There's plenty of groundwater, thanks to the irrigators, so it's a matter of working out the best way to access that. A windmill would do the trick.'

Luke grabbed a juice, closed the fridge and kissed his wife's cheek, managing to make the cream disappear. 'Mate,' he turned back to Jack, 'we're millennials. The progressive generation. You do realise that tilting at windmills is like stepping back a hundred years?'

'And you're going to argue that's such a bad thing?' Taylor hiked an eyebrow at Luke.

'Never dare argue with you, babe.' Luke wrapped his arms around her waist from behind, but shot Jack a wink over her head.

'Tilting at windmills,' Jack snorted. 'Nice one. Didn't realise you were that educated.'

'Same school as you, cuz.'

'Global warming isn't an imagined adversary, though.' Jack said. 'Tay's right: what our great-grandparents had going was a hell of a lot more sustainable than the way we're running the place into the ground.'

'"Tay's right",' Luke mimicked with an eyeroll. 'Man, I thought you'd have my back. What happened to the days of bros and beers? Time was, we were all playing footy together, checking out the girls. Now you're a dreadlocked greenie, Matt's a vego—'

'And you're an old married man,' Jack said, running a hand through his hair. Although a bit on the long side, it wasn't in dreadlocks. And it was easier to tie his hair back with a strip of flat leather he always kept in his pocket than rely on Samantha finding time away from the cafe to chop it for him. Besides, his sister had screwed up a couple of years back, leaving him with a bowl cut that wouldn't have looked out of place in a nineties' boy band. He'd taken it back to a number one before leaving her place, not sure whether to laugh along with her or be pissed he'd have to wear a beanie for months.

He scrubbed at his chin, fingers tangling in his beard. It was probably time he hit that with the clippers, though. 'In any case, I don't recall you doing too much checking out of the girls.' He gestured towards Taylor. 'You guys have been together since forever. Next thing we know you'll be producing generation whatever-we're-up-to. Alpha?'

Luke and Taylor exchanged a glance, and Jack winced. People round here were all over each other's business— largely because they *were* family—and he should know well enough to stay out of it.

'Yeah, together forever.' Luke kissed Taylor's cheek before releasing her waist. 'You want a hand with that pump?' He jerked a thumb towards the doorway, where two nosy

15

chickens cheeped and ruffled their feathers on the hearth-stone, occasionally pecking at the screen.

'Thanks, but she'll be right. I need to duck home first and pick up the ute.'

'So much for your carbon neutral footprint, mate.'

Jack clowned copping a punch. 'The Holden's a dinosaur, so I reckon that makes her exempt from emissions ratings.'

'Time for an upgrade?' Luke asked.

'I wish. But not unless my returns are ten times the expected. She'll do the job for now. I need to haul some rabbit wire out there, keep the damn yabbies out of the filter.'

'Bring us back a feed, then. They're sure to be clean, coming from your place.'

Jack brushed off his cousin's compliment, as though the low chemical load he maintained on his land was incidental rather than a result of bloody hard work and reinvesting every cent he ever made. 'They'd be floating if they weren't clean, mate.'

'They can't cope with a toxin load?' Taylor asked. 'I guess they're the farmer's version of canaries in the mines.'

'Don't know about that,' Jack said. 'Never heard a yabby sing.'

Taylor chuckled but lifted her chin towards the helmet he dangled from one hand. 'You make sure you put that on. I saw you out in the paddock the other day without it.'

'Yes, doc,' he responded contritely, though he grinned at Luke. Like they ever wore their helmets on the farms. In any case, he'd limited himself to a couple of beers, knowing that not only did he have to hit the road early but there was always the risk that Taylor would make him take a breathalyser before he left. She'd done a few stints in emergency in the city and was pretty hot on safety. But it'd be fine; he had no intention of being roadkill.

3
Monica

1990

Monica grinned at the blue-inked *Mon 4 Mack 4 Ever* inside the front cover of her ringbinder. The doodle was juvenile, but her feelings for Mack were far beyond any crush. She added a heart around the inscription, then a flowing banner at the bottom, centring the year, *1990*, in the middle of the ribbon.

Beneath the desk, Karen nudged her leg with a Doc Marten and lifted her chin towards the front of the hall. Monica sighed. Pharmacology lectures were mind-numbing and she'd far rather think about last weekend's high— mostly legal, although they had passed a bong around the smoky interior of Mack's silver Celica—than the effects of the drugs she would be responsible for administering when she graduated in a few months' time. She leaned back in the hard seat, then wriggled so the padded shoulders of her denim jacket didn't bunch under her ears.

The lecturer's drone switched up a gear as the end of the class neared. Monica glanced at her Swatch, the sunshine yellow band a cheery note in the bleak room. Bubbles of excitement fizzed in her chest and tweaked her lips into a grin: in just a few hours she'd catch up with Mack over the road at the Botanic Hotel. They'd first met there only nine weeks ago, their conversation shouted over the band cranking out Simply Red and B-52s covers. By their second date, also at The Bot, the occasional almost-accidental brushes of their hands turned to kisses, and by the third the conversation became talk of their plans. Three weeks later, on their eighth date—conducted mostly in the rear seat of Mack's car—their hands were roaming and, perfectly naturally, the talk was of *forever*.

'Daydreaming?' Karen said as the study theatre filled with the noise of scraping chairs and hasty escapes. She tapped the heart doodled on Monica's open folder. 'Don't suppose there's a prize for guessing what about. Or should I say who. Like that pash rash isn't enough to give you away.'

Monica reflexively lifted a hand to her jaw, although she knew her foundation, a shade lighter than the pale skin she'd inherited from her mum, was thick enough to cover the two-day-old chafing from Mack's stubble—just like her carefully contoured blush would cover the heat that raced up her cheeks at Karen's knowing grin. 'Bite me,' she said.

'Looks like someone beat me to it,' Karen laughed as she slung her tote over her shoulder and fluffed her teased hair. Thanks to half a can of Aqua Net, it crunched rather than moved, but she had Meg Ryan's sexy bleach-blonde tousle down perfectly.

'Hilarious.' Despite her sarcastic tone, butterflies fluttered in Monica's stomach at the thought of just where Mack's lips had been.

'I've never known you to hang with one guy for so long,' Karen said as she headed towards the door. 'You want to watch out, you'll be talking wedding bells soon.'

Monica cringed, but other than the lecturer still fussing at his desk, they were the last to leave the room. 'More like blue balls,' she muttered.

Karen whipped around to stare at her. 'You're kidding me? *You're* holding out?'

'Ouch. It's not like I never do.'

'Really?' Karen made her eyes huge. 'Not the way I've heard it.'

'Shut up,' Monica laughed.

'Seriously,' Karen said, halting dramatically as the lecture room door shut behind them with a hollow bang, 'Mack's pretty damn hot. You're willing to risk pissing him off and being dumped?'

'Not risking. I'm playing him.' Monica sucked in a quick breath as they stepped out of the foyer and into the autumnal chill. On the night she'd first spotted Mack, things had changed. *She* had changed. It was as though her entire life had been leading up to that point, that meeting. Her decision to leave home, to study nursing, to go to the pub right then—every movement had been orchestrated by some higher being, their togetherness preordained. Call it hormones, call it fate, call it whatever the heck you wanted, but the electric tingle that started deep in the pit of her belly had her instantly and completely invested in winning his attention.

And once she'd got it, she wanted to keep it. 'If keeping him means chastity knees, as Nanna says, I can handle it.'

'Chastity knees?' Karen giggled. 'What the heck is that?'

'Not surprised you're unfamiliar with the term,' she replied with mock primness. 'You know, like a chastity belt, but no risk of rust. Just keep your knees together.'

'Your nan's a hoot. Sounds like it would make walking awkward.'

The naked branches of the plane trees hung heavy beneath a charcoal-smudged pewter sky, the rain gluing giant bronze leaves to the footpath, dinosaur footprints in a cement swamp.

'Actually, it's kind of fun seeing how long I can hold out and how hard he'll beg. I reckon chastity belts probably weren't ever really for the guy's sake. It's super hot wanting to say yes but knowing I can't.'

'Well, it's not that you *can't* ...'

'Can't if this is going to go the way I want it to.' Besides, the tease of Mack's lips and hands were a thousand times better than sex had ever been, and she almost didn't want to go to the next level in case it was an anticlimax. Although, with a ring on her finger and knowing Mack was hers forever, she'd be willing to tolerate a fair amount of minor disappointment. Not that she believed for one second that Mack would disappoint her in any way.

'Wait, the way you want it to? You mean you *are* holding out for a ring?'

'Give it a few months,' Monica said. While Mack was keen for them to get a place as soon as she qualified, she was determined: there would be an engagement before she gave up her cramped room in the Nurses Residential Wing.

'Are you shitting me? What happened to Europe?' Karen's words came out punchy as she held a folder above her head, jogging through the drizzle towards the Residential Wing behind the hospital.

'Never said I planned to do it solo.' Besides, her fantasies of travelling the world had been a way of escaping her small-town life in Brooks Siding, where Dad worked at the grain silo and Mum, the perfect frumpy country mouse, scheduled her day around having his lunch and dinner on the table either side of the afternoon rerun of *Neighbours*. Now Monica's dreams were of a husband in a business suit coming home to tiny, sweetly scented babies in a beauti-fully appointed townhouse.

As they blew into the entry hall of the residential building, she ran her fingers through her shoulder-length hair, which needed a wash and blow-dry before she headed out. Back-to-back perms had left her hair a little frizzy and dry on the ends so she'd been toying with the idea of a pixie cut, but then Karen had said that the brown wash she'd put through her natural blonde made her look like Jennifer Grey in *Dirty Dancing*. As Mack rocked Patrick Swayze's fringe-heavy mullet, that pretty much proved they were perfect for one another.

'And Mack's up for it?' Karen pursued.

'Oh, he's up for it, all right,' Monica giggled. 'But you mean for travelling? Sure. I mean, I'm sure he *will* be. I guess it depends on whether his dad will give him time off when he's only just started with the company.' The memory of Mack in a suit and tie—so different to the guys she'd known at school or college—quivered determination through her. She had waited her entire life for the one man who would be her everything, always.

4

Lucie

'Muuuum,' Keeley hollered from their shared bedroom. 'Dash needs to go wee.'

Lucie pressed her head to her knees, trying to take deep breaths despite the cramping of her lungs.

Dead.

He couldn't be.

'Mum-mum-mum,' Keeley yelled again, turning up the TV volume over her own voice. 'Dash *really* needs to go.'

The envelope trembled in Lucie's hand.

Dad was dead.

Only minutes earlier she'd decided that their estrangement would be easier if he was dead, if she didn't have to wonder why he'd abandoned her, why he hadn't been in touch for years. But now she wanted to yank back that thought, to tear any hint of it from the air, as though her momentary disloyalty had poisoned the atmosphere. Because she had been wrong: she didn't feel relief or release. Not even a sense of karmic retribution.

Lucie pushed to her feet and tramped across the courtyard towards the Moroccan blue door.

She gasped as Keeley barrelled into her, flinging chubby arms around her hips, head butting into the softness of Lucie's belly. 'He did it, Mummy, he weed. I told him to wait for you, but he weed.'

Lucie allowed herself one long-suffering sigh. 'Geoff isn't up yet?' For his own sake, he had better not be: it had been Geoff who had sided with Keeley and argued they needed a pet.

'No. He still sleep.'

'Guess we'd better take care of your little monster, then, huh?'

Trailing Keeley, the dachshund pup immediately sat, then curled his elongated body into a ridiculously small ball, hiding his snout in his paws, one toffee-coloured eye regarding Lucie reproachfully.

'Look,' Keeley announced importantly, pointing down the short, white-tiled hallway. 'Look, there where he done it.'

'Did it,' Lucie corrected automatically, reaching for the bottle of orange oil spray and recycled paper towels alongside the bowl of crystals on the hallstand. With a three-year-old and a dog, she kept clean-up supplies in almost every room.

She mopped up, patted the pup's head to let him know that she accepted liability for his accident, washed her hands and then set two bowls out on the narrow stainless-steel kitchen bench. The industrial look was part of what had attracted her to this house—that and the fact that the rent was within her budget. Though having Geoff and, more recently, Finlay move in had helped with her finances.

She couldn't summon the energy to insist Keeley ate homemade bircher muesli before her treat today. Besides, the pancakes would be buckwheat with organic maple syrup, kefir cream and organic whipped butter. Keeley had never tried the white-flour commercial variety, and Lucie disguised the heavy, gritty texture of the buckwheat by folding in a generous handful of overpriced blueberries she picked up at the market in the next suburb.

She cracked the eggs single-handed, then ran the white through her fingers into one bowl and dropped each yolk into the second bowl with a satisfying plop. If only she could separate the facets of her life with such precision. Instead, her memories were a scrambled mess of having been loved, secure in the certainty that she was the most precious thing in her father's life, and then of the slow death of that affection. As she grew, as willowy and vigorous as the nettles Dad weeded from between the rows of strawberries, his callused hands immune to the sting, so had Blue Flag Strawberries. Dad employed an army of labourers to work from low wheeled buggies, planting the runners into high mounds tightly covered with ugly, shiny black plastic instead of the rich earth her hands had known. And there were no more rhymes. His face grey instead of sun-kissed, lined with concerns rather than good humour, Dad was imprisoned behind his desk in the packing shed, his hand frequently straying to the whiskey bottle barely hidden in the musty-smelling top drawer.

Eventually, Lucie's memories of sunshine and strawberries seemed to belong to another life, and the bond that had been an integral part of her existence unravelled to become the most gossamer of threads.

'Morning.' Geoff yawned as he padded into the galley kitchen and flipped the kettle on before tugging open the fridge door to hunt for food.

Lucie shivered as delayed shock hit her. She had to stop thinking about it, thinking about Dad, thinking about what was lost and could now never be retrieved. Her chin wobbled. If Geoff noticed, she was going to lose it.

Juice carton halfway to his mouth, he stopped. 'Luce? What's up? You're as white as magnesite.'

She tried to chuckle at his simile; it was a habit he had picked up from her, using crystal colours for comparison. Instead, the noise caught in her throat, erupting as a little sob. Magnesite enhanced psychic abilities. Had she somehow known her father was dead? Was that why she felt particularly homesick today?

Geoff shoved the carton onto the counter and had his hands on her shoulders in half a heartbeat.

She closed her eyes for a second, taking comfort in his firm touch. She certainly had a type: eleven years older than her, Geoff had been a stabilising force since soon after she moved east. Heavily pregnant, Lucie had advertised for a housemate to share expenses. But she hadn't expected the bonus of creating an odd little family with someone whose calm personality contrasted so strongly with her own.

Geoff's gaze travelled towards the lounge room, and she knew he was checking on her daughter, followed quickly by Dash. She felt the tension in his hands ease as Keeley's laughter pealed through the house and Dash gave a yip of excitement. 'What is it, Luce?'

She pulled the envelope from her pocket. 'My dad . . .'

'Finally extended the olive branch?' She heard the smile in Geoff's voice. 'Get it? Greeks . . . olives?'

He knew that she and Dad hadn't been on speaking terms, but she rarely shared details. 'He . . .' She couldn't finish the half-formed sentence.

Geoff tugged the letter from the envelope she held towards him, skimming it. 'Holy shit,' he muttered. 'You didn't tell me your mum had called about this.'

Lucie bit her lips together for a moment as she sought control. 'She didn't. This is the first I've heard about . . .' She couldn't bring herself to say the words; they would underscore her emotions in heavy ink, give them an unbearable permanence.

Geoff waved the page. 'So it's some kind of bizarre joke?'

'My mother doesn't have a sense of humour.'

'Then your dad is . . .' Geoff seemed equally reluctant to accept the news. He drew his fingertips across his carefully stubbled jaw, then ran the hand over his shaved scalp. For breathless seconds, the rasp of bristles was the only sound in the room.

'Dead.' The word had a cold, hard finality, starker than she had anticipated. Lucie sucked in a sharp breath, as though she could recall the utterance, erase the sentence, retract the diagnosis.

Geoff stared at her. 'Luce, I'm sorry. I know that doesn't help, but I don't know what else to say.'

She wanted him to know the right words, the magic that would make the pain blossoming in her chest go away. 'I've screwed this up so bad, Geoff. It's too late, too bloody late.' The words tumbled frantically, as though the acknowledgment would somehow wind back time. She clutched her crystal pendant, a sudden, ridiculous notion that drawing blood might relieve the pain locking her fist so tight, her knuckles ached. 'What is wrong with me? Why am I incapable of maintaining a relationship?'

Geoff hiked an eyebrow and tapped a forefinger on his chest, but she ignored him.

'It's not *all* my fault, though,' she insisted. 'I mean, Dad has no idea how to communicate. He simply doesn't talk.' She used the wrong tense but wasn't about to change it. That would infer acceptance of her mother's message.

'Apple didn't fall far from that tree, then,' Geoff said dryly.

Instead of being irritated at his comment, Lucie seized on the commonality, the proof that she and her father were still connected in a way that could never be ripped apart by distance or deceit or death. 'Fair. But Dad takes it way beyond the strong, silent stereotype. The only conversations we've had for years were him pressuring me about uni. And they weren't even conversations, just him completely ignoring my interests and telling me what I had to study. Because everything always has to be about Blue Flag Strawberries.' She shook her head, trying to unwind exactly what had happened, how she and Dad had grown so far apart. 'I guess it was predictable I'd eventually rebel.'

'Jeremy was part of that rebellion?' Geoff suggested.

Lucie winced; considering her ex-lover as nothing but a childish mutiny diminished what they'd had. Or at least, what she had once believed they had. 'Maybe. That and cutting Dad out of my life. Keeping my own silence, I guess.' That sounded better than the truth, which was that she'd been sulking. Sulking because Dad ignored her passions, demanding she study business management.

But Jeremy had listened, encouraging her to pursue her dreams, to take an extra year to study natural therapy alongside the uni qualification Dad had insisted on. 'Keeping secrets from Dad felt like I was scoring one up on him. But then the secrets became too big to share, and now . . . now it's too late to go back.'

'I didn't think you had plans to go back.' Geoff sounded worried.

Lucie gave a snort, which bordered far too closely on a sob. 'You want the truth? I've always wanted to go back. I need to be somewhere I can grow fruit and veg for Keeley, where I'm not worrying about air pollution or being under a flight route, or the traffic. Melbourne feels like . . .' She waved a hand around, as though indicating the city beyond their walls. 'Beige. Numb. Like a halfway house. I'm just sitting here waiting for permission to go home.' She shook her head in disgust. 'Like a kid who needs releasing from time-out.'

'Permission from your dad?' Geoff set aside the letter and reached for the teapot.

'From Mum. Or an invitation from Dad.'

A frown creased Geoff's forehead. 'Why would you need permission—or an invitation—to go back home?'

She groaned, cupping both hands over her face. 'I know. It sounds ridiculous when I say it aloud. Hell, it's ridiculous when I even think it.' For the past four years she had glossed over the dysfunctionality of her family, hiding the dirty secrets behind vague lies about minor disagreements.

She took a deep breath. 'The thing is, when Mum found out I was pregnant, she was . . . I don't know, resigned, I guess. It was like she'd always expected me to screw up, and at least I was proving her right. I figured she was thrilled to have an excuse to moan to her pals about what a disappointment I am.' She couldn't bear to describe the brief minutes when, seduced by the novelty of her mother's apparent acceptance, she had briefly hoped that the unplanned pregnancy might thaw the permanent frost that existed between them.

'But the second I told her that Jeremy was the father, she lost it.' Lucie shivered as the echoes of her mother's inexplicable hysteria rippled through her. 'She was wild. Savage. Acted as though I'd somehow betrayed her. Then she packed me off here like some shamed fifties-era single mum.'

'Your dad didn't speak up then?' Geoff spooned leaves into the teapot, a calming mix of chamomile flowers, vervain, schisandra berries, skullcap and tulsi.

At any other time, Lucie might have teased him about how much he'd learned from her. 'When I say Mum packed me off, I mean literally,' she said bitterly. 'Next-day flights, suitcase, hotel booking. I didn't even speak with Dad.' Drinking late in the packing shed, he hadn't been around anyway. 'Mum said that she'd take care of telling him, because I'd break his heart.' Her hand trembled on the mixing bowl and a tear slid down her cheek, landing in the egg white. 'But his heart broke anyway, didn't it?' she whispered, sorrow overwhelming the anger she was trying to hold close. 'And now I've missed out on my chance to tell him anything. Ever.'

'Luce,' Geoff's arm wrapped around her shoulders, pulling her close, 'it's not your fault.'

She leaned into the safety of his embrace for only a moment before deliberately straightening her spine. She had learned from Dad that you put up and shut up. Occasionally you blew up. No matter what, wallowing in misery wasn't an option.

Although maybe hiding that misery in alcohol had become one for Dad.

'I made my choices and I'll own them.' Determination vibrated in her words. 'Besides, at least here, Keeley is safely away from *him*.' She busied herself opening the container that held the sack of buckwheat.

'From your dad?' Geoff asked, his brow furrowed.

'No. Her dad. Jeremy,' she said bitterly. The blade shrieked on the counter as she slammed the cleaver through a block of butter.

'Has he been in touch since you broke up?'

'"Broke up" is a pretty shit term for deserting me when I was two months pregnant.' It hurt to rehash the memories, but she could avoid thinking about Dad if she talked about Jeremy. Lucie could recall perfectly the first time she had seen the suave businessman, looking hugely out of place in the messy, makeshift office of Blue Flag Strawberries. The moment her fifteen-year-old self had decided she was in love with him. She had been thrilled when Dad announced— despite Mum's furious disagreement—that he had hired a marketing manager to take over some of the paperwork he loathed. Of course, it had taken years to get Jeremy to notice her.

And now, years to get over him.

'You're right, it is a shit term,' Geoff said mildly. 'Sorry. But once he'd had time to get his head around the fact that he has a child, didn't Jeremy change?'

'Gee, it must be nice to have time to get your head around something like that,' Lucie snapped. She whirled towards the fridge, searching in there for anger, because hot fury did a fine job of chasing away the chill of hurt and abandonment. 'And no, he's never bothered getting in touch. Once it was over, it was over, a clean break as far as he was concerned.' She flicked up her fingers, counting off his failures. 'Apparently, his love for me had an expiry date, he had zero interest in having a family, and the only partner he wanted was my dad.' Her heart clutched at the mention of Dad, but she tried to keep her focus, her anger, on Jeremy.

'When he said he loved you, it would have been the truth,' Geoff said calmly. 'But people change. Circumstances change.'

Lucie stiffened at his disloyalty. 'You're supposed to be my best friend—you don't get to come to his defence.'

'I'm not defending him, just trying to keep it real. It's okay to feel whatever you need to, but make sure you hold on to the facts.'

'You can stick your screwed-up platitudes, Geoff.' Lucie slammed a jug of milk kefir down so hard that sour-smelling whey splashed from it. She usually controlled her anger, but occasionally it boiled over. 'The fact is that what's right and what's wrong doesn't change, even when it becomes an inconvenient truth. Jeremy didn't only hurt me, he deserted his daughter. He didn't want to know her then, and I'll be damned if he'll ever get the chance now. He doesn't deserve her.' Arms wrapped around Keeley in bed at night, breathing in the sweet baby smell, Lucie would allow tears of pure fear at the thought of anything ever coming between them, of sharing custody, losing her daughter even for a moment.

Geoff nudged the cleaver away from the edge of the counter. 'It's been four years. You don't think maybe Jeremy's grown up, that he would take responsibility now?'

'At his age, there's not much room for growing up,' she snapped.

Geoff gave her an approving grin. 'Seems maybe your mum was right in suggesting you come here, then, Tumbleweed.'

Despite the nickname, which Geoff coined the first time she spelled out her surname, Tamberlani, for him, Lucie couldn't force a smile. A white cloud rose as she sifted organic flour with far more energy than the job required. 'Suggested. Insisted. It's a fine line with Mum.'

'At least you don't have to worry about running into Jeremy.'

'That wasn't why Mum sent me here.' Dumping the tear-contaminated egg whites into another dish, she wiped out the vintage pottery mixing bowl and cracked another egg. Normally she kept her own counsel, but the suspicion was a hard, festering knot inside her. 'Mum is manipulative. She engineered it so I'd be isolated here, in a position where I'd have to terminate the pregnancy. Or at least, that's what she hoped.'

'Jesus. Have you confronted her with that belief?'

'It's not a *belief*, Geoff. And my mother isn't the sort of person you confront. It's just not worth it. She has this knack of making you doubt your own experience.'

Geoff blew out a low whistle. 'Gaslighting? That's cold.'

Lucie rarely thought about it: Mum had always been the same. She and Dad had learned to tiptoe around her. 'After I'd been here a couple of weeks, I told her I'd decided to keep the baby. And she was furious. No. She was *bitter*, as though my choice was somehow calculated to hurt her. She said Dad couldn't deal with the shame of having his daughter knocked up by his business partner, and that he wouldn't forgive me.' She felt dirty repeating the words, although they were carved on her heart.

35

'But I never should have listened to her. Dad would have been disappointed in me, for sure, and perhaps that's part of the reason I didn't go home: I guess I wanted him to beg me to come back, so I wouldn't have to explain or apologise. Because I won't,' she added fiercely. 'I'll never be sorry for having Keeley. I mean, it's not like I was a kid. It's just that Jeremy wasn't the partner Dad would have chosen for me.' She gave a bark of derisive laughter. 'Or, more to the point, apparently I wasn't the partner Jeremy would choose for himself.'

'His loss,' Geoff said.

'No. My loss. Because if I'd been honest, if I had told Dad the truth straight up, maybe Jeremy would have been the one to leave. And I would have been there. For Dad.' She ended on a sob as the real reason for her distress hit home again.

'Ah, Tumbleweed,' Geoff murmured, one hand stroking her back. 'I'll book our flights.'

She knew she should tell Geoff it wasn't his problem, that he didn't need to come. But his calm was reassuring, and he was the only person she allowed herself to lean on. She nodded, reaching for paper towel to blow her nose.

'Mummy?' Keeley piped around the thumb in her mouth as she wandered into the kitchen. 'You sad at Dash?'

Lucie gave her nose a quick rub. 'No, not at Dash, baby. He's only a puppy. But I had some bad news today that's made me a little sad.'

A hell of a lot more than a little, but how did she explain death to a child who had never experienced it?

Never even met the person she was talking about.

Would never know that person.

Fresh tears fell and Lucie fisted her hands, determined to regain control. There was no forgiveness to be found by encouraging her daughter to feel sorrow; it was her fault Keeley would never know her grandfather. And, although she had no desire to capitulate to her mother's demand that Lucie now return, she refused to be the reason Keeley didn't know her grandmother.

It was time to go home.

5

Jack

Even though he wasn't suffering from overindulgence, the icy blast of fresh air cleared Jack's head before he reached his bike. Rainfall was always low in the rain shadow east of the Mount Lofty Ranges, but the past winter had been the worst for a while: cold enough to freeze the nipples on a chicken but dry as bones. If the rain held off, the harvest would be early—and that lack of rain was all the more reason for him to get the pump cleared out. Again. Gus's crop was not only ridiculously unsuited to the area but also heavily water dependent.

The short ride on rough dirt tracks blew away his annoyance. Reaching the bitumen road, he wound parallel to the river, through the twenty-acre blocks the government had provided for soldiers returning from the First World War. There had once been fifteen dairies along this stretch, yet now there was only one. Small blocks simply didn't produce enough income, which was why he also farmed Pops' acreage up on the dry land.

The River Gum Twenty, though—named for the massive redgums along the banks of the Murray and with a nod to the size of the block—this was his passion and his home.

Jack leaned the bike to one side, taking the turn onto gravel faster than Taylor would have liked to see. The track narrowed as it climbed a rocky ridge before wriggling down the other side and snaking across a reclaimed swamp flat. His property was the last on the dead-end track, sheltered by an outcrop of sandy limestone that had been hollowed by time into a small cave, creating a natural courtyard on the far side of the house.

Whistling under his breath, he kicked down the bike stand and pulled off his helmet. The lopsided chain-wire gate dragged against the ground and he grimaced. He really should look at straightening it up. Prossers' cows had shoved right through it a year or so ago with a single-minded bovine intentness on reaching some delicacy that grew in his backyard. At least they hadn't headed for the orchard.

Jack let himself in the unlocked back door, tossing the helmet on the window seat that ran half the length of the covered-in porch his sister insisted was called a boot room. Sally padded sleepily down the central hallway, her dusty-red tail wagging with a lethargy that spoke of her age rather than any lack of joy at seeing him. He should make her sleep outside like other farm dogs, but he could see in the way she struggled to her feet that the slightest chill made her arthritic joints ache. Ten years of sheep work meant she had earned the hessian sack plump with wool offcuts that lay in the morning sunlight streaming through the front bedroom window. Despite Taylor's teasing, Sally was the only female who had shared his bedroom for the last few years.

Jack broke stride to rub her head, tugging her ears as she sat at his feet. 'How's my best girl? Been guarding the house? Want to head out for a drive?'

The dog's ears pricked at the magic word, tongue lolling as her tail swept the bare boards more vigorously. He could see a trace of the puppy she had been before grey peppered her red muzzle.

One final pat and he headed into the kitchen, snagging his Akubra from the scratched sideboard. Papers cascaded to the floor. He scowled as he noticed a couple of unopened window-faced envelopes among the avalanche. He'd have to get onto that stuff. Soon as he had a moment to himself, that was.

Beating a hasty retreat, he dropped the hat onto his head as the screen door slammed behind him. Sally waddled ahead, her matronly rear swinging from side to side. At the back of the dusty ute, she paused and cocked her head, looking up at the tray with a slight whine. Her eager demeanour changed, a defeated slump entering her posture.

'No tray for you, old girl.' The ute door creaked as he opened it. Placing an arm beneath Sally's haunches and another around her barrel chest, he scooped her up and slid her onto the cracked vinyl passenger seat. The window refused to roll down, so he forced the pane with one hand while he cranked the handle with the other, praying that neither the plastic nor the glass would break. He sure as heck couldn't justify the expense of repairs. But he also couldn't take old Sally for a ride without letting her hang her head out in the breeze.

As the crow flies, the dam wasn't far from the house, and it would have been quicker to walk or take the bike. But anything beyond the most leisurely wander down to the orchard was pretty much past Sally these days. By car, navigating a series of dried-up irrigation channels filled with thigh-high weeds, winding tracks and multiple gates ate another ten minutes out of his day. But Sally hung her head out of the window, snuffling the breeze as though it held all the scents of her youth.

He had been hoping the pump had managed to miraculously clear itself and start up again, but it sat on the bank, silent and dry as the Nullarbor. The water level in the dam had dropped further, the exposed, cracked mud riddled with yabby burrows. 'You'd think the buggers would stick to the river, huh, Sal?' he muttered as the ute chugged and farted to a halt. Preferring the still water and soft bank of the dam, the freshwater crays braved the spoonbills and ibis puddling through the swamps to make the trek across the flats.

'Bloody things are nearly as bad as the rabbits.' He yanked on the handbrake, squinting at the waterhole. 'No way round it, we need that windmill.' His fingers sifted through the few coins in the tray beneath the dash.

Hell, he'd put the windmill in himself if he could find the cash. But they'd need a bore, too. Which would require a permit. Which would cost more money. Everything about farming was a vicious cycle: didn't matter how damn hard he worked, money was required to make money.

He should offload The Twenty and focus on Pops' farm. He'd given the riverside block a red-hot go for the past three years, but while his stock and gardens were thriving, they were designed for subsistence living, not profit. And Gus's strawberries would always be a financial drain, so the property would never bring in a positive return. Yet Gus had shot down the sell-out the second Jack tentatively floated it.

He hadn't been too surprised. Although Gus never said anything to intimate he shared Jack's passion for the land— a deep connection to the earth and plants that made him feel more a guardian than an owner—he was always, in his terse manner, clear about two things: he had no intention of selling, and he wanted Jack in charge of farming. Although he didn't fully cotton on to Jack's principles, Gus supported his goal of transitioning from chemical-dependent farming to ecologically sound management. It had proved a pretty steep learning curve for them both. Even though he wasn't aiming for the practically unattainable organic certification, Jack felt he was playing an endless game of catch-up. Most landowners would bring in the equipment and cover a paddock with weedicide, insecticide or ferti-liser and be done, but following sustainable principles meant learning to read the soil, to balance the nutrients and find ways to handle insects and weeds without the relatively cheap chemical solutions of commercial farming. And that took both more time and more money than he had. Gus was rarely around to help out on the block; that wasn't part of their agreement. Come to think of it, it had been a while since Jack had seen him.

He clambered out of the ute, reaching back in to pull Sally across the bench seat and lower her to the ground, the earth baked into corrugated ridges by the cycle of wet and dry. 'Back, Sal,' he said as the dog hunkered down, haunches drawn tight as though she still had the agility of youth and was ready to spring after the plover who patrolled the far edge of the dam.

Any moment now, the bird would take to the air and start swooping, shrieking stridently as she tried to draw them away from her nest. Up until a few weeks back, the plover was always with her mate. They paired for life, but she was now trying to hold her territory alone. He hoped she had nestlings hidden nearby so she wouldn't remain lonely: the chicks tended to hang around for a couple of years.

Jack slapped his Akubra onto the roof of the ute, raising a cloud of grit. His flannel-lined Driza-Bone vest and long-sleeved shirt followed. Predictably, one of his dusty Redbacks skittered under the car as he kicked it off. He glanced around, as though there was a risk of anyone spotting him dead centre of the acreage, then shucked his jeans.

The mud at the edge of the dam, slimy with bird droppings, squeezed between his toes. 'Holy hell!' he grunted. The water was cold enough to make him glad Sally was the only female around. Cupping his tackle—as though that would make any difference—he waded chest-deep into the muddy water to find the end of the pump shaft.

He shook his hair clear of his eyes then ducked beneath the water, feeling for the end of the pipe. Trying to get anywhere near clean production—never mind organic—was not only twice as expensive but twice as much work as regular farming.

And that's why he was going under.

6

Monica

1990

'You know blue balls are a thing, right?' Mack said, using the steering wheel to push himself back in the car seat.

'You know I'm a nurse, right?' Monica replied. She loved it when Mack reacted so obviously to her. It gave her a sense of being desired. No, of power.

The leather of his biker jacket creaking as he shifted, Mack's Ralph Lauren polo shirt clung to his chest. He ran his palms against the sides of his head, making sure his new slick-back remained in place. 'Good. You'll know how to look after me, then,' he retorted, his eyes glinting under the carpark lights.

'I meant more along the lines of I know you're full of shit,' Monica said. 'But you know I'll look after you. I always do.' She slid her hand down his shirt to the tented crotch of his jeans. As she carefully worked down his fly and awkwardly leaned across the handbrake, he turned up Fine Young Cannibals on the tape deck and sang along with the chorus to 'She Drives Me Crazy'. Only a couple of lines, though, before his breathing became laboured, his hand pressing on the back of her head.

As she sat back a few minutes later, reflexively working her jaw from side to side, he took a bright pink packet of strawberry Hubba Bubba from the top of the dash. Unwrapping the cube, he pressed it against her lips. 'Least I can do for my favourite girl.'

'Only girl,' she corrected, moving the gum to her cheek.

'Yep. Only girl,' he grinned. 'But, Only Girl, cool as a couple of weekly BJs are, when are we going next level?'

'You know the answer to that.'

Mack stretched to the dash, rewinding to the start of the mixtape. Madonna's classic, 'Like a Virgin'.

Monica had never actually made that claim, but clearly it was what Mack had taken away from her refusal to have sex. 'Nanna says that if I give away the milk, you won't buy the cow.'

'Thought you weren't into farmers anymore?' he teased. 'Seduced by the suit, right?'

'Not wrong,' she breathed. Mack's mum was kind of hooked on buying him clothes, and he got a kick out of putting them together just right.

He cracked the fogged window. 'You know you quote your nanna a lot?'

She shrugged. 'She has a lot to say. And, like, who else am I going to quote?'

'You should try someone famous. Makes you sound more highbrow. Mum hosts loads of business dinners for Dad and goes to functions with him, so you'll have to expect that kind of thing when I take on my own accounts.'

Excitement tingled through Monica like tiny exploding stars. She loved it when Mack talked about their future, every bit as certain as she was. 'Marketing sounds so glamorous.' About as far from farming as was possible.

Mack chuckled, taking her hand and interlacing their fingers. 'Speaking of glam, Mum's booked us in on Thursday to look at a couple of venues for the engagement. It'll be high-end stuff. They're some of Dad's clients.'

Monica nodded. 'Thursday? I'll see if Mum can come down.' Mack grimaced and she knew where his mind had gone. 'And I'll tell her to wear something nice.'

'Just maybe not the slacks, okay, Mon? You know what Mum's like.'

She did. All David Jones and single-strand pearls, his mother was unfailingly pleasant. And absolutely terrifying.

But if being intimidated by her mother-in-law was the price of marrying Mack, she'd happily pay it ten times over.

7
Jack

Jack didn't like funerals. Of course, he thought, probably only undertakers did. Except, as he glanced around the crowded room, he realised that some of the older folk—those who should be subdued by the statistical likelihood of it being their own farewell service sometime soon—seemed to be taking a perverse delight in the occasion. Congregated in crusty huddles, they recounted with grim relish the number of funerals they'd attended this year, ticking off the deaths of their friends on gnarled fingers in grisly competition as they rated the events on attendance, service length and the quality of the refreshments. The gusts of sound eddied around Jack, the volume increasing as tallies were debated and news of other deaths greedily embraced.

'You're pulling my leg—Smithy fell off the perch? Did you hear that, Helen? Paul Smith died! Do you remember

him? I wondered why he wasn't at the bowls champion-
ship. What got him in the end? Was it his heart? I always
knew it'd be his heart.'

They discussed their anticipated deaths with the confidence of immortals, each secretly believing they would be the
one to attend every funeral, appallingly eager to outlast their
peers and claim a trophy cup overflowing with loneliness.

Jack avoided eye contact that could be mistaken for an
invitation to engage. With Gus's farm at Chesterton, more
than forty kilometres from Settlers Bridge, he knew few
people here. He found it awkward to speak to strangers
and had no desire to explain his connection to Gus. But he
had come to the service because it seemed the right thing
to do, particularly after Gus's widow sent a terse message
to that effect.

Many of the fifty or so people in the overheated hall
were older-generation farmers. Weathered to shades of
broken-capillaried redness, shoehorned and brushed into
suits that probably didn't even get a chance to be dry-
cleaned, they exchanged backslaps and shook hands as
their wives embraced.

'Don, how have you been? Haven't seen you for a while.
Did your pears cop much hail damage? I heard the Forsters
wrote off their entire crop.'

'Susan, was that your new great-grandie I saw in the
Herald? Another boy for Charmaine? Dan got her breeding
a footy team, has he?'

The greetings were quickly hushed, gossip becoming
furtive whispers illuminated by a burst of laughter or

punctuated by excited recognition as more people entered, making their way to their seats with an ease that spoke of macabre familiarity.

Jack tugged at his tie, loosening the knot. He'd learned that suits weren't necessary funeral attire for anyone under seventy, but Ma would have a fit if gossip made its way back to her that he hadn't put a decent shirt on with his moleskins. The CWA had a grapevine that covered more ground than caltrop weed.

He forced a deep breath in. Dammit, he could practically smell formaldehyde over the reek of chemist's perfume and supermarket aftershave permeating the almost-festive atmosphere. He scowled. It was as though half of the crowd were there to revel in the fact that they'd outlasted Gus, gloating that they, at least, had made it well into their sixth decade.

He'd thought Gus ten years younger than that, but, still, it was far too soon for any man to go—though it was a relief to have it confirmed as a heart attack. Too many farmers took their own lives.

Positioned against the back wall, as though the location would allow him a fast escape once the service was over, Jack's height meant he could look over heads, adopting a stoic, far-off gaze. It was preferable to glimpsing the expressions of pain and sympathy around the room, which twisted at his gut.

'Jack.' Luke nodded as he and Taylor made a beeline for him. 'You okay?'

'Yeah, mate.' Jack reluctantly let his gaze brush Taylor's. The doctor was one of the most intuitive people he knew.

Although she was always up for stirring the blokes, she also kept a close eye on their health, both mental and physical. As neither Taylor nor Luke knew Gus, Jack realised they'd shown up to support him. 'F-f-fifth one of these damn things in six years.' He lifted his chin towards the front of the room where the polished casket lay, in case they needed a visual reminder of why they were there. 'Do they still use formaldehyde, Tay?'

The question sounded bizarre, but he needed to talk over the sorrow that welled within him.

Taylor didn't miss a beat. 'Sometimes. You said it's been two weeks since Gus passed? Embalming definitely would have been an option, then.' As Jack scrubbed the back of his hand across his nose, she twisted her mouth sympathetically. 'You might just be picking up traces of disinfectant, though.'

He shrugged. 'Whatever, it s-smells like death.'

'Nah, man,' Luke disagreed. 'It's just that you've shorn all this,' he pinched his own chin, 'and can actually smell for the first time in years.'

'Could be it,' Jack replied, grateful for a ribbing to take his mind off why they were there. Maybe the need for distraction was the true reason the other mourners were so eager to chat? Noise meant life.

'You look really good,' Taylor said, appraising him so carefully that he knew she wasn't talking only about the close-trimmed shadow that was all he had left of his beard. 'I'd almost forgotten what you looked like under there. You should have had it like that when Becca came.'

'Becca?'

'Wow, Jackson, you lightweight.' Taylor rolled her eyes. 'You only asked about her a week back. My uni friend, remember?'

'Oh. Yeah. That'd be one *with* a partner? Not into hanging around for scraps, Tay. I'm fine with being alone.' He broke off as the lights dimmed and a slide show started on the large screen at the front of the room.

The first photo was unmistakably Gus, although he would have been in his late twenties, all white teeth and black hair as he grinned up at the camera from where he squatted in a strawberry field, a plant clutched in his grimy hand. In the next photo he was older, seated on a wooden crate, a dark-haired infant nestled in his lap. Those large hands, scoured until they were red, were now wrapped carefully around the child he gazed at, his face lit with adoration and wonder and maybe a touch of fear.

Jack scowled and looked away: the expression on Gus's face was made more poignant by the fact that this gathering was proof he would never again get to feel such joy. Never again feel anything, in fact.

Instead of watching the images that caused an unpleasant tightening in his chest, Jack focused on a blur of life that swooped beyond the frosted glass of the arched window to the left of the screen. He had noticed the rainbow lorikeets while he sat astride his bike in the carpark, trying to find the balls to enter the parlour. Even though the widow was the only mourner he would know here, the service would kick him in the guts. They always did. He knew the way it would play out, with the funeral director trying to smooth the grief with quirky reminiscences, offensive in his pretence that he'd known the person who lay in a wooden box beside him. The bereaved would nod their heads, eager to be placated by the nostalgia, and at least one friend would bravely take the podium, stoically recounting how Gus had been his best mate.

A smudge of green and yellow and red, the bird fluttered against the glass. The repeated flight path likely indicated it was building a nest. Which took his mind back to the plight of the lonely plover, out on the river block. Jack's gaze ranged along the front row of the mourners, sitting closest to the glossy black coffin. Although he could only see the backs of heads, Mrs Tamberlani's was easy to pick, her blonde hair pulled back into some kind of neat twist that looked like she'd taken a dip in a tub of the varnish his mate Justin used to lacquer his wood sculptures. Jack hid a cynical snort in a cough: her hair probably didn't dare move. In their few interactions when he'd been out to Blue Flag Strawberries to discuss management of The Twenty with his partner, he had found Gus's wife curt and dismissive. She'd made it clear that she didn't like him, and he had a fair idea why. But he'd keep that information to himself. Maybe she would be like the plover, spiky and vicious to outsiders, but pining for her life mate? Protecting her offspring at her own peril?

A frown crossed his face: from Gus's conversations around his plans for The Twenty, Jack knew he only had the one kid. Lucie. She would likely be here somewhere, too.

Intent on keeping his mind busy rather than dwelling on a sermon designed to bring tears, he searched the row. On either side of the widow were older women, probably her friends, turning to her with tight, sympathetic smiles as Louis Armstrong's 'What a Wonderful World' burst from hidden speakers at a volume calculated to wake anyone who had dozed during the eulogies.

As mourners stood, making their way in a subdued column to lean over the coffin and pay their last respects, the movement eased the pressure in his chest and Jack allowed his gaze to range further. Near the far end of the front row of burgundy velour padded chairs a young woman sat, her face in profile, the ridiculous chandeliers throwing up highlights in the rich darkness of her short, tousled hair. For a moment, Jack thought the chair to her left was vacant, but by shifting slightly towards Luke, he could see through the open back of the timber frame. A blonde-haired child nestled against the woman's upper arm. The woman leaned down to speak to her, then shot a tight smile at a guy seated on the far side of the kid.

With a shaved head and dude-pruning so meticulous that Jack was trying to work out whether the shadow was actual stubble or airbrushed, the guy looked both out of place and yet supremely confident. His shoulders flexed beneath what Jack, thanks to his upbringing, could pick as a damn fine suit. Jack tugged at the collar of his shirt, second-guessing his choice. If that was Lucie, Gus had neglected to mention his daughter had a wealthy husband. In fact, he'd never mentioned a husband or a kid at all.

The guy reached across the back of the child's seat, his fingers casually caressing the nape of his wife's neck, as though he was massaging the tension from her cappuccino skin. He tilted his head towards the casket, but Lucie shook her head, the movement unmistakeably adamant.

Luke caught Jack's glance. 'Any idea who that is?'

Jack ran a hand through his hair. He should have tied it back. 'Maybe Gus's daughter. And family.' Hot irritation ran through him at the words. He'd had it in his thick skull that the daughter would come home and take up the reins on Gus's share of The Twenty.

Not the daughter and *husband*.

He shifted impatiently. What the hell difference did it make to him? There was no reason to assume the husband would be anti sustainable farming.

'How's that going to affect the property?' Luke murmured.

'Shh,' Taylor warned, although theirs wasn't the only conversation. Tissues out, dabbing at reddened noses and leaking eyes, people milled around, the background noise amping up as they tired of waiting for their turn to drift their hands across the coffin.

He'd done a damn fine job of not listening to the remembrances and eulogies. They were always the worst part, even for people he didn't know, filled with guilt and angst as the sudden realisation of time wasted and opportunity squandered took root. He'd never understood why so many people failed to seize the day. That was one of the best things that had come out of his childhood: a realisation that the future wasn't assured.

'Don't know.' He shrugged, trying to give the impression that money wasn't one of the first issues that leaped to his mind when he heard the news about Gus. But money was always on his mind. Buying the nine hectares alone would have left him in the hole for over a hundred and ninety thousand, a loan he'd have had to provide the security for, putting Pops' arable land—the acreage he relied on to provide the family income—at risk of foreclosure. Gus's partnership meant he was still up to his neck owing almost a ton, but it was direct to Gus, no bank involved.

'It's messy as shit,' he muttered. 'Technically, Gus and I are equal partners. But he only needed a hectare or so to rotate berries across, so let me use the rest in exchange for managing the block. Plus, I get the house.' He blew out a frustrated breath, lifting his chin towards the dark-haired woman. 'I guess now she gets her four hectares to do whatever she wants. As long as it doesn't contaminate mine.' He stopped speaking as the music died away and the mourners hushed, their focus once again on the podium alongside the casket.

Jack fixed his attention on Gus's daughter instead. Even though she was probably about to screw up his plans, it made for a far more pleasant view than the bleak finality of the polished coffin.

She ducked her chin, raking a hand through the messy crop of her hair as though she was trying to force thoughts out of her head. Skewed slightly away from the macabre centrepiece of the room, her attention seemed fixed on the windows to the left, where trees threw stark silhouettes across the frosted glass. Twice she leaned down to press a kiss into her daughter's hair.

As her husband glanced across at her, sympathy twisting his features, Jack caught himself frowning again, jealous at their silent communication. Though the jokes around the footy club were that they needed to import women into the district just so the guys had a chance of getting their end wet, the need ran far deeper. But it was something they would never openly discuss because it sounded weak. Wasn't it supposed to be only women who longed for someone to share their lives with? Not that social media sharing kind of bull, either. He had no need to post a photo of his breakfast—not that Weetbix ever looked all that exciting. But he'd like someone to share that cereal with. Someone who'd discuss whether he was neglecting the family farm and putting in too many hours at The Twenty. Someone to tell him he was doing the right thing by the environment—or even to tell him he had it all ballsed up. Just someone to talk to.

Because he had told Taylor the truth: he was fine with being alone. But that didn't mean he was never lonely.

8
Lucie

'She's just tired, Mum,' Lucie said. Her throat was thick with unshed tears, but she was determined to sound neither offensive nor defensive in the face of Mum's disapproval.

'I wasn't expecting you to bring . . . her,' Mum said. 'This is hardly the occasion for a child to be present.'

Occasion? They were burying Dad, and Mum called it an *occasion*?

Mum redirected her gaze to the chapel, some distance from the anteroom where they were apparently being afforded a private moment with their grief before accepting condolences from the other mourners.

Not that her mother seemed particularly wrapped in grief. *No.* Lucie took a deep breath, trying to centre herself: she had promised Geoff she wouldn't go down that track. He advocated mindfulness, putting out the positivity she wanted to receive. Besides, although she envied those who could embrace their emotions, she didn't dare. Perhaps her mother was doing the same thing, shielding herself from pain.

'I bored, Mummy,' Keeley repeated, pressing her face into Lucie's stomach. The post-pregnancy softness that remained despite Lucie's perfect diet did nothing to mute the piercing whisper.

'I know, baby.' Lucie stroked her daughter's blonde curls, looking at her mother properly for the first time since they had rushed into the chapel, flustered and almost late.

Definitely late, by Mum's standards: the censure in her brief greeting before she moved back to join her huddle of cronies for the service had jolted Lucie back about a decade.

She was thinner than the last time Lucie had seen her, almost skeletal, with barely a skim of skin covering her bones. Not that *soft* was a word Lucie would ever have used to describe her. Still, she took her instinctive desire to attack down a notch: there was no point going off at Mum about a poorly chosen word, or because she couldn't deal with a slightly whiny three-year-old. 'Keeley's not used to travel.' She shot Geoff a scowl. Though he'd been invested in his favourite role as devil's advocate, defending her mother's behaviour, Mum's evident disapproval of Keeley now would be sure to stir his protective instincts.

Geoff didn't disappoint her, raising one elegant eyebrow, a quirk that never failed to remind Lucie that, short of both time and money, she had neglected her own. 'I'm sure Keeley would be more settled if we'd had a chance to shower and refresh,' he said drily, refraining from mentioning that, thanks to a hold-up waiting for the live cargo—aka Dash—to be unloaded, they'd had to make do with a quick scrub using dampened, scratchy paper towels at the airport.

Mum acted as though Geoff hadn't spoken, directing her reply to Lucie. 'If you had to wait for discounted flights, you should have mentioned it, Lucie.'

On one of their non-existent phone calls? The monthly missive? Emotional exhaustion dragged at Lucie, clawing at her resolve to not allow this interaction to devolve into an undeclared battle for no apparent prize. Mum's comment was typical: technically inoffensive yet barbed in intention.

Her mother flicked an appraising glance at Geoff, who Lucie had introduced as her housemate minutes before the service began. 'Of course, I suppose *three* tickets pushed the price up.'

Lucie recoiled: surely she wasn't imagining the condemnation that laced her mother's words? 'This was the first available flight, considering how late we received your *letter*. And Keeley's prone to earaches. The trip wasn't pleasant for her.'

Mum dug into the knock-off Gucci bag Lucie remembered from her own childhood. 'So then she *is* whiny?' she said, her tight smile triumphant.

Lucie tensed. Geoff could list whatever the hell positive affirmations he wanted her to recite but no happy thoughts or cleansing crystals would dilute her mother's acid. She made an art form of inserting snide criticisms with the stealth of a scorpion strike. Delivered in a disinterested monotone so superficially acceptable that the conversation had generally moved on, the sting in the words would catch the unsuspecting victim too late to allow an outraged reaction.

Mum pulled out a wrapped Ferrero chocolate and handed it to Keeley without looking at the child.

Lucie started to protest, her hand outstretched, but she caught Geoff's glance and reluctantly subsided. He was right. One chocolate wasn't going to hurt. And at least her mother finally acknowledged Keeley's presence. Lucie wasn't sure what she had been expecting—maybe for Mum to have come to terms with the fact that she had a granddaughter? Perhaps even be eager to meet her? Proudly introduce her to the clucking entourage that trailed her until she waved a dismissive hand? But clearly none of that was about to eventuate, and the deliberate disinterest cut more deeply than Lucie wanted to allow. Mum was out to prove a point, punishing the child for the sins of the mother.

Carefully not looking at Lucie so that she couldn't be reprimanded, Keeley already had the treat unwrapped, her left cheek bulging as she popped the entire chocolate in her mouth.

'If she can't fly, it obviously would have been better for you to leave her in Melbourne,' Mum said, as though Keeley was an extra bag or a troublesome pet.

'Geoff is the *only* person I trust with her,' Lucie laced her words with meaning, 'and he came to support me, so that means Keeley came. In any case, I wouldn't have stayed away from her overnight.' She never had; the days were hard enough. As she took the tram to work, Geoff dropped Keeley at day care on the way to his office. But knowing Keeley enjoyed day care didn't prevent Lucie checking the time, imagining where her daughter was every moment that they were separated.

Separated. God. She clenched a hand into a fist in her jacket pocket. Her fingers closed around the purple teddy bear Keeley and Dash took turns carrying around, and she gripped it tightly, as though it was a talisman. As Geoff repeatedly pointed out, gently trying to prepare her, regardless of what she said or how loudly she declared it, Jeremy had rights.

Lucie had barely been able to bring herself to furtively look around the chapel during the service, breathlessly dreading the moment she saw Jeremy. Not because of the old hurts resurfacing—she'd grown way beyond him—but because of the potential he had to damage the new life she had created for herself.

Even though it was only delaying the inevitable, relief had turned her knees weak when the service ended without him making his way forward to pay his respects at the coffin. Not that she had, either.

Because that wooden prison could only hold an inanimate, waxen effigy. Not the Dad she remembered. Even as he became distant towards her, increasingly consumed by the farm, still Dad had been vibrant and alive. They had grown apart, but the chasm had never been insurmountable. Not until now.

'See?' Mum said, as though she had been advocating how to soothe Keeley for the last half hour. 'She's perfectly happy. She was grizzling to get a treat.'

'Luce,' Geoff said, his low voice urgent as she bristled in maternal affront, 'I'm going to let Dash out of the car. It's been an hour, and even though it's not hot and the windows are down . . .'

She scowled. He was deserting her. But he was right: although the dog had been happily curled in the centre of the sky-blue stuffed donut she had made from an old crocheted blanket Keeley chose at the op shop, he couldn't stay in the car. 'Sure,' she responded brightly. After all, Geoff hadn't known her dad; there was neither need nor point in him being there. 'Actually, do you want to find us a B&B? Take my phone, there're screenshots of a couple.'

There weren't: it hadn't even occurred to her she would need to stay anywhere but her childhood home, but it was a deliberate jab at Mum.

'Dash?' Mum said, unnecessarily smoothing her French twist. She had always worn her hair the same way, taking it down to brush out the hairspray and then plait it over her left shoulder each night.

'Keeley's puppy. I sent you and D-Dad photos of them last Christmas.' Damn, his name hadn't been that hard to say before being so close to him made the new finality of the distance between them so obvious. 'We had to bring him because our flatmate was working, and there wasn't enough notice to get him in kennels.'

'A dog?' Mum waved a hand, as though shooing away the invisible animal. 'Oh, yes, please do find somewhere to stay. I don't care to have animals in my home.'

Her home? 'We've always had pets.' A yard full of chickens. Rabbits. Cats. Even a goat, which Dad had sworn was for Orthodox Easter feasting. He had made the same threat for at least eight years—and had then dug a deep hole to bury the nanny when she eventually died of fat old age. He planted a rosemary bush on top of the mound, saying he'd finally got around to seasoning her the way he had always planned. A sigh shuddered through Lucie at the bittersweet memory. It didn't matter that they had drifted apart: he was still Dad.

Her mother held up an authoritative hand. 'Not now, Lucie.' Her mouth tightened with the inconvenience of it all.

Lucie knew the look and her mother's *not nows*. They were unsubtle code for 'not ever'.

'Mummy,' Keeley moaned, 'I wanna go.'

'Children should—' her mother started.

Be seen and not heard. Lucie knew the adage by heart, one of the hardcore favourites of a mother who raised her on restrictive axioms. 'Be permitted to politely share their thoughts,' she finished firmly. 'Keeley, Mummy needs to stay here for a little longer.' *Mummy needs to face up to your daddy,* her brain interrupted, rebelling against her attempts to ignore the reality. Oh god, how could she do it? For months she had hated Jeremy for his desertion, yet within a few weeks of Keeley's birth, that hate had turned to aching disappointment, a sense of loss that was almost as much sorrow for what Jeremy was missing out on as it was a lament for the family life she and her daughter would never have. She had discovered she couldn't hate the man who had given her Keeley. But that didn't prevent her being terrified of the risk that perhaps now he would want his child.

'Luce, how about Keeley comes with me and Dash?' Geoff murmured, so that Keeley wouldn't hear the suggestion.

Lucie hesitated. She wanted Keeley with her, but was that because her daughter provided a buffer? If she busied herself with the child, she couldn't allow herself to *feel* all the emotions that were battering at her insides, trying to find a way to escape her deliberately calm façade. With Keeley there, the fear of seeing Jeremy had to be controlled, just as the grief about her own father had to be hidden, and the disappointment she felt towards her mother politely disguised. Being so very busy keeping everything concealed helped her to pretend she was strong. But if she allowed Keeley to go with Geoff, it kept her daughter safe from Jeremy. For today, anyway.

The darkly garbed crowd now oscillated around the main hall, casting longing glances towards them as they waited for the funeral director to signal they could press forward to share their condolences. Prove who was the most upset, who grieved the hardest. She couldn't expose her daughter to that. She nodded at Geoff. 'Good idea.'

'Yup,' he said with a wink. 'Some days I'm awesome like that.'

'And other days you can't even find your pants in the dryer,' she shot back, grasping at the flash of levity he offered. She had managed not to cry during the service, but that was only because the fear that made her fold in on herself, the thought of losing Keeley, chased away her grief. 'Keeley, go with Geoff and find us somewhere *nice*—' she emphasised the word with a scowl at her mother, which was wasted as Mum pasted on a sorrowful smile of elegant bereavement and turned towards the crowd '—to stay. Somewhere with a garden for Dash to run around in, okay?'

Keeley stretched up, placing her palms on Lucie's cheeks as she bent, so she could draw her closer to whisper loudly, 'Mummy, I didn't like Nanna's chocolate. It was yummy in my mouth but now is yucky.'

'Never mind. I'm sure Geoff will get you a big drink of the water kefir from the cool bag. It's a nice fizzy orange one. Here, take Purple Ted with you.' She pressed the well-washed toy into Keeley's hand. 'Off you go, quick. Skedaddle.'

Keeley turned to Geoff, putting up her chubby arms. 'Carry.'

'Sure, princess.' Geoff scooped her up, then moved closer to speak softly to Lucie. 'You'll be okay, Tumbleweed?'

She managed a smile through gritted teeth, warily surveying the crowd beyond him. How could she be this scared of a man she had known so intimately? A man she had loved, no matter how foolishly? And why, at this most inappropriate of moments, were her thoughts all about him instead of her father?

Probably because he posed the most imminent threat to her happiness. 'Sure.'

Geoff kissed her cheek. 'Remember, be good. Manifest. I'll be back as soon as I've found us a place.'

'And gotted me kefir,' Keeley reminded him.

'Yes, and that.'

As they moved away, Lucie felt immediately alone. Vulnerable. Which was ridiculous. Jeremy had never lifted a finger to harm her, he simply refused to take responsibility for their accidental pregnancy, even asking if she was sure the baby was his. He hadn't been angry, just coldly articulate and determined in the manner she had previously considered a mark of his maturity. He had calmly stated that as he had messed up raising his own kids—said as though Keeley wasn't his—he wasn't about to do it again. End of story. No rebuttal allowed, no negotiation, no consideration for how she felt about the child growing within her.

'Tidy your hair, Lucie,' her mum chided, as though she hadn't been gone for four years. As though she wasn't an adult. As though she didn't have a child of her own. 'Appearance is everything.'

Lucie squared her shoulders instead. It might have been the end of the story as far as Jeremy was concerned, but it had been the beginning of hers. The business qualification Dad insisted on had, surprisingly, helped her land a job in Melbourne. She was making ends meet—although sometimes that was a bit of a close-run thing—and had found unlikely family in Geoff and, more recently, Fin.

But still she had to face the man she had loved. With her stomach knotted tight enough to make her hunch, she scanned the crowd making their way past to reach the buffet of sausage rolls and sweet no-bake slices in the foyer. 'Have you seen Jeremy?' Her heart tripped as she uttered his name, as though she was summoning the demons of her past. Or worse, the demon of her future.

'Jeremy?' Her mother's face pinched, she spat the name as though it was an unripe persimmon. 'You're pining after him *now*?'

'Hardly.' She was arming herself, readying for the confrontation.

'Then it's probably fortunate that he is currently overseas,' her mother said icily.

Lucie sagged in relief, taking a stumbling step towards her mother. 'He's away? For how long?'

Her mother immediately retreated. 'Months. So perhaps now you could focus on your father?' She brushed nonexistent fluff from her black jacket; her hands, so thin now, cabled with blue veins, as though they belonged to a much older woman.

Lucie caught their tremble and realised that her mother was lashing out to hide far deeper emotions—*That* she could understand. And, with Keeley safe, she had more room for empathy. 'Mum—'

'If you had given a little more thought to your father in the first place, maybe we wouldn't be here now. You know he relied on you. The pair of you were always thick as thieves, and then . . . well, time is the cruellest thief of all, isn't it? Especially when you waste it.' An angry, spiky stick insect, her mother stalked across the room to greet the mourners, leaving her unusually direct attack hanging in the air like a cloud of acid.

Lucie's blood flashed cold and she screwed her eyes closed as she concentrated on controlling the venom-fed nausea that swept through her. It wasn't as though guilt hadn't already taken her there, wondering whether Dad's heart attack was linked to overwork. As Blue Flag Strawberries had taken off as a commercial supplier, Dad came to increasingly loathe the bookwork and had insisted Lucie study business management. He reckoned you could trust no one but family, and even then you had to choose carefully. 'Strength is in loyalty, not numbers,' he often said, apparently borrowing from Mum's book of aphorisms. Yet Lucie had gone straight from uni to the office job Jeremy had arranged for her in Adelaide. He'd warned that crossing paths in the office of Blue Flag would make their secret impossible to keep. Thrilled by the seemingly illicit nature of their tryst, she had been eager to please him.

Jeremy, not Dad. Where had she left her loyalty?

'Are you all right?'

Lucie flicked her eyes open at the unfamiliar voice. 'I . . .' Words escaped her because she was so very far from all right. Was Mum's accusation, for once, fair? Was she the sole reason everyone was gathered here, the reason her father lay in a coffin? And, on so many levels, the reason Keeley would never know her grandfather?

The guy standing almost toe-to-toe with her pulled an apologetic face. 'S-sorry. That was a dumb question.' He waved a hand towards the main chapel, where the coffin sat alone, a stark foretaste of what was to come for her father. 'Given the circumstances.'

'No, it's not that. I just . . . kind of zoned out,' she gabbled, trying to drag her mind from the image of Dad being interred in the cold, hard earth. Reclaimed by the soil from which he had drawn so much life.

People shuffled past, avoiding intruding on her apparent grief by murmuring their sympathy without making eye contact as they headed for the buffet. But the guy who had interrupted her thoughts just . . . stood there. Oblivious to the crowd eddying around him.

Lucie stepped back, instinctively creating distance between them.

The small of her back hit the flower-bedecked side-board, bringing her up hard—but the timber also provided support, and the impact gave an excuse for her soft gasp. When Geoff asked for input on his wardrobe, she routinely told him she didn't care: Jeremy had cured her taste for sharp-dressed men. Yet apparently you could take the girl out of the country, but you couldn't take an appreciation for the country out of the girl. Because, holy heck, this guy planted in front of her in his clean-cut cream moleskins, button-down shirt with rolled up sleeves and Cuban-heel boots rocked the perfect mix of cowboy and culture.

A slight frown between his eyes, he shoved shoulder-length hair back from his tanned face. And, unfortunate gasp aside, she felt she could finally draw breath, as though he brought fresh air and sunshine into the sombre room that sought to suffocate her with its reek of death, guilt and grief.

9

Jack

Hell, he was a certifiable idiot. What kind of moron asked a woman at her father's funeral whether she was 'okay'? Was she supposed to smile sweetly and assure him she was just fine?

Instead—and understandably—Lucie looked confused and . . . lost.

Though maybe she only seemed that way because she was surprisingly tiny. Probably actually the same height as her mother, yet he'd never thought of Gus's wife as particularly petite. Close up, although Lucie had Gus's Mediterranean colouring, she didn't share his features. Hers were far finer, a dusting of deep colour along high cheekbones, her nose a little tip-tilted. Her thickly lashed brown eyes might have been exactly the same as Gus's, he wouldn't know. He hadn't been in the habit of staring into the guy's eyes. Not like he was hers.

'J-Jack,' he said, thrusting out his right hand. 'Jack Schenscher.'

She lifted one shoulder, indicating the name meant nothing to her, then put her hand into his. 'Lucie Tamberlani. You know—knew . . .' A flash of pain crossed her face and her nostrils flared. 'You knew Dad?'

So she hadn't taken her husband's name. No reason why that should be at all interesting. 'We've b-been working together for the last three years or so,' Jack replied.

Lucie nodded, her smile tight, lines of sorrow etching her eyes.

Jack gave himself a mental shove. As now was definitely not the time to talk business, he needed to move along. He could feel the widow's glare spear him as the shuffling mutters of other people waiting to speak with Lucie increased in volume and frustration. 'I g-guess we'll c-catch up later.'

Lucie looked shocked and withdrew her hand, and he started to stutter an explanation, but a woman crowded into his space, throwing her arms around Lucie.

Probably just as well. He was sweating like a pig, and his bloody stammer was out of control. He could go for days, maybe weeks, without it cutting in, but if he was tired or nervous, all hell was likely to break free.

And now he had every reason to be nervous: Lucie and her husband could destroy his farm before it ever had a chance. If she wanted to use her share of The Twenty, it could affect his near-organic production, and if she chose to sell, he was totally screwed. He couldn't afford to buy her out.

The widow cut across his thoughts, summoning him with an imperious wave. 'Jackson. We will have to discuss business, of course.'

His guts sank. 'Of course,' he agreed, surprised that she'd bring it up now.

'But not until after the grant of probate.'

'Probate?'

'Sorting out Georgius's will.'

It took a second for Gus's proper name to click. 'Sure.' Man, even allowing for what she held against him, the widow was a cold piece of work. Other than a slight redness to her pale blue eyes, she didn't betray any emotion.

'Then we shall see where we stand.' The widow's words sounded vaguely threatening.

∾

The farmhouse kitchen always seemed like home. Which wasn't surprising, considering how much of their childhood he and Sam had spent here, even when Mum lived in Settlers. Ma only baked on special occasions nowadays, but Monday dinner with her and Pops was their family tradition. Sam didn't open the cafe as she reckoned everyone had treated themselves enough over the weekend and wouldn't need to eat out. Instead, she headed over to Ma and Pops early to do what she could for them around the house. Jack suspected she made it a dinner thing because her husband, Grant, had a weekly bowls meeting with the rest of the guys from the meatworks so couldn't hassle her about what she was doing with her time.

'So how dire was the funeral?' Samantha asked, sliding a huge wedge of Ma's fresh-baked steak and mushroom pudding onto his chipped blue plate.

'Is there some kind of rating?' he asked. 'Like, do you say, "I went to this awesome funeral last week"?'

'Whoa, calm your farm there, bro,' Sam said as she moved around the table to pile the suet dough on Pops' plate. 'I was just making conversation. It's what civilised folks do, you know.'

Jack surreptitiously scratched a bit of dried food from his plate. Sam raised an eyebrow and pulled a disgusted face. He noticed that her laughter lines were carved deeper than they used to be, maybe as a result of the weight she had dropped over the last year or so. He didn't generally take time to look at his sister, but now he noticed that although the weight loss went some way to dispelling the comfortable, matronly look she'd had for more than fifteen years, looking more her age wasn't doing Sam any favours.

He turned his attention back to the dirty plate. Well, hell, no time like the present. 'Pops,' Jack said, raising his voice so his grandfather would look up from where he was intently focused on cutting his steamed pastry and veg into bite-sized morsels. He would then swap his fork to his right hand and not pick up the knife again during the meal. It annoyed Ma because, she said, it was horribly American. But there was little chance Pops would change now. 'Pops,

I got some brochures on in-home support when I went to pay the dogs' regos.'

Pops dropped his cutlery with an impressive clatter. 'Told you, Jackson, we don't want to hear about that kind of stuff. Your ma and me, we do just fine.'

Just fine, except Jack had to be out there on a daily basis taking care of chores he didn't want Pops tackling, and Sam helped out with the laundry and as much cleaning as she could squeeze in without Grant getting on her case. It hadn't bothered Jack too much until a couple of years ago; after all, the farm machinery was kept in the sheds near the old farmhouse, and he had to access that most days. But since he'd started setting up The Twenty, time had become almost as precious a commodity as money. Not that he would begrudge his grandparents either. 'I know that, Pops. But a bit of help round the place wouldn't hurt.'

'Help? Having someone pry through my things, you mean,' Ma said. Her faded blue eyes settled on him, though she squinted across the table to force them to focus. 'Jackson, we've talked about this. If I was to have someone in here to clean, I'd have to tidy before she came. And how do you think it would make me feel, having someone clean everything I've already cleaned, as though I'm not capable?'

Thanks to his father, Jack knew what it was to have someone make him feel less than capable. And Ma had always been houseproud. He and Sam had pretty much grown up here, as their mum found it impossible to settle in any one place for long. She had managed to park for a while when he was in primary school and Sam starting high school, but other than that short stint, she had always been on the go, chasing a career in journalism that offered something more exciting than reporting on crop yield, wool grades, driving misdemeanours and the footy scores in the local rag.

Jack's earliest memories were of Ma insisting they take their boots off at the door and wash their hands before entering the kitchen. The problem now was that she didn't see too well anymore. Little things escaped her, like the dirty plate—because no way could he ever persuade his grandparents that a dishwasher wasn't the biggest waste of money known to man, when they had a perfectly good stainless-steel sink and plenty of Palmolive.

He spooned peas from the Pyrex dish in front of him. 'It's not like that, Ma. The council subsidises these packages, kind of a payback for all the years you and Pops have paid rates. Since Pops got sick,' he wisely left out Ma's funny heart turns that had landed her in hospital three times in the last year, 'Narelle at the council said you might be entitled to extra assistance.'

Pops grunted as though 'assistance' was a dirty word, and Jack switched his focus to Sam, hoping to get her involved. When his speech impediment led him to be reticent, Sam had always stepped in, her chattiness making up for her little brother's silence, and occasionally even succeeding in deflecting their father's anger over the defect.

Today, though, focused on her untouched dinner despite not even having picked up her fork yet, she missed his cue.

'Sam?'

She glanced up, startled, but spoke quickly. 'Ma, what was on at the CWA last week? Are you gearing up for the lamington challenge, or is that later in the year?'

'I wouldn't know, love,' Ma said. 'I didn't go.'

'Again? That's the last two meetings you've missed, isn't it? Is that Christine Albright staging another coup?' Sam picked up her corn cob and bit into it, chewing nonchalantly, as though disinterested in the reply.

Jack made a business of shovelling in his dinner to hide his grin. Sam was the smart one. She knew better than to tackle the problem directly, like he had.

'It's not that,' Ma said. 'But Pops was a bit under the weather, so he couldn't drive me in.' Ma had failed her senior's eye test two years back and wasn't allowed to drive anymore.

'Oh, that's a shame,' Sam said. 'You know, council has volunteers who would run out here to pick you up and drive you to your meetings. Then you wouldn't miss out. And Christine would have no chance of taking over.'

Jack wanted to cheer his sister on but held it in as Ma set down her fork with far less drama than her husband had. 'Firstly, Christine isn't taking over. The youngsters are pretty much running the place. Roni and Tracey have it in hand, and Dr Taylor helps out when she can. Even Christine knows when she's beaten. She had her chance when Marian died and she was branch president. Briefly.'

She loaded the last word, her arthritic fingers tapping on the oddly out of place glass-topped kitchen table for emphasis. Jack's entire life, they had been warned to be careful of scratching the table, which Pops had picked out at Le Cornu's furniture store in Adelaide, before it closed down.

'Secondly, if Pops isn't well, I would hardly be leaving him here while I go off chatting, would I? And thirdly, no one does macramé anymore.'

'Macramé?' Jack stiffened warily. It threw him when his grandparents' conversation went off tangent.

Ma nodded, picking up her fork again. She used her other hand to indicate the knotted ropes of the plant-pot holder hanging from the ceiling above the window. An anaemic-looking spider fern straggled over the sides of a burnt orange terracotta pot, the spiderettes dangling in bushy tangles from the ribbon-like leaves. 'Macramé. All of us were into it in the seventies, but rope tying seems to be a dying art.'

'Not if you read *Fifty Shades*,' Sam sniggered.

'That's more cable ties and duct tape,' Pops said matter-of-factly. 'Quite a rush on at the hardware stores when that book came out.'

'Pops!' Sam screwed up her face.

Ma laughed at her. 'Goodness' sake, Samantha, we're old, not dead.'

'Oh my god,' Jack groaned. 'Come for a nice family meal and this is what I get? I mean, the pie's good and all, but the conversation . . . is not what I expected. Not even at the footy clubrooms.'

'Serves you right,' Ma said pertly. 'And enough of your nonsense now. Have some more peas and tell us about the funeral. Were there many at the service?'

There it was again, that fascination with attendance numbers. 'Didn't really count. Paid my respects and hightailed it out of there.'

'And you met the girl that Gus was setting the block up for?' Pops asked, his interest far more in the farming side than 'the girl'.

'Briefly. Didn't discuss anything with her, obviously. But Gus's wife said we have to wait for the, ah, grant of probate?' He looked to Sam to see if he was using the term correctly. With all the traffic at her popular Settlers Bridge cafe, she was far more in the know than he was.

This time she was inspecting her wrist and missed his question. He scowled at her: over more than thirty years, he had become accustomed to her bailing him out. 'Anyway, for the will to be sorted.'

'I suppose everything goes to the widow?' Pops said. 'Gus didn't have any partners at the strawberry farm?'

Jack lifted one shoulder, uncomfortable, as always, with talk of death around his grandparents. 'I don't have a clue on the ins and outs of Gus's business, because I wasn't expecting it to be an issue any time soon. I only know he was setting up his share of The Twenty for Lucie—though he didn't mention she has a husband and a kid.'

'And the problem with that is?' Sam said, suddenly jumping back into the conversation. Right when he didn't want her to.

'Only that Gus said his daughter is "into natural stuff", as he put it, so now I have to hope her husband is too or I'm in the shit. I went into shares with Gus knowing he planned to let Lucie take over when she came back from wherever, but I guess I never figured on her having input from someone else.'

'Lucie, is it?' Sam teased.

'Told you—married with a kid,' he said.

'Too bad.' His sister pulled a sympathetic face.

'It's just business, Sam.'

'Sure. Hey, I was chatting with a couple who passed through town the other day. They met on eHarmony. Have you—'

'Nope,' he said before she had finished. 'I'm not into online shopping.'

'That's the site that advertises late at night on the TV?' Ma said with one of her awkward flashes of understanding. She saw the look he exchanged with Sam and shook her head. 'Again, we're old, kids, not senile. You trying to speak in codes around us is like Pops and me still spelling out your birthday gifts to keep them secret after you'd started school.'

'Reckon Jack was in high school before that stopped working,' Sam said, grinning.

'Only because I couldn't hear their whispering over your constant yakking,' he shot back.

'Anyway,' Ma interrupted the bickering they had never grown out of, 'why don't you try one of those companies, Jackson?'

'Not interested,' he said gruffly. 'It's all bullshit. Everyone is on there selling themselves as something they're not.' Exactly like he'd have to. At least if he met a woman in the flesh she saw upfront what she was getting into, and he wouldn't have to spell it out. His mouth twisted at the irony of the phrase: if he spelled anything out, there would be double the number of necessary letters. Not that it was ever an issue around here—he knew every woman in the district, and they were either accustomed to his stammer or it didn't play up in front of them because they'd been mates forever.

10
Monica

1990

For the past ten years, Monica had seized every opportunity to escape the hick railway-siding town on the Eyre Peninsula and stay with Nanna in her one-bedroom half-house in Hackney. When she was younger, she loved that the unit was a five-minute walk through the Botanic Park to the Adelaide Zoo. From the moment she turned eighteen, she loved that it was three minutes to the Hackney Hotel.

Now that she was based in the Nurses Residential Wing only a kilometre away, she loved it for the sense of safe familiarity the combination of the flower-filled house and Nanna's presence evoked. Thursdays were a comforting routine of a simple meal—replete with the vegetables she loathed but always ate without argument—served on the slightly wobbly circular pine table in the minuscule but immaculate kitchen.

At the moment, the Scrabble board took up the centre of the table. Nanna was thrashing her. The deep purple box full of yellowed tiles also held a well-thumbed dictionary—Nanna wouldn't countenance the use of any word that didn't appear in the Oxford, except for *qi*, which she used almost every time she picked up the Q—and scribble pads with their scores from 1979 right through 1990. Recorded in Nanna's neat script, the addition done with calculator speed and accuracy in her head, each of the sevens had a neat, slightly angled horizontal line across the vertical, in what she assured Monica was the French fashion.

Recently, every tenth page or so had the total heavily circled in biro: Monica's wins were so rare, she made certain they were obvious.

'Daisy said she's coming down with Rose and the girls,' Nanna said, steam misting her glasses as she raised her brows over a cup of tea.

Hands wrapped around her own cup, Monica nodded. It was really too warm for tea, but it never occurred to Nanna to serve anything else. Breakfast came with tea in a china cup, while lunch and dinner were followed by tea in a mug. There was an additional mug mid-morning, and the china cup resurfaced for afternoon tea, accompanied by two sweet biscuits from the Arnott's Family Assorted selection. Never cream biscuits: they were for Christmas.

It was easy to drink lots of tea, though, as Nanna insisted every teabag was good for two cups. Before she accepted a drink, Monica always checked the kitchen side for a used bag draped across the teaspoon-sized china plate. The thought of the soggy bag sitting around for a couple of hours before being dunked in her boiling water being particularly unappetising, she only had a drink when a fresh bag would be used. 'Yeah, Mum didn't really give them much choice. Said both my aunts and all the girls had to come.'

'And your uncle and the boys?'

Monica shook her head. 'They were excused. Though I don't suppose they could get enough time off to make the trip down south, anyway.'

'No, it's a long haul from Queensland. I take it Ivy is using your engagement to show her sisters how things should be done?'

Monica grinned, too familiar with the never-ending minor feuds between her mother and aunts to let them puncture the bubble of happiness that had been expanding within her since she and Mack set their date. 'She did say something along those lines.'

The windchimes on the small verandah outside the kitchen window tinkled, and Monica squinted through the lacy scrim. In winter, they took their tea by the gas heater in the lounge room, separated from the street by less than a metre of verandah and an anorexic footpath. But as soon as the weather became warmer, Nanna preferred to use the kitchen overlooking the handkerchief-sized cottage garden. Filled with a wild assortment of flowers and self-seeded cherry tomatoes, the plot was sheltered by double-storeyed red brick apartments on three sides, so the windchime rarely made a sound as the dangling teardrop crystal flung shattered rainbows across the garden.

'Must be a storm brewing,' Nanna said as she refilled her Scrabble rack.

Monica arranged her tiles on the board, unnecessarily waiting a moment for Nanna to add up the score. 'Mack's mother is organising everything, so Mum could just chill a bit.' She drummed her fingers on the table to release the excitement that thrilled through her. The pine glowed golden through the layers of varnish Nanna lacquered on to prevent scorching, though she insisted cups be placed on the coasters that she changed as though they were art. This month, the cork tiles were laminated with pictures of native birds. Last month they had been twelve-centimetre square slices of bucolic English village life.

Nanna bent to wedge a sliver of cardboard more firmly under the table's pedestal base. 'That woman has some interesting notions,' she said. 'I gather we're off to sea in a hundred-and-fifty-year-old ship?'

'The *Buffalo* doesn't sail, Nanna. It's a recreation vessel and in dry dock.' Mack's mother had put a deposit down before telling them about the venue, as it was regularly booked out. Her own mum had pretended that she had never considered holding the event in their backyard at Brooks Siding.

'Shame,' Nanna said wryly. 'Though I'm sure there's still opportunity for jokes about avoiding shipwrecks when setting sail into the next part of your life.'

'Getting engaged isn't really a "next part of life" deal,' Monica said, trying to play it cool though clouds of butterflies shivered into flight in her belly. 'It doesn't change anything.'

Nanna snorted, arranging her word on the board. 'Licence to lust, we used to call it. Of course, it's different now. With all your premarital sex and carry-on.'

'Nanna!' Monica wasn't so much shocked at Nanna's words as at the hypocrisy. 'You and Joe weren't married. Or you and Hank.' She barely remembered Joe, only that he'd been bald and had a date palm outside the guest bedroom window, where doves made the most unholy racket from early in the morning. Hank she didn't remember at all, but Mum brought him up often enough. She had never forgiven Nanna for divorcing Grandad.

Nanna shot her a sly grin. 'I'd been married, so it wasn't premarital sex. Besides, men are like boxed chocolates—there's no way to tell what's inside the attractive packaging. Sometimes you have to sample a whole lot to find the one you want.'

'I'm not at all sure that's how it works,' Monica giggled, pushing the tiles into place on the Scrabble board. Her nails were cut short for work: she'd need to get acrylics to show off her engagement ring. She and Mack had spent half of last Saturday staring in the jewellers' windows in Rundle Mall. While she would be happy with almost any ring, Mack's mum said a traditional solitaire would be best. 'Mack and I are waiting, anyway.'

'Until you're married?' Nanna's pencilled eyebrows shot into the straight fringe she tucked under with a curling iron each morning. She'd had short hair forever, but until a few years back it had been a different colour each time Monica saw her. Nanna had an odd, artistic side and had worked the purple rainbow through shades of burgundy, violet, carmine, lilac and blue.

'Well, until we're engaged.'

'That explains the rush, then.' Nanna focused on the board. 'There you are: "coercion" with the C on a triple.'

Monica rolled her eyes at Nanna's triumphant grin.

Her grandmother waggled one finger from side to side. 'Wedding, engagement, there's no real difference. Once you've got that ring and his commitment, a white dress and a church are neither here nor there. Whether he chooses to honour his promise is up to him, not some notion of God.'

Nanna's cynical words made it seem like a good opportunity to ask what had happened all those years ago with her grandfather, but wasn't history always better forgotten? Monica knew that if she had ever been dumped, she sure wouldn't carry the hurt into her future.

11
Lucie

'I can't just stay!' Lucie blurted, before realising she needed to lower her voice so Keeley wouldn't hear her from the next room, separated from the kitchen by a brick archway and two carpet-covered steps. 'It's not an option.' She clutched at the blue-clouded larimar strung on a piece of braided leather around her neck. It was pointless, though: she would need a crystal the size of a car to have even the slimmest chance of adopting any serenity in her mother's presence.

Her dreams of limiting any further contact had been crushed by her mother's insistence that she needed to look through some paperwork. The more Mum suggested Lucie leave Keeley at the B&B with Geoff and come out to Blue Flag by herself, the more Lucie had dug in her heels, insisting they accompany her. Mum had finally agreed Keeley could settle in front of the television in the sunken lounge room as long as the dog remained on her lap and Geoff watched over them both.

Actually, Mum's reluctant words had been: 'I suppose you can bring her by, if you must. It will be boring for her, though.'

Bring her by.

Lucie's hand tightened on the crystal. Her child, to the home of her birth. The home of her entire life, up until four-and-a-half years ago. When Mum had forced—well, persuaded—her to leave. Her gaze roamed the familiar room, the glossy cherrywood cupboards showing no sign of wear, the flecks of colour in the polished black granite countertops dancing beneath the downlights. It wasn't the kitchen of her childhood, as Mum had extensively remodelled it a few years earlier. But Lucie could still link it to events of her past, try to focus on those memories rather than think about Dad.

Except how could she not think about him when, within hours of finding out about his death, she had become certain that he would have accepted Keeley, if only she had come home? Geoff said it was masochism: her guilt tortured her with what *could* have been, regardless of the actual likelihood, and there was no way forward in allowing such thoughts. But Geoff had no idea how impossible it was to block the insidious wondering, the sneaky little daydreams of a life made almost perfect. And if she couldn't allow herself to embrace memories of Dad here, then where?

Panic washed through her, and her gaze searched the room almost frantically. It suddenly seemed that, if she was ever to ease the grief that roiled like a malevolent cloud within her, she needed to connect with Dad, to touch places he had touched, sit in his chair, drink from his cup. Find some way *back* to him, so that she could say goodbye. Yet already the kitchen was showroom sterile. Dad's boots weren't near the door, his cap not on top of the brushed-steel fridge, his huge bunch of keys not on the countertop. 'I can't stay here,' she murmured, although now the words were plaintive rather than the decisive response she intended.

'Why is staying not an *option*?' Mum asked icily, making it clear that Lucie could have nothing more important to do.

'I have a life, Mum.' She waved a hand towards the east, narrowly avoiding knocking one of the glass-fronted boxes from the wall. The six black-framed cubes housed Mum's souvenir teaspoons, each capped with a tiny enamel picture disc and mounted on a burgundy velour background. Lucie had always thought teaspoons from countries Mum had never visited an odd thing for her to collect. And she had never been allowed to touch them. Even before the renovation, when the spoons had hung in neat rows from the dresser shelves, she had been forbidden to touch. Mum said she didn't want them to oxidise beneath grubby fingers, but as she grew older, Lucie wondered if there was a subtext. What memory did the spoons hold that could be tarnished by the touch of a child? Why did Mum slump into a days-long depression each time they arrived with the mail?

Lucie tapped the frame. 'No new spoons?'

'No need,' Mum said.

'You had a *need* for ornamental spoons?'

Mum sighed, sounding unusually defeated. 'Not really. They were a symbol. It doesn't matter now. Anyway, as we were discussing, you need to be here to sort out the paper-work.' She snapped down the lid on the plastic container of Arnott's biscuits. She ate two each afternoon, always Milk Coffee or Nice. Only at Christmas were cream biscuits allowed in the house. She arranged six plain biscuits in a careful pattern radiating from the painted sunflower in the centre of the stoneware plate. Evidently, Keeley wasn't invited to the uncomfortable afternoon tea.

Lucie ran both hands through her hair, mussing it. She knew it irritated her mother, who considered short hair unfeminine. 'And I'm telling you, I have a job, a house, a *life* in Melbourne.'

'A life? Well, wouldn't that be nice.'

The insinuation snatched Lucie's breath, a hard lump forming in her throat. Was Mum inferring that Lucie was responsible for Dad's lack of life or that Mum had been forced to give up the life she wanted? Either way, the claustrophobic press of guilt tightened Lucie's chest. Over the past few days, the emotion came in waves. Yet, unlike the ocean, it washed nothing clean. The guilt remained, the footprints in the sand that had led her away from home.

She willed her voice not to tremble. 'And Keeley has day care and is enrolled in kindy from her birthday. She has friends and playdates that I don't want to disrupt.'

'For goodness' sake, Lucie,' Mum snapped. 'I'm not asking you to move over here. Just to take care of whatever paperwork needs to be done for probate. Send Keeley back with your . . . friend.' She slapped slices of white bread onto another stoneware plate.

'Send her back? As in send her *away*? Like you did to me, you mean?'

'I have never done a thing that wasn't in your interest, Lucie.' Mum rounded on her, voice suddenly low and furious. 'Not a damn thing, and I'll thank you to remember that. I *protected* you by sending you away as soon as I found out what you were up to.'

Geoff's hands pressed onto Lucie's shoulders, firm and reassuring. 'I'm sure your solicitor will be able to handle the probate legalities.'

Neither his measured words nor Keeley's proximity were enough to hold back Lucie's pent-up anger. 'What I was *up to*? I was in love, Mum. Though I guess it seems maybe you don't know what that's like.' She hurled the barbs with all the vengeance of a hurt child. 'Don't you even miss Dad? Aren't you sad that he's dead? Because he's gone, Mum, gone!' She knew she was trying to provoke her mother to shed the tears she herself held back. She was terrified that if anyone but Geoff caught her crying for her father, the questions would come: where had she been for the last four years? Hadn't Gus put her through uni so she could help him in the business? Why had she deserted him when he was—with the harsh judgment and infallible knowledge of hindsight—so apparently unwell?

Her mother staggered back a couple of steps, her pale face a shade whiter than normal, her eyes hard with fury. 'How dare you,' she hissed. 'I loved your father—and you—as well as I was able.'

'As well as you were able?' Lucie mocked. 'What sort of measure is that? Shouldn't you love with everything you have?'

'What do you know of love?' her mother shot back, her tone loaded with vitriol. 'Do you think that's how you loved Jeremy? Are you trying to fool me, or are you still pretending to yourself? As soon as I separated you, it was all over. You left and you forgot him, didn't you?'

'Do I bloody well act like I've forgotten him?' She had spent the last twenty-four hours jumping at shadows, certain that, despite her mother's claim that he was overseas, Jeremy would appear to claim Keeley.

'He was a conquest,' her mother continued triumphantly. 'A man twice your age—'

'How would you even know how old he is?'

'You were determined to prove that you could have whatever you wanted, regardless of the cost to others.'

'What the hell are you on about?' Lucie gasped. 'What cost? There was no one else involved, Jeremy has been divorced for years.' Maturity had added to Jeremy's thrillingly illicit, urbane attraction. Though Dad had said the new marketing manager obviously didn't know *skata* from sugar if he thought suits appropriate attire for business meetings in Blue Flag Strawberries' packing shed, Lucie had been captivated

94

by the debonair, confident man. But it had been years before he'd noticed her. Eventually, she'd used her uni studies as a pretext to meet, seeking his career advice. 'The only cost was to me. In case you've forgotten, Jeremy left me. And you basically forced me to go and live alone in another state.'

Her mother snorted. 'Don't you dare try to play the victim. That right doesn't belong to you. I'm not saying Jeremy is blameless, but it's not like you were innocent, is it? You knew what you wanted.'

'Why is that so wrong? I believed we had a future, that we were planning to build a life together. Here. With Dad— and you—at Blue Flag.'

'Yes, well, those kinds of dreams have a habit of turning sour,' Mum remarked bitterly, seeming to regain her composure. She bent to one of the cupboards, pulling out Tupperware tubs and rummaging around before withdrawing a shaker of multicoloured hundreds and thousands. 'They belong in books. You should never let yourself fixate on one man.'

'But I loved him,' Lucie said desperately, trying to persuade herself of the strength of the almost-forgotten emotion that had turned her life upside down.

'You were a foolish child, Lucie. You wanted your toy. And Jeremy? Well, he most certainly wanted to play a game, didn't he?'

'A child? I was practically the same age you were when you had me.'

'After I'd been married for a year, you mean?'

'Jeremy and I were together for fifteen months!' Lucie defended. Yet her mother's words provoked an almost-buried memory of the night they first kissed.

'Lucie, you know you can't tell anyone about us. About this.' Jeremy moved a hand the few centimetres between their chests, stirring the air in the close confines of the car. 'Okay?'

Her lips still burned from their kiss. 'I'm not exactly jail bait, you know.'

'I'm not messing around,' Jeremy said sternly, his finger twirling a ringlet of her hair.

'I'd argue that you are,' she teased, wondering whether her frantic pulse was visible. She had fantasised this for so long, it was hard to accept the reality.

Deep grooves lined Jeremy's cheeks as he shot her a rueful grin and scrubbed one hand through the perfect fade of his salt-and-pepper hair. 'You're right. I am messing around. Because that's exactly what this is.' The leather upholstery creaked as he leaned in to run his fingertips from her elbow up to her neck, his sea-blue eyes intent. 'Right?'

Had it all been a game to Jeremy? Had she imagined more into the relationship than he ever intended? He often said they were nothing more than a May–December fling, but she laughed off his teasing.

Mum shrugged. *'Love is only a dirty trick played on us to achieve continuation of the species.'*

'You're quoting Somerset Maughan at me? If that's what you really think, did you ever bother to tell Dad?' Lucie snapped. Yet, despite her swift retaliation, Mum—or, more precisely, Somerset Maughan—may have been correct. She had believed she loved Jeremy—and the consequence of that delusion was Keeley. The most beautiful continuation of the species ever.

The familiar desolation hit the pit of her stomach, a yearning for something she had so briefly experienced and knew she would never feel again. 'No matter how you try to brush it off, Mum, I *did* love him. And you know what's truly terrifying? Even though Jeremy hurt me, maybe that was the only time in my life I'll ever get to feel love like that.'

'*Love makes the time pass. Time makes love pass.*' Mum's icy gaze flicked to where Geoff stood behind her.

'Got me beat,' he muttered.

'It's just some pretentious wank she gets off the desk calendar,' Lucie snarled.

'Euripides,' Mum said. 'The thing is, you only *thought* you loved Jeremy. He was lying to you, and you are still lying to yourself. I knew I couldn't talk to you about it— for goodness' sake, you haven't listened to me since you were six years old. You have your father's stubbornness to thank for that.'

'Dad, stubborn? Jesus, Mum, you ran him like a bull with a ring through his nose.' Her mother was the only person she had ever considered her father to be afraid of.

Mum shook her head. 'Dad had a temper, just like you. But his was a cold, hard fury that you never saw.'

'And you're trying to say that's why you sent me away, to protect me from my own father?' Her mother was off the planet. Sure, Dad had been introspective; they'd stopped talking. But cold and hard? Never.

'Partly. But also so you could get some distance, some perspective, and recognise the truth for yourself. You have to be careful, learn to guard your heart.' Mum spread margarine on the bread with short, sharp movements.

'Oh my god,' Lucie choked. 'You're really going to pull out that old crock of shit? Say that you sent me away for my own good? I thought your whole story was that it was for Dad's sake, but now it was supposedly for me? You see who the common denominator is in both of those stories, Mum, the one person who wanted me gone?' Yet, even as she flung the half-formed accusations, she knew they made no sense: her mother had nothing to gain by banishing her. Nothing except having Dad all to herself, but then she had never seemed particularly keen on his company.

Brightly coloured sugar balls rained over the bread. 'I'm not saying that you can't love at all. Despite what you seem to think, I did love your father. But I was careful about it, cautious about how much I allowed myself to get invested in the relationship. I made sure never to lose my sense of self in either you or your father.'

'Jesus,' Geoff muttered behind Lucie. It was the first time she had known him to be lost for words.

'Mum, do you even hear yourself? You were *careful* about loving? What kind of life is that?'

'It's a learned life, Lucie. And that's what you need to do: take your mistakes and learn from them. It's the only way to survive. And no, that doesn't mean that losing Georgius doesn't hurt. But it means I can compartmentalise that pain. I deliberately didn't allow him to be my everything. Yet it seems like you still haven't learned the lesson. Perhaps you could do with some distance.' Mum jerked her chin at Geoff.

Lucie frowned. 'Distance? From Geoff? We're not—' She broke off, shaking her head. 'You know what? It's none of your damn business.'

'Of course not.' Mum's gaze rested on the teaspoons on the wall. 'You must be everything only for yourself, Lucie. Never allow anyone to take that from you, don't allow them to rob you of a sense of self, don't model your dreams on their desires, don't hide yourself in the role of girlfriend or wife or mother. Everything else is fleeting; everyone dies, leaves, changes. *You* are all you will ever truly have, so you have to be faithful to yourself above all others.'

Lucie shook her head vehemently. 'You're a freaking nut job. And you're so wrong. Keeley is my everything. I'll never hold any portion of my love back from her.'

Her mother looked disappointed. 'Then you're setting yourself up to be hurt.'

'You want to know what really hurts? What totally fucks a kid up and leaves her crying in her bed at night? Knowing that her mother truly doesn't give a damn about her, that she's always going to be remote, aloof, untouchable.' Lucie could barely breathe for the pressure crushing her chest, forcing the words from her mouth. 'Being the only teenager who gets excited because her mum suddenly engages in her life for the briefest moment. But even those good times—holidays, working in the garden, shopping trips, it didn't matter what, literally every single thing was spoiled by the knowledge that you would withdraw from me again.' She heaved in a jagged breath. 'But I never realised that your choices were deliberate, that you were actively working at not loving me.'

Her mother slammed the shaker onto the counter. It toppled, then rolled across the hard surface and fell to the floor, edible confetti spreading across the tiles like the sad refuse of a ruined party. She grasped Lucie by the upper arms, her bony fingers digging through her jumper. 'You're not listening, Lucie. I never said that I don't love you. I've never done a thing to make you believe that. I gave you absolutely all that I could afford to. Emotionally, I mean. I've always loved you. I simply said that I'm careful to hold a piece of myself in reserve. Is that so greedy? I make certain I have a place to fall back to within myself when everything turns to shit. If I had invested everything in your father, if I had tied myself to him emotionally, how would I survive now?' She released Lucie's arms and gave a harsh, dry laugh. 'Believe me, I know what it's like to crumble when you realise you've lost everything, everything that you were pinning your hopes and dreams on. But, see, that's why you never give it all: then you can't lose it all. I can say goodbye to Dad, and I can carry on with my life. I know how, now. I know how to protect myself, how to endure.'

Lucie slapped a hand against her own chest, pressing the useless crystal into her neck. 'But *I* don't get to say goodbye,' she said brokenly. 'You sent me away, Mum.

You sent me away, and I never got to say goodbye, and that's just not fair!'

Her mother rolled her eyes. 'Why does everyone have such a preoccupation with what's fair? Life isn't fair, Lucie. We aren't born *deserving* some kind of easy ride. About the only guarantee is that those you love will desert and disappoint you.'

Lucie shook her head incredulously. 'How can you be so bitter? Dad didn't desert you, he *died*. And why am I such a disappointment? It's not like I committed a crime, or got into drugs or something. I had a baby. That's it. Plenty of my friends have kids without being married. And you know what?' Her lungs aching, she almost choked on the words. 'Their mothers are happy to be grandmothers. There's no judgment, none of this bullshit condemnation and *disappointment*.'

'And where are these friends now?' Mum said smugly.

Lucie flinched: although she claimed to own her mistakes and choices, she had distanced herself from her friends in favour of licking her wounds in private. It was as though she had started a new life in Melbourne. A half-life, where her existence was tied only to Keeley. She pushed the thought aside, wrapping herself in her anger. 'Did you know Dad was sick? Did you know he was living on borrowed time? Did you deliberately keep it from me, while you were so busy nursing your *disappointment*?'

'He wasn't sick, Lucie. And borrowed time is a ridiculous phrase. We have whatever time we have. It isn't borrowed, it is bestowed. Yes, Dad had high blood pressure, but

101

there was nothing serious that we knew about. This was just a . . . a . . .' Her mother waved vaguely around the kitchen, seeking inspiration, then picked up a dishcloth and presented them her ramrod straight back as she scrubbed at the bench, shoving the plate of fairy bread to one side. 'A horrible tragedy. There was no way to predict it, no way to prevent it. If I'd had any inkling this could happen, don't you think I would have brought you home? Even though you come with . . . baggage.'

'Baggage?' Geoff murmured ominously. His arm caged Lucie's ribs, pulling her protectively back against his chest.

'She means her granddaughter,' Lucie said scathingly, the tears instantly disappearing. 'Right, Mum? My baggage is your only grandchild.'

'And your feelings, clearly,' Mum said levelly, any hint of emotion suddenly smoothed from her tone. She held the plate of fairy bread out to Geoff and lifted her chin towards the lounge. 'Take this to . . . her.'

'Keeley. Her name is Keeley!' Lucie snarled.

As Geoff reflexively reached for the plate, Mum snatched it back, slammed it onto the counter, and severed the crusts, the blade hitting the porcelain with a series of four harsh cracks. With two swift strokes she triangled the stacked slices. Then she passed the plate back without looking at Geoff. 'Indeed. Lucie, I need you here until all this legal palaver is sorted and we can move on.'

'No,' Lucie said decisively. 'I'm so done here. Dad was all I ever wanted to come back for.' If her mother wanted to hurt her through Keeley, Lucie wasn't above fighting back.

'And your father would expect you to help out now.'

Lucie sagged in despair. Even though she had known Mum would pull that card, there weren't enough crystals or positive affirmations in the world to protect her from the instant guilt.

'I'll organise accommodation for you,' Mum closed in on her victory.

Exhaustion washed over Lucie, debilitating and numbing. 'It's wild that knowing I'm being manipulated apparently still doesn't protect me from it,' she muttered. 'You know what, why don't you just banish us to Settlers Bridge? That's where you hide your dirty little secrets, isn't it?'

12
Monica

1990

'Is it about the sex?' Monica folded her arms across her chest as though she was angry, but really she was desperately holding the halves of her heart together. 'Because if it's about the sex, we don't have to wait. I just thought that it would be nice, kind of an extra, you know? Like our engagement present to ourselves.' Her voice was high, her tone frantic. But still Mack wouldn't meet her eyes.

He stared at the bitumen path that wound through the Botanic Gardens alongside the hospital where she had spent so many hours studying. 'It's not that, Mon. Jeez, if it was about the sex, I'd have been out months ago. You know I liked that about you, the fact that you aren't an easy lay. It's just . . . I don't know. The whole thing. It's kind of all too much.'

Liked. Past tense. Shit, she shouldn't have pushed him to plan the wedding before they'd even got engaged. Monica wiped a trembling hand across her mouth, swallowing down the sudden excess saliva; she was going to be sick. 'It's fine,' she blurted. 'We'll put the whole thing off. I mean, we haven't booked anything for the wedding, there's no reason we can't postpone.'

Mack nudged at the creeping lawn with the toe of his loafer but didn't speak.

She couldn't breathe. Her throat closed, her lungs filled with cement. Tears blurred her vision and she shook her head, forcing the words out. 'I mean, we can even put off the engagement too, if you want. We'll lose our deposit with the *Buffalo*, but that's no biggie.' She was clutching at straws—or, in the face of Mack's silence, clutching at their relationship. This couldn't happen, they hadn't even argued. Hadn't *ever* argued, in fact. From the moment they met, they had been perfect.

Mack lifted his head, but the difference in their heights allowed him to avoid her eyes, gazing over her, into the distance. His tongue darted out to wet his lips. The perfect lips, full and firm, that she'd planned to spend the rest of her life kissing. 'It won't make any difference, Mon. I think . . .' He screwed up his face, the grimace carving furrows into his closely shaved cheeks. 'Maybe we burned too bright, you know? It was so good, so perfect, it's like we've reached the peak of what we could be.'

'What the hell are you talking about?' she gasped. 'But—but we have *plans*, Mack. I've already given notice on my room.' They were moving into a unit in St Peters, one suburb from Nanna, in two weeks' time, right after the engagement party.

Mack lifted one shoulder, the camel-coloured Hugo Boss suit bunching. His icy eyes met hers. 'You'll be qualified soon, Mon. You can go anywhere. Work anywhere. You want to go overseas, you told me that the night we met.' He gripped her upper arms, and she couldn't help but lean in closer to him. 'There's no way I can take time off in my first year, we've got loads of new accounts coming in and Dad would kill me. I'm holding you back.'

'You're not holding me back,' she burst out. 'Travelling was just my dream because I'd been stuck in Brooks Siding all my life. It doesn't matter, it's not important. It's what we have that's important, Mack. You're my dream, now.'

The corner of Mack's mouth lifted in a pained smile, loaded with regret. 'I can't do it to you, Mon. It wouldn't be right. We have to call this off.'

'Off?' The word echoed around the gardens, startling a flock of noisy miners foraging in the ivy beneath the trees. 'Everything?' A wave of fury sliced through her anguish, tightening her mouth until she had trouble pushing the words free. 'You're dumping me and yet you have the nerve to try to make it sound as though you're doing me a favour?'

Mack glanced at the TAG Heuer his parents had given him for graduation then ran a hand through his hair, which she'd persuaded him to have bleached and wear teased out like Peter Blakeley's, ready for their engagement. She'd also chosen a load of Blakeley's songs to be played at the party, including 'Crying in the Chapel'. Which, right now, seemed horribly prophetic. 'I've got to get back to work.' Mack moved to take a step away from her but then paused. 'You're young, Mon,' he wheedled, as though there were more than a few months between them. 'You need to travel. Do some stuff with your life before you settle down.'

Ducks in the lily pond a short distance away erupted into a cacophony of quacking laughter.

'Like you have, you mean,' she sneered, the anger washing through her in bitter waves. How could this be happening, when everything had been so perfect only minutes ago when she darted down the sun-splashed path, eager to spend her lunchbreak with the man she loved? Her almost-fiancé.

He lifted one shoulder. 'I've travelled.'

'With your parents.'

His jaw hardened and he snorted through the back of his nose. 'Seriously? I took the opportunities that were offered me, Monica. You're going to throw that back in my face? Jeez, Mum said you'd have problems with the differences between us.'

'Differences? Mack, we're practically the same person. You know we're always in sync.' Until now, that was. Fear threatened to chase her anger away: Mack was serious and she had a horrible premonition that this wasn't just their first lovers' tiff, to be smoothed over with kisses and cuddles. 'What differences?' She shoved her hair back behind her ear as a warm breeze, laden with the perfume of flowers and new growth, teased her sinuses with a whispered lie of permanent spring.

Mack stuffed his hands into the pockets of his suit pants, careful not to dislodge the tail of his tie tucked into the waistband. For the first time he seemed uncomfortable instead of exuding his usual overt confidence. 'You know. Upbringing. Education. Lifestyle.'

'You're kidding me.' She staggered back. 'It's nineteen ninety—what bloody century are you living in?'

'It's not me. It's—'

'Your parents? You're twenty-one and you're blaming them?' She clutched onto her fury, the only thing stopping her from falling to the path in a puddle of misery and tears.

Mack blew out a long breath. 'Come on, Mon. We can still be friends. We'll just back this whole thing off a bit, okay? Maybe see other people.'

She stilled; even her heart stopped. 'You're already seeing someone, aren't you?'

'No, of course not. Not exactly seeing, anyway. Michelle's a friend of the family, so she's always been around. It's not like I'm . . . hooking up with her or anything.' Mack thrust his hands deeper into his pockets. His expression belligerent, he trained his gaze on a family picnicking near the lily pond.

Monica stared at him in absolute silence. The traffic on North Terrace faded to nothing, the birds disappeared.

She had never truly known this man. 'I trusted you.' A wealth of hurt and broken dreams burgeoned in a dark cloud within her, suffocating her love. 'And I will never forgive you.'

13

Lucie

'How am I going to manage without you?' Lucie said, adding weight to the mournful proclamation by thrusting out her bottom lip in imitation of one of Keeley's sulks. Her daughter waited—not exactly patiently—in the car parked against the kerb at the rear of their Melbourne townhouse. Despite having returned from South Australia only days earlier, Keeley was eager for the road trip.

'More to the point, how am I going to manage without the pair of you? Three of you,' Geoff amended as Dash yipped excitedly from the back seat.

'I'm sure you'll have plenty of distraction.' Lucie tilted her head to where Geoff's partner, Finlay, lounged against the red-painted front door, politely pretending not to be able to hear their parting.

Geoff gave a slightly embarrassed grin, lowering his voice. 'Yeah, Fin is being a bit of a princess about coming over. He doesn't seem to consider Settlers Hill—'

'Bridge,' she corrected, pressing a hand against the car window so Keeley would know she hadn't been deserted. 'Settlers Bridge. I don't know whether Mum ignored my sarcasm or if she honestly thinks that's where I want to stay.'

Geoff raised an eyebrow. 'Told you before, you're not as hilarious as you think you are. No wonder the poor woman was confused.' He ducked an imaginary blow from her. 'Anyway, Fin doesn't rate Settlers Bridge as a tourist destination, but we can make it over there in a couple of weeks' time. Even though your mum scares the absolute hell out of me.'

'She's a bit of a ball breaker, isn't she? It's like she hates men. My dad included.'

'That makes me feel a bit less special,' Geoff joked. 'But terror aside, the offer stands.'

Lucie shook her head, the wind ruffling her hair and icing the flash of naked ankle between her boots and jeans. Even though winter was a month gone, still Melbourne's pervasive gloominess dragged on. 'No, you already took time off for the funeral. And it'll be good for you guys to have chance to be together without a house full of dogs and kids.' Finlay had joined their household only a few months earlier, and the chaos of living with a three-year-old probably wasn't the best way for anyone to start out in a new relationship.

Geoff's hands chafed her upper arms, warming through the thin sweater. Keeley liked the car super-heated, but Lucie couldn't risk getting sleepy on the trip so had dressed minimally. 'You know I'm going to miss both of those elements. And you too, Tumbleweed.'

'I could always leave the dog,' she suggested, although there was no way Keeley would be separated from the pup. It was hard enough to convince her that Dash would have to be strapped into his own tiny harness, not share her booster. 'Anyway, we'll be back before you have a chance to miss us.'

'Doesn't look much like it.' Geoff tipped his head towards the older model Toyota RAV4, packed to the windows with clothes, Keeley's toys and books, and the dog's belongings, which, for such a small puppy, took up a surprising amount of space.

Instead of having Geoff fly home and freight her belongings back to South Australia, Lucie had figured she needed the trip back to Melbourne with him to unpack her feelings before packing up her life. She pulled a face. 'Blue Flag has managers, so I'm choosing to think that things can't have got too screwed up in such a short time, but . . .' She lifted one shoulder rather than finish the sentence. Because if Dad had been waiting for her to come back and look after the accounts, maybe it was more like years of mess, rather than weeks. 'But once the will is sorted, Mum can organise accountants or whatever she wants.' She stopped short of saying she would never have anything more to do with Mum because, bizarrely, given the way her mother had ripped into her, she wasn't quite ready for that. Some tiny part of her was still clinging to the hope that the mother of her earliest childhood memories would re-emerge, that the increasingly cold, hard stranger would thaw like the blooms in the frozen birdbath. Yet she knew that the recollections of infancy were unreliable: in truth, her mother had always been insular. But until she had a comparison point, for years Lucie hadn't recognised her mum's shortcomings and had loved her unconditionally.

Although their street was quiet, only a block away the mid-morning traffic throbbed by, the white-noise drone occasionally interrupted by a squeal of tyres or jarring melody of horns. Mrs A's cat appeared from the side passage, making for one of the potted rosemary plants Lucie kept at the front door. Dash yapped and the tom sauntered towards the car. The dachshund bolted from the back of the vehicle to the front seat, using the armrest to wedge himself up high enough to see out of the windows. His long, silky ears almost tripped him as he tap-danced his front paws from one end of the armrest to the other. The cat sat on the sidewalk, washing himself nonchalantly while keeping his startling golden gaze on the dog.

'Looks like the cat knows he's got the place to himself now,' Finlay said. He did a fair job of not sounding too gleeful, Lucie thought, although considering his wiry build, he was managing to fill the doorway in a very proprietorial manner.

'Yeah, he'll be a monster now,' she agreed. 'You've no hope of Mrs A keeping him under control, so I suggest you buy your herbs from the market.'

'Market?' Finlay sounded shocked. 'Hon, you know we'll have to eat out without you here to take care of us.'

'Without me here to moderate your diets, you mean.' Finlay was not a fan of the wholesome, organic food she served. Lucie circled a hand airily in a royal wave. 'In which case, to you I bequeath Geoff's chronic indigestion.' Then she flung her arms around Geoff's neck, revelling in his familiar, comforting squeeze. She lowered her voice. 'Seriously, take it easy on the crap, Geoff, okay? That *Helicobacter pylori* is not something to mess around with—you don't want an ulcer. Remember, loads of green tea and liquorice root. And don't kill your kefir.'

'Yes, Mum,' he said meekly. He gave Lucie another squeeze and kissed her cheek before releasing her. 'And speaking of, say hi to yours for me.'

She grimaced. 'When I turn up without you, I'm pretty sure she'll be convinced I've managed to drive away another good man. Even with all her lecturing about maintaining my emancipation and making sure I don't ever fall in love, I'll no doubt have failed to live up to the expectations of her stone-cold heart yet again.'

Geoff pointed a long finger at her, adopting a stern tone. 'You tell me you're like your dad, but I see a lot of your mum in you.'

'Wow, way to make it easy for me to leave, Geoff! I just called her a cold-hearted bitch and you're comparing us?'

Geoff shook his head. 'I meant because you've both built this façade, whether it's to protect you from being hurt, or to protect you from grief. But the thing is, you don't know what lies ahead, Lucie, you only know what lies behind. You let past experience—whether it's with your mum or with a partner—colour your expectation. For four years I've watched you push away every guy on the basis that Jeremy proved all men are untrustworthy. Now you'll do the same with your mum.'

'I trusted you,' she pointed out sulkily. 'Though I'm rethinking that right now.'

Geoff pinched her chin between thumb and forefinger, shaking her head a little. 'Just give her a chance, Luce, is all I'm saying.'

She laughed, but the sound was made short by her annoyance. Geoff was the only person she would ever tolerate giving her a hard time, but even he could push it a bit far in his determination to help her better herself. 'I'm pretty sure I exist only to make her miserable.'

'Come on. Manifesting, remember? Positive thoughts. At least she rings you now.'

The heavy breath she puffed out misted in the damp air. If only she could find the rose-coloured glasses that must have been in the dress-up box of her youth, then she'd find the parents of her memory. 'I guess the truth is I miss Mum horribly. Right up until the moment I see her.'

'Ah, Tumbleweed, I wish I had some way to make this easier on you,' Geoff murmured.

His ankles neatly crossed, Finlay lounged indifferently against the doorframe. But his arms, tightly folded over his chest and the hard jut of his chin gave him away. He often seemed uncomfortable with the rapport she and Geoff shared, and around him she was usually careful to maintain a little distance, both emotional and physical, from her best friend. But not today, because leaving Geoff, even for a short time, hurt a damn sight more than she had expected. 'It is what it is. Just something to be got through, I guess.'

Geoff glanced up as a bellbird chimed its distinctive loud *tink* from one of the eucalypts that softened the harsh grey angles of the road, gutter and footpath. 'Maybe it won't be all bad. Seems to me you've mentioned a particular guy a few times since the funeral.'

'Only because that whole thing was weird,' she defended. 'Some random farmer saying we'd catch up later. It was . . . creepy.'

'Uh-huh. Sure,' Finlay sang out.

As she frowned, Geoff turned her slightly away from Fin and pulled a small burgundy jewellery box from his pocket, pressing it into her hand.

'Wow, I didn't realise we were that serious.' She tried to joke, but all this felt too much like goodbye. Her hand trembled as she popped the velour lid open. A tiny purple crystal stud lay pinned to the white satin interior.

'Amethyst for safe travels, right?' Geoff tapped the side of her nose. She'd removed her stud the previous week, deciding that bringing attention to the piercing would invite a level of judgment from Mum that she just didn't need. 'Remember to be yourself. You're adorable and woman and strong and every single thing you need to be.'

14
Lucie

Even with Dash determined they wake early each day, and Settlers Bridge only a little more than three hours from their overnight stop at Bordertown, it was after lunch by the time the broad pewter sweep of the Murray River came into sight at Tailem Bend.

As she gazed across the water to the distant smudge of the Mount Lofty Ranges a sense of homecoming coursed through Lucie. Unlike the flight last week, where the distance was swallowed by the tin-can loungeroom atmosphere of the plane, each kilometre she travelled west eased the constriction of her chest. Now she had the curious notion that once she crossed the river, she would be transported to where she belonged. Not necessarily a place, but a period in time when love had still seemed possible and loss was unknown.

The slow travel had a lot to do with her passengers—
a three-year-old and a puppy who couldn't match their
wee-stop needs meant for a lot of exploring of roadside
laybys and every town they passed through. When they
reached Settlers Bridge, Lucie could have pushed on for forty
minutes, gone to Mum's for afternoon tea. But that's all
it was now: Mum's place. The lack of welcome for Keeley
had unravelled any tie Lucie felt towards the home of her
childhood. Instead, she located the real estate agent—a
single room in the front of a house—and picked up the
keys to the rental her mum had organised for her, along
with an assurance that the place was fully furnished. Then
she doubled back to the IGA that she had spotted on the
main street as they crossed the bridge from the east.

A flowering gum stood opposite the grocery store, and
Lucie pulled the car into its dappled shade. As she opened
the window a sliver, she recoiled. The bright sunshine and
cloudless blue sky were deceptive: the breeze still held the
chill of winter, but the air smelled crisp and clean. 'Come
on, sweetie. We'll have to leave Dash in the car for a minute
again. Purple Ted can keep him company.'

'I needs beanie,' Keeley proclaimed with a hint of accusation, crossing her chubby arms over her chest and shivering
dramatically. The real estate office had been heated by an
old-school three-bar radiator, but the twelve steps from car
to front door had evidently been too chilly for her daughter.

'You do *need* one,' Lucie agreed. 'And I've got it right
here. When we get to our holiday home, you can choose

a jumper for Dash to put on, too. But for now he can stay in here, nice and snuggly, while we get some yummy food.'

She glanced over her shoulder before cracking the car door. The caution was unnecessary as there were only three other vehicles in the street, two of them on her side facing the grey river at the end of the road. On the other side was a decrepit ute that looked like it hadn't moved for a decade. Although Settlers Bridge wasn't quite a ghost town, unlike the oddly named Ki Ki or Culburra, both of which they had passed through earlier, it was evidently headed that way.

Lucie scowled at the Australia Post sign that took up most of the nearest shop window, behind glass greyed by decades of scratches and sticky-tape residue. Geoff would say there was no such thing as coincidence, that she had subconsciously parked here because it was time she addressed the desertion she had felt every month for the last four years as each impersonal letter from her mother arrived postmarked by this remote office.

It was lucky for her then that Geoff wasn't here, she thought, although his imagined commentary had been degrees of annoying and entertaining in her head throughout the long drive. She thrust the door wide, the car flooding with a heady floral scent.

As it was Saturday, the post office had a red-and-white 'closed' sign hanging from a suction cup on the glass front door. 'No such thing as coincidence, remember, Geoff?' she gloated. Over the course of the road trip, she had realised two things: one, there were only so many times she could sing along with the *Sesame Street* theme. And two, it was easier to win a debate with Geoff when he was present only in her mind. A fact that was nowhere near compensation enough to stop her from missing her best friend.

She clambered from the car, sticking her hands into the pockets of her sleeveless jacket, wondering whether she had remembered to pack her own beanie.

Although mainly comprised of squat buildings with verandahs hunched over the footpath like a permanent frown, the short street had a few substantial buildings. A pair of pubs near the bridge faced off across a four-lane road divided by a paved pedestrian island. Gutters made of stone slabs ran the length of the street, their depth ludicrous given that this was a low rainfall area. On her side of the road, smaller shops sat between the pub and a sandstone building with the Commonwealth Bank logo jutting out like an erupting pimple.

Her gaze travelled to the opposite pavement then darted back in disbelief: each building seemed to be mirrored across the road, the counterpart similar both in purpose and appearance. According to the signage, the post office doubled as a general store: on the opposite side of the street the IGA had an identical shopfront, right down to the scratched glass and access ramp. A few buildings down, a shop window adorned with a cartoonish representation of a farm machine and emblazoned with *Tractors and Tarts* in gold paint faced its twin, *Ploughs and Pies*, the window decorated with a stencilled wheatfield and burgundy lettering. A newsagent stood opposite a butcher, the magazines laid out on a sloping window display that mimicked the geometric lines of the empty butcher's trays.

Lucie glanced from one side of the road to the other, uncertain whether to be amused by the symmetry or bemused by the surreal effect. She shook her head and unbuckled Keeley, then carried the pre-schooler across the deserted road and up the ramp to the IGA. As Lucie fought her way between orange plastic fly strips hung across the doorway, Keeley captured her face between her hands, making sure she had her mother's full attention. 'I big now, Mummy. I walk by self.'

Her hands smelled doggy, and Lucie wrinkled her nose. She would have to remember the bamboo wet wipes before they ate, although a little grot was important for a robust immune system. 'You can walk, but you have to hold my hand. Or the trolley, because we're going to need one,' Lucie added as she surveyed the shopping list on her phone. She had brought along her cultures, the kefir and kombucha, as well as chia and hemp seeds, nori and other staples she suspected would be hard to get outside of the city, but still she needed to stock up on a lot of stuff if she was going to be here a few weeks. She didn't want to turn up at Mum's tomorrow acting as though she had any expectations, including that of being fed. And she also didn't want Keeley getting fairy bread again. Of course, Keeley had been thrilled with the treat and Geoff eager to point out that her mother thinking to feed Keeley was surely a step in the right direction.

He didn't realise that Mum was trying to undermine her strict views on nutrition and win Keeley over, while still refusing to acknowledge her existence.

The trolley had a mind of its own, all four wheels determined to pull to the left. Fortunately, the three aisles were only about ten metres long, and it didn't take her much time to collect the groceries.

Although not holding either her hand or the trolley, Keeley skipped happily alongside, keeping up a constant monologue that switched from what games Dash liked to play, to how interesting the food on the shelves looked.

Within ten minutes, Lucie trundled the trolley towards the checkout, the sides of the scratched wooden counter cluttered with stands of garishly coloured Lifesavers and Tic Tacs. 'Will you help me chop up carrot sticks and celery to go with the hummus when we get to our new house?' she said brightly, hoping to circumvent Keeley's wide-eyed wonder. They did most of their shopping in the wholefoods store or online, so this was a new world for Keeley.

Keeley nodded, although she didn't take her eyes from the lollies.

'Well, that sounds yummy.' The magenta-haired woman at the checkout did a great job of making her tone believable. 'Though I really like French onion dip, myself.'

Suddenly shy, Keeley pressed against Lucie's side, her thumb against her closed lips.

That was a good sign: when she was upset or overtired, Keeley would suck her thumb, but right now, she just had it in a 'ready' position.

'Did you find everything you need, love?' the woman asked Lucie.

'Almost. I don't suppose you have raw goat's milk?'

The cashier frowned. 'Isn't unpasteurised illegal?'

'Goat's milk is approved. Just hard to come by.'

'Well, let me see now.' The woman tapped her bottom lip with a pen. 'Matt Krueger would know who has goats round here. He's the local vet. I can give him a call if you like?'

'Oh gosh no,' Lucie said, taken aback. 'It's not important, don't bother.'

'It's no trouble.' The cashier's hand hovered over a brick-sized telephone alongside the register. 'Are you sure?'

'Absolutely.' Lucie held up one hand. 'We've plenty of other options.'

The woman nodded and her gaze shifted to Keeley. 'Speaking of Matt, how old would you be, possum?' she said. 'I'm guessing about three, because you look the same size as Roni and Matt's littlies.'

Keeley's eyes widened and she knuckled her mouth, glancing up to Lucie for permission to speak. Lucie nodded encouragingly. 'I four,' Keeley proclaimed.

'Four? My goodness, you are a big girl, then!' The woman leaned over, her ample bosom pressing against the counter as she craned towards Keeley.

Keeley nodded proudly, stretching up a hand displaying all five fingers. 'I this big.'

'Nearly four,' Lucie corrected, gently folding in Keeley's thumb. 'It's your birthday in November, isn't it?'

'Oh, are you having a party? That'll be exciting.' The woman straightened, starting to put the groceries Lucie unloaded through the register. There was no conveyor, and she rang up each item manually.

'We're not sure yet,' Lucie said quickly. 'It depends whether we're still here.'

'You're staying locally?' The renewed interest in the woman's perusal and tone was unmistakable.

'We've rented a house for a few weeks.'

'Oh, you'll be in one of mine, then,' the woman said. 'Claire at the real estate mentioned she'd set up the house for a young family. I'm Lynn,' she added with a smile. Then she turned her attention back to Keeley. 'And I'm guessing you must look like your daddy.'

Lucie winced. No one would ever pick the blonde cherub as her daughter. 'I've never thought about it,' she said quickly, then bit her lip, knowing how transparent her lie was. 'Actually, she's the spitting image of my mum.'

'Well, how lovely for your nan.' Lynn leaned over the scratched wooden counter again, a slight frown between her eyes, as though she needed to see Keeley more closely. 'Who would your mum be? This little one does look familiar.'

Lucie tossed the groceries into one of the fabric carriers she'd brought in. 'Mum's not from around here.'

'Looks like you're settling in, though.' Lynn tipped her head towards the shopping. 'Quite a pantry fill-up.'

How had she forgotten that small-town folk operated without a filter, and everyone's private business was offered up for public consumption? The complete opposite to

Melbourne, where you could wait with the same people at the tram stop every day for three years without ever acknowledging them. 'We drove over from Melbourne, and this Mother Hubbard doesn't even have a bone for the dog,' she grinned at Keeley, holding up the packet of Dentastix that Dash loved. Or at least, he loved them when he ran out of slippers, toys and furniture legs.

'You have a puppy?' Lynn said to Keeley. 'What's his name?'

'His name Dash. Cos he little. Littler than me. But biggerer than a dot, Mummy says.'

Lynn nodded as though that made perfect sense.

'And I'm going to put his jumper on when we get home,' Keeley added, gaining confidence. 'To our new home. Just for holiday.'

'Dash likes jumpers, does he?' Lynn said. 'I'll have to tell the girls at the CWA that. Might be a fundraiser for next winter. I don't suppose the working dogs will get a look-in, but a few of the older folk here have the little orna-mental pups.'

'The jumpers certainly cost enough at pet stores,' Lucie said. Not that she paid for Dash's wardrobe; buying outrage-ously priced dog couture was one of Geoff's passions.

Lucie wished she had purchased fewer groceries so they could escape before Lynn returned to the subject of Keeley's parentage. Better still, she should have shopped in Murray Bridge. It wasn't far away, and she would have been safely anonymous in the larger town. Without the risk of encountering Jeremy, the crushing fear that had numbed her last visit had been removed, but she still didn't need reminders of his existence or rights. For now, she wanted only to have to deal with the grief that re-emerged in odd moments, odd memories.

And with her mother.

Lynn rang up the total and took Lucie's card. 'You should find everything you need already in the cottage,' she said.

'You get a decent tourist trade here, then?'

One purple apron strap slipped down Lynn's plump arm. 'Maybe we would if we advertised, but I just buy the properties and keep them nice so the town doesn't look like it's falling into wrack and ruin, you know? I'm hoping that one day it will repopulate, but until then I like to make sure it stays neat and tidy.' She handed over a receipt. 'Claire won't open up the office again until Wednesday, so if you're missing anything, just come looking for me. If you can't find me here, I'll be over at the pub.'

The familiarity was comforting: Wednesday schnitzel nights at the local pub had always been part of Lucie's life at home. 'Thanks.' She bundled the bags into the trolley, belatedly realising how hard it was going to be to navigate the four lanes and centre strip, even without traffic. 'Come on, Keeley, let's go find our new house.'

She pushed the trolley down the ramp, Keeley clutching the hem of her vest. Somehow she had to get six bags of groceries and Keeley safely over to the car.

'Look, Mummy,' Keeley tugged her jacket and pointed at the footpath in front of them. 'Bug.'

Lucie angled the trolley so it wouldn't roll onto the road and stepped around it to see what had caught Keeley's attention. A large black beetle was stranded on its back, six legs waving feebly in the air. 'It's a rhinoceros beetle,' she said. 'I haven't seen one of those for ages.'

'Why he doing that, Mummy?'

'Waving his legs? Because he's stuck. Sometimes they get blown over by the wind and they can't get back the right way, because they're not nice and bendy like you.' She ran her fingertips up Keeley's spine, and her daughter giggled.

'Tickly. We help him, Mummy.'

'We will.' She crouched down on the pavement. 'We need to pick him up very carefully, and then I'll show you something really special.'

With her thumb and forefinger, she lifted up the large beetle then placed it flat in her palm. 'See, he has a big horn. He looks a bit like a unicorn, doesn't he?'

Keeley screwed up her face doubtfully but stroked the beetle with a tentative fingertip.

'Oh, listen,' Lucie said, making her eyes huge. 'He's talking.'

'Talking? What he saying?' Keeley hopped from one foot to the other, excitement sweeping away her hesitation.

'Listen and see if you can hear.' She closed her hand gently around the beetle, like Dad had done for her so many times. The bug vibrated noisily, and she held her fist to Keeley's ear. 'Can you hear him, baby?'

'I hear! He saying . . . he saying . . .' Keeley's face screwed up as she tried to make words from the beetle's frantic buzzing.

'I think he's saying, "Thank you, Keeley, for saving me from being squashed." But now you've rescued him, we need to find somewhere nice for him to live.'

'There are flowering vines growing in the alley alongside the shop,' a deep voice said behind her. 'Though, of course, that's not their preferred habitat.'

She startled, putting a hand on the ground to catch her balance as she jerked around.

The guy nodded at Keeley. 'Bet your mum brakes for butterflies, too,' he said, then looked back to Lucie. 'Or are you just looking to improve your karma?'

She lurched to her feet, the bug still in her hand. 'I'd need to do a lot more than rescue a stranded beetle.'

15

Jack

She had no idea who he was. The sharp breeze, heavy with the scent of the jasmine that grew in many of the narrow alleys between the buildings in Main Street, lifted Lucie's hair as she turned back to her daughter. Jack was surprised at the flash of cobalt blue and hot pink hidden beneath the top layers of rich chestnut. Maybe she tried to hide her true personality beneath the conservative colour?

And maybe he'd spent too long alone with Sally and his books over winter if he was going to imagine entire scenarios into some girl's haircut.

He realised Lucie was now staring up at him, no doubt wondering why he still lurked over them and their bug. 'We met at the—m-m-met last week.' 'Funeral' would be no harder to spit out than any other word, but even he wasn't idiot enough to open a conversation with that.

Lucie shook her head, a puzzled frown between her eyes. 'I don't . . .' She trailed off, inviting him to explain.

A tiny purple gem glinted in the side of her nose. He wondered how he had missed it before. With a flash of irritation, Jack realised that meant his daydreams had been off kilter. Because, yeah, he had spent time thinking about her. It was nothing personal, just that talking to anyone new was a rarity.

Not that he'd managed anything brilliant in the talking department, either then or now.

'Jack Schenscher,' he said. As the owner of the Settlers Pub strode past, headed for the IGA, Jack seized on the diversion to ease the awkward moment. 'G'day, Ant. Run short again?' He was pretty sure Ant had a thing for Lynn in the grocery store. As Lynn had been widowed for a few years now, Ant was obviously a slow-burn kind of guy.

'Jack,' Ant nodded, his bald head hidden beneath a beanie.

Normally Jack would stir him a bit, but instead he turned back to Lucie. The recognition that now lit her dark eyes pleased him for a second before he reminded himself that it meant nothing.

'I remember.' Lucie's short nails gleamed soft pink against the dark tan of her hands, like the inside of the cockles he collected down at Goolwa Beach with Pops. 'Just you look . . . different. It threw me.'

His mates took the mickey about his liking for decent clothes, but he was suddenly absurdly happy that he'd originally run into Lucie while presentably dressed. Even if it was for a funeral.

He jerked a thumb at the quilted red plaid shirt he wore with jeans that had seen better days. 'Work gear. Though I guess I could ditch it now winter's done.' He groaned silently. Seriously, he was discussing the weather with her? No, not even that: he was having an entirely one-sided conversation about the weather, while Lucie stared at him.

'Is cold,' her daughter informed them. She looked up at him. 'I got a beanie.' She turned to Lucie. 'Mummy, he got beanie too. And he gotted a funny—'

Jack's heart froze. The kid was about to remark on his stammer. They were like that, no filter. And usually it didn't bother him. But not now—

The girl poked at her own face. 'He gotted funny eyes.'

'Keeley!' Lucie gasped. 'Oh god, I'm so sorry.'

Relief made the comment easy to shrug off. 'It's fine. Kids tell it like it is. And you're right, Keeley,' he glanced at Lucie to make sure he had the name right, 'I do have funny eyes.'

'They're not funny, they're beautiful!' Lucie exclaimed. She flushed, although he wasn't certain whether it was because of Keeley's statement or if she regretted her own.

'Well, thanks. Can't say I've heard them called that before,' he lied. It seemed plenty of girls considered heterochromia beautiful, comparing him to Henry Cavill, although Jack's hazel eyes each sported a splash of blue rather than a brown splotch. He couldn't recall ever caring about the other women's opinions, though, beyond being slightly embarrassed when his mates gave him shit for it. He gestured at the beetle in Lucie's hand but directed his words to her daughter. 'I think that little guy may be a bit lost, don't you?'

'He a unicorn,' the kid said solemnly.

Jack leaned in close to check out the unicorn. Lucie smelled fresh. Not a perfume scent, but somehow wholesome. As though her clothes were washed in sunshine. 'I can see that,' he said eventually, realising it was his turn to speak. 'The horn, huh?'

'He should be purple,' Keeley said. 'Or maybe somefing blue, like in your eye.' Again she jabbed at her own eye, and he reflexively reached out to grab her hand before she poked herself.

He released her quickly, flashing Lucie a grin of apology. 'I can see that those colours would look nice on him. But the thing is, he's this colour so that he can hide.'

'He not hid,' Keeley said, looking dubiously at the patchy grey cement footpath.

'No, not here. But this isn't where he lives. Maybe he was just visiting and got kind of lost?'

Keeley had become bored with his conversation and was dragging Lucie's hand down so she could chatter at the beetle. 'Is that your story, too?' he asked Lucie, in what he figured was a pretty smooth transition. 'You're day tripping? Or lost?'

'More like ordered back to face the music,' she said with a wry smile that grooved a dimple in her left cheek. Somehow, the dimple looked more like a crease of sorrow than a mark of humour. 'Mum needs me back to take care of some paperwork.'

He was struck by the way her gaze never wavered from his. She reminded him of Gus, who had seemed a deep thinker, quiet and calm most of the time. Even when shit went wrong on the block, Gus rarely became truly angry—though when he did, it was monumental. 'Back? I didn't realise you'd left.' Her raised eyebrow made it clear that there was no reason why he should either know or care. 'Y-you're passing through Settlers on your way to Chesterton?'

'We're renting here.' Lucie's hair flashed blue and pink as she shook her head. 'It seems a nice little town, and we could do with a break from Melbourne. It gets pretty glum there over winter, and spring is taking extra long to kick in this year.'

Jack frowned. Chesterton was much the same as Settlers, just further from the river, though perhaps Lucie's husband was into fishing. Not that there was anything but carp left in the lower Murray, maybe the occasional redfin, and they barely rated as edible.

He took a second to think through his words before opening his mouth again. It never guaranteed he wouldn't stammer, but his father had thumped it into him that his silence was preferable anyway. Now he often didn't bother sharing his thoughts, unless he was with good mates. 'Speaking of p-paperwork, do you and your husband want to come by and have a look at the block?' He was clinging to a vague hope that, if he made the property an unattractive proposition, they would decide to lease him back Gus's share. For a peppercorn rent, because he couldn't afford much else.

Of course, it was more likely they would choose to call in the loan Gus had made him. In which case, he was screwed.

Lucie looked confused. 'I don't have a husband.' His gaze followed hers to Keeley, and he watched as her jaw tightened.

Damn, how old-fashioned was he that he had gone straight for the husband assumption? Obviously been hanging out with Pops too much, who set great stock in marriage, never missing an anniversary. Ma always laughed that at least one of them remembered the date, although she always happened to have Pops' favourite meal on the table on special occasions. 'Sorry . . . partner.'

Her eyes grazed his, as dark as rich loam. 'Not anymore.'

'Oh. S-s-sorry. I thought . . .' He let the sentence trail off, hoping she would save him from his stammering awkwardness. Last time he'd seen her he'd put his foot in it about her dead father, now he was banging on about some dick who'd obviously bailed on her right after her dad died.

Her cheeks flushed a deep apricot beneath her olive tan, but her tone was firm. 'Nope.'

For a moment his heart leaped, but he shoved it down to the bottom of his dusty workboots. Every idiot knew there was nothing but a one-night stand and a whole lot of baggage to come from a rebound romance. He wasn't interested in buying into that. 'Ah.'

Hell, sometimes the stammer would be better than being tongue-tied.

She gave him a sideways glance, a frown furrowing between her eyes. 'What is this "block", anyway? I have no idea what you're talking about.'

'Mr Unicorn is cold,' Keeley piped up, tugging Lucie's arm down so she could see the beetle more closely. 'He wants go to his new home. I want go mine. Dash wants go too.'

'Oh shit—sugar,' Lucie corrected with a guilty glance at Keeley. 'The dog is in the car.'

'Let me give you a hand with all this.' Jack nodded at the laden trolley. 'That's your car across the road?'

'How did you know?' she scowled, as though he'd been stalking her.

'Doesn't require any detective work. That's me,' he nodded at his ute. Sally sat in the front seat, her nose pressed to the window, regarding him intently. 'And that's Matt and Roni's Landcruiser next to Tracey's hatchback down by The Overland. Which makes the RAV4 yours, right?'

'Mr Unicorn wants to go home *now*,' Keeley interrupted again.

'Jack,' Sam hollered from the doorway of Ploughs and Pies. 'Ma needs those groceries. Today.' She was laughing at him, no doubt dying to know who he was speaking to.

Lucie flinched. 'Sorry, we're holding you up. Your wife . . . ?'

'Sister.' He dropped to his haunches alongside Keeley. 'But she'll understand that rescuing Mr Unicorn is more important. Because we have a bit of a problem here. We could put Mr Unicorn in the jasmine, but that's not really where he likes to live.'

Keeley looked at him suspiciously, then glanced at her mother, as though seeking confirmation.

'Why not the jasmine?' Lucie asked, almost as mistrustful as Keeley.

'Because, along with being quite a cool unicorn, this guy is actually a dung beetle. I'm not too sure how he hitched a ride here, but he prefers to be out on farms.'

'Oh!' Lucie looked down at the bug. 'I've always called them rhinoceros beetles. We don't get many up at Chesterton.'

'Probably because there aren't many cows out that way,' he said. He liked the way she wrinkled her nose in distaste but wasn't freaked out by the insect she still cupped carefully in her hand. 'Though you do have some non-introduced species of dung beetles up there.'

'Why would anyone introduce dung beetles?' Despite her rather adorably wrinkled nose, Lucie did a great job of sounding interested.

'Native dung beetles have evolved to deal with native animal waste. You know, roo and wombat pellets. Obviously, cow dung is rather a different . . . well, matter.'

'What is dung?' Keeley asked innocently.

Jack looked to Lucie. She lifted one shoulder in a shrug. 'It's poo, Keeley. Animal poo.'

'Like Dash poo?' Keeley asked. 'Dash done a poo on the kitchen floor once. Mummy was mad. I don't do that. I'm big girl.'

He blinked. Whoa. And he thought he'd been dishing out an information overload?

Lucie gave a little snort of laughter. 'He did, and I was cross. But no, we're talking about cow poo. Aren't we, Jack?' She pulled a comical face, then dimpled a smile at him. 'Can't say this is one of the first conversations I expected to be having in my temporary home town.'

'Can't say this is a conversation I expected to have in my permanent home town,' he grinned back like an idiot. 'No one has ever been interested in tapping into my vast knowledge of dung beetles before.'

She laughed aloud this time, a deep-throated, unashamed gurgle. 'Okay, I'll bite. Just why is it that you have such a vast knowledge of these bugs?'

'Not only these guys, plenty of others. But Mr Unicorn here is particularly important because he makes cow pats disappear, which saves manually removing them.' He flicked his wrist as though frisbeeing a pancake-sized, inch-thick clod off the paddock. 'Cows won't graze dirty land. But this little guy tunnels into the ground to bury dung balls for his larvae to hatch in. While he's doing that, he's aerating the soil and increasing the fertility. Plus, getting the dung off the surface almost completely eradicates the leeching of phosphates and nitrates into waterways.' Man, why couldn't he just shut his trap? It would be better if he was stammering unintelligibly than, quite literally, talking crap.

Lucie's nose stud sparkled as she gazed up at him. 'You're really into this stuff, aren't you?'

'Everyone should be *into* sustainability. But yeah, sorry. I get kind of over the top about it.'

'Cool,' she breathed. 'That's so freaking cool.'

His words completely dried up.

16
Lucie

Lucie knew why Jack was suddenly speechless: she had put far too much enthusiasm into her appreciation of his interest in nature. But that was only because it happened to intersect with her own passions.

'So what do you suggest we do about Mr Unicorn?' she said brightly, glossing over his sudden awkwardness and her own embarrassment.

'Well,' Jack sounded relieved she had asked something concrete, 'I suggest that, if Keeley agrees, maybe he comes back to my farm. There's plenty of, uh, *places* for him to live there.'

Keeley looked like she wasn't in any hurry to part with her new pet, so Lucie quickly added, 'And maybe, if it's okay with Jack, we could visit Mr Unicorn out there.'

'Absolutely okay,' Jack said, with a whole lot of depth to his voice.

Lucie checked that thought swiftly: it was probably the way he spoke all the time.

'Awright,' Keeley said uncertainly.

'I can't carry him in my hand while I'm driving,' Jack said, 'so how about you tuck him up nice and safe in here, Keeley?'

As he spoke, he yanked off his beanie. Sun-streaked hair brushed his shoulders, rainwater-soft and fresh. Lucie dragged her attention to his beanie instead. Mottled grey in colour, the thick cable knit could only be handcrafted.

He caught her looking at it. Lucky that was all he caught her looking at. 'Keeshond wool.'

'Pardon?'

The corners of his eyes creased. And she stood by her earlier involuntary and unfortunately verbal assessment: they were beautiful. If they were one colour, his thickly lashed eyes would have rated as attractive, but the unusual splash of blue across each hazel iris made them mesmerising. However, a sudden, intense interest in iridology didn't excuse her staring, even though his eyes reminded her of brown-and-blue-swirled pietersite, the tempest stone that brought short-term upheaval leading to long-term change and healing.

She didn't have room for any more upheaval in her life.

'Sorry,' Jack said, clearly not realising that she should be the one apologising. 'That sounded like a curse. But I meant the beanie is knitted from keeshond fur. It's like angora wool.'

His explanation didn't unconfuse her any. 'Keeshond is a type of sheep?' Though she was a country girl, Chesterton wasn't sheep territory, and she couldn't tell a ram from a ewe. 'Or goat?'

Jack gestured down the road with the beanie. 'Keeshonds are dogs. Tracey's dog, to be specific. If you're going to be here a while, you'll no doubt meet Bear—and Tracey. Kees have an undercoat that can be spun into wool. My gran is a gun spinner, so Tracey trades her a share of the wool in return for spinning it into chiengora.'

Lucie's head was doing the spinning. 'Bear is a dog and the sheep's wool is dog hair and angora goats have nothing at all to do with this story?' She couldn't resist reaching to touch the beanie. 'Wow, it's so soft. Don't you wish we could do this with Dash's hair, Keeley?' Her daughter put a tentative finger on the beanie. 'Keeley's puppy is a long-haired dachshund, so I'd looked into donating his hair to an organisation that collects animal hair, along with fleece and fur, to filter waterways. But I've never heard of anyone spinning it. That's awesome.'

'Filter waterways?' Jack looked at her strangely, but Lucie was used to her interests getting that kind of reaction. Or perhaps the odd look was because she was letting her mouth run away with her. She always did that when anyone touched on one of her passions. She made an effort to get her conversation back on track. 'Some American guy came up with the concept and teamed with an organisation called Matter of Trust. They make oil and petrochemical spill mats out of felted hair. The mats are hydrophobic, so they put them across gutters and the water runs off them, but the petrol from the road soaks in.' She lifted Keeley with one arm, struggling to get the child onto her hip without crushing the dung beetle in her other hand. 'They also manufacture stuffed booms to buffer beaches from major oil spills.'

'So they've created the perfect link of surplus and need.'

'Exactly! A symbiotic relationship.' She shivered as a frisson ran through her, lifting the hairs on her arms. Geoff pretended to listen to her environmental lecturing, but it was with amused tolerance, not true interest. This guy, Jack, he . . . understood.

Lucie took a step away from him. 'Anyway, look them up sometime. It's interesting. I'd better get going.'

'Not with Mr Unicorn.' He held his beanie out to Keeley. 'Are you going to put him in here, nice and safe? Then he can go in my car.'

Keeley nodded, her legs gripping Lucie's waist as she leaned to take the insect from her mother's palm. Her heel shoved into Lucie's belly, and Lucie found herself hoping her sleeveless jacket covered any unattractive bulges.

Her bottom lip held between her small white teeth, Keeley transferred the beetle to Jack's hat. Then she dramatically let out a long breath, and clapped her hands. 'He happy now!'

'He was probably happy in your mum's hand, but I'm sure he'll be really keen to get to work on the farm,' Jack said.

Of course, he didn't mean anything by saying the bug was happy in her hand.

'And I visit him?' Keeley double-checked.

'Soon as your mum wants to,' Jack replied.

'Yeah, um, well, we're going to be pretty busy,' Lucie hedged. She needed to leave this conversation. Now. She was far too intrigued by this man.

'Mummy, we has to see Mr Unicorn!' Keeley's voice took on a sharp edge.

'Yes, we will,' she quickly soothed. She grimaced apologetically at Jack. 'I guess we'd better swap numbers and I'll let you know when we can make it?'

'Sure,' he said. 'Let me just put Mr Unicorn in the ute.'

Beanie-caged bug in hand, he strode over to the dilapidated ute parked nearby.

Lucie lowered Keeley to the ground so she could haul the grocery bags from the trolley. There was no way she could get the recalcitrant carriage over the island in the middle of the deserted road.

Jack returned as she hefted the last bag and reached to take them from her.

Keeley grabbed his outstretched hand. 'Up,' she demanded.

Lucie cringed. Great, her kid had just adopted this hulking farmer while his sister watched from a couple of doorways down. He probably thought she trained Keeley to be cute for precisely this purpose. 'Sorry. She's used to Geoff carting her around.'

'Ah. Geoff,' Jack said with an odd edge. 'Well, up you come, then.' Taking both of Keeley's hands, he lifted her straight into the air, to her giggling delight. 'Like this?'

'No, silly,' she squealed, kicking her legs into his chest. 'Not this!'

'Keeley!' Lucie remonstrated, as the booted foot came dangerously near Jack's chin.

He laughed and drew Keeley against his chest so she couldn't do any damage. 'Like this, then?'

'This,' Keeley agreed. She pressed her hands to Jack's cheeks. 'Your eyes *is* pretty.'

Oh god, was it possible she could die inside while still maintaining a politely smiling façade? Lucie started towards the kerb but Jack closed his free hand over the straps to several of her carriers.

'Here. Let me,' he said. And he strode ahead, bearing her burdens across a deserted country road to her car.

With Keeley and Dash reunited and phone numbers exchanged with Jack, Lucie drove off. She only went around the corner out of Jack's sight, though. There, she pulled into the kerb and blew out a long breath. She made eye contact with Keeley in the mirror. 'Mummy just needs to call Geoff, okay, Keels? Then we'll get going.'

Happy to have the pup released from his harness and busy tongue-washing her face and hands, Keeley giggled agreeably.

Lucie put the phone in the cradle and left the car engine running so she could use the hands-free.

The phone rang only twice before Geoff answered. 'Tumbleweed! I was beginning to worry. I thought maybe the banjo players got you.'

'It's not quite that backwoods remote here, Geoff. But in any case, I'm going to have to come home soon.'

'Excellent. But first, how did Keeley travel?'

'She was fine,' Lucie lied. She would never, not even for the briefest second, wish her life without Keeley, although Dash might be a slightly different matter. But it had been every bit as hard as she expected, driving and simultaneously entertaining both the child and the dog over six hundred kilometres. She was dreading the next few weeks of completely single parenting, more than ever aware of how much Geoff helped her out. Yet she knew that if she told him that, he'd come running. And that wasn't fair to him or Fin. Or even to Keeley. She had to stop pretending they were some neat little three-person family with Finlay tacked on as a temporary extra. Geoff deserved his own life.

Lucie rolled her head from one shoulder to the other, her neck stiff with tension. 'We both miss you, though, obviously. Also, I'm allergic to South Australia.'

'What? Do tell.'

She took another deep breath, avoiding her accusatory reflection in the mirror. 'You've got to talk me down, Geoff. I have no idea what's going on but, seriously, five minutes here and I'm practically throwing myself at the first guy I come across.' Something of an exaggeration, but she was shocked by her reaction to Jack.

'Whoa, Tumbleweed.' Geoff's voice was amused. 'About time, too. I was beginning to think I was house-sharing with a nun. So this is some old flame you've uncovered?'

She closed her eyes. 'Jack Schenscher.'

'Who—wait.' Geoff gave a low whistle. '*The* Jack? The one you've been banging on about?'

'Shh,' she hissed, glancing at Keeley.

'Let me get this straight. We are talking about the guy you said was creepy, right?'

'I'm sure I didn't say that. Just that the conversation with him was weird,' she said crossly. Then she sighed. 'Seriously, Geoff, what is wrong with me? I haven't looked at a guy in, you know, *that* way for . . . well, more than four years.'

'I'd say that is precisely what is wrong with you then, hon. A drought only lasts three years, tops.'

'You're not helping,' she said, though Geoff's humour always lightened her mood.

'Okay, okay,' he soothed. 'Well, I assume you've not pledged your troth to this strapping young farmer or anything like that, right?'

'We did swap numbers,' she said glumly.

'You did what?' Geoff's voice lifted in surprise.

'So I can go visit his dung beetle.'

There was a long moment of silence on the other end of the phone. 'I'm going to hope that isn't any kind of euphemism. Although, I think I also hope that it's not a statement of fact.'

'It is,' she groaned. 'The latter.'

'Do you want to explain?'

'Not really. What I want is for you to tell me what's going on. I'm not some ridiculous seventeen-year-old, so why do I suddenly have these . . . feelings?' She spat the word out.

Geoff chuckled. 'You've always had *feelings*. You just work very hard at channelling them in one direction.'

'As I should.' She slammed the steering wheel with the flat of her hand. 'That's what being a good mum is about. You know I've seen the alternative.'

'Mmm,' Geoff said, his tone laden with doubt.

She closed her eyes, recognising the prelude to one of his lectures. But wasn't that precisely what she had rung for? To get him to sort out her life, yet again?

'Lucie, I get why you've compartmentalised and turned yourself over to caring only for Keeley for the past four years. But you have to accept that she's growing up. She'll be off to kindy in the new year. Which, I agree, is sad. But good. And it means it's time for you to find yourself again.'

'I haven't lost myself,' she muttered.

'Okay. Then how do you describe yourself?'

She shrugged, although he couldn't see it. 'I'm an almost twenty-nine-year-old single mum to a gorgeous daughter.' She caught sight of Dash in the rear-view mirror. 'Oh, and to a daft puppy, courtesy of my best friend.'

Geoff allowed one of his long silences, intended to make her reflect on her words. But she refused to consider that she had just described herself and her entire life solely in terms of her relevance to her daughter.

'Is that all, Lucie?' Geoff said gently.

She groaned rather than reply.

'There is no facet to you other than your importance to Keeley?'

'That's how it should be,' she said, knowing the lame response would get her nowhere.

'No, it isn't.' There was a rustle as Geoff moved the phone.

'Do you have that on speaker?' she said sharply. 'You know the EMF from mobile phones is linked to brain cancer.'

'Yep, you've sent me enough links and information to make your point.'

'It's from credible sources,' she huffed. 'If anyone would know, I should think a neurosurgeon would.'

'And if anyone would know a deliberate attempt to derail the conversation, I would. Lucie, you're using Keeley as an excuse to hide from the adult world.'

'I'm not hiding,' she flared. 'I'm out working, I go to all of Keeley's playdates, I have you and Fin.'

'Yep. All nice places to hide, Luce. You are adulting in as much as you're a wonderful mum to Keeley. Literally, the best. But you're not doing yourself any favours. In fact, I've been waiting for a chance to speak with you about this. You can't become a hermit, nor can you make Keeley everything that is important to you.'

'But she is,' Lucie said stubbornly. This lecture sounded far too close to Mum's.

'She is now, but you need to be prepared to loosen those reins as she grows. It's fine for her to be dependent on you, but you can't define yourself solely through that lens. You have to watch out for your own mental health or you'll end up relying on her as the one place you can invest all your affection and attention. Ultimately, that won't be healthy for you. Or her.'

Lucie's silence obviously tipped him off that she was pissed. Geoff sighed. 'Look, Luce, all I'm saying is that it's well past time for you to allow feelings for other people. You're not taking anything away from Keeley by letting someone else into your life. You'll possibly be enriching hers. I mean, even if this guy doesn't work out, you don't want her growing up afraid of socialising, or mistrusting everyone's intent, do you? You have to lead by example, show her that it's fine to have friendships and relationships, that people can come and go without her world turning upside down. She needs to trust that you are her constant, but that doesn't mean you have to be the only influence in her life. We both know that you'll not let anyone within a million miles of her who sets off the slightest tingle in your spidey senses, so where's the harm in allowing yourself to feel whatever you're feeling?'

'Because I'm clearly such a bloody good judge of character, right?' she snarled. 'Besides, that's just it: I don't know what I'm feeling. Because it's ridiculous and childish and pathetic.' At least, what she thought she was feeling was certainly all those things.

'And terrifying and dangerous and exciting?' Geoff said.

'Geoff, I've met him for fifteen minutes. Total.'

'Every love story starts with a split-second meeting.'

'So does every axe murder,' she said dryly.

Geoff hooted with laughter. 'Tumbleweed, this guy worked with your dad, right?'

'He said something about it. He must work out at Blue Flag.'

'And did you trust your dad's judgment?'

'Ish. Sometimes,' she said begrudgingly.

'Then maybe let that be enough for now. Feel whatever it is you're feeling. Stop trying to shut yourself down.'

'Let's not forget, Jeremy also worked for Dad. I just wanted a bit of input into why I'm reacting this way,' she grumbled.

'Because you're human. And humans have needs. And desires, both physical and emotional. And—'

'And Keeley's in the car with me, so this conversation had better wait for later.' In this case, her later meant the same as Mum's—never.

17

Monica

1991

Monica leaned her elbows on the pine table, chin in hand. Over the last few weeks, Nanna's kitchen had provided regular dinners—light on vegetables, so she knew Nanna empathised—but no comfort. Because there was neither comfort nor joy to be found anywhere. Her life was pointless. She should have been engaged by now, setting up house with Mack and planning the wedding.

The ivory tiles clicked as Nanna arranged them on the board. *Aftermath.* 'There,' she said, taking her cup of tea from the pale pink hollyhock. Monica's coaster was similar, though the bloom was burgundy. 'That's a lovely mouth word, isn't it?'

Monica shrugged despondently. She didn't need tea. She needed a brandy and Coke. She hadn't gone to the pub in weeks, but Karen had brought a couple of bottles home to the St Peters unit she'd moved into with Monica. Neither the alcohol nor the fact that Karen was living there, when Mack should have been, had helped ease her sorrow. 'What's a mouth word?'

'One that exercises your mouth when you say it. Go on, try it. Aftermath.' Nanna contorted her face around each syllable, then grinned at Monica.

Monica didn't react.

Nanna clucked her tongue. 'Speaking of exercise, you look as though you've done nothing but sleep and cry for months.'

'Thanks,' Monica said. Her mouth felt heavy and tired, permanently pulled down at the corners. Actually, her whole life felt like that: heavy, tired and pointless. She had lied when she said she'd never forgive Mack: she would take him back in a heartbeat.

Nanna pushed herself up from the table. 'We'll have the last of the Christmas trifle for dessert, out in the garden. Before the mozzies start up.'

As Nanna loaded up the bowls—trifle was one of the few foods she did not believe required moderation—Monica heaved a sigh. Christmas. It would have been the first one with Mack. With her fiancé.

Although the last traces of sunlight still reflected from the dull red bricks of the surrounding townhouses and warmed the tiny verandah, Monica was cold. Chilled to her soul, as though nothing would spark her to life again.

'Wait,' Nanna said, as though there was a chance Monica was going to move from the outdoor chair she'd slumped in.

Nanna disappeared inside then reappeared moments later, carrying her precious cut crystal sherry decanter, two delicate thimble-sized glasses and a large box of chocolates.

She poured the honey gold liqueur and then lifted her glass, toasting Monica. 'To the aftermath of after Mack.'

'Hilarious.' Defiantly, Monica tossed the drink back, knowing Nanna advocated sipping and relishing. She was being petulant but, much as she loved Nanna, it seemed unfair that everyone else's life simply continued as it had been when her life, even her dreams, lay shredded like torn party streamers.

Nanna didn't rise to the bait, though. Instead, she nodded at the chocolate box. 'Open it.'

As Monica peeled the cellophane and lifted the lid to reveal the foil-covered treats, Nanna's tone gentled. 'Look, Mon, they're all pretty and shiny and tempting when they're wrapped in their finery—and your Mack certainly knew how to do that wrapping, didn't he?'

Monica's shoulders stiffened. She remembered Nanna's chocolate box analogy, but it wasn't going to fix a damn thing.

'Go on. Help yourself.' Nanna nudged her chin at the box.

As Monica disinterestedly picked up the lid to read the contents list printed on the inside, Nanna shook her head. 'No. Choose blindly. The thing is, you can always have more than one.'

Monica pushed the box across the plastic table squeezed into the two square metre verandah nook. 'I don't want *any*, Nanna.'

❧

Two weeks and five boxes of chocolates later, Monica watched Karen prowl the gloomy lounge of their flat.

'Come on, Mon,' Karen said. 'I don't want to go alone.'

'Helen's supposed to be your old school friend.'

'Yeah, but I haven't seen her *since* school. And she's bringing about a gazillion of her cousins along that I don't know, so it'll be weird me being the odd one out. Come on, it's dinner for free,' Karen wheedled. 'You don't even have to chip in for her present, I'll get it.'

'I wasn't planning on putting in.' Over the past year, most of her friends had turned twenty-one, and it had become so expensive she'd started turning down invitations.

Karen ignored her. 'Just have a couple of drinks, then. Hang with me till I loosen up, then you can cut.'

Monica blew out an annoyed breath. She had no interest in socialising, but she was sick of the routine of work and returning to the dingy unit that had seemed so cute when she and Mack were going to live there. 'What are you wearing?'

❧

Karen's promise to keep the drinks flowing was pretty shit, Monica decided, scowling into the dregs of her third brandy and Coke. The Greek cafe in North Adelaide was crowded with friends and relatives of the birthday girl— who Monica had avoided—and she'd been propping up a wall for an hour.

A glass appeared in her peripheral vision, and Monica straightened. 'I'm getting a taxi. This is boring as.'

'Shame,' a male voice said, and she snapped her gaze sideways.

The guy holding the glass was average height, his skin darker than any tan won on Brighton beach. 'Georgius. Gus,' he said. Both hands full, he tipped his head towards the pageant of flippy skirts with tight lycra tops and slinky sheath dresses. In her high waisted jeans, black v-necked bodysuit and flats, Monica was way underdressed. 'Helen's my sister.'

Monica shrugged. 'I'm a ring-in. I don't know Helen.'

'That explains why you're standing over here all alone.' Georgius offered the glass. 'It's years since I've been to one of these. I'd forgotten how loud they are.'

Monica gave him a second glance, not bothering to be subtle about it. Georgius definitely looked a good bit older than the guys she knew. Than Mack. She threw back the drink deliberately. 'Too loud. Do you have a car? Want to get out of here?' She angled with a hand on her hip and breasts thrust out.

A slow smile tipped Georgius's lips. 'Did you want a ride home?'

'Definitely.' The hell with chastity knees, they'd got her nowhere. Mack's mother had made sure of that.

She directed Georgius to the unit in St Peters, surprised that he didn't try to pull over in a quiet side street during the ten-minute drive. He didn't chat much, though when he did speak it didn't seem that he was nervous or uncertain, just that he didn't feel a need to fill the silence with words.

She deliberately didn't ask anything about him: she didn't need to know a damn thing, she just needed to get her mojo back. Before Mack, she'd had an unblemished record of six times the dumper, never the dumpee. Until his mother forced them apart.

She tugged her bodysuit top lower, as though she could expose the ache deep in her chest and have Georgius eradicate it.

He pulled the car into the short driveway, made dark by overhanging trees and a wall of diosma bushes. 'I'll walk you to your door?'

'Sure,' she said. Not many guys would bother with the bullshit line, but whatever.

Georgius stood back as she fumbled the key in the dark. Once she had the door open, she stood to one side to let him in.

'Good night. It was nice meeting you,' he said.

And walked away.

He bloody walked away.

She slammed into the unit, snapping her head around as though she could find someone to direct her anger at. Of course, there was nothing. No one. No Mack.

Not even some crap substitute named Georgius.

Neither of them wanted her.

She froze, the thought banging inside her head. She hadn't been good enough for Mack—or, more realistically, for Mack's mother. But Georgius?

Suddenly, she needed to prove that she was desirable, that she had control of her life. Before Mack she'd been confident, sexually self-assured. But it all turned to shit when she decided that not having sex with a guy was the way to keep him.

She strode into the bathroom, reaching for her makeup bag. She knew how to fix the problem. And she knew where to go: Saturday nights at either the Bot or the Hackney were a meat market, a sexual smorgasbord. She and Karen had learned years back that they only needed to pay for their first drink, knowing there would be guys willing to buy for the rest of the night.

And she only had to give a nod to be guaranteed a hook-up.

Chase, conquest and sex would fix the ache deep inside her, banish the aching insecurity. At least for a few minutes.

∾

It was three days before Georgius called. Three days that had passed in a blur of alcohol, aching limbs and barely remembered calls in to work to claim she was sick.

Monica wanted to pretend she'd forgotten Georgius, though Karen had warned that he'd been chasing her number through Helen. She couldn't for the life of her work out if that was good or bad. She only knew that she needed to win: she needed him to want her.

'Hi,' she said, turning her back as though that would limit Karen's eavesdropping on the phone conversation.

'I'm going to the Greek Festival this weekend. I'd like to take you.'

She frowned. Georgius sounded offhand, as though either he didn't care to talk on the phone, or her reply wasn't really of any importance. 'No, thank you. I'm busy,' she replied curtly. There. Let him make of that whatever he wanted.

'No problem, another time,' he said.

And hung up.

'You couldn't have gone, anyway,' Karen said, not bothering to pretend she hadn't heard both sides of the conversation.

'Why not?' Monica scowled.

Karen tilted her head to indicate Monica's neck. 'I don't reckon the bite patterns even match, do they?'

Monica slid a hand up her throat, as though she could hide the myriad bruised and welted lovebites. 'So what if they don't?'

Karen stirred a cup of Nescafé extra noisily, as though determined to make Monica's hangover ten times worse. 'Nothing. Just, you might want to go a bit easy. Whoever it was hightailing out of here this morning was number three in three days, right?'

'Four, actually,' she snapped back. Potentially five, but the alcohol made numbers fluid. 'Anyway, why are you getting all preachy now? You're the one who said I shouldn't hold out, remember?'

'I'm not being preachy.' Karen handed her a mug. 'I'm just saying pace yourself. There's not that many guys in Adelaide, you know. Don't burn through them all at once.'

'Jealous much?' Monica sneered. Karen didn't understand. It was only with a man inside her that Monica felt complete and was able to forget Mack for a few minutes.

No, that wasn't even true: she didn't forget him, not even for a second. Instead, her arms wrapped around some nameless, faceless guy, she pretended he was Mack. That all her dreams had come true.

∾

A week later, Georgius rang again. He didn't bother to identify himself when she answered, as though she should recognise his voice.

Which she did.

That was her friends' fault, though. Rallied by Karen, they were in unanimous wet-knickered excitement at the prospect of her hooking up with someone as exotic as the dark, quietly confident Greek.

Which meant she had to date him, if only to prove herself with quantity over quality.

Yet she didn't *want* any of them. They served a purpose, but she dreamed of Mack at night, cried over him every day. She fantasised his mother dying, and Mack being free to admit that Monica was the only person he truly cared about. At one point, she wished he had died, because then her friends wouldn't have an excuse to act as though Mack was just another guy, comparable to the men who'd dumped them. Even Nanna with her stupid chocolate box analogy was determined to minimise what Monica had lost. How was it that no one understood that she would never move on? Mack owned her heart. It wasn't his fault that his mother had torn them apart.

She hung the phone up, planning what she would wear. Something easy access. She hadn't seen *Sleeping With the Enemy*, but a movie date was a dead cert for at least heavy-duty making out.

It always had been with Mack.

Georgius picked her up, took her to the movies, then for a yiros, lamb roasted with garlic and herbs and then wrapped with bucketloads of parsley in flat bread. Then he took her home.

He kissed her goodnight on her doorstep.

Then he left.

He bloody left again, and she was just about stamping her feet in frustration. His unwillingness to take advantage of what she was offering perversely made her want him. Not only to reclaim her winning streak or prove to her friends she still had it. Definitely not to spite Mack, because Georgius would have to remain a secret until Mack was ready to defy his mother. Yet Gus had somehow ignited a spark in her. Not of passion, oh hell no, it'd never be that with anyone but Mack. But a competitive spark. She needed him to want her, crave her, desire her.

Like she did Mack.

And then she would drop him. Punish him for being a man while she gave Mack time to realise what he'd thrown away, time to remember how perfect they were together.

∽

Karen glanced up as Monica emerged from the bathroom, wiping her mouth on the back of her hand. She was going to have to dial back the drinking—this was the second time she'd been sick this week, and it was starting to feel like she had a permanent hangover. But at least she was numb. Had been for months now. It was as though life slipped by her. Painless but dim.

'Did you see this?' Karen slapped *The Advertiser* on the breakfast bar, open to the classifieds.

Monica shoved the paper away, nursing the cup of tea she'd made before her bathroom dash. Georgius was hassling her to meet his family that weekend and she couldn't see the point. They'd been occasionally dating for months, but even though he was decent company, kind of sweet in his own way, and had certainly given her a lot of cred in her friends' eyes with his gifts of flowers and chocolates, he was temporary.

Until Mack could find a way to escape his mother.

Besides, Gus wasn't even exclusive. At least not as far as she was concerned. He refused to be coerced into her bed, so she found that positive feedback elsewhere. Frequently. Except for the few heady seconds of orgasm, sex was satisfyingly numbing.

'No, look,' Karen insisted. 'It's Mack.'

Monica's blood ran cold. She snatched at the paper, scanning the death notices.

'Here,' Karen said, jabbing at a column.

The wrong column.

The engagement notices.

'That's him, isn't it?' Karen said. 'I can't believe he's engaged again already. Well, not really again, but you know what I mean.'

Monica didn't reply, her eyes devouring the details as bitter acid clawed up her throat. She didn't need to read Mack's name, the photo told her everything.

Michelle Parsons.

The girl he'd claimed to be just an old friend only a few months ago.

Without missing a beat, she picked up the phone and dialled Georgius's number. 'Hi. I've swapped out my shifts this weekend, so I can come to your family thing.' If Mack was engaged then she'd get married before him.

18
Lucie

It only took Lucie a couple of minutes to find Lynn's rental cottage, two blocks behind Settlers Bridge main street.

'Wow.' She pulled up the handbrake and leaned across the passenger seat to peer out of the window. 'Look, Keeley, it's like something from a fairytale.'

'A castle?' Keeley asked.

'Not quite. But maybe a princess's cottage. Like the one Snow White lived in.'

'There are dwarfs?'

'Probably not, but how about we go and see?'

She clipped the lead onto the dog's collar, and then let both Dash and Keeley out of the car beneath one of the red-flowering gums that almost spanned the broad street. Keeley immediately started collecting the blossoms from the sun-dappled footpath. 'Look, Mummy, fairy dresses and elf hats!' she said, holding up the tutu-shaped flowers and a handful of the shiny red caps from the buds. 'It *is* a fairy princess castle.'

'You could be right,' Lucie said, gazing at the cottage. 'Seriously, white picket fences are a thing outside of Instagram?'

She led the way through a latched gate, pausing to take in the striking continuation of the white theme. Countless rose bushes created an ocean of whitecaps across the deep front garden. Crisp, tulip-shaped blooms stood proud, while huge, heavy heads curtsied like Victorian ladies to low bushes sprinkled with ruffled rosettes of pink-tipped white.

The roses were linked by pristine crushed-gravel paths that twinkled like fresh snow in the sunshine. Dark olive, symmetrical borders of box hedge, no higher than her knee, contrasted the white, and a row of strappy butterfly iris spread open white, orchid-like petals to reveal soft mauve stripes.

Lucie's shoulders relaxed, the tension of her conversation with Geoff easing as the serenity washed over her.

'Is pretty, Mummy!' Keeley twirled between the plants, skipping along the meandering paths.

A trace of cinnamon scented the air from borders of dianthus interspersed with low, grassy clumps of thrift, the pink fluffballs of flowers seeming to hover above each knoll. Pink and white, truly a garden fit for a little princess, Lucie marvelled. How incredibly lucky that this house fell into the budget Mum had set.

She juggled Dash's lead so she could pull the bunch of keys from her handbag, groaning as she realised she would need to unpack the car to find the box of kitchen goods that contained her tea blends and pot.

Keeley and Dash raced ahead after she succeeded in getting the old-fashioned key to slowly turn the tumblers in the lock and pushed the heavy door open.

At least Mum had noted her preference for hard floors; carpets didn't do well with small children and an even smaller dog. Keeley paused in the first doorway leading off the central hall, her mouth hanging open. 'Mummy,' she stage-whispered. 'I think is Sleeping Beauty's house.'

Lucie suppressed a smile, edging the dog out of the way with her foot so she could see into the room. 'Oh,' she gasped, possibly even more stunned than Keeley.

Like the outside of the house, the colour scheme was shades of white and pink. Creamy walls with ice-white wooden trims highlighted pink-patchwork curtains in what looked like a soft suede, the nap swept in different directions on each square. A pink beanbag filled one corner, a white rocking chair another. But the centre of the room was what had Keeley's eyes the size of fifty-cent coins.

There was no denying the lacy, canopy-covered single bed had to be for a princess.

'Our room, Mummy?' Keeley whispered. In Melbourne, they shared a room with space only for their two single beds.

'I think it must be *your* room. Let's see the rest of the house first, though.'

With Dash and Keeley running ahead, Lucie checked the remaining rooms. The neutral colours continued throughout, although the sun-filled family room had more practical beige couches grouped to face an open fireplace piled high with a pyramid of pine cones. Cabled cream and rust–coloured throws were arranged diagonally across the lounges, and Lucie made a mental note to check whether they were washable. Otherwise, she would buy some cheap blankets to make sure the furniture didn't suffer from dog and daughter.

Keeley barely spared the TV a glance, although she had missed her usual allowance of screen time while they had been travelling. 'Come see, Mummy,' she said, tugging Lucie towards the back door.

'Wait a minute, Keels. Let's finish looking inside first.'

'No,' Keeley said obstinately. She caught Lucie's raised eyebrow. 'Cos there is a *swing*, Mummy,' she wheedled, turning to press her nose against one of the small windows that framed the back door.

'No way,' Lucie chuckled. Keeley had grown up in a suburban world where swings belonged only in the local park.

'Way,' Keeley pronounced gravely, borrowing one of Geoff's favourite expressions. 'Out there. We go?'

'Sure.' That cup of tea could wait five minutes. Peppermint, for energy.

As always, she was aware of making the most of every moment with Keeley; not forever would her daughter be thrilled by the little beauties and oddities of life, not forever would everything be a discovery, a mystery waiting to be unravelled. Not forever would her daughter find the magic in a raindrop, in a snail's silvery trail, in the unfurling petals of a flower.

Although perhaps she would, as Lucie still found enchant-
ment in those things. Maybe even more so since Dad's death,
the mundanities of life made precious by loss.

In contrast to the elegance of the front garden, the rear
was an explosion of joy, the kaleidoscope of colours and
textures a visual feast. Everywhere she looked there seemed
to be another tree, another bush, another flower, the air
loud with the chorus of bees plundering the riot of blooms.
Honeyeaters hovered like hummingbirds in a flurry of whir-
ring wings or clung to stalks with delicate claws as their long
beaks probed the folds of bright petals in search of nectar.
Thanks to Mum's love of gardening, she recognised many
of the plants that crowded the area, spilling across brick
pathways and sprinting to the top of the rusted corrugated
iron fences surrounding the yard. Yellow and lilac Dutch
irises stood tall among the maidenhair-fern foliage of deep-
blue granny's bonnets nodding in the breeze. A Chicago
Peace rose sprawled across a four-metre expanse of fence,
each bloom the size of small cauliflower, while in front of
it a cascade of deep pink Peter Frankenfeld blooms wound
over the rusty patina of a wrought-iron archway.

Keeley raced through the tunnel. 'Mummy, fishes!'

Dash and Lucie followed as Keeley dropped to her knees
on a carpet of jade green baby tears beside a rock-edged
pond. She leaned to trail her fingers in the water, and
Lucie darted forward. 'Careful, Keeley, it might be deep.'
Or shallow. Either could be dangerous. Keeley had gone to
swim classes since she was six months old, but still Lucie
would never leave her unattended near water. She clucked

her tongue in annoyance: she had stipulated to Mum that the accommodation needed a fully enclosed, safe backyard for both Keeley and Dash. In fact, she'd had a whole list of requirements, which Geoff said were a not-too-subtle attempt to frustrate her mother to the point that she no longer demanded Lucie come over.

'I can't get him,' Keeley pouted. 'Is in the way.' She pointed at the pond.

Lucie kneeled alongside her. 'Oh.' Just below the surface of the water, disguised by the lilies that thrust their waxy pink and yellow flowers through the barrier, shiny weldmesh covered the pond. Keeley giggled as palm-sized orange-and-white goldfish bubble-mouthed at her, as though they expected food.

Warily, Lucie pushed on the weldmesh. It didn't have a centimetre of give and refused to move when she tried to jiggle the frame. Keeley couldn't fall through. The fish immediately shifted to directly beneath her hand, their begging clear.

'We feed them, Mummy?' Keeley asked.

'When we go back to the shops, we'll ask the nice lady there if it's okay.'

'Okay,' Keeley agreed easily. Her mouth fell open as a huge dragonfly darted with erratic movements down to the water's surface. It flew towards her, then quickly reversed and disappeared between the strappy leaves of dianella that overhung the far edge of the pond, the berries a glossy purple-black interspersed with tiny yellow star flowers. 'A fairy!'

'Maybe,' Lucie agreed.

Keeley clambered to her feet. 'The swing, Mummy,' she squealed as she spied it.

The bright blue swing looked new, strung on thick ropes from a purple-leafed branch, the ground beneath a carpet of deep pink cherry plum blooms. Lucie lifted Keeley onto the wooden seat. 'Okay, ten pushes,' she said hopefully. 'Then we need to unpack the car.'

'Ten is for me, and ten is for Dash,' Keeley wheedled.

'If you do the counting,' Lucie agreed.

Ten minutes later—and far more than ten pushes, each one accompanied by Dash racing beneath the swing, struggling to turn his ridiculously long body at the apex—Lucie insisted they go in. 'I'm going to have a cup of tea, and you're going to have some kefir and a snack. Then we'll arrange to visit Nanna.' Because, unfortunately, life couldn't always be these sweet moments. She had learned that with Dad.

'She gived me fairy bread,' Keeley said.

'She *gave* you fairy bread, yes,' Lucie agreed. 'Maybe we should make a treat to take as a thank you.' She could whip up some protein truffles and with some luck persuade Keeley they were just as exciting as the illicit delicacy.

'Okay.' Keeley skipped ahead of her. Dash had exhausted himself chasing the swing and was happy to follow at her heels, pausing to nose beneath the daisy bushes.

Keeley slammed to a halt. 'Buff flies,' she breathed.

A cloud of lavender butterflies, the size of Keeley's fingernail, rose from the thick lawn.

'Buff flies,' Lucie agreed in awe.

The purple wave lifted, then settled again.

'Come back this way carefully, baby,' Lucie murmured, as though they risked frightening the creatures.

Keeley stepped slowly backward, her little bottom tense with the effort, her breath held in concentration. 'Did I hurt them, Mummy?' she whispered as Lucie scooped her up.

'Not at all,' Lucie assured her. 'They're clever enough to flutter out of your way. But you don't want to squash their flowers, because that's what they're drinking from, see?'

'There's the big mummy one,' Keeley gasped, pointing at a daisy bush.

Like a faded relic of the seventies, a wanderer rested on a wilting bloom. Mottled orange and brown wings, tattered at the edges like the raggedy hem of a boho peasant dress, drooped to match the broken antennae crooked to one side. With pained, deliberate movements, the insect went through the motions of life, still collecting nectar despite the futility.

'Oh, the poor thing.' Lucie's heart twisted at the reminder of the fragility of life. Had Dad been like the butterfly in his last days? Had he slowed down, moved more carefully, known the end was near? Or had he kept working with his strawberries, oblivious to the fact that he had his own broken antenna?

Lucie pressed trembling fingertips to her lips. If she had been there, she would know when Dad stopped flying . . . although perhaps that moment had been long ago, when the bottles of whiskey first appeared.

Hidden behind the mountains of paperwork he loathed.

The ones she was supposed to help with.

The thing was, she had always known Dad was going to die. Over the years they grew apart, she told herself the emotional distance was a good thing: it would hurt less when that final separation came. Mum had unwittingly helped, arranging physical distance, and Lucie had assured herself that, as long as her own child was safe, she could accept the inevitability of death.

But she'd lied.

It would never matter what words they had spoken in anger, or the things they had stubbornly left unsaid: the bond formed in her childhood was unbreakable. With no distance far enough or separation long enough to destroy her attachment to the father she had adored, now she dared not allow her grief, knowing it would tear her apart.

And yet, despite recognising how she had missed her chance with Dad, she was reluctant to spend time with her mother, already counting the days until she could escape. What did she even want to escape to? Beyond Geoff's company, which she claimed with a greediness that threatened to alienate Fin, Melbourne held nothing for her. The truth was, Lucie didn't care where she was, as long as she was with Keeley.

19

Monica

1991

Monica huddled in the bath, arms wrapped around her scarlet legs. Head bowed to rest on wet knees, her wracking sobs tore at her chest.

This had to work. She didn't know what else to do. Not short of a coathanger, anyway.

There was no point taking a pregnancy test. She possibly could have pinched one from work, but in any case, she knew.

What she didn't know was what the hell to do about it.

'Mon?' Karen thumped on the door again. 'Come on, you're freaking me out. What's wrong?'

Monica groaned. She struggled to her feet, flicking the door lock and quickly dropping back into the searing water, gasping at the heat.

Karen barrelled in, batting at the steamy air as though she could push it away. 'What the hell, Mon?'

'I'm pregnant.' There. No sugar-coating it, she'd said the words.

'Oh.' Karen looked suitably horrified. 'But how? You're on the pill?'

'Of course I am. But I guess I must have chucked it up one day. Whatever, the damn thing didn't work, did it?' It felt good to blame the chemicals rather than herself. There was a good chance she'd forgotten to take the little yellow tablet, but an even better one that she had thrown it up after binge-drinking.

'Gus's?' Karen asked, her hand to her throat. 'His family will freak. You know how religious his mum is?'

Monica shrugged. Then she shook her head. 'Not unless immaculate conception's a thing. Gus won't touch me, he's too freaking busy being a gentleman, as though that's going to win me over.' The irony of having Gus treat her the same as she'd treated Mack wasn't lost on her.

'So whose?' Karen said, sliding onto the edge of the tub.

'Mack's,' she blurted.

'What the hell? You've been over for nearly a year. Don't tell me you started seeing him again.' Karen grabbed her wrist, pulling her hand from her knee, where she'd been digging her nails in as she tried to tolerate the burning water. 'You're scaring me, Monica. Did you hook up with Mack?'

She shook her head. 'But it's still his. It's his fault, Karen. It's all his fault.' If she hadn't been so desperately trying to prove to him—to herself—that she was desirable, this would never have happened.

'Oh. I see,' Karen said uncertainly. 'But, like, really, whose is it?'

'Don't know. Don't care. What I need to know is how to get rid of it.'

'Wow. Are you sure that's what you want to do?'

'Of course. What the hell else am I supposed to do?' she snarled. But she wasn't sure, not even a tiny bit. Because she couldn't forget her dreams of raising tiny, powder-fragranced babies with Mack.

Mack. If he hadn't left her, the child would be his. Her life would be perfect.

∾

One arm protectively across her stomach—although there was no longer anything to protect—Monica froze in the discreetly unlabelled doorway of the clinic.

Leaning against his duck-egg blue car, Gus waited on the footpath.

She should run.

She didn't need him. Didn't need anyone.

Except Karen, who had promised to be here to collect her.

The firm click of the door behind reminded her of the nurse's instruction to leave the premises quickly and quietly. She lurched towards the steps, sucking in a sharp breath as her stomach cramped. The doctor had promised she'd have enough time to get home before it started.

A moan caught in her throat as she took another step, the pain bending her double.

Gus was by her side in an instant. 'Your place, or do you want me to take you to hospital?' he asked as he slid an arm around her waist.

'Mine,' she gasped.

She didn't recall much after that. Nothing but the pain, anyway. After blabbing to Gus, Karen had done a runner, heading home to her parents for the weekend. In retrospect, Monica didn't blame her. Well, not too much, anyway. With non-medical abortion illegal, it wasn't something a nurse could afford to be mixed up in.

Gus didn't leave her. He drew a bath, rubbed her back, held her when she cried and writhed. Measured the painkillers the clinic had provided, brought her water, helped her to the toilet.

Held her again after the unwanted life slid from within her, when she suddenly doubted her decision.

It was Sunday afternoon before he finally asked anything of her. His face drawn with fatigue and darkened by two days of growth, he hunkered down at the foot of the chair he'd carried her to, bundled in a dressing-gown. 'You didn't have to do this alone,' he said gently.

She shook her head. Was he some kind of crazy? 'But it didn't have anything to do with you,' she muttered.

'Yes, it did,' he said stolidly. 'It did, because I love you.'

She flinched. Those weren't words she wanted to hear from anyone ever again.

But it had been nice to allow herself to be cared for over the weekend. To pretend to be cherished.

No, not pretend, because she instinctively knew that Georgius loved her just as she had loved Mack. Immediately, unstintingly, unquestioningly. Forever.

And maybe, after having her heart broken, she had done her penance and deserved that? If she had Georgius, no one would ever hurt her again. Yet still she couldn't bring herself to utter a barefaced lie. Georgius would have to understand that he could never have the part of her heart that Mack had stolen. It was cold and dead.

Instead of speaking, she nodded acceptance of his declaration.

Georgius gave his slow smile, taking her hands. 'Good. That's settled.'

She hadn't expected the rush of relief that washed over her: it was as though she had been tied in a giant knot for the last year and Georgius snipped through it, released all of her tension in a magnificent rush. His thumbs caressed her hands. 'I'll only ask one thing of you, Monica. Well, two.'

Her hands clenched. 'What?'

'His name.'

She nodded. 'Mack.' As soon as she uttered it, she realised Georgius meant the name of the baby's father, not the name of the man who had broken her heart. But it didn't matter. Mack was the one to blame.

Georgius gazed at her for a long moment. 'Then the other thing I ask is your word that you'll never see him again.'

She caught the underlying demand in his tone and intuitively understood that this was non-negotiable. But it didn't matter.

Mack was dead to her.

20
Lucie

'I don't believe you ever told me why you chose that particular name.'

'I don't believe you ever asked,' Lucie shot back, eyeing her mother over the rim of the coffee mug.

Mum shrugged, her elbows on the kitchen table in a manner that had never been acceptable when Lucie was a kid. She seemed too exhausted to notice the barb. 'Maybe not. But I'm asking now.'

Lucie darted a glance through the archway into the lounge, where Keeley played on the carpet with Dash. Although Keeley loved the dog, her attention span was that of a typical three-year-old: the 'I'm bored' would soon start and no doubt be like fingernails on a blackboard for Mum.

And not only for Mum.

Lucie had been shocked to discover how hard truly single parenting was. The realisation that she now had to time her bathroom visits so she would know where Keeley was gave her a whole new level of appreciation for Geoff's help over the years. His presence had given her a break from the role of carer, provider and nurturer. She had been able to soak in the bath, read a book, even occasionally sleep in, knowing that Keeley was safe. Now, although she adored her daughter more than life itself, there was a vague sense of terror that she couldn't ever be enough, do enough, provide enough. Raising a small human alone was . . . constant. Exhausting.

'I just liked the name,' she said, begrudging her mother the answer.

'So it was your choice?' Mum asked. 'Not anything to do with—' She canted her head to one side, as though indicating someone outside the back door.

A prickle of wariness ran through Lucie, but she quelled it. He was overseas. 'Jeremy? Not at all. Unless you told him, as far as I know he isn't even aware he has a daughter.' Would it have been different if he realised his baby was a girl? Lucie almost wanted to persuade herself so, as though that would redeem him, but Jeremy had been adamant about his complete disinterest in any child.

Mum frowned. 'He must know. I can't believe he wouldn't have contacted you. Well, no,' she amended. 'I can believe that—'

'Oh, thanks very much,' Lucie muttered, trying to rein in her temper.

Mum's lips pursed into a bitter-lemon pucker of annoyance, her cheeks hollowing ghoulishly. 'I meant,' she said, with irritating clarity, 'I can well believe he'd be self-centred enough not to contact you, once he made up his mind that you were no longer what he desired. What I can't believe is that he wouldn't want to claim his daughter. I would have expected him to have at least a sense of . . . well, obviously not of moral obligation, considering his behaviour. But perhaps of ownership.'

'I wasn't aware that you know him well enough to have an opinion of his ethics,' Lucie said acidly, though she would have cheered on anyone else taking a shot at Jeremy. 'I thought he pretty well kept to the office in the shed.' Mum never bothered to mix with any of Dad's colleagues or acquaintances. 'Which reminds me, the paperwork? You wanted me to look at something for probate, and I'd better check the automated pays are running smoothly. The sooner I get in there, the sooner we're out of your hair.' More like the sooner she could escape, even though Melbourne didn't call to her. Perhaps she wouldn't head directly back. She knew the only cure for this new insecurity about her ability to raise Keeley alone was to simply do it: thoroughly invest herself in the role of sole parent as she had never before needed to. She had arranged to take her full entitlement to annual leave from the office, padded out by a couple of weeks of compassionate leave, so maybe they'd take a leisurely wander home via the Great Ocean Road. Keeley and Dash both loved the beach, and the rainforests fringing the coast would be grounding and revitalising.

'It takes little effort or time to know someone so shallow,' Mum sniped back. She picked up a teaspoon, inspecting the enamelled handle. It must have been a double as she would never use one of her precious collection for their coffee.

'Moccona?' Lucie tapped her cup. Dad always had his coffee brewed in the *briki* on the hotplate. He took it *sketos*, straight up, unsweetened. She preferred *glykos*, the sugar mixed in with the ground coffee and water, then heated until it foamed. When she was very young, Dad would sprinkle extra sugar over the grounds left in the bottom of her cup, then laugh as she used a finger to scoop it out to eat. Now there was no sign of the coffee pot in the austere kitchen.

'It's easier,' Mum said, a flick of her hand waving off Lucie's attempt at diverting the conversation. 'In any case, Jeremy rather makes my case for me, doesn't he? When did you last speak with him?'

Lucie sighed. Four years ago, she would have loved the opportunity to discuss what had happened with her mum: now there was no point. 'The day after I told him he was going to be—' She broke off, aware of Keeley in the next room. 'The day after I told him. When he said that he had messed up raising his other kids and had no intention of repeating the experience. I guess he agreed with you: I should have had an abortion.' Although she wanted a fight, wanted to air her grievances, wanted to offload the cancerous suspicion that had been growing inside her, deep down she longed to have her mother deny the accusation. Her gut tensed in anticipation of Mum's reaction. 'Because that's really why you sent me away, isn't it? You hoped this *problem* would just disappear, and I'd come home like I'd popped over to Melbourne for a shopping spree.'

'*A problem is a chance for you to do your best.*'

'What?'

'Duke Ellington,' Mum said. 'In any case, I didn't have a problem that needed to disappear.'

'And neither did I,' Lucie retorted hotly.

'That was for you to decide, Lucie. I merely gave you the space to do that.'

'Four years of space, Mum—in fact, more than four years. You said you would tell me when I could come back.'

'Oh, Lucie, for goodness' sake,' Mum said wearily, her finger marking time on the edge of one of the coasters she insisted they use. 'Since when have you ever waited for my approval? You were quite capable of packing up and coming home any time you chose. You simply did not choose.'

'How could I?' Lucie slammed her palm on the table. 'You said I'd break Dad's heart. Was I supposed to risk that?'

Her mum pinched the bridge of her nose. 'Stop being so dramatic. I might have said something along those lines in the heat of the moment, but it's a figure of speech. Yes, your father would have been disappointed. As I am. We supported you through your education—'

'Wait, what do you mean "would have been"?' Lucie turned so cold her jaw clenched, making it difficult to get the words out. 'You said Dad was devastated. That he couldn't face me.'

'I'm sure I didn't state it quite like that.'

Lucie shoved to her feet, her entire body trembling. 'You didn't tell him, did you? You never told Dad about Keeley.'

Her mother huffed. 'There would have been no point hurting him, Lucie. After thirty years, I like to think I knew the man well enough to understand how he'd feel, how devastated he would have been by the truth. It was far better that he thought you'd decided to take a job inter-state and had simply chosen not to tell him because you felt guilty about leaving him to handle the business alone. He knew you, knew you'd be back when it suited you.'

Lucie dropped back onto the chair, a hand pressed against her madly accelerating heart. She had suspected Mum of playing some kind of game, of trying to manipu-late her, but this? Never this. 'But—but if Dad didn't know, then he didn't reject me. Reject Keeley. Oh my god, what have you done?' The room spun around her, the edges blurring into darkness.

'Lucie, we've already been through this. I did what was best for you. And for your father.' Her mother stood, wincing as she straightened. She was only fifty yet seemed older. Jagged, as though grief had torn her around the edges. Not a clean cut, but shredded paper with layer upon layer exposed. 'Would Keeley like a drink of milk? I bought Paris Creek organic. Ridiculous price, but it's what you prefer, isn't it?'

'What I'd prefer is if you just tell me what paperwork needs taking care of, so I can get the hell out of this night-mare.' Lucie dropped her head into her hands, suddenly utterly defeated.

'I was getting the impression you wanted to be home.' Mum's triumph trumpeted across the noise of Keeley's TV program.

'Home. Not this empty shell.' Anguish welled up inside Lucie. 'Home like it used to be.' Except had that home ever existed or was it just a fairytale of her childhood? The happy memories, she now realised, were the same small handful, played on repeat in her mind.

Milk slopped from the glass Mum set carefully on the table. She took a serviette and dabbed at the white pool. 'I'm sure we all want a lot of things we can't have. Including love that will never be reciprocated.'

'You're doing my head in,' Lucie groaned from behind her hands. 'Do you mean I don't reciprocate your love, or that you refuse to reciprocate mine? Because that would be assuming I even have any for you.' The words burst from her as she fisted her hands.

She didn't care.

Except that it damn well hurt. Surely she should feel victory at finally being brave enough to speak her mind? Instead, blood thundered in her ears as she waited for Mum to tell her she was wrong, that she was mistaken, that they did love each other. Like a normal family. Or what remained of one.

Silence.

She couldn't wait any longer, couldn't pathetically hope that, just this once, her mum would be there for her. Lucie planted both hands on the table, shoving to her feet, the chair tipping over and clattering to the floor. 'You know what? Don't even answer that. Because I don't care. I'm back because I owe *Dad*. As you're so eager to point out, I have a debt to pay.'

Mum met her gaze in unblinking silence for a long moment. 'Does Keeley need something in the milk?' she said eventually, her voice a little uneven. 'I bought some Nesquik. Chocolate and strawberry.' She moved to the kitchen cabinets, stretching up to take out a can of the powdered flavouring that Lucie had never been allowed as a child. 'I'm sorry, Lucie.' Back ramrod straight, her oddly uncertain voice was almost too quiet to hear as she faced the cupboard. 'I should never have inferred that you owed your father, or that he expected anything from you. I spoke in anger. Or perhaps, I suppose, in panic. I just wanted to make sure you came home.'

'Why? Why now, when it's too late?' Lucie snapped, the released anger white hot within her. She wanted to lash out, to punish her mother.

'Mummy, I need you,' Keeley piped from the living room.

'Right now?' Lucie called back, an edge of panic to her voice as she struggled to get her emotions under control, her mask in place.

'Mummy!' Keeley yelled louder.

'It can be consuming, can't it?' Mum said, with what momentarily sounded like empathy. 'This parenting business.'

'How would you know?' Lucie snarled.

'Mummy!' Keeley's voice was piercing. 'Dash has eated my sock and my toes is cold.'

Okay, so it wasn't anything urgent. 'I'll be there in a minute.' Lucie took a deep breath, her hands shaking as she reached for her cold coffee.

'*Never do for a child what he is capable of doing for himself.* Or, in this instance, herself,' Mum said. 'Elizabeth Hainstock.'

'I know who said it. But how do you know a Montessori quote?'

Mum lifted a narrow shoulder, the bones pouching her blouse like a broken bird wing. 'I toured the local school. I assume that's where you'll place Keeley.'

'Maybe. In Melbourne.'

Sudden fear locked her lungs: had Mum made some kind of arrangement with Jeremy? Was that why she was pushing for information and pointing out his rights, after all these years? She smacked the cup back down on the table and stood. 'The paperwork can wait. I'll be back. Sometime.'

21
Monica

1996

Raising chickens in the bathtub had seemed like such a good idea. She could keep them neatly contained and set the heater lamp so that it was at a safe distance from them on the edge of the bath: close enough to warm them but far enough away that they wouldn't singe their down. Above all, the enamel tub would keep the mess contained while she made the finishing touches to the lovely outdoor coop she'd had built for them.

All good in theory, except who knew the chicks could fly so early?

Monica leaned over, trying to catch one of the white bundles of fluff that madly scrambled from one end of the tub to the other, repeatedly letting out an ear-piercing peep that the other five chicks echoed in abject fear.

Standing behind her in the doorway, Georgius chuckled. 'You'd have more luck herding cats.'

Trust him to see the humour in the situation—from here, all she could see was shit-smeared enamel. 'I've only fed them the chick crumbles from the fodder shop. How can there be so much crap?' she gasped, instantly regretting speaking. The air was foul with the smell of wet, singed feathers and excrement. Apparently, the light was not far enough away when the little buggers somehow managed to fly-jump up onto the side of the bath, and they had taken turns dunking themselves in their drinking bowl, then toasting dry beneath the naked bulb. Georgius had said he'd pick up a proper heat lamp from the fodder shop, rather than use the bedside light from the guest room, but as usual she had gone her own way.

Grabbing one of the warm, squirming bundles, she thrust it into the shoebox she had ready. Although her movements were abrupt, she was careful of the straw-like legs. 'You can say "I told you so",' she muttered to her husband, knowing he wouldn't. Georgius never gloated and rarely argued, although when he did, he would explode in a display of ethnic passion. When truly furious, though, Georgius would go quiet. Now she frequently found herself nagging him, picking fights simply to spice up the relationship. Anger was preferable to nothing.

'You're probably loving them a little too much,' Georgius offered. He often made pronouncements like that, as though he believed her capable of more affection than she revealed.

He was wrong. He had grown on Monica, and she did love him. But it wasn't the all-consuming love she had known. It was more peripheral, dutiful. Gratitude to him for proving that she wasn't unwanted. For rescuing her, for marrying her before Mack got married. Though that had been a near-run thing, with Georgius insisting they not only be engaged for over a year but be celibate for that time.

Not that the lack of sex had bothered her. Not since the abortion that should have proved to Georgius that she was incapable of loving anyone. Mack had taken that from her, along with everything else. He had ruined her past and stolen her future, and all she could do was wish the same pain on him.

Georgius lounged against the doorframe. Little seemed to faze him, not even this destruction of the bathroom in the home they'd moved into a little over three years ago, right after they married—and right before Nanna died. 'Mama always says that chicks should be fed on gruel to start with,' he offered. 'She boils potato peels and mixes them with cold polenta or oats.'

Monica felt a brief twist of guilt at the introduction of the one subject guaranteed to steal the light from Georgius's dark eyes: his family. The rift had nothing to do with her, but she had tried to fill the void in his life. Although she could never offer him more of herself, she had given him the child he desperately wanted, helped him to create his own family.

And that should be enough for her, too. Yet, although she loved her daughter, still her life had an emptiness, a sense of unfulfilled promise, as though she was merely marking time, waiting for the best bits to happen. Waiting for an exhilarating finale when the soundtrack to her life was nothing but elevator music.

But the truth was, maybe the best bits had already happened. Maybe they had disappeared, along with the lost baby. The baby she blamed Mack for yet still felt, deep inside, had somehow been his child.

Their child.

Like their love, irreplaceable.

Georgius and Lucie could only ever come a pale second best to the loves she had lost.

A full-throated scream from the next room almost made Monica drop the final chick. That was always Lucie's way; no slow, gentle waking, she was passionate and demanding, determined to display all the fire Georgius deliberately kept bottled up.

Georgius spun, as though he couldn't bear to hear his daughter cry, and returned seconds later, tossing the giggling, squealing toddler into the air and carefully catching her each time. The look of adoration on his face mirrored that on Lucie's, her chubby cheeks plumped as she chuckled in toothy breathlessness. As always, vague envy dug dull talons into Monica's chest. Why could she never experience the love that these two obviously shared? She always felt slightly . . . distanced. It wasn't that she didn't love them, just that she didn't have the same overwhelming attachment they evidenced.

Monica rarely felt extremes of emotion. She was neither happy nor sad. Simply grey. Or beige. Yes, that was more apt. Her life wasn't miserable enough to be grey, but nor did it have more colour than the dullest of browns.

It hadn't since Mack had ruined her life.

22
Jack

'Watch the fly strips, Ma,' Jack said as he swept the orange plastic aside. It was ridiculous, he'd never spent so much time in town in his life. At least, not since he had attended the small primary school there.

'Lynn,' Ma raised her voice querulously, 'you know you really don't need the fly strips down until summer.'

The cashier looked up from the till and smiled. 'Back again, Jack? Tell you what, if you're going to be here every day, could you run a sack of kibble out to Hayden for me? I spoke to him this morning and he reckons Trigger's right for a couple of days yet, but I'm thinking it wouldn't hurt to have someone drop in on him, y'know?'

'Course. Not a problem.' Running the dog biscuits out to his mate, who was in a bit of a dark place, certainly wasn't a problem. Having Lynn notice that he'd been in town every day was. 'Ma wanted a bit of a wander in the shops today,' he said by way of excuse.

'Ma is quite capable of speaking for herself,' his grandmother observed.

'Perfect timing, Evie,' Lynn called cheerfully. 'I've got Chloe coming to take over in a few minutes so I can pop out to the CWA meeting. Care to ride with me?'

'CWA?' Ma sounded a little shocked. 'Is that today? Dear me, I've lost track.'

Jack frowned. That was a refrain he was hearing far too often from Ma lately.

'We're finalising the spring trading table. Christine's still arguing against Tracey's theme. Not because it's a bad idea, simply that it's Tracey's idea.'

Jack automatically filtered out the gossip. The local CWA was notorious for the power battles between a couple of the senior members and their faithful cohorts. The fly strips behind him made a distinctive soft swish, and he jerked around.

'Hey, Jack. Lovely to see you out, Evie,' Roni smiled.

'Hey, Roni.' Jack stifled his disappointment. In a town the size of Settlers Bridge, it only seemed fair he would have run into Lucie by now.

'How are those babies of yours?' Ma asked as Roni pulled a trolley from the queue of five rickety-wheeled carriages.

'Not so much babies now, Evie,' Roni said. 'They're almost three. I've dumped them with Tracey for a few minutes so I can shop without reaching the checkout with a load of unexpected things bunged in my trolley.'

'Three? No! Where did that time go?'

Jack pushed down his rush of concern. 'What was it you wanted, Ma?' He assured himself that the question didn't sound as though he was testing her.

Ma waved a gnarled finger. 'Toilet paper, cornflour, butter if you want bacon and eggs this weekend. Did Young Eric drop off any fresh duck eggs?' she added to Lynn.

'I think I'm out,' Lynn said. 'I've not seen him for a couple of days.' Along with the standard grocery lines, Lynn stocked local produce, adding a small margin to cover her time. 'Actually, if you'll take Hayden's kibble, Jack, I'll look in on Eric after the CWA.' She glanced out of the window, squinting between the posters advertising Vegemite and bung fritz. 'Oh wait, here's Chloe now. I'll have time to go before the meeting.'

'I've loads of eggs at the moment, Evie,' Roni said. 'The ducks have just realised it's spring, though no doubt they'll be broody soon enough. If you can wait until tomorrow, I'll pop some by the farm?'

'Lovely. Don't tell Young Eric but your eggs are nicer. I'm quite sure he lets his ducks eat mice, you can always taste it in the yolk,' Ma said, likely prompting a minor feud once that tale made it around town. She turned back to Jack. 'And I must find something for arthritis. Pops doesn't like to bother Taylor about it.'

As Jack had been drinking milk all week, having forgotten to buy coffee despite his repeated trips into town, Ma seemed to be doing better with her shopping list than him. He was clearly worrying about nothing, in that regard at least.

He didn't turn as he heard Chloe bat her way through the fly strips behind him. 'You know Taylor will fix Pops up. You only need to ring.'

'*I* know that,' Ma said, managing to infer the issue was all Pops'. 'But he insists the arthritis isn't bad enough to bother the doctor. He's a little stiff in the morning. And when he's been sitting too long. Which he does far too much of now, anyway. But he doesn't like to take medicine, it messes with his bowels.'

Jack grimaced at Roni. Far too much information.

'I don't mean to eavesdrop—'

The lilting voice sent a shockwave up his spine. He whiplashed around. 'L-L-Lucie. Hi.' Hell, he sounded like an idiot.

Lucie smiled at him, but it seemed a polite gesture, nothing more. 'Hello, Jack.' She turned back to Ma, tucking her short hair behind her left ear, the gesture oddly uncertain, as though she regretted having spoken. 'I overheard you saying something about mild arthritis? I have a tea that may give your husband some relief.'

'Tea?' Ma laughed. 'I think he'd rather a stiff brandy.'

Dusky colour mounted Lucie's cheeks. 'Sorry, I didn't explain that well. I'm a natural health therapist. I can put together a blend of herbs that have anti-inflammatory properties. Or, if your husband is on blood thinners or other medication, I can look into making an ointment that might give him some relief.'

'I'm sure he'd far rather an ointment, especially if it comes with someone to rub it on for him.'

Jack rolled his eyes. 'Ma . . .'

Lynn guffawed. 'I'm sure Paul will be quite happy to have you do that, Evie.'

'Small children present,' Jack warned, tipping his head towards Keeley, who was partially hidden behind Lucie.

'Oh, this is who you were talking about at lunch the other week?' Ma suddenly cottoned on with a flash of understanding he could do without.

'Well, not so much talking *about*, Ma,' he muttered, 'as talking about business.'

Ma seemed to realise she'd planted her Homyped in it. She leaned down to Keeley. 'Jack told me he had met a lovely young lady.'

Not true, but a decent save, as long as Ma didn't also mention the funeral, where he had *not* met Keeley.

There was an awkward pause, then Lucie said, 'Anyway, I was popping in to say thanks for the groceries I found in the kitchen, Lynn.'

Lynn waved off the thanks. 'No problem. I like to make sure my guests have the basics in stock. Though considering what you bought last week, I don't suppose it was really much use to you.'

Lucie looked flustered, as though she wasn't used to having her spending habits discussed in public. 'Oh no, it was fabulous. That's why I've not been in again, you set us up really well. I just like to supplement our diets with organics and stuff . . .' She trailed off, seeming to realise she was sharing even more of her shopping list than Lynn had. 'The cake was delicious.'

Lynn held up a hand. 'Can't take credit for the cake. Sam down at Ploughs and Pies delivered that.'

'Sam?' Jack blurted. His sister had known for over a week where Lucie was staying? Not that he'd asked her, or even dared make a passing mention of Lucie.

Lynn cocked an interested eyebrow. 'She came by for the key on Saturday morning. Said she had a phone order from out of town.'

'Out of town?' Lucie seemed oddly perturbed.

Lynn shrugged. 'Sorry, love, can't tell you more than that.'

'Cake was pretty,' Keeley piped up. 'Was pink for fairy princesses, like me. I has a fairy garden.'

'It was a Napoleon cake,' Lucie clarified. 'With pink icing, right, Keels? My dad always used to buy it for my birthday.' Though she smiled, the tightness of her lips and the deepening dimple somehow looked unutterably sad. 'Oh, remember, Keeley, you wanted to ask Lynn something about the goldfish?'

Keeley nodded solemnly and straightened, as though she had rehearsed lines to share. 'I can feed fishes, please?' she said to Lynn.

'Sure you can, sweetie. Their food is under the laundry sink.' Lynn added to Lucie, 'They don't need feeding, they catch enough insects. But they'll no doubt appreciate it.'

Recognition had dawned in Keeley's golden face as she stared around the group of adults, her gaze finally resting on Jack. 'And I visit Mr Unicorn now?'

'You mean "may I visit",' Lucie corrected. 'And I'm sure Jack's busy, so we'll make it another day, okay?'

'Oh, Jack's not busy,' Ma said slyly. 'He's just brought me in to go to the CWA with Lynn here, so he's quite at a loose end.'

Like there was ever a farmer who had nothing to do. Even one who had driven into town every day for a week on the off chance of running into Lucie—to whom he now couldn't think of a bloody thing to say. 'I, uh, yeah. I just have to drop some kibble at a mate's place.'

'Chloe can take that with her, right, Chlo?' Lynn called to the teenager who was now held up behind the crowd standing around the register. 'I'll give your mum a ring to pick you up and get it.' Apparently, Lynn's concern for Hayden's welfare had taken a back seat to interest in Lucie. And him.

'No worries,' Hayden's youngest sister replied, edging around the group to get nearer the register. 'But what's this about a unicorn?'

'Jack has Mr Unicorn,' Keeley said. 'Him live in poo, and Jack has poo.'

'Is that so?' Roni chuckled. Out of everyone there, she would be the most accustomed to the way kids spoke. Yet she was clearly not about to let him off the hook.

'Don't ask,' Jack groaned, aware of everyone's gaze on him. Except Lucie's. The one he would have welcomed. Instead, she looked as embarrassed as he felt. 'I'll, ah, draw you a mud map of how to get to The Twenty,' he said to Lucie. 'Just give me a thirty-minute head start.'

She shook her head. 'It's okay, Keeley knows Mr Unicorn could be out visiting.'

Clearly, she didn't trust him to have looked after the dung beetle.

Lucie continued quickly, as if making sure he realised she did intend to come out. 'I saw the dog in your ute. We have Dash with us—is it okay to bring him, or will that be a problem?'

She'd remembered which car was his? That probably wasn't great, given the old Holden's state. 'It's fine. Sally's a lover, not a fighter.'

'Like master, like dog,' Ma said, nowhere near enough under her breath.

Roni finally took pity on him, speaking loudly before the silence had a chance to get more awkward. 'I'm Roni. You're new to town?'

'Sorry, yes. Lucie.' She held out her hand and he felt a stab of jealousy. He hadn't found an excuse to touch her yet, and it was a bit late to do introductions. 'And Keeley.'

'Hi, Keeley,' Roni said. 'I have a little girl who's about your age. Maybe you can come for a playdate sometime?'

'Does she be a princess fairy?' Keeley asked.

'Hmm. She is most definitely both of those things, on occasion. And she has a twin brother you can play with as well.' Roni looked up at Jack, her eyes dancing with amusement, and he groaned inwardly. A few years earlier, when she'd been new to the district, Roni had been slightly aloof to hide her shyness. What he wouldn't give for a serve of that right now. 'Jack, put my number on that map you're drawing, okay?' She turned to Lucie. 'We're not far from Jack's, once you get to know the back roads, so get him to point out the direction when you're out that way. If you have time, that is.'

He scowled at the sly glance Roni shot him. She grinned unrepentantly. 'I'd better get my shopping done before the kids drive Tracey nuts, though that woman has the patience of an angel.' She looked back to Lucie 'Seriously, if you're ever looking for a babysitter, Tracey is awesome. I'd be so lost without her. She'll be taking my two after the fireworks in a couple of weeks' time, so Matt and I can catch up with some friends without worrying about the combination of marshmallow toasting sticks and little eyes.' She gave a dramatic shudder. 'You are bringing Lucie and Keeley to the fireworks, right, Jack?'

So many people were getting struck off his Christmas card list right now.

'I can babysit, too,' Chloe put in. 'I mean, if you guys want to go to the fireworks without kids.'

He stared in horror as she gestured between him and Lucie as though they were a couple.

Lucie gave a small gasp but then pulled her shoulders back, stood a little taller. 'Thanks—Chloe, was it? But Keeley has never seen fireworks, so I'm sure she'd love to go.' She pulled her daughter against her thigh and looked down at her. 'And maybe Geoff will come too?'

Geoff? Great. The guy must have patched his relationship with Lucie. 'I'll put the map under your wiper,' Jack said brusquely. 'See you out there whenever.'

23
Lucie

Lucie stared in dismay at Jack's back as he strode away. Why did she have to go and mention Geoff?

Mostly because she was trying to keep things normal for Keeley, and Geoff had always been part of her daughter's life. But, if she was completely honest, it was also because she had panicked a little at the insinuations she imagined into the conversation.

'I'll make a blend for your husband and drop it at Jack's,' she said to his mother. Although Jack seemed to be around her own age, maybe thirtyish, his mum had to be over seventy. But many country women, exposed to the elements while working alongside their husbands, aged prematurely. 'I'll make a tea, too, but if he's on medication, warn him to check with his doctor first.'

'For your Paul, Evie?' a voice behind her asked. She cringed inwardly at the addition of yet another person to the burgeoning group. Surely about half the town had to be crowded into the supermarket by now.

'Hi, Taylor,' Lynn and Evie chorused.

Chloe glanced beyond her with a shy smile. 'Hi, Doc.'

'Yes, for Paul,' Evie nodded. 'His arthritis is playing up, and he doesn't want to bother you with it.'

'Lucie here is a naturalist,' Lynn volunteered.

'Natural health therapist,' Lucie corrected, twisting to include the newcomer in the circle she wished she could extricate herself from. The grey-eyed woman smiled, but Lucie knew well enough most of the medical establishment's aversion to alternative medicine.

'Oh, cool,' the woman said. Then her gaze sharpened. 'Actually, do you know much about burn lotions? I've a patient who really isn't responding as well as I'd like to the prescription creams. I suspect he doesn't use them as much as he should.' She flicked a glance towards Chloe, as though the younger woman would confirm her suspicion. 'If I could limit his scripts to the more serious burns and have him use something else to ease the itching and scarring of the lesser ones, maybe I can win him over. Do you have any suggestions?' She slapped a hand across her mouth. 'Oh my god, I hate when people waylay me for professional advice, and I've just done exactly the same to you. Sorry. I'm Taylor. Local doc and apparently local foot-in-mouther.'

'Lucie. Depending on the burn, I'd probably look at an aloe base and then some essentials, like chamomile, lavender for healing, juniper for scarring. Peppermint oil for pain. And some oregano, if there's minor broken skin, because it's microbial.'

Taylor nodded eagerly. 'That's the kind of thing I'm talking about. We could do with some complementary medicine around here. Something a bit more grassroots, old-school, you know? As much as modern medicine makes surges forward, I think we're losing ground by throwing out some of the tried and tested remedies. I have this vague memory of a really sticky, gooey cream that was used for burns years ago—smelled like an air freshener. Do you have any ideas on that one?'

Lucie nodded, more comfortable in familiar territory. 'It would be pine oil, or a pine decoction. Pine is an all-rounder—reduces scarring, kills pathogens, eases pain.'

'We really need to get together,' Taylor said. 'You're from Adelaide?'

'Melbourne. But we're staying here, actually.'

'In my buff fly fairy garden,' Keeley put in. 'But Mr Unicorn isn't there. Jack's got him in his poo.'

'I'd love to explain,' Lucie said with a laugh, shaking her head to signify that she really wouldn't, 'but I was only popping in for a moment. Lynn's got my details if you want them.' Chances were, the doctor was just being small-town polite.

'If that Jack of mine forgot to put the map on your windshield, you come back in here and get it,' cautioned Evie.

'I will. I'll get the blend to him,' she said. Because that was the whole reason she'd agreed to go to his place—wasn't it? That and the dung beetle visit.

'Don't forget the babysitting offer,' Chloe called after her as Lucie beat a retreat through the fly strips.

If Jack hadn't bothered putting the map on the windscreen, it would be his way of getting out of the arrangement. She would simply drop the treatments in to Lynn to pass on to Evie's husband. She had time to kill; she was nowhere near ready to see Mum again yet.

Mum. The pink-iced Napoleon. Her favourite cake. Had Mum organised that? Yet she hadn't mentioned it when they turned up with the protein truffles earlier in the week.

Any thoughts about the cake disappeared in a rush of relief as Lucie spotted the scrap of paper on her windscreen. She buckled Keeley in her car seat before retrieving the note, penned on the back of a receipt from a local stock fodder shop. No reason for the lack of notepaper to seem cute and country, yet it did. The fact that there was no message, only a map, was a bit disappointing, though.

But what the heck did she expect him to write?

Jack wanted a thirty-minute head start—no doubt so he could locate a dung beetle to replace Mr Unicorn—but by the time she had worked out which blend and form would be best for his father, he'd get a lot more than that. Which was good. She didn't want to look too eager.

Back in the kitchen at their cottage, she settled Keeley with a book, then pulled out her stock of essential oils. She could produce a vaporiser concoction or oral drops, but as Evie hadn't said whether her husband was on medication, massage oil to reduce inflammation would be safer. The unguent the doctor wanted could wait a day: she'd harvest Vera, the potted aloe she had brought with them, to create the base.

She measured drops of lavender, juniper, and a third less of ylang-ylang and rosemary into one of the cobalt blue homeopathy bottles she kept specifically for her 'witches brews', as Geoff called them. Sweet almond oil came to hand, but she hesitated. It was her favourite carrier, but possibly too nicely scented for a man, particularly of a certain age. She chose coconut oil instead, measured a hundred millilitres into the bottle, capped it and shook vigorously. With her free hand she pulled her labelling folder from the top of the microwave. She had put all of her naturopathy supplies where Keeley couldn't get to them. Although her daughter liked to play herbalist in the garden, picking petals and leaves and mashing them with a rock and water to produce potions, she wasn't about to graduate to the potentially lethal distilled oils anytime soon. Selecting a label, Lucie wrote *Not for consumption* with a thick marker, stuck the label on the bottle and gave it one final shake.

She packed everything back out of reach, pausing with her hand on the sweet almond oil. Jack wore a woodsy cologne that gave off notes of sandalwood and cedar, putting her in mind of summer days and lush forests— and reminding her that she hadn't brought any perfume with her. But the sweet almond was a good base and would do fine for now. She dabbed it onto her wrists and neck.

Tonight she'd revisit her knowledge of perfume making, add the right heart and head. Perhaps something fruity for spring, like orange and grapefruit? Or more earthy, like vetiver and musk, which she could order online.

Like Jack would care how she smelled. Irritated with her line of thought, she recapped the bottle and put it away. In any case, perfume would need to sit for a month for the fragrances to mellow.

'Dash,' she called, knowing she had a better chance of the dog responding than Keeley. Within seconds, the dog appeared from Keeley's bedroom, his paws scrabbling on the boards as he tried to gain traction, and hurtled towards her on stubby legs. 'It's okay, little guy, slow down.' She reached to take her jacket and Keeley's from the hooks in the hall. 'Keels, it's getting colder by the minute. I think Dash needs a jumper on, too.'

'I pick it, Mummy,' Keeley called, far more interested in dressing Dash than she was in dressing dolls.

'Sure, but make it snappy or Mr Unicorn will have gone out visiting.' She had to work in an excuse for when Jack was unable to produce the dung beetle.

'Snappy' turned into four costume changes for Dash, the final one when Keeley realised she could wear her bright purple wellington boots but decided they didn't match Dash's jumper.

The car was toasty warm, and Jack's place, despite being further into the countryside, looked like it would be as easy to find as the town was to navigate. Lucie had quickly discovered Settlers Bridge consisted of the main strip, with its oddly mirrored shops, and a couple of parallel backstreets on either side that housed organisations including the local council chambers and library. Beyond that was a grid of wide, tree-lined streets with solid stone homes. The road she had arrived on crossed the bridge and ran straight as a die up the main street, then out of town, towards a low range of hills. Near the bridge was a T-junction, the side road coming in from the north. According to Jack's map, she needed to take that road, winding out of town and then cutting across orchard and dairy flats. The first dirt road to the right after the apricot packing sheds would hug the serpentine edge of the river and eventually reach his farm in the next valley.

Keeley and Dash bounced up and down on the back seat, both straining against their harnesses to see the black-and-white or rusty red cows in paddocks of uniform size, bordered by irrigation trenches. In her excitement, Keeley forgot how to count, repeatedly missing the number seven and groaning with frustration as she reached ten with a finger still curved into her palm.

Lucie waited until Keeley said 'six', then said, 'Oh, look at that baby cow over there, Keels, isn't he cute?' As Keeley leaned against her seatbelt straps to see, Lucie added, 'Sorry, I interrupted. You just counted six, so you're up to seven.' She repeated the trick a few times, and by the time Keeley was once again confidently counting to ten, they were pulling off the rapidly narrowing dirt track.

She drew the car to a halt in the shade of a massive river red gum, the trunk as wide as her car. A few metres away stood an asymmetrical, red-roofed cottage. On the far side, a wind-hollowed cave in a sandy hill hugged the house, so she knew she had the right place: according to Jack's map, he was the end of the road. Plus, his decrepit ute was almost hidden beneath a rampant, deep purple bougainvillea sprawled across the roof of a rusted lean-to garage slightly down the yard.

'We see Mr Unicorn now?' Keeley asked hopefully.

'If he's home,' Lucie hedged. She had been hoping the calves would be distraction enough that Keeley wouldn't be disappointed by the lack of a bug. And Lucie wouldn't be disappointed by Jack letting them down.

Which was ridiculous. He owed them—her—nothing. He'd been as embarrassed as she was by the scene in the IGA, couldn't get out of the place quick enough.

Although he had put the map on her windscreen.

'Let's find Jack.' Taking Keeley's hand, and making sure Dash's lead was around her own wrist, she scanned the area for signs of the farmer. Even if he hadn't heard their car, the furiously barking dog inside the house should have alerted Jack to their presence.

'Hello?' she called tentatively as they approached the house. A low stone wall surrounded an overgrown flower garden, larger than an entire Melbourne house block, at the front of Jack's cottage. The house appeared to be only two rooms wide and perhaps three deep. One of the front rooms was set forward, with a small, galvanised iron canopy over the pair of windows. The recessed room alongside was shaded by a bullnose corrugated iron verandah, creating a porch sectioned from the garden by a hip-height, cement rendered wall, sculpted in a deep, smooth swoop. Three concrete steps led up to the porch, passing beneath a rough-hewn timber sign engraved with *River Gum Cottage*. She had seen a few similar timber signs around Settlers Bridge, including the one in Sam's shop directing customers to place their order at the counter. Apparently, someone in town had a gift for woodwork.

They moved towards the garden, still alert for any sign of Jack. Against the far garden wall were the evergreen needle leaves of rambling rosemary, while at the bottom of the plot a hedge of thick, knobbly-branched English lavender was crowned with a profusion of short, purple-flowered stems. Daisies in white, pink, purple and every shade of yellow perfumed the air with musky sweetness, interspersed with a variety of lavandin growing wild and unharvested. Lucie's mouth watered at the thought of baking with the fragrant blooms of the English lavender, but it was the smaller, more delicate lavandin bushes that caught her attention: French lavender held more oil than the English variety, and the naturopathic uses for the herb were endless.

Still standing in the yard outside the garden, Lucie placed her hands on the stone wall, leaning over to gaze greedily at the abundant tangle of vegetation. She caught her breath. Surely the silvery, downy foliage of the nearest bushes were wormwood? She pinched a leaf between forefinger and thumb and sighed with pleasure at the sweet scent. There was so much she could do with fresh wormwood . . . perhaps Jack would allow her to cut some?

'Mummy. Smell?' Keeley asked.

'Sure, baby.' She tucked a sprig of the plant through the buttonhole in Keeley's jacket. 'Okay, so no Jack.' Lucie straightened, staring across the flats stretching down to the river. Here, the land was fenced into plots, each area seeming to have a defined purpose. To the left of the house, across a tussocky expanse of grass and dirt, was a huge bird-netted orchard. The near side was open to a coop, layer boxes jutting from the back of the building like a Victorian bustle. Multicoloured chickens scurried down a ramp to scratch and peck through a wild jumble of bushes beneath the fruit trees, the undergrowth in stark contrast to the parade-ground precision and austerity of the commercial orchards they had passed. A dense hedge bordered the lower end of the orchard, and grapevines sprawled along a wooden frame on the side opposite the hen house.

But it was the plot to the right of coop that caught Lucie's attention.

The market garden was a wilderness of bamboo canes and trellises. She could make out various kinds of beans and the tall, ferny fronds of asparagus. A patch of straggly, knee-high plants with dark green, almost purple leaves could only be potatoes, and the green straps of garlic with their dandelion-burst flower heads lent a distinctive aroma as she was drawn towards the garden. With the magic brought by the turn of seasons, juniper green, white-stemmed English spinach and the finer silverbeet grew only a row from small, pale oakleaf and burgundy radicchio lettuces.

The garden puzzled her: she had thought Jack a farmer, yet this plot was too small to be commercial and too large for one person. The women in the IGA had definitely made it sound as though he was single. Hadn't they? Or had she just chosen to read that into their conversation?

Areas of the garden were bare, the rich earth mounded high. Lucie instinctively knew why, and the jagged shards of memory tore at her heart: like Dad, Jack waited for the soil to warm before bedding his precious plants.

With Keeley urging her on, they walked along a short row of cauliflowers, surely the last of the season, their outer leaves pulled together and tied with string to keep the hearts white. The borders of the plot were planted with sweet alyssum, and mint bushes interspersed the brassicas. A thrill ran through Lucie as she recognised the organic techniques: the tiny white alyssum flowers attracted hoverflies, one of the fiercest natural predators of aphids, and the mint brought in parasitic wasps who would decimate caterpillars on the brassicas.

Excitement swelled within her at the realisation that Jack's interest in permaculture had not been faked. This garden, with its potential to nourish both body and soul, could only have been created by someone who shared her longing to find fulfilment and meaning in life, someone who wanted to step off the treadmill of thoughtless consumerism. The bounty and beauty surrounding her held so much more promise than her few cat wee–infected pots in Melbourne.

Keeley tugged on her hand. 'Mummy, baby lambs!'

With rows still to explore, Lucie was reluctant to leave the vegetable garden, but Keeley dragged her down the slope, towards a wire gate that opened to a paddock containing a low, iron-roofed stone building. Strident bleating almost drowned the buzz of a motorbike on the dirt road behind the house, but before she could fully pinpoint either noise, a familiar sight caught her attention. Beyond the paddock were strawberries. She would know the look of those lush, dark rows from miles away. And the smell. It could be her imagination, but even from this distance, she thought she caught the fragrance, the scent that awoke the poignant memories of her childhood.

'Mummy, lambs!' Keeley insisted louder again, tugging on her fingers until they cracked.

'Not lambs. Kids,' a male voice corrected.

24
Lucie

Lucie snapped around to look at Jack. She had been so focused on trying to repress the melancholy evoked by the sight of the strawberries, it hadn't registered that the noise of the motorbike had stopped somewhere behind them.

Jack's hair hung in dripping sandy blond strands, brushing the shoulders of his flannelette shirt. 'You're wet,' she said, as though the chill breeze wouldn't tip him off.

'Yup.' He hiked a thumb across the paddocks. 'Had a fight with the pump down at the dam. Hang on a sec.' As he strode back up the slope towards the house, passing a red ag bike, he tugged off his sopping shirt and gave his hair a quick rub.

Lucie trailed him uncertainly, though Keeley was reluctant to leave the animals she had discovered. Eventually, slowed by Keeley, Lucie stopped in the middle of the market garden, watching Jack's retreat.

Metal screeched as he pushed open the side gate and disappeared from view, re-emerging seconds later with a dusty red cattle dog glued to his heels. He headed across to the ute parked beneath the lean-to, ducking beneath the cascading bougainvillea to toss his shirt into the tray, then reached through the open car window and retrieved a bundle of grey marle.

As Jack pulled the dry sweater over his head, Lucie turned away, trying to steady her breathing. It wasn't like she hadn't seen a half-naked man anytime recently: Keeley loved the beach, and they spent a good part of each summer there. But she hadn't spoken with any of them, hadn't had to survive that awkward moment of making it ostentatiously clear that she was focusing on nothing but their eyes. And nor had they looked quite like . . . this.

Although what 'this' was, she wasn't entirely sure. There was something effortlessly athletic about Jack's physique, as though the finely honed, sinewy muscles were a result of work, rather than gym. Which, logically, they probably were.

As Jack returned, he gave an exaggerated shiver and shook his head. Keeley squealed as droplets sprayed on her, and he grinned. 'Sorry, Keeley. Doesn't your dog do that?'

'Him not big enough,' Keeley said crossly, bending to wipe a spot of water from her gumboot.

'Fair enough, I guess he wouldn't make you too wet.' Jack pointed at the cattle dog 'Sally is plenty big enough to make you wet when she shakes. I had to leave her in the house or she would have been in the dam taking a swim with me.'

'You was swimming?' Keeley said, round-eyed.

'Uh, yeah, you were swimming?' Lucie echoed, finally finding her voice.

'Not this time.' Jack dug a strip of flat leather from his pocket and tied his hair back.

'You was swimming with other kids?' Clinging to the notion, Keeley sounded outraged, as though she had a right to claim him.

'Kids? Oh, yeah.' He nodded at the yard Keeley had been dragging Lucie towards. 'The kids are over here. Baby goats,' he added to Lucie, as they walked back down the slope.

'Goats?' Lucie breathed. 'Do you have a nanny?'

'Sure do. I wanted organic milk, but cows are tough on the pasture. Goats are browsers, so as long as I keep their cradle filled and grow a tagasaste hedge for them, they don't rip out the grasses. And they're light enough on their feet to not churn up the ground,' he added with a laugh as a fawn goat, the size of a medium dog, launched itself stiff-legged into the air, then ran a quick lap of its enclosure before leaping onto a wooden structure that sprouted straws of leafy olive-coloured hay in all directions. 'That's Marilyn.'

'Hush, Dash,' Lucie said as the pup barked and pulled on the lead, eager to join in. 'Marilyn is your nanny? I asked Lynn at the store if she knew of anyone selling goat's milk.'

'No, Marilyn's one of the kids. And I don't sell Pamela's milk.' Jack caught her raised eyebrow and ran both hands

213

over his hair, shoving the errant wet strands into place, and gave a bashful grin. 'Don't ask. It was a pub dare.'

'Ah.' Blokes and boobs. 'That one is a *Baywatch* reference?'

Jack flushed a bit deeper under his tan. 'Yeah. Anyway, most people only want cow's milk, and they want it in a plastic bottle. Pamela was a rescue, and not really the best kind of goat for milking. But she produces enough for me, and Ma and Pops take a bit. Though Ma won't use it in baking. She says it's not rich enough.' Lucie must have looked disappointed, because he added, 'I mean, I intend to produce only enough for myself, but there's plenty to spare. You're welcome to it, if you don't mind the fact that it's raw.'

'I'd pay extra for that.'

'Can't be paying anything,' he said. 'Only a handful of places are licensed for selling unpasteurised goat's milk. How about we call it ground rent?'

Lucie lifted one shoulder, not sure what he was getting at. 'Ground rent?'

'Well, partial, anyway.'

Marilyn leaped from the haystack and darted towards a far corner of the paddock, beneath the shelter of a low tree covered with white flowers. A flock of round, soft-lavender birds scuttled across the paddock.

'Chickies,' Keeley squealed.

'Not quite,' Jack said wryly. 'I brought in guinea fowl to help keep predators away from the rest of the flock, but mine clearly didn't read the same info pack as I did, although they do all right with the mozzies. Unfortunately, they aren't selective, so they're just as likely to eat the bees and ladybugs.'

Lucie needed to guide the conversation back to the ground rent, to find out what Jack was talking about, but the fowl had caught her attention almost as much as they had Keeley's. 'I thought guineas were black with white dots?'

'Can be. These are lavenders, though. Same white dots, they just don't show as clearly. I'm trying to create a closed-loop system. You know, grow the food for the animals, then use their manure to fertilise that production chain.'

Did she imagine that he looked hopeful she understood? 'Turn waste into resources.'

He nodded. 'You've got it.' A cacophony of bleating and clucking and whistling filled the air, and he groaned. 'Though I'm still not sold on the guineas. Bloody things know Marilyn and Arnie are going to chase them if they get in the tagasaste trees. I'm sure they only fly up there to stir shit.'

'Arnie?'

'The Terminator,' Jack grinned, seeming pleased with himself. 'He's something of a menace. I really need to move him on.'

'Aww, but he's cute,' Lucie watched as the goat, whose coat of mottled brown seemed to be half falling off him, leaned his forelegs on the low tree, stretching nibbling lips up towards the branches. Pamela and Marilyn, who looked identical, circled, seeming to encourage him.

'You won't think that when you get close,' Jack warned.

'Because of his coat?'

'No, he's a cashmere cross, so the coat sheds like that, rather than needing shearing. But he's coming into his first rut. Which is back-to-front because he should have held out until autumn.' Jack grinned at her obvious incomprehension. 'He wants to mate. And a rutting goat likes to spray on a particular cologne.' He glanced at Keeley, whose attention was on the two female goats, who had become bored watching Arnie and now bounced stiff-legged across the paddock. 'He'll pee on his beard and face to make himself more attractive to the girls.'

'And that works?' Lucie said, not trying to hide her disgust.

'Hopefully not, given that he's related to these two. That's why I have to move him on. Not many folks want to take on a buck, though.'

'You won't—' she lowered her voice '—eat him?'

Jack shook his head. 'You want to pat the girls, Keeley? We'll pick some of the tree lucerne they can't reach and they'll love you forever.' He led the way down the block as he spoke. 'Nope, can't make him into dinner.'

'You're a vegetarian?'

'No. Not at all. Actually,' he looked embarrassed, as though it was a secret he rarely shared, 'I'm more of a nose-to-tail eater. That means—'

'That you don't waste anything when you kill an animal. Sustainable eating, smaller environmental impact.' The excitement that thrilled through her was ridiculous.

Except it wasn't excitement; it must be the freshening afternoon breeze blowing in off the river and clearing her head. 'You've got your mum talked into cooking the offal dishes, then?' She winced at her less-than-subtle attempt at finding out if Jack had any female other than Evie in his life.

Jack looked puzzled. 'No, Mum's much handier with an Uber Eats order than a cookery book.'

'Surely you can't get Uber Eats out here?' She looked down, untangling Dash's lead from around her legs.

'No, but I'm pretty sure they do in Singapore.'

A hollow river gum alongside the cottage formed a natural amphitheatre for a concert of juvenile galahs, and their raucous argument covered her confusion. 'I brought the tea and rub for your dad.' Hopefully, the nudge would remind him that she'd met his mum. Most definitely not in Singapore.

'Dad?' Jack barked, as though the word flicked a switch. Then his countenance cleared. 'Ah. That was Ma you met in the IGA. My grandmother, not my mum,' he clarified.

'So the rub isn't for your dad?'

A muscle in his jaw twitched. 'W-w-wouldn't waste the stuff on that bastard,' he muttered. Then he seemed to throw off the brief mood, reaching up into one of the blossom-laden branches. 'Here, Keeley. This is their favourite food. Even though they can reach the lower branches, they're pretty sure the higher ones taste better.' He snapped a thin branch, shaking it to one side to remove the thickly busy coat of bees.

'Is it a fruit tree?' Lucie asked. 'I noticed the same kind in the orchard.'

'Tagasaste. Tree lucerne. It's great browse, high in protein. Plus it's perennial, so no unnecessary soil disturbance.

Terrific windbreak, puts nitrogen back into the soil, and protects the young fruit trees from frost.'

Lucie tried not to stare. Every word Jack said made complete and immediate sense, as though she'd finally found someone on her wavelength.

He gave the branch one more shake. 'And the flowers are awesome bee forage, so it's a cool all-rounder.' He handed the branch to Keeley, waiting as her stubby fingers fastened around it. 'Have you ever been to Adelaide Zoo?'

Keeley shook her head, her eyes huge, as though he'd given her a gift, then squealed in delight as the two female goats nibbled on the leaves. Arnie seemed more interested in Dash, pushing the pup with his nose.

'The girls have horns as well?' Lucie asked.

'Cows, sheep and goats,' Jack nodded. 'It's part of their thermoregulation; blood pumps into the core of the horn and cools down. Not that the temperature here is extreme enough to make that necessary, but I see no reason to dehorn them.'

Dash sprawled on his back, stubby legs pawing at the air as Arnie nuzzled him. Lucie bent down to scoop him up, but gasped and quickly straightened. 'Oh. Phew. My goodness.' She fanned at her face, her eyes watering. 'Oh, that smell is way beyond pee.'

Jack grinned. 'It's so bad, right? I really need to let him go, but he's bloody hilarious.'

'So, you won't eat him . . . but you'll sell him for meat?'

Jack stroked the goat with his boot. 'I'd have to separate him from the girls for a month so the rut hormones leave his body or he'll taste as gamy as all f—ah, as all get-out. And they're herd animals, it's cruel to separate them. The other option would be to castrate him, so the meat doesn't get rank.'

She tried not to wince. 'Which will you do?'

'I've patted him, so he's not gonna be food for anyone. Roni—you met her at the IGA, she's married to the local vet. Anyway, they run an animal rescue. Well, it's supposed to be a kennel and cattery, but Roni's a soft touch. She has a crazy sheep that's getting on a bit and maybe would like some company. I figure if I pay for Arnie's upkeep, they'll make space for him.'

'You'll fund him for . . . ever?'

'Ten years, I guess.' Jack gave a sheepish grin. 'Maybe not the best investment strategy, particularly if Pamela here throws a buck every year. But what am I gonna do? It's not his fault he was born a guy.'

Jack's easy acceptance of the animal's right to a place in the world reminded her of Dad and the Easter goat he could never kill. With the memory came a new surge of sorrow.

She turned away quickly as the impermissible tears stung her eyes. God, she hated this, the unexpected stabbing grief that stole her breath and shook her control.

Since Dad's death, she'd thought about him more than she had for the last four years. And it was just too damn late to do anything about it.

25
Jack

Jack tried not to stare at Lucie.

What had he said?

Whatever it was, Lucie's expression had darkened, her mouth tightening and shoulders hunching, as though she hid within herself.

Why was he rabbiting on about the animals on land that he stood to lose once Lucie inherited it, anyway? He could at least be business-like about the whole damn shitshow. He gestured towards the river about eight hundred metres away, distinguished by the high levee bank and the broad, white-and-russet-striped trunks of river red gums. 'The block ends before the river, the border's where the darker grass is. There's an irrigation channel through there. The dairy owns the bottom paddock, along with everything south. It's around nine hectares or twenty acres, hence the name, 'The Twenty'. It has good fencing all round and the soil's excellent; the only real problem is the lack of water.' Lucie looked a bit non-plussed but dutifully squinted in the directions he indicated as she bent to put the dog on the ground. The pup waddled over to Sally, who gave him a couple of tentative sniffs then looked up at Jack, as though not convinced the long-haired sausage was a dog. 'If I had a water licence, I'd have liked to turn some land over to hemp production. The returns per hectare are good, but more importantly—'

'It can be sustainably grown and is nutrient-rich.'

'And suppresses weeds and improves the soil,' he finished, trying to quell the lurch of excitement, the urge to share. But it was like she was inside his head.

He gestured back at the cottage. 'The house is plumbed to rainwater, so you have to go a bit careful on it. I've been living here the last three years, but we'll work something out if you want to move in.'

'What?' Lucie gasped. She took a quick step back from him, pulling Keeley with her. 'Why would I—?'

The cottage could do with some work. He never had time to spend on prettying up the gardens, and somehow a fair bit of farm equipment had found its way into piles on the cracked concrete porch—although that mess should be hidden by the hip-high wall—yet it wasn't as bad as Lucie's reaction made it seem. 'I mean, I know Gus wasn't interested in the house, but a share of it comes with the property, I reckon.'

Lucie kept Keeley tight against her. 'I have absolutely no idea what you're talking about.'

Was she serious? 'Gus only cared about the strawberries, but technically half of everything is his.'

'Dad . . . owns this?' Lucie asked slowly.

'Half-owns,' he corrected quickly. 'Equal partnership.' He tapped his chest, in case she still didn't get it.

Lucie shook her head, looking around with what he hoped wasn't renewed interest. Though wasn't it better if she liked the place? She clutched the stone on the cord around her neck. 'So Dad—and you?' she paused. 'You both own this?' One tanned finger hesitantly described the perimeter.

'Ah, yep.' He'd thought the concept pretty clear; it was only when the use of the land was taken into account that it got messy. And that's where he'd better go right now, lay it out for Lucie before Geoff poked his nose in. 'But Gus was hands-off, beyond having a plot—'

'For strawberries,' Lucie breathed. 'But why? I thought Blue Flag was already too much for him.'

Why the hell hadn't Gus had these conversations with his daughter? It wasn't his place to explain it all. 'He figured the way I manage the land would interest you.'

'He mentioned me?' Lucie's head snapped up.

'Sure. He said this "had to be done right by Lucie".' Gus had often muttered the phrase as though it was a mantra. 'He reckoned you were, well . . .' He rubbed his arm. 'He said you're *oneiroparménos*.' He butchered the Greek word, but at least he got it out without stammering. 'I had to Google it. A—'

'Dreamer,' Lucie finished.

'Yeah. He figured you didn't fit in at Blue Flag—' He broke off. Hell, his own father was right, he should never open his damn mouth: Lucie looked on the verge of tears, her dark eyes glistening. He stumbled on, not pausing to choose his words. 'But he said the same thing about me, too. The dreamer bit. Every time he couldn't see the logic in some principle of sustainability, he'd say that I'd have to talk it through with you when you came home. It was like he didn't care that it made no sense to him, just kept coming back to the fact that you'd understand.'

Lucie dropped to her haunches to untangle the dog's lead from around her feet, but he was pretty sure the move was to hide her face. 'I never even told Dad I studied natural therapies. He wanted so desperately for me to study business, and I wanted so desperately to follow my passion, I figured doing it on the side was sort of an unspoken challenge to him.' She gave a bitter laugh. 'Not much of a challenge when I still got the qualification he wanted. But Dad's part of the "there's a pill for any ill" generation, so I knew he'd see the interconnectedness of mind and body as a whole load of woo-woo.' She gave a soft, sad laugh. 'For dreamers.'

He stared at the river, pretending not to notice her use of the wrong tense or her distress, because he didn't have a damn clue what to do about either. 'I doubt there's anything he didn't know about you. Certainly managed to bring you into every conversation.' *Shit.* Now he couldn't pretend not to notice her fisted hands and silently quaking shoulders.

'Mummy. Mr Unicorn,' Keeley demanded.

He blew out a tense breath. Heck, he could really get to like that kid.

Lucie swiped her nose with the back of her hand. 'Did I ever tell you that grass makes Mummy sneeze?' she said to Keeley.

'Like my allengies?' Keeley asked.

'Exactly.' Lucie managed a watery smile, and Jack dragged his gaze away. Geoff was a bastard, leaving her to cope with losing her dad on her own.

Arnie chose that moment to launch himself at Lucie's back. Unbalanced from her squatting position, she tumbled onto her knees, her hands planting in the barnyard muck.

Jack grabbed her elbow, helping her up and expecting tears. He shot a stern look at the too-boisterous animal. As though that was going to do any good.

Instead of tears, Lucie's peal of laughter rang out as she held her hands towards Keeley. 'Look, Keels. If we ever want to make mud pies, I know just the right place.'

'Looks like chocolate,' Keeley said.

Lucie snatched her hands back. 'Uh-uh. Most definitely not.' She glanced at him. 'Mum gave her chocolate for the first time the other week. Keeley wasn't keen but now thinks it falls in the category of things you shouldn't give up without a second try.'

'Nothing wrong with a little tenacity,' he said gruffly, trying to cover his reaction to her sorrow. 'You've managed to get that chocolate on your face, though.'

'Oh no. Where?' She automatically reached towards her face but stopped, pretending to gag at the close up of her hands.

'Wait, you'll get it in your eye.' He cupped the side of her face with one hand, holding her still.

Couldn't miss the quick intake of her breath.

He wiped away the speck of mud with the ball of his thumb.

Lucie's liquid-chocolate eyes never left his. 'Thanks,' she murmured.

'Mr Unicorn. Now,' Keeley demanded, tugging on the hem of his sweater.

Lucie startled at the piercing sound of her daughter's voice and she took a half step back. Okay, maybe he didn't like the kid quite so much.

'Keeley, just wait. Remember your manners, please,' Lucie said. She shot a glance up at him from beneath long lashes. 'Is there a garden tap?'

'Use the bathroom.' Damn, he should have cleaned up. The place was definitely *comfortable*.

'I don't want to intrude.'

'Can't intrude when the place is half yours.' For the first time, that circumstance didn't seem a huge issue.

She fell into step alongside him. 'I'm not sure how that'll work out.'

'You and Geoff won't be interested in staying in the partnership?' Bloody hell, straight back to it being an issue.

'Geoff? Oh.' Lucie's colour deepened and she focused on Keeley. 'Geoff's our best friend, isn't he, Keels?' Her gaze flicked back to him. 'He and his partner might come and visit, if they find time. What I meant was, I don't know how it'll work out with the will. Mum said she and Dad always had their wills set up to leave everything to each other. That's why she's called me back over here, to help sort out what this probate stuff is about, because she'd expected the will to be straightforward.'

Right now he couldn't give a damn about the property. Because Geoff had a partner? One who evidently was not Lucie? Geoff was nothing but a *best friend*? Holy shit. Despite the dry, icy wind, it may as well have been the middle of summer because he was suddenly sweating buckets. 'Ah. I-I-I m-misunderstood,' he finally managed.

He gestured for Lucie to precede him into the boot room at the back of the house, where he had his wet weather gear piled on the floor. Along with most of his dirty washing, he now noticed. He averted his eyes, hoping Lucie would do the same. 'On your left,' he nodded towards the bathroom.

Lucie froze, her gaze on the coat hooks on the back wall. 'Is that . . . ?' Her voice trailed off. Gus had always been neater than him and kept a few odds and ends at the cottage. Lucie pointed at the black cap stitched with bright blue Greek letters. 'May I?' she said.

'Sure.' He crossed to unhook the cap, realising she couldn't reach.

'Thanks.' She didn't look at him, just crushed the hat against her chest with her forearm as she turned to her daughter. 'Keeley, do you need to go to the toilet?'

'Yep,' Keeley agreed, and thrust the dog's leash at her, leaving Lucie trying to juggle Gus's cap and the lead without touching either with her dirty hands.

'Here.' He slid his hand down Lucie's forearm to unhook the lead. He could have snagged the nylon rope without touching her. But, holy shit, she didn't have a partner.

As Lucie closed the bathroom door, Jack muttered, 'Come on, you,' to the dachshund, who was threading himself between Sally's paws, and headed for the kitchen.

A couple of minutes later, Keeley bounded up to him and grabbed his hand. 'Mr Unicorn now, please.'

Gus's cap held between her teeth, Lucie ran wet hands through her hair, pushing the choppy locks from her face. Then she tugged the cap on firmly. 'It might be hard for Jack to find Mr Unicorn,' she cautioned her daughter.

'I've got a pretty good idea where to look. This way.'

He led them out of the side gate and back down to the orchard. At the lower end, near the strawberry patch, sat one lone cow pat. 'I reckon that looks like a good home for Mr Unicorn, don't you?' he said.

Keeley looked doubtful, so he picked up a stick. 'Let's knock and see.' He tapped on top of the sun-baked dung, then cocked an eyebrow at Keeley. 'Nothing? Maybe you need to knock.' He handed her the stick, and she rapped on the pat four times, exactly as he had done. Then she stared up at him, all big blue eyes. He shook his head, looking disappointed. 'Nope, still nothing. Maybe he's out—oh, wait! Did you hear that?' As the girl looked back at the pat he made a faint, high-pitched squeak between his teeth.

'I hear it,' Keeley whispered.

'I think he wants us to open the door,' Jack said. He took Keeley's hand and helped her flip the dung with the stick. For a heart-stopping moment he thought he really had lost the beetle. Then he spotted its shiny carapace burrowed into the dirt. 'Ah, there he is. Wait, I'll grab him for you.' He dropped to his haunches, retrieved the beetle, and put it in Keeley's cupped hands.

As he straightened, Lucie gave him a smile. Like, a full smile. Not a smirk, not a tentative grin. A smile that lit her entire face. 'Lucky Mr Unicorn managed to find what appears to be the only suitable home for him on this entire property,' she said.

'Lucky Mr Unicorn wasn't here for too long, or he'd have disposed of the pat,' he said. 'If he'd had some mates to help, he could have made that "house" disappear inside twenty-four hours.'

'How have you kept him in the one place for the last week, then?' Lucie asked.

Apparently, all of his deepest conversations with her were going to be about dung beetles. 'He was living in my bathroom,' he admitted.

'Eating . . . ?' Lucie screwed up her face yet still managed to look cute.

'Yep. Eating. Lucky I live next door to a dairy, huh?'

'You hand fed him?'

'No choice.'

'So dung beetles actually eat dung?' Lucie said, looking more closely at the bug.

'They do, but only the, ah, tasty bits. The rest is made into balls with a beetle egg in the middle and shoved into the tunnels. The aeration caused by tunnelling—plus the fertiliser balls—improve pasture.'

'And gets rid of cow poop,' Lucie said, sounding fascinated rather than disgusted.

'Which limits the flies. That's one of the best things about The Twenty: having a dairy next door can be on the nose, but Prossers' set-up is organic, and they're all over the dung beetles. They brought in colonies. No stink.' He inhaled deeply. 'And no flies in summer. We just need some more biological controls for the mozzies and we'll have paradise.'

'Bats and dragonflies,' Lucie murmured, looking around. The crisp breeze off the river stirred unruly tendrils of hair that escaped Gus's hat. 'And then you'll have paradise.'

The mention stirred something in his memory: didn't dragonflies eat mosquito larvae? He'd have to look into that.

Lucie's gaze paused on the strawberries, and the haunted look returned. 'But why the strawberries? Your stuff, that makes sense. Sustainable farming, permaculture, paddock to plate. It's perfect. But it's the wrong microclimate here for strawberries.'

'Yeah, Gus and I knocked heads over them a bit. They're water thirsty, and the soil is nitrogen heavy because it's had cows on it for years.' Jack had gone through litres of seaweed tea trying to control the resulting fluffy grey mould of botrytis.

'Then why did Dad persist?'

He'd thought about that a lot. Gus was far from being any kind of idiot, but still he'd been hellbent on growing a more environmentally sound version of the crop he had successfully produced in the Adelaide Hills for the last three decades. 'I reckon he was trying to find a connection between what he knew and what he thought you'd be interested in.'

Lucie closed her eyes for a long moment. Jack's chest tightened. He wanted to take the hurt from her, to ease her pain. Because although they'd only met a handful of times, she got him.

Gus was right: together they would make a perfect team.

Yet, as fast as the realisation hit, so did the reason it could never happen. In trying to push them together, Gus had forced them apart: if Jack made any kind of move on Lucie, it would look like he was trying to secure his right to The Twenty.

26
Lucie

Only when Keeley eventually tired of chasing guinea fowl, patting goats and exploring the orchard and asked to go back to her fairy princess room, had Lucie left Jack's place. She was drawn to Jack on a deep level, something far beyond the hormone-driven desire she'd felt for Jeremy. And that had led to some very unpleasant soul-searching over the last two days, which she had unsuccessfully tried to find distraction from by busying herself with Keeley and experimenting with new concoctions for Jack's grandfather's arthritis.

She didn't need to analyse what it was she liked about Jack because it was . . . everything. He was environmentally ethical, passionate about his land and animals, dedicated to sustainability. But discovering that synchronicity meant she had to question why she had ever been attracted to Jeremy and his overt dedication to consumerism and appearance. Could her mother be right? Had Jeremy been a conquest? Or, super-disturbingly, had she been searching for a replacement for her increasingly distant father? Although, considering his plans for The Twenty, maybe Dad had never been as distant as Lucie imagined.

Zipping the crystal along her necklace, she stared at herself in the bedroom mirror. The rose quartz complemented the pink-and-white-striped button-through tucked into her jeans—and that was the sole reason she wore it. Not at all because of its ability to enhance romance and heal heartbreak.

She took a flat box from the dressing table drawer, opening it to reveal a felt-lined tray holding an assortment of crystals. She chose black tourmaline for confidence and peace, added warmly glowing deep red carnelian for communication and purple-striped fluorite, which had better be worth its weight in sorting out the chaos of her mind, and hopefully guide her head and heart to exist in harmony. Because, right now, they were at war. Down-to-earth and forthright, Jack exuded a sense of *rightness* that she instinctively knew would balance and complete her. Every cell in her body yearned to be near him, to share their passion and enthusiasm.

Every cell, that was, except for her brain, which insisted on wretched rationality: neither her instincts nor desires could be trusted. She had misjudged both Jeremy and her dad—maybe she should just lock herself away in her room.

She threaded the crystals onto her leather cord, hesitating a moment before adding a chunk of shiny hematite. Might as well go for broke and throw in some protection from negative energy.

'Keeley,' she called, 'have you finished your bircher yet?'

The soft scrape of china on lino had her racing through to the kitchen, snatching the bowl from the floor. 'Keeley, remember I told you that Dash can't have this? Sultanas are poisonous to dogs. He has his own special food, just like you do. You don't want to eat his biscuits.' She recognised the error the second she uttered the words; Keeley definitely believed the sharing should go both ways. 'Or even if you do, and even if Dash does want to eat your muesli, you mustn't. You don't want to hurt him, do you?' She struggled not to let frustration colour her tone: solo parenting was unimaginably hard. Being the only person responsible for this small bundle of energy, twenty-four seven, was exhausting. She didn't have time to complete a thought, let alone pursue a fantasy.

Keeley shook her head. 'Do you think Sally can share with Dash?'

'Sally? Oh.' She'd forgotten Jack's dog, who had, after the first half hour, adopted the pup trailing her as they explored the nine-hectare block. 'Yes, I'm sure Sally can be his special friend and share his food.'

'Like Geoff be our special friend?'

'Exactly.' She pressed a kiss into her daughter's blonde curls.

'And Jack be our special friend?'

Keeley's hair tickling her face, Lucie froze. 'Would you like him to be?'

'Yes.' Keeley's definitive nod clunked Lucie's teeth together. 'Him has animals. And Mr Unicorn.'

And any number of other attributes, Lucie thought wistfully. 'Okay, coat and boots on, let's get to Nanna's.' Her mother hadn't chosen an honorific, but Lucie was sure she wouldn't appreciate being called Nanna. Using it was a petty and unsatisfactory retaliation for Mum inexplicably robbing both her and Dad, an act that couldn't be revoked or forgiven.

The insidious poison of grief ran in her veins now, and if she allowed herself to dwell on thoughts of Dad, the trickle would become a torrent. Today she would head straight over to the Blue Flag office and get stuck into the paperwork. There was no point sitting over cups of Moccona with Mum, pretending a closeness that had evaporated years ago—and even less point airing her grievances to a mother who had no issue with lying and gaslighting.

As generally happened with a three-year-old, getting Keeley into her jacket and Dash into his car harness took another twenty minutes, although Lucie had to admit she wasn't rushing either of them.

As they moved towards the front door, a knock at the back halted their footsteps. She and Keeley exchanged a glance, as though either of them could know who the unexpected visitor was. Dash, however, scuttled down the hall, uttering the deep bark that in no way matched his size.

Lucie reached the door seconds behind him, opening it and simultaneously trying to restrain the dog with her foot.

'Goodness, what a big voice for a little feller,' Lynn greeted them cheerfully. 'Don't mean to bother you, lovey, just wanted to drop off this for the little miss.' She shook a cylindrical tub near her ear, the bright blue plastic flattering her hair, which Lucie was sure was several shades closer to magenta than the other day.

Lynn beamed as Keeley pushed in front of Lucie. 'Ah, there you are. I thought the fish might like some fresh treats now they have someone here to feed them again.'

'We feed them now?' Keeley said hopefully.

'Hi, Lynn,' Lucie smiled. 'Keeley, say hello properly, please.'

'Hello,' Keeley chimed, her eyes glued to the fish food container. 'Now?'

Lucie shook her head. 'You've already fed the fish today. They might get a tummy ache if you give them too much.'

'Oh, I'm sure they'll be fine with a little bit more of a treat,' Lynn said as Keeley took her hand. 'I was always a bit "all or nothing" with them, and yet they've survived for years.' She passed a shopping carrier to Lucie, calling back over her shoulder as she allowed Keeley to drag her down the path. 'I was in Murray Bridge this morning, so I popped into the health food shop and picked up some of that spirulina you were asking for the other day. Just in case you still need it.'

Lucie clutched the green carrier bag, looking at Lynn's retreating back in surprise. Then she scurried after them. 'That's lovely of you, Lynn. How much do I owe you?'

'Nothing, lovey.' Lynn held up her hand and wiggled her fingers so that her sparkly purple nail polish caught the light. 'I had an early appointment for a mani pedi so was headed there anyway. If you're going to be staying a while, I'll add spirulina to my regular orders, if you like.'

'I'm not sure how long we're staying,' Lucie hedged. A week ago she'd had a firm exit plan, but now it seemed that giving Geoff and Finlay as much time alone together as possible would be the decent thing to do. And, providing she didn't have to spend too long with her mother, if that meant she needed to slow everything down and stay in Settlers Bridge—near a certain farmer—for the remaining five weeks work had given her off, well, maybe that was fate.

Still clutching the spirulina, she followed Lynn and Keeley to the pond. 'You come by to feed the fish when the house isn't rented out?' she asked Lynn.

Keeley was on her knees by the pond and Lynn joined her, rather more slowly. 'No, like I said, they do all right with bugs and such. But when we lived here, Michael and I used to feed them while we had a cuppa.'

'Oh, this was your home? That explains why it feels so . . . inviting,' Lucie finished, knowing the word wasn't quite right. In truth, the house was too large, and she'd taken to occasionally sleeping in the beanbag in Keeley's room. 'We were so lucky to find somewhere furnished, especially with your daughter's room all set up.'

Lynn unscrewed the fish food. 'Oh, that's not my furniture, lovey. Never had any littlies. And probably a bit late for hoping. Not to mention Michael's been gone a few years, so unless there are stables and stars involved, I don't think it'll happen now.' She gestured at the white-painted bench. 'But when he was here, we'd sit in the sun for hours, watching the fish being daft. I swear, they were better trained than any dog, used to wait for their breakfast every morning, blowing bubbles up at us. We'd feed them, then sit and chat about everything, from ships and shoes to ceiling wax, as they say. Or is that s-e-a-l-i-n-g wax? Not that either make much sense.'

'That would be *Of shoes—and ships—and sealing wax. Of cabbages—and kings,*' a crisp voice corrected.

Lucie jerked around, pressing a hand against her chest. 'Mum! I wasn't expecting you.' Her gaze darted beyond her mother, and she gave a soft grunt of relief. Given their last interaction and Mum's penchant for lying, Lucie wasn't entirely convinced Jeremy was overseas.

Keeley looked up from the pond. 'I has fishes, Nanna.'

Despite her passive-aggressive determination to have Keeley use the title, Lucie flinched. She didn't want Keeley hurt by her grandmother's rejection.

Her mother gave Keeley a tight smile but spoke to Lynn. 'Lewis Carroll, I believe you will find. And completely nonsensical, of course.'

'Terribly.' Lynn apparently missed the inference that her conversations with her husband should be considered ridiculous. 'But then Michael and I liked to discuss everything,

237

serious or otherwise. You know how it is. But perhaps I should have said we spent hours solving the problems of the world, because that we most certainly did.' She sprinkled flakes on top of the water. 'It's just we never got around to sharing our solutions with anyone.'

Lucie's mum regarded Lynn for a long moment then gave a sharp nod. 'Monica.'

'Oh.' Recognition lifted Lynn's pencilled brows as she struggled to her feet. 'You'd officially be my tenant then, lovey? I'm Lynn.' She gestured between Monica and Keeley. 'I can see the likeness. It must be lovely having both your daughter and granddaughter close to home again.'

'Perhaps not so much, given the circumstances,' Mum said frostily.

Lucie clutched at her necklace. There was nothing like having your mum tell a near stranger that you weren't welcome home.

'Ah, I did hear about your husband,' Lynn said as she pushed to her feet.

Lucie lifted an eyebrow. News travelled fast in small towns, but as no one here knew her, they had no reason to gossip. Not that it had stopped them from shoving their oar in when it came to Jack. And not that she had minded that meddling. She blew a long breath between pursed lips, forcing her attention to the brewing storm.

'I'm very sorry for your loss,' Lynn continued. 'I do know how you feel.' She raised her right arm. 'Like you've lost this, yes?'

Mum's gaze narrowed, her lips thinning. 'Well, maybe not quite—'

'It's the little things, isn't it?' Lynn went on without skipping a beat. 'Like when you pour two cups of tea instead of one—although I can't say I ever have a problem working out what to do with the extra slice of cake.'

Her smile invited camaraderie, and Mum gave a tentative nod. 'Habits are hard to break. Like waking before Georgius, so I can turn the alarm off so it doesn't startle him. Or watching television in the dark, because he finds it hard to nap with the light on.'

'Or putting out their toothbrush,' Lynn added.

Mum made an odd sound, somewhere between a chuckle and a sob. 'Oh, I do miss the toothpaste! Georgius always put mine on, twice every day. It drove me mad because the paste would be hard by the time I cleaned my teeth, but he would never leave it for me to do when it suited me.' She shook her head and tightened her lips, as though reining in her runaway emotions. 'I had to clean everything out of the house straight away, I was driving myself mad with things like putting his cap where he could find it, or stuffing newspaper into his boots near the door so the earwigs wouldn't crawl in.' She gave a wobbly smile. 'Undoubtedly the worst thing, though, is being forced to accept that the empty toilet roll might be my own fault.'

Lucie stared. She had never imagined her mother capable of such feelings.

'Grief leaves an odd emptiness that never seems to quite go away,' Lynn sighed, bending to stroke Dash as he pawed at the mesh cover of the pond. 'My Michael had a passion for the garden. And for white, as you can see—though I used to joke that the irises looked like crumpled tissues. I let him have his way in the front garden—' She broke off with a girlish giggle as she straightened. 'Well, so to speak. But colour is life, you know?' She patted her vibrant hair, then nodded at Lucie, tapping her own nose. Lucie fought down the urge to cover her piercing before Mum remarked on it. She knew it wouldn't be a compliment. '*You* understand,' Lynn continued. 'You can't go through life just sucking all the colour from it—you have to add back, right? Else your entire world ends up drab and grey. Anyway, eventually we compromised. Michael could plant whatever he wanted in the front garden, but back here it had to be all colour.'

'It is . . . lively,' Monica agreed.

As she tried desperately to think of something to add that would deflect her mother's customary backhand insult before it arrived, Lucie took the fish food container from Keeley, hoping a warning shake of her head would be enough to stop her daughter's imminent complaint.

'But see, despite that emptiness that never leaves, the garden is how I know that Michael is still with me.' Lynn pointed to a jumble of bushes against the back fence. 'I thought I should let him have a little something out here, so he planted a hedge of white roses. But within three years of him passing, every one of them turned deep red. Exactly as I had always wanted.'

'Oh, that's just—' Mum started, and Lucie's chest cramped in dismay. The profusion of small, scruffy roses shooting from the base of the bushes were the flat-petalled burgundy of briar. Her mother, with her passion for gardening only surpassed by her passion for being right, would inform Lynn that the colour change was a result of neglect, with the grafted plant reverting to the hardy rootstock.

'That's just incredibly beautiful,' Mum finished. 'It reminds me of a quote I once read. I probably don't have it word perfect, but it was something like *Death leaves a heartache no one can heal, love leaves a memory no one can steal*. I don't know who wrote it, but it is the most perfect sentiment. Memories only ever have room for the best of the person we've lost.'

Lucie was speechless. This was not the woman she knew.

'Oh!' Keeley squealed as her hand plunged through the weldmesh and into the water.

Lucie lurched forward, but her mother stooped and pulled Keeley upright.

'I wet!' Keeley held up her sopping sleeve to show the three women, her face a comical mix of interest in the phenomenon and a wary glance at Lucie to see if she was about to get into trouble.

'Goodness me,' Lynn said. 'If you ever wanted proof that you made the right call when you told Claire the pond had to be covered . . .'

'I didn't—' Lucie broke off in astonishment as she realised Lynn was speaking to her mother.

Monica ignored both of them. 'You are wet,' she said to her granddaughter. 'I'm sure you're big enough to go and get yourself changed, though, aren't you?'

Keeley switched her glance between Lucie and Monica for a second, as though weighing up her options. Then she nodded. 'I big. I has my clothes in my fairy princess room. You come see?'

Tears thickened Lucie's throat. Though she could never forgive her mother's betrayal, Keeley was the cure for, rather than the cause of, the new distance between Lucie and Mum. No crystal could match the disarming charm of her small daughter.

Her mother raised one steel-grey eyebrow at Keeley in chilly surprise. 'No, thank you. I'm speaking with the adults.'

27
Jack

'How long do you reckon this probate stuff will take?' Jack said, keeping his tone nonchalant and not making eye contact with anyone at the kitchen table.

'Not even sure what probate is,' Pops said. 'Guess if it involves lawyers, it's a finger-up-the-bum experience.' He paused for a laugh, but Ma just shook her head at him. 'Last I knew, you scribbled a list of who you wanted to get what, signed it, and that's the end of the story. That's the way this lot will be going.' Pops waved his fork around to indicate the homely room, yellow-flecked formica countertops crowded with newspapers, barley board reports, an overflowing bowl of plastic bread-bag ties Pops felt certain would be useful one day, and a stack of recipes wedged behind Tupperware containers that Ma said were waiting for their lids to turn up. She had been saying that for as long as Jack could remember, and the pile never seemed to get either larger or smaller.

Sam didn't look up from the beef schnitzel she was trying to drown in gravy. 'I asked Claire at the real estate office about probate. Didn't get a whole lot out of her, but it was along the lines of it's got something to do with proving the will is legal before the inheritance can be handed out.' She started spearing peas one at a time, loading them on the tines of her fork. 'Try googling. You can find anything on the internet.'

'Including women,' Ma added. Jack groaned as she directed a meaningful nod at him. Sometimes he wished Sam was single so Ma's matchmaking attentions could focus on her.

'What's that?' Pops said, puffing out his chest. 'Women? Why don't we have this Google, then?'

Ma waved a slice of buttered bread at him. 'You've all the woman you can handle right here. It's Jack we need to get sorted. Speaking of, tell Lucie that stuff of hers seems to be working. Doesn't it, Paul?'

'Certainly no complaints about the application,' Pops grinned.

'Ew,' Sam said. 'You two. How about we just keep the focus on Jack?'

'Pass.' He needed to know how long the grant of probate would take because it was the only way he could work out how long Lucie might hang around for—short of actually asking her. 'I googled, but one site says four weeks, another says it can take months.' He tried to pull off a disinterested shrug, but the truth was, if he knew how to stretch it to months, he'd be on it in a heartbeat.

'The longer the better for you, though?' Pops said. 'Give you a chance to work out how to buy the girl's share?'

Pops had never come to grips with the way the growing popularity of 'lifestyle' farms—which saw properties divided into blocks for city folk looking for a weekend retreat, or a paddock for their two alpacas and fancy dog to run around in—had hiked the value of small acreages. In Pops' book, it made sense that only big estates were worth big money.

'Wish I could,' Jack lied. He had an eye for what worked on the property, an intuitive understanding that guided him to plant for shelter, shade and feed, living in harmony with the land rather than stealing from it. And, as Lucie turned to him with a smile when he'd come home the other day, he'd experienced the same flash of *knowing*. He—and the property—needed her. He didn't want to buy her out, even if it had been possible.

'Those strawberries are failing, though?' Pops said, sucking on his teeth disapprovingly. Pops had always been cereal and sheep, he couldn't fathom fruit and vegetable growing being for anything but personal use. 'That should make her happy enough to offload the property.'

'She straight up knew it's because the climate's wrong for them.'

'What did she think of what you're doing with the rest of the property?' Sam asked.

Normally he'd blow off his sister's nosiness, knowing she was baiting him, but any opportunity to talk about Lucie was too good to pass up. 'Gus was right: she's totally down with sustainability.'

'That makes one of us,' Pops grumbled.

'It's the first time I've not had to try to explain what I'm aiming for.'

Pops snorted. 'Keep telling you, get out the herbicide to take care of the ryegrass and dandelions. That's what you should be aiming for. You're wasting good land by not using the spreader to put down a load of fertiliser.'

Lucie had literally clapped at the sight of the golden-headed dandelions he allowed to grow unchecked to aerate the soil. Listing the teas and tinctures she'd create, she had harvested flowers, roots and leaves, pausing to tug on Arnie's ears despite the goat's eye-watering stink. Jack gave his grandfather a tight nod. 'I'll use the sprays here, Pops, though I still say we need to look at rotating the crops or we're just setting ourselves up for a problem with herbicide resistance. But I'm not spraying on The Twenty.' He turned to Sam, trying to avoid the looming disagreement that never went anywhere. 'Lucie mentioned she has a bit of time off work, but I don't know how long she can afford to stay here waiting for this legal stuff to be cleared up.'

'Why would she?' Sam asked, pushing the peas under her schnitzel.

Jack frowned at her plate. Was she on some stupid diet again? Sam had always been sensitive about her weight. When they were younger, and their arguments more heated, he'd used it as a way to strike back against his sister's quick tongue. It'd been years before he realised that Sam never attacked his stammer, even though it was an easy target.

'Hang around, I mean,' Sam waved the empty fork at him. 'Shouldn't a solicitor take care of all that stuff?'

'Lucie said she's got to help her Mum to sort something. I remember Gus telling me that she's got a degree in business.' He'd invested a lot of time trying to remember everything Gus had ever said about her. Yesterday he'd damn near taken his finger off with the wire-cutters because his mind wasn't on the job.

'She should be getting paid, then,' Sam said. 'Seeing as it's a business.'

'It's not always that cut and dried, you know that, Sam,' he said, with a warning glance at Pops. Though Jack increasingly handled all of the main farm, he only took a split of the profit when the grain cheques came in. That had been okay when there were two of them doing the work and Jack could supplement his income by hiring out to do the seeding and reaping on larger properties, but now that Pops wasn't capable of much, Jack had to work like two men to bring in the family income. And then he had to find time for The Twenty.

'Maybe that's not the only reason she'll hang around,' Ma slipped in.

Sam shot him a sympathetic grin. Though she'd tease the crap out of him, she generally knew when to tone it down. Ma, not so much.

'She seems a lovely girl,' Ma continued. 'Lynn down at the shop said she's definitely single, so I don't know why you had your jeans in a jumble worrying about how to sort out her husband. Lynn said her mother seems lovely, too.'

'Lynn down at the shop is tripping,' he muttered. 'Lucie's mum is a hard arse.'

'Seemed nice enough to me,' Sam said. 'Though I only spoke with her on the phone.'

'Yeah, thanks for the heads-up on that, by the way,' he said.

'Don't think I generally share my shop talk, do I?' Sam asked, assuming an innocent expression.

'Reckon you generally do bore me with some such crap,' he snorted. 'Speaking of shop talk, how's business?'

Sam's face hardened. 'Depends whether you ask me or Grant, I guess.'

'Well, it's your shop, not his,' Ma said, her tone unusually curt. She planted her hands on the table, trying to shove upright, as though ending any discussion of Grant having a say in her granddaughter's business. She lifted a couple of inches, then sank into her chair. Grunted, and tried again.

'I'll get dessert,' Sam said, already out of her seat.

'You'll do no such thing, young lady,' Ma snapped. 'My house, I'll dish up.'

Jack and Sam exchanged glances. Both knew Ma's annoyance had nothing to do with the dessert. 'My dessert, so I call it,' Sam said, laying a hand on Ma's shoulder to press her back into her seat. 'Besides, it's a lemon meringue, and I know you don't like browning them.'

'I can cook, you know,' Ma grumbled. 'You don't have to bring food every week.'

'It's not like I'm the one up at sparrow fart doing the actual work.' Sam took her plate to the sink and then lifted a large brown paper bag out of the cardboard box on the counter alongside. 'You know I leave that to the bakery. And you're doing me a favour using up anything I have left in the cabinet. Otherwise Grant gets all up my butt about over-ordering and waste.'

Jack knew damn well that although Ploughs and Pies was closed at the start of the week, Sam ordered in fresh on a Monday so she'd have a treat to take to their grandparents. With his diabetes, Pops shouldn't be touching the stuff, but like he always said, life was for living.

'Turn the oven on to finish the meringue if you like, love,' Ma said, leaning back creakily to keep an eye on Sam.

'No need,' Sam said. 'I brought a blowtorch with me. That way I can get just the right colour on the peaks.' Thanks to growing up in the shadow of their dad's constant criticism, Sam rarely baked, but she had a knack for plating up food so that the simplest meal looked like a feast.

She probably served meals in her cafe with clean cutlery, too, Jack thought with a grimace as he noticed his dessert fork. While Ma was distracted overseeing Sam, he palmed the fork and stood, pulling together the remaining plates and carrying them to the sink.

Sam caught his glance at her plate and moved to quickly scrape the others on top of it, as though their morsels would disguise the fact that she'd left most of her meal. 'Just going to make a chicken run before I do dessert,' she said, taking the plate of leftovers to the door.

He waited a few seconds then grumbled, 'She forgot half the scraps. Typical.' Taking an empty plate he held it near his chest, above his grandparents' heads. They were too busy readying for the latest episode of *Call the Midwife* to notice him.

Sam had already done the chicken dash and was mounting the steps to the verandah as he exited the screen door. He nodded at her plate. 'What's the story?'

She paused with one foot on the top step. 'I know. Shouldn't feed the chooks at night, it'll bring in the mice. But better that than leaving it on the kitchen sink and ending up with the house infested with the buggers.'

He stared down at her. Maybe because Sam was so talkative, or perhaps because she'd spent years listening to him stammer, trying to get a word out, it unnerved her when he went quiet.

Eventually, she huffed her annoyance. 'Don't get on my case, all right, Jack? I can't deal with it at the moment.'

'What's the go, Sam? You're lucky Ma's too worried about Pops to notice you didn't eat.'

Sam rolled her eyes. 'For crap's sake, Jack, it's not like I can't afford to skip a few meals.' She patted her newly flat stomach.

He shook his head. 'But you're not, are you? Skipping a few?'

She screwed up her face. 'Haven't you heard? Misery's better than a gym workout.'

'You and Grant?' His brother-in-law was an A-grade tosser, but Sam always seemed happy enough. Though maybe over the last couple of years she'd been more snappy, made more negative mentions of Grant's legendary tightness with money.

Sam grimaced. 'Told you, don't worry about it. Anyway, we've got bigger issues. Ma and Pops can't keep living like this, it's not healthy. The bathroom is bloody disgusting, and the fridge is full of out-of-date crap.'

'You know I keep us all fed, Sam,' he retorted immediately, arcing up. The fact that he got to indulge his passion while providing for his family always made him defensive.

'You do. But Ma and Pops love their convenience food. It's generational, I see it in the shop all the time. Folks their age are always buying the markdowns in bulk. I guess they must have had tough childhoods.'

He gave a cynical snort.

'Tough in a different way,' Sam said, knowing his mind had gone straight to their own less-than-perfect upbringing. 'Ma and Pops are always going to want potato chips and frozen hash browns and cheap plastic cheese, that's their comfort food. You provide the good stuff—the veg, fruit, meat—but it's wasted because Ma says it's not worth cooking for two of them.' She waggled a finger at him, warming to her topic. 'And food aside, Ma refuses to let me strip their bed, but I can't tell you when I last saw any linen on the washing line.'

'I'm sure that's no big deal.' He couldn't remember when he'd last changed his own sheets. He didn't have time to put them through the machine and, in any case, they'd take forever to dry. Though maybe, as the days were stretching longer and warmer, it was time for a clean-up. Besides, he needed to clean out the boot room before Lucie came back. She had promised to come by to exchange kefir for goat's milk. Though he wasn't sold on the health benefits of the probiotic drink, he'd give it a red-hot try. 'At least Pops' arthritis seems better, did you notice? Lucie's stuff must be working.'

'Oh my god,' Sam rolled her eyes. 'Does she have to come into the conversation every five words?'

'I just think it's cool that she gets my take on farming.' Not only had he not needed to explain his philosophy to Lucie, it was probably the first time he'd not had to defend it.

'Is she going to *get* it enough to let you keep running The Twenty?'

'I was thinking . . .' He stared out at the chook yard, the high, fox-proof mesh catching glints of moonlight. 'I was thinking maybe Gus was right, Lucie would get into running it with me. But she reckons her mum's going to inherit everything, anyway—and Monica will be happy to screw me over for every last cent.'

'You actually *like* Lucie, don't you?' Sam gave a harsh laugh. 'Trust me, you don't want to mix business and relationships. Which reminds me, I'm going to have to cut back what I bring in for Ma and Pops. It's stuff all, but because it comes as a separate delivery, Grant notices it on the accounts.'

'You know Ma doesn't expect you to bring food every time, Sam—'

'Yeah, but I should be able to, right? I mean, they did everything for us, Jack. I should be able to bring them a treat once a week without copping shit about it.'

'Why don't we switch out what day we have dinner? Make it when you've got leftovers from the cafe?'

Sam shook her head. 'Aren't you listening? It's not just about the food. The house is falling down around them. I know they don't see it, but it's filthy; Ma's bucketing water out of the kitchen sink because the drain is blocked, there's mould on the ceiling in the front room, and don't think I didn't see you ditch your fork. Hell, how bad is it when I'm considering bringing paper plates along with the food? Coming here one night a week isn't enough, Jack. We can't keep pretending that Ma and Pops are going to be able to manage forever.'

Jack squared his shoulders against her attack. 'I-I-I'm here a hell of a lot more than once a week. Fair enough, I'm not in the house helping out, but this—' He waved a hand at the acreage beyond the yard. 'It's bloody killing me, Sam. I can't spare time to do maintenance around the house as well.'

'Yet you can spare it to go prancing around The Twenty, showing it off to Lucie? You can spare it to babysit Gus's strawberries?' Sam shot back.

He was used to arguing with his sister. Though she would defend him against everyone else, their father included, Sam had a temper and didn't pull punches when they got into it. But her reaction this time was something more than their usual sparring and, thanks to decades of dealing with his stammer, he recognised it: fear.

Fear of not being able to control something, fear of not meeting expectations, fear of being inadequate. 'Have you heard from Mum lately?' he asked, trying to rechannel Sam's anger.

She shook her head, using a thumbnail to scratch at dried muck on the edge of the plate. 'Of course not. In any case, she won't help out, you know that, Jack. We have to sort this ourselves.'

'I've got those brochures from council,' he said, feeling useless.

Her anger quickly giving way to despair, Sam groaned. 'You can't just keep throwing that one out there. A gutter clean once a year won't cut it. And it's not like we have Meals on Wheels around here.' She rubbed a palm across her forehead. 'Look, realistically, the food is the least of our problems. Screw Grant, I'll bring as much food as I want for my grandparents. I'll make up meals and freeze them, though it'll be hard enough to get Ma to accept it. You know what she's like, still thinks she's the adult and has to look after us. But even if I get that sorted, it's more the day-to-day things that are an issue. Did you see Ma organising Pops' medication earlier?'

He shook his head; he'd been working the back hectares and by the time he got there, dinner was already on the table.

Sam tipped her head back, as though she was studying the stars, but he knew she was keeping the tears in check. 'She was counting out his pills for the week, putting them in one of those flip-top containers with each day marked on it. Some of them look practically identical, so she simply divided them up by colour. You know, a white tablet in each compartment, a white capsule in each, a yellow and so on. Then she passed Pops today's tray and he downed the lot. Eight pills. In one go. I tried to explain that they might need to be taken at different times of the day, some with food, some without. And I picked up one of the bottles to read.' She mimicked the action with her free hand, bringing the imaginary bottle close to her face. 'And I realised that the dose was half a tablet.'

She looked at Jack, her breathing ragged. 'Ma didn't have any half tablets. I asked her why, and she said it's too difficult to break them in half. So she just gives him one every second day, instead.'

'Jesus,' he muttered. 'I guess we could give her a pill cutter, or maybe get the chemist in Murray Bridge to cut them. But it's b-b-bigger than that, isn't it?'

Sam nodded. 'They need someone here with them, Jack. We can't desert them. We both know what that's like.'

Hell yeah, he knew all right.

Sam stared at him, and the unspoken words hung in the air between them: one of them would have to give up their dream to care for the grandparents who had raised them.

28
Jack

Jack raked a hand through his hair, determined not to head back to the cottage to check his reflection. He'd spent the last hour trying to distract himself by straining a new top wire across the goat yard—Pamela had discovered she could pretty well get airborne when the mood suited her—and now he was finished, he finally allowed himself to pull out his phone to check the time. Just happened to thumb onto Lucie's message, as though he'd not read it more times than he could count. Couldn't stop the stupid grin spreading over his face again.

> Hey, Jack, I know we only just came out to do our kefir/milk swap, but is there any chance we could drop by again? I have an order from Chloe at the IGA, and I'd really like to pinch some of the aloe you have growing in the front garden. And Keeley, of

course, wants to visit Mr Unicorn again—sorry about
you still having to handfeed him—I'm hoping THAT
attraction gradually fades!

He was fairly sure he shouldn't read anything into her
capitalisation.

He was even more sure that he wanted to.

Still grinning like an idiot, Jack packed the wire strainer
Sam had bought him for Christmas into its black kitbag
and slung it over his shoulder. 'C'mon, Sally.' As the red
dog lumbered to her feet, Jack could hear the faint churn
of wheels on gravel. That was the beauty about being
at the end of the road: if a car crossed the flats, it was
for him.

He sucked in a steadying breath. Ridiculously, he felt
like he was headed out on a first date. And apparently, the
feeling wasn't getting old anytime soon: he'd felt the same
the last two times Lucie had swung by.

By the time he reached the cottage, Lucie was out of her
RAV4 and leaning across the back seat to unbuckle Keeley.

He looked away.

Not before he'd copped a decent eyeful of her backside
packed into tight blue jeans, though.

Dash and Keeley somehow managed to eject from the
vehicle at the same moment, the kid running to him. 'Jack!
We bringed you somefing!'

'Well, that's a coincidence. I have something for you, too.'
Though he put a hand on Keeley's back as she wrapped her
arms around his thigh, his gaze was on Lucie.

'Hi, Jack,' she said. Simple words, but he was pretty sure the colour in her cheeks wasn't from the warmth of the breeze curling around them. She held up a shallow pie dish. 'You're going to have to trust me on this. Chia tart. It looks like something Mr Unicorn would be interested in, but I promise it tastes amazing. It's basically dates, sultanas and chia seed on an almond meal base.'

Jack nodded. 'I grew some chia last year.' He grabbed at the plate as Lucie almost dropped it.

'You're kidding? It grew here? Why?'

'It's hydroscopic, so as long as it doesn't get wet when it's setting seed, it does fine here.'

Lucie shut the car door. 'I mean, why did you grow it?'

He lifted one shoulder. 'Wanted to see what all the fuss was about. Look at diversifying my output. The soil is a bit heavy, but it's a salvia, so pretty hardy.'

'And you got a crop?' Lucie said breathlessly.

'Sure. It'll still be in a jar in the kitchen somewhere. Once I'd harvested the stuff, I didn't really know what to do with it.'

Lucie held the tart up, the top decorated with nuts, seeds and dried fruit to look like a sunflower. 'Taste this and I promise you'll have a use for your chia.'

'Or I could just trade you? The seeds for home-baking?'

Lucie looked at him for a long moment. She had a habit of doing that but, instead of finding it disconcerting, he liked it. It meant she was careful with her words. 'I'm sure we could come to an arrangement,' she finally said.

'You like chia, Jack?' Keeley tugged on his jeans, and when he glanced down, held up her arms. 'I like chocolate,' she confided as he swung her up.

'Are you sure about that?' he raised his eyebrows. 'Because I think that pie your mum has looks more yum than any chocolate I've ever tasted.'

Keeley chewed on her lip for a moment, her forehead furrowed as she looked from him to the tart. 'Awright. We has some now, Mummy.'

'We will *have* some when Jack wants some,' Lucie said, then mouthed, 'Sorry, bossy' to him.

'I think we should go and say hello to Mr Unicorn first, and then we'll have some pie.' He was keen to get the bug viewed and then safely back in the shoe polish tin in his pocket.

Keeley nodded and Jack inclined his head towards the window. 'I think he's probably down near the strawberries again.' He saw the shadow cross Lucie's face, and his gut clenched. Because she was usually so bubbly and enthusiastic, he tended to forget she was still grieving. He set Keeley down again and as she raced down the slope with the dogs, he turned to Lucie. 'Sorry, I didn't think. It was stupid of me.'

She gave him a brave smile. 'Not your fault or your problem.' She put the tart back in the car and started across the paddock after her daughter. But he caught the sideways glance she shot him. 'I wanted to come out here. I mean, here—' she gestured between the two of them, apparently oblivious to the way she made his heart lurch '—but also

259

here.' She pointed to the strawberry plot. 'It's like . . . the only place I feel close to Dad.'

'Not at Blue Flag?' he said.

She gave a crooked smile as they walked through the vegetable plot, the peppery scent of crushed nasturtiums filling the air. 'I haven't even made it out to the sheds yet. My mum is . . . a lot. She's being weird about handing over the details of what's needed for probate. And about a bunch of other stuff.' Lucie ran a hand through her hair and took a deep breath. 'I like it here. It's . . . does *balancing* sound too wanky?'

Jack shook his head. Not the way she said it.

Keeley and the dogs waited by the gate into the goats' paddock, and he flicked the latch to open it. With all the confidence of several visits, Keeley raced down the field as the goats galloped up to meet her.

Lucie stooped to pick a dandelion clock, twirling the stem between her fingers. She closed her eyes and blew, and he suspected she was making a wish as the tiny seeds flew high and free on their intricate parachutes. 'Everywhere else is claustrophobic, like sadness is seeping through my skin and I'm being suffocated by sorrow. As though nothing in life will ever be right again. And then I get angry—angry that I'm wasting energy on feeling this way when it's so damn pointless. And angry that I let the situation get to a point where it's too late to fix it.'

He tensed. 'What situation?' Did she mean The Twenty? It seemed maybe she was trying to tell him there was no way to continue the farm.

'Me and Dad. When I moved to Melbourne, we weren't talking. He didn't—' She darted a glance at him, and he saw her jaw tense, as though sharing thoughts didn't come naturally. Hell, he could empathise with that given he'd stayed silent so much of his life. 'He never knew about Keeley. And now I have to live with the knowledge that I robbed him of that opportunity. Robbed Keeley of knowing her grandfather.'

She stopped talking as he lifted Keeley over the fence, then held up the bottom wire for the dogs to wriggle under before holding apart the top two for Lucie to duck between.

'At least you're here with your mum now,' he said. Not that Monica was any kind of stand-in for Gus. He couldn't imagine two more dissimilar people, and that Lucie was a product of them seemed bizarre.

'Mmm,' she agreed, unenthusiastically. 'That's a whole other story. Anyway, all that was just a really long way of saying I like it out here. I feel closer to Dad here than anywhere else. Which is nice. But also sad.'

This time Lucie looked directly at him, her dark eyes huge and liquid. And he wanted to take her in his arms, to hold her until the pain had passed. 'Y-your dad was a good man. And if it helps even a little bit, I never got any hint of a rift between you from him. His entire focus was always on doing right by you, as far as The Twenty was concerned.'

She gave him a wobbly smile, but Jack knew he hadn't helped. He'd never been any damn good with words. He pointed at Lucie's tawny forearm, below the bunched sleeve of her apricot sweater. 'Y-y-you've picked up a ladybug.'

Keeley squealed with delight but Lucie raised her other hand to calm her daughter. 'Don't scare him, Keeley. We have to wait until he flies off and then make a wish.' She glanced at Jack. 'Dad always said ladybugs were for luck and love.'

'And he had a whole heap released here.' Or, more correctly, Gus had agreed to it. 'I thought it was for biological control, but maybe your dad had another reason.'

Lucie gave him a gentle smile. 'Thank you.'

The bug flew off and Keeley jumped up and down. 'Make a wish, Mummy.'

'You can have my wish, baby.'

'I wish . . .' Keeley swivelled to eye him. 'I wish Jack has somefing for me.'

'Keeley,' Lucie groaned.

'Your wish is my command,' he said. 'Let's quickly say hello to Mr Unicorn, then I'll show you what I have back in the cottage.'

Apparently, quickly was a pretty loose concept with a three-year-old. It took them about half an hour to meander from the far end of the strawberry plot to the chicken coop. He and Lucie were collecting the eggs from the layer boxes at the back when a commotion at the front made them race around the small structure. Keeley had one of the fluffy white bantams in a fair approximation of a death grip, dunking the bottom half of the bird into the water bowl. Dash yipped excitedly, trying to dart forward, though Sally kept the younger dog under control, blocking his attempts to reach the squawking bird.

'Keeley, what are you doing? Oh my god, Jack, I'm so sorry,' Lucie gasped.

'He has poo feet,' Keeley said prosaically. 'He need a wash.'

'You could be right,' Jack said consideringly. 'But how about we do it in warm water, up at the cottage. I bet you like your bath to be nice and warm, don't you?'

'With bubbles,' Keeley agreed, releasing the chicken and taking Jack's hand instead.

'Okay, we'll see what we can do.'

Familiar with the layout of the farm, Keeley tugged him towards the vegetable garden. By the time they reached the cottage, both his arms and Lucie's were filled with fresh-picked produce and a multitude of companion plants Lucie said had herbal uses.

'I feel guilty taking all this,' she said as they piled spring onions, calendula, bok choy and sage into the back of the car.

'No need for guilt. Just more tart,' he said. More tart meant more visits.

'Done deal.' She passed him the pie dish to carry to the house.

'Look, Keeley,' he said, sliding the dish onto the kitchen table and picking up the piece of wild honeycomb he'd impulsively collected at Pops' the previous day. 'This is what I wanted to show you.'

'It's to eat?' Keeley said.

'Oh, wow.' Lucie seemed far more impressed than her daughter. 'This is what bees make honey in, Keels.' She moved close to him, cupping her hand under his to bring the honeycomb closer to her nose, as though she was afraid she would damage the wax creation if she touched it. 'It smells like honey. And . . .' She frowned as she tried to pick the other scent.

'Mallee,' he said. 'The honey smells like whatever the bees are foraging.' Right now, he was dealing with his own urge to forage in almond blossom, the sweet scent wafting up as Lucie bent over their hands.

'I can eat it?' Keeley asked again.

Sally gave a soft 'oof' as Dash headed off down the hall to explore. 'That's okay, Sal, you go with him,' he said. The old dog gave him a measured look, as though asking why she had to babysit, but then went after the pup, her tail slowly wagging. 'Not this one, Keeley. It's not fresh. You need one where the bees have filled each of these little rooms with honey.' He pointed at the hexagonal chambers.

'That's so cool,' Lucie said. 'I've never actually touched honeycomb before.'

'I'm heading out to Matt's on the weekend,' he lied, surprising himself. 'They've got a decent acreage of untouched scrub and Matt mentioned they've loads of wild bees, so if you and Keeley want to come along, we could go and find some hives. They're pretty awesome to see, usually wedged in between rocks or in hollow trees.'

'Really? Are you sure Matt won't mind us lobbing up?'

'Not at all. Roni said for you to come out, remember?'

Recognition lit Lucie's face. 'Oh, Roni with the twins? Sure, that'd be fantastic.'

And just like that, he'd made an actual date with Lucie.

At least, that's how he was choosing to think of it.

29
Lucie

Grief came in waves, Lucie had realised. And this morning, it was a tsunami. It would be one of the days where she had to drag herself out to the kitchen to make a cup of tea, barely able to see through eyelids swollen shut with the acid sting of tears.

It was the choughs' fault. There was a family outside, foraging in the leaf litter along the picket fence beyond her bedroom curtains.

As the birds' chatty, strident calls filled the early morning, her mind flashed back. When she was little, she spent hours listening intently to the white-winged choughs because Dad insisted they were having a conversation, using actual words. His gaze would range across the strawberry mounds to an ancient gum that stood proud of the others, Cinderella rags of stripy, peeling bark cast off in favour of a smooth silver gown.

'Listen, Luce,' Dad would say. 'Close your eyes and let your heart hear.'

Eyes squeezed tight, she'd concentrate on the calls, trying to find the words of the large black birds.

Dad's low translation added a bass undertone, rather than interrupting. 'That's the father talking now. He said it's a great day to go down to the creek for a splash, and maybe they could visit with the kookas. Oh, but wait! Did you hear the mum? She said the kids need to clean up the nest before they can go anywhere.'

She'd slit one eye open to watch Dad. He grinned, deep lines crisscrossing his brown skin, and held up a hand for silence. 'Ha, now the dad's promising Mum the juiciest grub he can find, if she'll let the babies do their nest later.'

'What did the mum say?' she'd ask breathlessly, as though her own happiness hinged on the answer.

Dad would listen attentively for a long moment, then nod as though satisfied. 'Mum said that it's a great idea, and a beautiful day to get some wind under their wings.' His dark eyebrows lifted as he turned to her. 'How about we walk down to the creek and sit in the shade for a while and watch them? We'll hunt for blackberries and take some back to your mum.'

Although she knew it was nothing more than Dad's version of a fairytale, even now Lucie held her breath as the choughs talked to one another. Secretly, childishly, she wished they'd bring her a message from him.

As the birds took wing and the song faded into the distance, she tried not to think that perhaps they'd gone in search of a creek she would never again explore with Dad. Those days had been long gone, anyway, so why did they rip at her heart now, as though they were a new loss?

She should have slept in Keeley's beanbag again, so she didn't feel so alone.

Pulling the covers over her head, she tried to stifle her sobs so she wouldn't wake Keeley in her fairy princess bedroom down the hall. Keeley, who would never get to hold her grandfather's work-roughened hand, who would never know the magic of tucking the baby strawberry plants in their soil beds, or of listening to the choughs' stories.

Despite the size of the house, Dash heard her. His outsized paws skittered across the wooden floors as he raced into her room, emitting a funny growl-bark as he barrelled towards her bed. Lucie extricated herself from the doona and sat up. Dash hadn't yet learned that he shouldn't jump and could hurt himself trying to scramble into the bed. She reached down to scoop up the pup. Despite his diminutive size, his length made it a two-handed job.

Delighted with the unusual treat of being allowed in her bed—although she strongly suspected he was frequently in Keeley's—Dash wiggled beneath the covers, tucking his silky head beneath Lucie's chin. She fondled the floppy ears that always seemed in danger of tripping him, winding the soft tendrils of long fur around her finger as he lazily licked her hand.

The tightness of Lucie's heart eased a little, and she pressed a kiss onto the hard ridge of Dash's head as she leaned over him to pick up the mobile from the side table. She flipped airplane mode off. It was a half hour later in Victoria, so Geoff would be up getting ready for work.

''Lo?'

His sleep-laden voice made her double-check the time. 'You having a lie-in? You know it's after seven there?'

'Tumbleweed.' As usual, the smile came through in Geoff's tone. 'No, I had a rough night, so I'm taking the day off.'

'Partying during the week now I'm not there to keep you in line?'

'More like doing penance for takeaway Thai,' Geoff said.

'Oh no. Have you been taking the aloe juice? And the slippery elm?'

'Both of the above. Self-inflicted, it'll pass,' Geoff said, sounding glum. 'Anyway, I feel better just for having my favourite nurse call.'

'That's home care assessment manager to you,' she corrected. 'Or, more specifically at the moment, unpaid layabout.'

'You've still not started into the farm paperwork?' Geoff's surprise was obvious. 'I thought you wanted to knock it over by the end of the week.'

'I tried to go after Mum turned up here—because I really needed another cup of crap coffee and a heaped serve of criticism. But Mum said it wasn't convenient. Like coming all the way over from Melbourne *was*.'

'Mmm,' Geoff said. 'And how many times have you been out to this river block?'

'The Twenty? Only three. Keeley wanted to see Mr Unicorn.'

'And how was Farmer Thor?'

'Thor?

'Yeah, didn't you say he rocks his hair tied back with a leather strip or something? Definitely Thor-like.'

'Trust you to fixate on that.' She couldn't quite keep the giggle from her voice. 'He does have a way of dressing, though. Not like a farmer. I mean, he dresses like a farmer sometimes, but other times . . .' The sentence trailed off as she grimaced at herself. 'Anyway, I needed to get some aloe vera—did I tell you he has basically an entire wall of the plants that must be donkey's years old? No need to strip poor little Vera anymore.' Instead, she had put the potted aloe out on the edge of the pond in the back garden, where it could catch the sunshine. 'I've made a couple of burn creams for the local doctor, and an acne treatment.' She had been flattered when Chloe cornered her in one of the short aisles of the IGA a few days earlier, whispering her request as though her smattering of pimples was a cause for embarrassment. 'I made a face mask using honey and Jack's lavender.'

'Sounds like you're building up a clientele,' Geoff said.

She flicked a thumb over Dash's paw, the dog jerking back as though it tickled. 'Yeah, go figure. Country South Australia is about the last place I'd expect to find interest in alternative therapies.' Or a traditional farmer trying to commit to sustainable principles. 'Seems more of a trendy city thing.'

'Byron Bay isn't a city. I hear they're sort of big on alternates.'

'It's a city compared to Settlers Bridge,' she chuckled. 'Anyway, Jack said he'd take us out to see some hives. I'll find out about sourcing raw honey then.'

'Whoa,' Geoff exclaimed. 'Back up there, Tumbleweed. Did you say Thor's taking you out?'

'Not that kind of taking out, Geoff.' She swallowed the urge to add 'unfortunately'. She was sure Jack had noticed how well they clicked, how their shared interests made for easy company over hours that passed too fast. She was equally sure he'd have no interest in a single mum he had met only weeks earlier. One who had a life in Melbourne. 'We're going out to his mates' farm so Keeley can see how honey is . . . made? Produced? Happens? I'm not even sure what the correct term is.' She was waffling, trying to lead Geoff away from any hard questions. 'That's on the weekend, though. Today we're going to Blue Flag. Mum's going to have to give me something to prove why it is I need to be over here twiddling my thumbs.'

'Doesn't sound like you're doing too much thumb-twiddling. I told you why, Luce—she misses you. You are each the only connection the other has with your dad.'

'The dad she lied about, you mean?'

'From what you told me, I think she honestly believes that she protected him. Which is not to say her process wasn't misguided.'

'That's way too generous, Geoff,' Lucie warned, her temper rising. 'She didn't even apologise.' Not that any apology could excuse all that had been stolen from her. Yet deep down, Lucie wanted her mother to rationalise, to persuade her that the secret had been well intentioned.

'Maybe she can't. Perhaps anger is the only emotion she dares allow; it's her way of processing the grief.'

'Processing? That's not even a thing, Geoff. Grief isn't something you can work through, or work towards resolving. There are no KPIs, no targets. I mean, some days I'm just fine. I haven't seen Dad for years, so why wouldn't I be? In fact . . .' she pulled at the silky strands of long hair on the dog's ears as she considered the wisdom of admitting her feelings. 'In fact, I kind of feel guilty because I'm just . . . numb. It's like nothing has changed. But then other days—like today—I'm bloody well drowning. I feel like . . . like . . .' She thumped a hand against her chest as she struggled to find words to explain the emotions, the suffocating darkness that had again welled without warning, chasing away the brief warmth which had flooded her at thoughts of Jack. Maybe that was why she liked him? Because, like a ray of winter sunshine, his presence seemed to dispel her melancholy for a time. 'It's like I can't even breathe because of the weight of the sorrow crushing my chest. Yet I can't get past the feeling that there should be a logical solution, that I should be able to think my way out of this. That if I'm smart enough to realise what I did wrong, then I should be smart enough to find a way to fix the situation. But this is the one time that's not possible, isn't it?' Her words ended with a gulp.

'Death has a horrible finality, Luce. But maybe you need to focus on dealing with the future, not mourning the past. Change what you can and accept what you can't.' Geoff paused. 'And perhaps think on whether there is any reason your mum should feel any differently to you. Could she also be beating herself up over her mistakes, wishing she could change history? Maybe longing for a second chance?'

Geoff's insistence that she give her mother the benefit of the doubt was exhausting. 'Give it a rest, will you?' she groaned. 'I'm your friend, not a client.'

'Lucie, grief and love are so similar. Neither can be controlled or predicted, the emotions come in waves and then recede. Just because your mum doesn't show her love all the time doesn't mean that she doesn't *feel*.'

'*All* the time? You mean *any* of the time. But you got the waves bit right: she leaves dirty great tidemarks on my heart,' she said bitterly. 'You know, when she came around the other day, I thought she was warming towards Keeley. Hell, for a few minutes there, I actually thought she was human. But she went right back to her nasty, spiky self.'

'Back to her protective armour, then?'

'Are you forgetting the gravity of what she did, how she lied to me? And you straight up heard her say that she doesn't love me, Geoff,' she snapped.

'That's not exactly what I heard, Luce. Anyway, speaking of love, tell me more about The Keeper of Unicorns.' Geoff knew when to let the subject go, but it was a deliberate technique, leaving her to mull over his words so that her usual knee-jerk reaction was tempered. 'Seems Keeley's pretty smitten with this guy, too.'

'I'm not—oh, whatever,' she said, rolling her eyes. 'Keeley likes him because he has a million animals.'

'And Lucie likes him because . . .' Geoff prompted.

For a second she fluffed herself up indignantly, but then gave a rueful shake of her head. She'd already admitted to Geoff that she liked Jack. 'Lucie likes him because he's different. He's smart, but not in that "listen to me quote all my book-learning" kind of way.'

'Ouch,' Geoff said drily.

She ignored him, because sometimes he deserved to be taken down a notch. 'It's more a kind of . . . connection to the land, to the environment. He knows what he's doing, what he wants to do. He's not just existing, he's contributing.'

'And that's why your dad went into partnership with him?'

'It's more than that,' Lucie said slowly. 'Dad loved the land, but it's not like he was into organics or the environment. Jack said he and Dad were introduced by a mutual friend, and Dad took on The Twenty because he knew Jack and I would click, that we shared the same values.'

Geoff stayed silent. She heaved a sigh, which came out as wobbly as chia pudding. 'He knew, didn't he, Geoff? Not only about my studies, but Dad knew me better than I realised.'

'More than that,' Geoff said gently. 'He cared, Luce. He cared more than you realised.'

30
Lucie

Maybe it was Lucie's imagination—or purely wishful thinking—but Mum seemed less prickly this morning.

They had carried their cups of Moccona outdoors, where Keeley and Dash danced ahead of them through the garden. It was better out here: the gardens had always been Mum's province, so there was less evidence of the deliberate erasure of Dad.

'See these plants, Keeley?' Mum pointed to the three-metre-tall spires of hollyhocks, which she prided herself on coaxing into early bloom against a sheltered wall. 'Be careful if you touch them because they're quite prickly. But look how much the bees love the flowers.' Tight green buds studded the length of each thick stem, the flowers opening in flushes from the bottom of the plant right up to the tip. In Mum's usual retentive fashion, the colours were separated: a patch of white, one of deep crimson and another of flighty pink.

'Do you know my favourite colour, Nanna?' Keeley said, leaning back to look up at the blooms on the very tip.

'I think I can guess,' Mum said, bending down a tall stem of fragile pink flowers nestled among large, sandpapery leaves. 'This one?'

Keeley nodded eagerly. 'Like my fairy princess bedroom.'

'I thought you might be a fairy princess kind of girl,' Mum agreed.

'Wait,' Lucie gasped. 'Her bedroom? That was your doing?'

'It's a large house. It needed to be more welcoming,' Mum said, as though furnishing for a short-term rental was normal.

'Welcoming? Why banish us to Settlers Bridge then?'

Mum didn't meet her gaze. 'You know that you and I don't do well in a confined space together.'

Mum's words were true enough but still hard to hear. Wasn't it a mother's job to tolerate the myriad small hurts inflicted by a child, to pretend her own kid was a little closer to perfect than was true? But that had never been Mum's style: she was always quick to take offence, in a rush to attack. 'It's hard to "do well" when you blatantly don't want me around,' Lucie flared.

Her mother still held the flower low for Keeley, the tissue-thin, transparent petals each textured by tiny ridges running out from the centre. 'Look in the middle, Keeley, where the fluffy white part is. That's where the bees and butterflies come to drink.' As Keeley reached a tentative finger in to touch the filaments, Mum glanced at Lucie. 'It's not that I don't want you around, Lucie. It's never been that. But you've always been independent. You have Dad to thank for that. He was the same, determined to prove he could do everything his own way. That's why he left the family orchards and dropped us in a mountain of debt to set up this place.'

Lucie flicked away an errant fly. 'I always had the impression that Dad fell out with Yiayia and Pappous because . . .' She hesitated, her anger not hot enough to allow her to be deliberately hurtful. 'Well, because of you.'

Mum shrugged. 'It didn't help that I'm not a good Greek girl. But no, it was because he knocked heads with his father all the time. He wanted to be his own man, and this was the place for him to prove that he could be. And you're so similar, you have that hot-headed streak in you. Except Dad learned how to channel it.' She raised her voice. 'Keeley, why don't you take Dash over to the cherry tree? Check if there's any water for the birds in the bath.'

As Keeley raced off, her mother gave a reminiscent chuckle. 'Georgius never cared what anyone thought of him, he just—' She made a slicing movement with her hand. 'He just ploughed ahead, did what he wanted his own way.'

'Except that he always worried about making you mad,' Lucie disagreed. She recalled from her youth her father's eagerness to keep Mum happy, the little secrets they'd kept just between the two of them, to avoid her mother's ire. And later, when Dad became withdrawn and silent, he simply stayed away from the house. Away from Mum.

Away from her.

A line furrowed between Mum's eyebrows. 'I hardly think so. Your dad had this trick of going silent when something displeased him, and that was far worse than his temper. If he was angry, that was fine, I could argue. But when he went quiet, I'd be scurrying around,' she tapped her fingertips against her temple, 'trying to work out what was wrong. Honestly, between the two of you, I never knew whether I was going to get frozen out or if Santorini was going to erupt.' She pantomimed a volcanic explosion. 'You're so like him with your stubbornness. From when you were thirteen or fourteen you were set on your path, and you'd give me a dead-eyed stare if I dared say anything to contradict your plans—even though you never bothered sharing them.' Mum blew a long breath between pursed lips, shaking her head. 'Remember how determined you were to move to the city when you started uni?' She gestured with the garden shears at the small greenhouse they approached. 'Did I mention I've joined the African violet society?'

Lucie waved away the gardening news, although she matched her mother's slow pace along the pebbled pathway. 'When I enrolled in the degree Dad insisted on, you mean? I recall you said it was a waste of money. I was never sure if you meant moving to the city or going to uni.'

'*How sharper than a serpent's tooth,*' Mum said, her face tightening.

It is to have a thankless child, Lucie finished the Shakespearean quote in her head. But she refused to bite.

'Why would I not want you to go to uni?' Mum obviously wasn't letting it go, though.

'You tell me. Dad was the one pushing for me to get a degree. You were never interested.'

Mum let out a sharp 'humph' of cynical laughter. 'Not interested? Lucie, if I'd shown the tiniest bit of enthusiasm, you'd have run off and joined some hippie commune instead of going to uni.'

'Oh my god, you're exaggerating,' Lucie huffed. 'Besides, I don't think there are any communes around here,' she added with grudging humour, a tiny acknowledgment of the truth in her mother's accusation.

Mum paused to snip off a rose. 'My only comment about money would have been that there was no point you moving out. Starting life with a HECS debt is bad enough; the last thing you need is to have to work to pay rent while you're studying. That was one thing Dad agreed with your grandfather about: family should stay close. It broke his heart when Pappous died without them making good and Yiayia and his sisters moved back to Greece. He thought they had time. Time for him to prove that he could make his own way with Blue Flag, and time for him to smooth things over with his parents.' The blooms in her hand trembled. 'Time is fleeting.'

Mum broke off her reminiscence to shoot Lucie what seemed to be an apologetic half-smile. 'And that one's courtesy of *The Rocky Horror Picture Show*. We used to catch the bus from the city to Goodwood to watch it at the cinema every week. In costume. My god, what we must have looked like.' Her chuckle sounded dry and unused.

'You lived in Adelaide?' Lucie was having trouble following her mother's conversation. 'I thought you lived on the peninsula with Nanna and Grandad until they moved to New Zealand?'

Mum ran her fingers up the closed bud of a rose, squeezing gently. The green blood of aphids stained her fingertips. 'No, I was at the Royal Adelaide Hospital when I met Dad.' A shadow crossed her face. 'Or rather, I was working there, though I had just moved out of the nurses' residential wing.'

'The residential wing?' Lucie repeated. 'You have nursing qualifications?'

'Had. I stopped work before you were born, so my registration lapsed.'

Lucie didn't miss the insinuation that this was yet something else that was her fault.

Keeley raced over, her legs bare above the purple wellington boots she wore at every opportunity. 'Nanna, Dash has done poo in your flowers.'

Lucie groaned. Mum would flip out.

'Better in the garden than in the house,' Mum said. 'Just make sure he doesn't get into the agapanthus, Keeley. Those bushes over there.' She pointed towards the strappy green plants. 'They'll make him itchy. But later, when Dash is having a nap, you must clean up after him. Then perhaps you'd like to go snail hunting? Your mum used to love doing that. Cost me a fortune.'

Lucie snorted, the memory as much pain as pleasure, reminding her of what had been lost. 'I'd forgotten that. Five cents for every snail I found, wasn't it?'

Mum nodded. 'Remember that year when you filled the fertiliser bucket so full, Dad had to carry it up to the house for you?'

'And I cried because you wouldn't take each snail out to count.'

'And then you refused to let me feed them to the chickens. You told Dad to release them at the back of the property, so they could go next door and make happy families.'

'Yeah. Because relocation takes care of that,' Lucie muttered.

Mum sighed tiredly as Keeley moved out of earshot. 'Lucie, parenting is hard. Not the way it is now,' she lifted her chin towards Keeley, 'where it's physically exhausting but still rewarding. But hard mentally and emotionally, trying to keep everything balanced as your child develops into an adult with their own beliefs and expectations and demands. There comes a time when no amount of logic, no amount of rational discussion, no amount of reason seems to percolate.' She shot Lucie a meaningful look. 'You grew away from me. And that's fine, that's the way it should be, so, yes, I took the opportunity to encourage you to go to Melbourne. Of course, I also thought you might not want to stay close to the memories here.'

Lucie couldn't pinpoint an accusation, yet she had the feeling that Mum had neatly blamed her for all of their problems. 'Memories of my childhood? Why would I want to avoid them?'

'No. Memories of . . . him.'

'Jeremy?' Lucie scoffed. 'You do realise I live with the permanent memory of him?' She waved a hand towards Keeley. Why did Mum think life could be so neatly changed by her manipulations?

'Of course. But that memory at least has compensations, doesn't it? Compensations that would have seemed vastly different if you'd remained here. Compensations that I can promise you would have weighed, wondering whether they were enough to balance the pain of having to watch Jeremy go on with his life without you.'

'If I'd stayed, maybe his life wouldn't have been without me,' she flared. 'Have you thought of that? When you were busy scheming, did you bother to think that perhaps I would have done anything to make our relationship work? That maybe it was my one chance at love?' Lucie slammed her hands on her hips. It didn't matter that she now questioned her own feelings for Jeremy, this was about *right*. Her mother had no right to mould Lucie's life.

Mum squared up to her. 'One chance? You have no idea what it's like to face the realisation that you will never love again. *You* can have more children, carry on with your life. For me, this is it.' She threw a hand wide, as though indicating the farm. 'I've already lost everything I could ever want.'

The anguish in her mother's tone forced Lucie to step back. 'You stood in the kitchen only the other day and gave me a bloody lecture about how it's so emancipating not to bother loving anyone.'

Her mother shrugged the statement off. 'I also said that I had loved you to the best of my ability . . . but we both know I could have done better.'

Lucie ran a hand through her hair, spiking it up in a tiny act of defiance. 'I'm so confused. You're saying that you do love me?' Despite their uneasy relationship, she couldn't quell the leap of hope.

Mum hunched one shoulder. 'Sometimes, the truth we *know*, stripped of all the questions and misunderstandings and angst and pain, is far more important than the truth we can explain.'

Was that a yes? God, she wished Geoff was here to unravel Mum's twisted half-statements. How could a woman so fond of sticking her two cents in be so ambiguous?

'Nanna, is your bees making Jack's honey?' Keeley interrupted.

Mum blinked in surprise, though whether it was at the question or the way that Keeley grabbed her hand to draw her attention, Lucie couldn't guess. 'Jack's honey?' she echoed.

'Jack gave Keeley some honeycomb the other day,' Lucie explained, reluctant to share any part of her happiness with her mother.

'Jackson?'

Mum managed to load the single word with judgment, and irritation—never far from the surface when she dealt with her mother—prickled up Lucie's spine. Her fingers ranged across the crystals on her necklace as though she could invoke their properties as she replied, 'I guess so.'

'I see,' Mum said, her face tight. 'Come over here, Keeley. This is where I grow vegetables.'

Lucie stared after them. Her mother and daughter looked . . . natural together. But it would only be seconds before Mum said something to destroy the image.

Mum didn't look up as Lucie followed. 'I've made spanakopita for lunch. Dad's favourite.'

Typical. She knew Lucie loathed it.

Her mother pointed at the garden. 'I used silverbeet, though. It'd have Dad turning in his grave, but you always hated the bitterness of spinach, and I thought Keeley might be the same.'

Longing aching in her chest, Lucie turned away. Allowing herself to think that maybe Mum actually cared would only lead to more heartbreak.

31
Jack

'First time you've brought a girl out here, mate,' Matt said as he plonked a mug on the table.

'Couldn't miss a chance to sit out on the verandah with you, chatting over tea like a pair of little old ladies,' Jack said, tapping the wrought-iron table that matched their chairs. Three steps led down into the fenced garden and, beyond that, chickens scratched around a shed about halfway down the yard, while ducks and geese splashed in a large dam. The home paddock was sheltered by impressive stone sheds stationed along the boundaries and a row of gums at the bottom. 'Besides, it's the first time I've known a girl who'd be interested in seeing your bees,' he added.

He knew Matt was hanging to tease him, but he couldn't drag his gaze from the yard. Or, more specifically, from Lucie. Sally had deserted him to waddle alongside Dash as Roni showed Lucie and Keeley around the stone sheds now fitted out to home surrendered pets in air-conditioned luxury. Jack chuckled. 'Keeley's gonna go nuts when she sees in there. She thinks The Twenty is awesome, and I've only got a fraction of the animals you have.'

Matt groaned good-naturedly. 'She'll find there's now a Shetland and two alpacas in the barn.'

'Don't suppose you want to add a goat to that herd?'

'Flock. I refer to any of our animals as a flock because that way Roni's never entirely sure whether I'm swearing about them. And *want* is a strong word.' Matt shot him a grin. 'I'm trying to rein Roni in a bit, but you know what she's like: heart as big as the sky.' He smiled down the yard, to where his wife was showing Lucie around.

'Like you'd refuse a home to an animal in need. Probably the only vet in the country who provides free care.'

'Gotta do what the boss tells me,' Matt said, though he clearly had no issue with the fact that Roni owned the property where they ran their business.

Matt's twins raced across the yard towards the dam, and Keeley stared after them, obviously torn between following or going to meet the animals. Lucie bent down and said something, then Keeley nodded and took off after the kids, her purple gumboots flashing and Dash chasing behind. Sally lumbered along behind Dash. The old cattle dog seemed to have taken on a new lease of life with the pup around. Instead of being annoyed by his spontaneous behaviour, she joined in—or, if she was tired, she mothered him, using a heavy paw to hold down his wriggling brown form while she gave him a good tongue-lashing.

'Sam and Lynn mentioned that Lucie's single,' Matt said, taking a swig from his mug.

'You need to stop hanging out with the town gossips,' Jack shot back, making a mental note to tell his sister to shut the hell up.

Matt stretched his legs and pushed his shoulders back against the wall. 'Seems everyone in town's talking about her. Tay's going crazy about some kind of cream Lucie's made, and Lynn's about ready to put her stuff on the shelves.'

'Pops is fully into the gear she made him, too.' Jack tried to keep the unwarranted pride from his tone. 'Settlers Bridge, the new Byron Bay. You vegos will fit in well.'

Matt ignored his dig. 'Anyway, I have to get my info from somewhere. It's not like you've been available for a drink the last few weekends.'

'Not like I have time anymore,' Jack said. 'Between my grandparents, the farm and The Twenty, I don't get chance to scratch myself.'

'And yet here you are, hunting for honey. So to speak,' Matt chuckled.

Jack kept his eyes on the yard. 'K-Keeley's a city kid. Had no idea where honey comes from. And Lucie's keen on getting some raw honey for her natural therapies.'

'Uh-huh. And what else is Lucie keen on?'

He blew out a long, exasperated breath. 'Wish I knew, mate,' he said, shaking his head. 'Wish I knew.'

'Why don't you ask her, then?'

He huffed a laugh, although he felt instantly resentful. His mates forgot how hard this kind of stuff could be for him. 'You make that sound pretty straightforward.'

'Kind of is.'

'Hardly. I mean, look at her.' He gestured to where Lucie was laughing at something Roni had said, both women watching the children playing in the mud. The sun caught Lucie's hair, flashes of pink and electric blue dancing through her choppy cut. 'She's smart and totally into the same kind of stuff as me. And cute as hell.'

'Don't know about the first, the second sounds like a plus, and I'm not gonna comment on the third because either you or Roni will have my balls for it. What about her kid?'

'Keeley? I don't know how Lucie keeps up with her.' He chuckled. 'Caught her the other week trying to wash my bantams because they had dirty feet.'

'How did the birds take that?'

He shrugged. 'Didn't seem to mind a bit. Out preening themselves in the sun, showing off. Not too sure they were as thrilled about the dye job they got the next day, though.'

'You serious?'

Jack nodded, laughing at the memory. 'Lucie bought some food dye and we made each of the silkies a different colour.' He would have agreed to dye the goats if it meant Lucie would come back again. Seeing her two days in a row had been a mixture of heaven and hell.

'You should get her to enter them in the pet section at the Settlers Bridge show.'

'End of next month, right? If they're still around.' He tried not to sound too hopeful. 'Keeley named all the birds, but the names have no relevance to the colours. We've got Beaky and Feathers and Pinkie, who is actually blue. I'm just gonna pretend I remember the other names. Kids, huh?'

'I live with an ancient sheep who was named Goat by a septuagenarian, remember? But yeah, kids are cool.'

Matt's self-satisfied grin said more than his words, Jack thought. Until Roni came to Settlers, the local vet had been insular, working through some pretty dark shit. Obviously, life had done a one-eighty for him.

Matt lifted a questioning hand. 'But what I actually meant was, what about Keeley's dad? Is he still in the picture?'

'No idea. Kind of an awkward question to lob into the middle of a conversation.' He wasn't about to admit that he was hoping the father was some deadshit no-show. He, who knew the pain of being abandoned, was wishing it on Keeley. Just because it would make his next move easier.

'So why don't you straight up ask her if she's keen?'

Jack's heart dropped into his gut. 'You forgetting her old man owns half of The Twenty?'

'That should make it better, not worse.'

Jack shook his head. 'Except Gus bankrolled me for my half.'

'Shit,' Matt groaned. 'Mate, I know where you're going. Been there myself.'

Jack flexed his shoulders, making them crack. 'So, words of advice?'

'Not much I can say. People will talk. They'll question your motives, whether you're really into Lucie or just looking out for yourself. But you know the truth of it: are you in it for the property or the girl?'

'One hundred percent the girl,' he said without a second's hesitation. If Matt could help him out, this wasn't the time to pussyfoot around being shy. 'Lucie doesn't reckon she'll inherit, so that'll make it less messy. Sort of.' With The Twenty in Monica's hands, he knew he'd be punished for a past he couldn't change, and that would determine his future.

'There's your answer then,' Matt said, standing and collecting their mugs. 'Doesn't matter what anyone else thinks as long as you know the truth. I'll just chuck these in the kitchen, and then we'd better go search for your honey.'

'You realise I've only known her a few weeks?'

Matt held the screen door open with his boot. 'I didn't say you have to marry her, dude. Tell her you like her. See how it plays out. Besides, time is irrelevant: plenty of folks are married for decades and then divorce.'

'Cheerful thought.'

'I meant, what's the point of waiting? There's no such thing as a right or appropriate time. Life is for living. You like the girl, so make a move. Before someone else does.'

∾

'I can't believe I've never seen wild hives before.' Lucie gazed up at the honeycomb hanging from the boxthorn.

'This looks like the splayed open pages of a book hung from its spine.'

Her description was perfect, Jack thought. Four sheets of honeycomb, each about a metre across, their ragged edges stretching half a metre towards the ground, hung one behind the other from the bush.

Simon tugged at his mother's hand. Marian stood beside him, the twins, as usual, inseparable. 'We have some?' He pointed to the comb.

'Hmm . . .' Roni scrunched her face, warily watching the apparently random path of the occasional bee.

'It'll be fine,' Jack said. He'd grown up stealing from the wild hives on Pops' property. 'They won't mind sharing a little with the kids.' Avoiding the sections of comb that were white and waxy, he broke off a small portion of the darker hexagons. He showed it to Lucie. 'See the wax caps over the top of each chamber? Scrape them off like this.' He pulled out a pocketknife and uncovered the prisms. 'And there you have the honey. You can melt the entire comb in a pot or the kids can just tip it into their mouths.' He waved Simon closer and flipped a piece of the stripped comb upside down on his outstretched tongue. 'You can eat the wax, too, it's like chewing gum.'

'These are native bees?' Lucie asked, studying the honeycomb intently.

'Never thought about it,' Jack said, cursing silently. So much for impressing Lucie with his knowledge.

Matt shook his head. 'They're European gone wild. Native bees generally burrow into the ground or build their hives in hollow trees, depending on the variety of bee. But it's good, raw, wild honey.'

'So cool,' Lucie breathed. 'I mean, it's not like I've never seen honeycomb in markets and stuff, but this is so . . . natural. And the wax, even that's fragrant.' She glanced shyly at Matt and Roni. 'Do you think I could take some of the fallen combs, the ones on the ground?'

Roni grimaced. 'The ants have already been in them, there'll be very little honey. And plenty of dirt.'

'I don't want them for the honey,' Lucie said, her tone breathy with excitement. 'With a little coconut oil, I can make a hair setter. Add some shea butter and essential oil and it's the best lip balm ever. Oh, and your front garden is full of marigolds, Jack. I'll dry some and make a salve for your grandmother's psoriasis—she said she's never found anything that deals with it properly. With access to clean wax, I can do just about anything.'

'Don't suppose you have something for bruising?' Roni nodded towards her son, who routinely sported egg-sized shiners on his forehead. 'I don't think Simon ever uses his hands to open doors.'

'Arnica,' Lucie said promptly. 'I have arnica-infused oil at home. With this wax,' she hefted the lump in her hand 'I can get a salve to you tomorrow.'

'In that case, take as much as you need,' Roni said. 'We're never going to run out of a use for bruise cream around here.'

'Jack's right, you're like a chemist on steroids,' Matt chuckled.

Jack flinched, wondering if Lucie would be ticked off knowing they'd talked about her.

She looked across at him, her high cheekbones flushed. 'Steroids? Hope that won't make me too bulky for you.' She modelled a body builder's crab pose, arms bowed outward, fists close together at her abdomen, but all he could do was grin like an idiot. Because hadn't she just said, in front of his friends, that the way she looked *to him* was important?

'D-definitely not an issue,' he finally said.

'You're actually a chemist?' Roni asked as they started to pick their way back through the scrub towards the farmhouse.

Lucie shook her head. 'I have quals in natural therapies, along with a bachelor in business management.' She chuckled. 'Pretty whack combination, right?'

'I reckon they're both skills we could use around here,' Matt said. 'I know I'd like to bring some alternative therapies into my vet practice.'

Jack took Lucie's hand to help her over a fallen tree, and she reached with her other hand for Keeley. The three of them were connected in a line, an ellipsis leading . . . to where?

Wherever it was, as his eyes met Lucie's, the moment felt perfect.

They neared the farmyard and Keeley broke away, racing ahead with the twins and the dogs. But Lucie didn't take her hand from his.

'I-I was thinking,' he began, wishing Matt and Roni weren't close enough to hear his fumbling, 'have you and

Keeley been out to the Mannum Waterfalls? It's a nice picnic spot.'

'Oh, that'd be awesome,' Lucie said, and his hopes soared. 'But I've got to buckle down and get some work done at Blue Flag. I've been bumming around a bit and promised myself that after today there'd be no more days off till I'd got some work done.'

'No worries.' He didn't pull off the nonchalant tone he hoped for, but hell, he felt like he'd been kicked in the guts. Though at least Lucie was making an excuse to let him off the hook without shooting him down in front of his friends. 'J-just a passing thought. It's only a few minutes out of town, you can go there anytime.'

'Oh!' Lucie flushed. 'Sorry. I thought you meant with you.' She took her hand from his, waving it around, sounding embarrassed. 'Like, you'd show us where it is.'

'That's exactly what I meant,' he said. Damn, he never should have taken Matt's advice, he should have planned out what he intended to say.

'Maybe a raincheck?' Lucie asked.

'Why not go today?' Roni butted in while he was still trying to process whether Lucie was interested or just intent on not hurting his feelings. 'You can do a loop from here to the waterfalls and back to Settlers.'

'No good,' Jack said reluctantly. 'I haven't organised any food, and Keeley will be getting hungry.'

'Easy fixed,' Roni said. 'I'll throw something together for you. Come on, Jack,' she wheedled. 'You know you never refuse my baking.'

That much was true, but had Roni trapped Lucie? He glanced sideways, afraid to catch her reaction.

Lucie clutched her pendant. 'I can't let you feed both of us, too, Roni.'

'Okay, tell you what,' Roni said. 'I'll swap you a quickie picnic for that arnica salve. And anything you can make that'll moisturise these.' She displayed her hands as though proving she was driving a hard bargain. 'The food will be nothing flash, though. Some cold vegetarian pastie slice, salads, pickled eggs and a fresh sourdough. Maybe some liverwurst,' she shot a grin at Matt, and by the look on his face, the last bit had some hidden meaning.

Still Lucie hesitated. He needed to let her off the hook, find a way for her to escape. He'd say he was busy: it was a permanent truth.

'Besides, it'll be too hot and snakey to go out there soon,' Roni continued. 'And once Reedy Creek stops running, it's pointless, anyway.'

Lucie nodded and his heart gave his ribs an almighty whack. 'Deal,' she said. 'I mean, if that's okay with you, Jack? If you have time today . . .'

He'd have time, all right. Like Matt said, he had to make a move.

32

Lucie

'Wow,' Lucie breathed, gazing at the rough-hewn granite formations reflected in the pool they had reached after a short walk along a tree-lined track. 'We didn't crawl up so much as an anthill on the drive, so how can this gorge even be here? It's . . . mountainous. Looks like it belongs in the Flinders Ranges.' She turned in a slow circle, trying not to appear too much like a tourist as she took in the spectacular valley of cliffs and boulders. 'We're, what, about sixty kilometres from Chesterton? But the climate, the vegetation, the landforms—this could be another world.'

Jack grinned at her reaction, and instantly the scenery wasn't the only thing that had her captivated.

'You'd think a place like this would be crawling with tourists,' she said, dragging her attention back to their surroundings. Though theirs were the only vehicles in the carpark, the valley pulsed with life as water rushed, trickled and splashed between boulders and smooth granite slabs further up the gully, charging the air with ions. Red-rumped parrots in the gums called to one another across the billabong—distinctive, loud squeaks that made her think of fingertips dragged down glass—then continued their conversation with melodic whistling and peeping. Birds hidden in the scrub trilled loudly. Complex, earthy and dynamic, it seemed that if she pressed a hand to the ground, she would feel the heartbeat of the world. Yet despite that lifeforce, she could almost pretend the three of them were the only people for hundreds of kilometres, that there was no risk of anyone intruding on this moment, this place. This new memory.

'Is it some kind of local secret?' she asked, catching Keeley's hand as her daughter splashed one booted foot in the water.

Jack settled his Akubra more firmly, his sandy hair curling loose beneath it. 'Not so much. More a case of not promoted. We can follow the path a ways, but then we'll have to do some rock-hopping if you want to reach the actual waterfall.' He gestured at the dirt track winding along the edge of the reed-fringed creek. 'It's only 'bout a kilometre. There's another carpark closer to the falls, but the walk from that side is crazy steep and slippery. I doubt Sal would make it.' As he spoke, Dash plopped onto his side, exposing his stomach for Sally to nuzzle. The old dog obliged, then nudged the pup back onto his feet.

'Let's try this path, see how far we can get with kids and dogs.' Lucie eyed the path dubiously. 'And, in my case, rather unfit adults.'

'You look perfectly fit to me,' Jack murmured.

His words thrilled her to the point of not being able to respond, so she covered up by pointing out various birds and plants to Keeley, who was still trying to get her gumboots wet in the shallow edge of the lagoon.

'We're in luck,' Jack said as they strolled, frequently stopping for the dogs to sniff or Keeley to poke at things. 'Even during winter there's no guarantee the falls will be running, but there's plenty of water coming down.' He lifted his chin to the torrent splashing through a rocky neck and into the lagoon. The gully above had been landscaped by a giant, the car-sized boulders made tiny by the sheer-sided ravine.

The path narrowed and he dropped behind so she could hold Keeley's hand as they tackled the increasingly steep incline. The water cut channels through slabs of granite larger than buildings, the streams occasionally disappearing, then foaming in white chutes from unseen tunnels, or dropping in waterfalls that ranged from only a handspan to more than a metre wide.

'Must have been a storm up in the hills.' Jack raised his voice over the noise of the water. 'After a dry winter the ground's baked and the rain runs straight off.'

'It's so beautiful,' Lucie called back over her shoulder, trying to take it all in. She wanted to get her phone out, but photos could never do justice to the sheer scale of the vista. Besides, she was clutching both Keeley and Dash wherever the track narrowed and the drop to the river came a little too close for comfort.

'A family got stranded the other year,' Jack said. 'It was barely raining, so they'd hopped across the rocks to a boulder in the middle of the creek. Then a flash flood hit, and they had to be winched out by helicopter.'

'Sounds excruciatingly embarrassing. Don't let that happen to us, okay?' she laughed.

The gully widened, the calm, tea-coloured water mirroring the scudding clouds. Keeley tugged free of her hand. 'Dash, is your turn carry Purple Ted,' she said, tossing the raggedy toy onto the ground.

Lucie grabbed her hand again. 'Keeley, you have to stay close. It's dangerous.'

'Probably not as dangerous as the city,' Jack said.

Was he trying to point out the benefits of living here, as opposed to going home? She shoved the thought down: years ago she had projected her own desires onto Jeremy, and she refused to make the same mistake twice. If Jack was interested, he was going to have to make it clear.

The gully here was scattered with perfectly rounded boulders and angular granite outcrops. Spumes of white bubbles flung horizontally from clefts between the stone, splashing down onto rocky platforms worn smooth by centuries of the water's caress. 'This place would be a geologist's wet dream,' she marvelled. Jack snorted with laughter as he came up alongside, and she shot him a reproving look. 'In that it *is* wet.' Yeah, sure that was all she meant. It wasn't like she was trying to titillate him, provoke his interest. Much.

'Uh-huh,' he chuckled. 'Don't get too excited yet—the higher we climb, the more spectacular it is.'

'I'm not so fond of that word *climb*,' she cautioned, pointing at Keeley's purple wellingtons. The boots were an excuse: she didn't much fancy humiliating herself by panting harder than the dogs.

'I'll help you over the slippery bits.' Jack held out his hand.

Lucie slid her hand into his, though they'd moved onto a broad, smooth part of the path, several metres away from the water. 'Never mind the slippery bits, you have to promise to haul me up the steep parts,' she said, forcing herself to act normal. They'd held hands earlier; this was no different.

Except that this was completely deliberate. They were adults, strolling along a scenic path, *hand in hand*. And that was so different to her normal. She blew out a tremulous breath, careful to look at the creek so Jack wouldn't catch her. 'This is . . . really nice.'

'I don't recall it ever being this *nice*,' he responded.

The dog's leash around her wrist, she touched one finger to her yellow citrine, the crystal of happiness and sunshine. Despite the clouds of dark grief banked on the horizon, joy filled her. Or maybe it was hope. She had been in a rut in Melbourne, existing in a cycle of work and self-denial to make sure she was doing the best she could by Keeley. Yet it seemed now that she could find her way out of that pit. Dad had sent Jack so she would know that he not only loved her but that he had understood her. Mum, well, she was still unfathomable. Yet she showed glimpses of having far more empathy than Lucie had credited her with. Perhaps the Napoleon cake had been some sort of pink-iced peace offering? And she seemed to be slowly, rather erratically thawing towards Keeley. As long as Jeremy kept to the other side of the world, Lucie could see no reason to leave South Australia in a hurry.

And one very specific reason to hang around.

'Hold hands, Keeley,' she called as the path neared the water course again.

'Here, Keeley,' Jack said. 'Hang on to me and I'll help you across this bit.' Her daughter's tiny hand was engulfed by Jack's fist, and he swung her across a trickle of water onto a flat-topped rock. 'We have to climb here.' He indicated an easy scramble over large rocks. 'Do you think Dash can manage it?'

'Sally will helps him,' Keeley said authoritatively. 'She loves him.'

'I think she does,' Jack agreed as the cattle dog nudged the pup across the trickle. 'I'm not sure she realises he's a dog, but she definitely thinks he needs rounding up. I haven't seen her this interested in anything other than her food bowl for a couple of years.'

'You've had her a long time?' Lucie asked, watching her footing. She'd noticed that Jack rarely commanded Sally; instead he clicked his fingers or simply tilted his head, and the dog seemed to intuitively understand what he wanted.

'Twelve years. Since she was born. She was one of Pops' pups; he still has a couple of her great grand-nephews over at the farm. Sal was a runt and Pops said she had to go. So she did. Straight into my ute. She lived there for a couple of months while I fed her up.'

'Your grandparents didn't notice?'

He grinned. 'Ma would give me the fattiest bits of meat to feed her, right in front of Pops, and he never mentioned it. When I turned twenty-one, he said, "Guess you'll be wanting that dog for your birthday, then," and that was an end to any question of her *going*.'

She suspected Jack wanted to air quote the last word, but he didn't let go of either her or Keeley to do so.

'Once I moved out to The Twenty, Pops started asking after Sal. She's outlived her siblings, so I reckon he's beginning to doubt his eye when it comes to choosing the best pups.'

'He still breeds them?' she said, her calves aching as the slope inclined more sharply, the gravel rolling under-foot like marbles as they moved back onto a section of dirt path. 'Come on, Dash,' she called as the puppy paused to sniff at the sparse grass.

Jack clicked his tongue and lifted his chin, and Sal doubled back to hurry the dachshund along.

'I take Dash, Mummy,' Keeley said.

The path ahead was clear for some way before they'd have to make their way back onto the rocks to cross the small streams. 'Just for a little bit,' Lucie said. 'But you still have to hold Jack's hand.'

She passed the leash across to Keeley, aware as she did so that the hand Jack still gripped—in fact, her entire arm—was crushed against his side. As she straightened, Jack threaded his fingers through hers. Somehow, the gesture seemed even more intimate than a hand clasp. His hand was dry and strong, a little work-roughened. And she knew she had never been so safe in her life.

'Yeah, Pops still breeds them,' Jack said, picking up their conversation as Dash waddled in front of them, tongue lolling as they crested one of the undulating hills that flowed like waves beside the river. He shook his head. 'Leaving the farm is going to kill him.'

'They're leaving? Where are they going?'

Jack scowled, a flash of sunlight catching the blaze of blue across his irises. 'I d-don't know. Sam and I are trying to work something out. Maybe some kind of supported accommodation, I guess. There are a few retirement home kind of things in Murray Bridge.' His mouth twisted despondently. 'But it won't much matter where, because we'll have to drag them off the farm kicking and screaming.'

'Then why are they going?' she asked.

'Getting too old to look after themselves. Sam's busy with the shop and I'm out at The Twenty. Though I could chuck in the block and live with them again. I mean, I *should* do that.'

It was obvious from his tone that he wasn't enthusiastic about the prospect.

'You didn't like living at their place?'

303

'Loved it. But The Twenty is my dream. I've got—sh-shit, I'm not trying to twist your arm—'

He broke off and she hurried to reassure him. 'Don't worry, I'm untwistable. In any case, like I told you, the estate will pass to Mum.'

A fairy-wren flitted onto the path just in front of them, and Dash dropped the teddy bear. They paused as the bird cocked its bright blue head, the rich chestnut patch on his shoulder flashing as he spread his wings and danced off across the path. Dash started forward, but then paused to pick up the toy before moving more quickly after the flitting bird.

'Good,' Jack nodded, though a deep frown furrowed his brow. 'I've found out the local council can offer a bit of help, cleaning gutters, that kind of stuff. But it's not enough anymore.' He glanced at her, looking embarrassed. 'Sam and I are getting to the point where we always make sure to take food with us, because Ma can't see well enough to notice whether the dishes are dirty, or the food mouldy. And I don't know about Sam but I'm never using their loo again.'

Hope surged through Lucie. She had seen Jack tend her father's strawberries on The Twenty as though they were his own passion, rather than an inherited burden. With Dad gone, Jack could have let the crop die: no one would judge him for it, the berries were a drain of resources and time. Yet, when she'd said as much, Jack had straightened from where he kneeled between the fragrant plants, pushing back the long blond hair that escaped its leather tie so that he could meet her gaze. 'Gus wanted strawberries for you,

Lucie. While I'm on The Twenty, your dad's strawberries will be, too.'

Had she now found a way in which she could repay him for that quiet kindness, for keeping part of Dad alive? 'Do you know if your grandparents have been assessed for a government home care package?'

Jack looked a bit lost. 'I remember Ma said that Pops' stroke gave him a level-three rating on some system. But she couldn't work out what that meant, only that a lot of people from different organisations contacted her, and she figured it was a con. Sam was going to look into it, but she's been preoccupied.' A shadow crossed his face.

Lucie pulled on his hand so he and Keeley would stop walking. 'Jack, this is literally my job, back in Melbourne.'

'Natural therapies . . . ?' He raised an eyebrow in question.

'No. Working with natural therapies is my passion, but my business qual got me a job as a manager with a home care provider. I help clients understand their entitlements, identify their needs, coordinate services and access the funds. If Paul has a rating three on the system, he's entitled to assistance.'

'We go,' Keeley demanded, dragging on Jack's hand.

Lucie waggled her fingers and Keeley swapped to her hand.

'Won't do any good,' Jack said. 'Ma refuses to have people she doesn't know in the house. Besides, since when does the government help out?'

'I guess since they're frantic to prop up our health system by keeping senior citizens independent and at home rather than in a care facility. It's cash assistance—and a decent amount, too, at least if your pops is a rating three. It doesn't have to be people coming into the house to help, either— it can be used for things like, I don't know, say a scooter if Paul's arthritis gets worse and he can't get around. Or rails for the shower, a commode for the bedroom.'

Jack grimaced and she laughed, slightly breathless from the climb. The noise of the water had become louder as the flow increased, and she knew they must be nearing the main falls. 'Hey, they're lucky to make it to an age where stuff like that is necessary. But the thing is, they can also use the money to hire home help. Pretty much any kind they choose, whether it's cooking or cleaning or yard work. Anything that makes it possible for them to stay in their own home.'

Jack shook his head. 'Settlers is small; even if I could get Ma past her whole "ain't no one coming in my house" mindset, there's no one to take on the jobs.'

'That's where I can help.' She'd never been happier to say those words. 'My employer is national, so I can pull up lists of providers, agencies with staff who are willing to travel—'

'Dash!' Keeley shrieked. She tugged her hand from Lucie's and darted towards the ravine.

'No!' Lucie yelled, but terror swallowed the word, nightmare quicksand cementing her feet.

Jack leaped forward, snatching Keeley's arm before she reached the edge of the cliff.

'Dash,' Keeley screamed again, struggling against Jack's grip.

The quicksand let go and Lucie stumbled to her baby. She crashed to her knees, locking her arms around Keeley.

A blur of rusty red fur brushed past her, and Sally launched herself into the gorge.

'Jesus, Sal!' Jack shouted.

The dog slammed into the churning water below and disappeared. Nearby, Dash bobbed up like a cork, his legs too short to paddle effectively. Sally surfaced, surging through the water towards him. She seized the scruff of his neck in her teeth.

'Come away, Sal! Come away!' Jack bellowed, gesturing frantically, trying to get the dog to swim to the side of the pool.

Her eyes wild and white with fear, Sally struggled to obey, but the current had her trapped, pulling both dogs towards the cascade.

'I didn't mean to let go, Mummy,' Keeley sobbed.

'Shh, shh,' she said, trying to press Keeley's face into her shoulder, so her daughter wouldn't see the tragedy below them.

The dogs hit the edge of a whirlpool formed by the spill of water plunging over the rocks. Lucie caught her breath in sudden hope: they would be pushed close to the shore, where deceptively soft-looking froth hid the boulders beneath the deluge.

But though Sally paddled valiantly, the current snatched the dogs, sucking them under the waterfall. Pummelled by the torrent, they disappeared.

'Sal!' Jack roared. He ripped his shirt over his head, his hat cartwheeling over the cliff, and toed his boots off.

'No!' Lucie gasped. 'The rocks!'

Jack plunged over the edge of the cliff feet first, arms braced across his chest.

'Oh my god, oh my god,' Lucie edged forward so she could look down. 'Jack?' The water swirled below, threatening and ominous, the rock teeth surrounded by rabid foam.

His wet hair dark, Jack surfaced, looking around blindly, and her breath sobbed out.

The dogs were nowhere to be seen. Three strong overarm strokes took Jack to the falls. He paused, then dived deep.

Keeping Keeley twisted away from the drop, Lucie instinctively moved to her haunches, as though she could somehow help.

Almost immediately, Jack reappeared, clutching a bundle of dark red fur high against his chest. His powerful legs propelled them away from the waterfall, towards the centre of the pool. Fighting against the current, he shook his head to flick the hair from his face. As he trod water, he hefted the cattle dog's sodden form over one broad shoulder. In his other hand he had Dash, the chocolate brown bundle motionless as Jack struggled to keep the three of them afloat.

Lucie pushed to her feet, sweeping Keeley up. Carrying her baby, she raced back down the path, constantly glancing to her right to make sure Jack was swimming to the downstream end of the pool. As soon as the cliff gave way to steep, muddy banks, she dropped onto her bottom, still holding Keeley as she slid down the slope.

The rocks at the base brought her to a stop with a painful crunch, but she shoved upright. 'Keeley, stay here. Right here!' she yelled, but there was no time to soften her tone. Water like this was so dangerous, with snares and snags, currents that could pull Jack under and—

He was already staggering out of the shallow end of the billabong as she pushed through the reeds and raced across the mud. 'Jack!'

He gave her a tight grin, though his chest heaved with exertion. 'Yours?' he said as he thrust the now-wriggling pup towards her.

Dash yipped excitedly, as though he'd had an adventure, then covered her face in puppy kisses.

She felt sick. So many emotions, so much fear in the space of a few minutes, spiked her adrenaline and now it crashed. She closed her eyes for a long second, though her ears were trained on Keeley, still sobbing behind her. 'Oh, Jack, I thought . . .' She shook her head, unable to put her fears into words without crying. And she wouldn't allow that to happen.

She opened her eyes, determined to finish the sentence, to find the words to thank Jack. And to tell him how desperately concerned she had been about him. Because maybe, instead of protecting herself by insisting she be certain of his feelings, she needed to be brave enough to admit her own and accept the consequences.

On his knees, Jack huddled over Sally's sodden form in the mud.

He looked up, his face stark with grief. 'She's gone.'

33
Jack

He buried Sal in the front garden, as close to his bedroom as he could break the earth.

Lucie had driven off from the waterfalls with Keeley and Dash, leaving him to take Sally home on the front seat of his ute, where she belonged.

He assumed the girls had gone back to Settlers, but within the hour he heard gears changing down as Lucie's car wound along the road to the cottage. Felt her presence as she walked the dirt path at the side of the house, carefully lifting the gate to open it quietly.

He didn't turn. Instead, he kneeled to rub Sally's grizzled muzzle for the last time. 'You'll always be my b-best dog, Sal,' he murmured. He wanted to promise that he'd never have another, but he was a farmer: a dog was as necessary as a tractor. But there would never be another like her.

He had dried her damp, rusty red fur and wrapped Sally in the cover he'd taken from his bed, tucking the blanket carefully around her cold, too still form. Now he took one final look at her familiar, faithful face, then closed the fabric protectively around her. Reluctantly he pushed to his feet and took the shovel, working slowly and making sure the dirt landed softly on his best friend.

When he had mounded the earth high, Lucie stepped up beside him. She bent and scooped a depression in the dirt, then pressed a small plant into the hole. Alongside it a baby pink rock glowed softly in the last of the sunlight. Then she scattered bright yellow dandelion flowers across the mound. 'Pink calcite,' she said. 'The stone of peace. Rosemary for remembrance. And dandelions for emotional healing.'

He nodded, unable to look at her.

'I'm so sorry, Jack,' she murmured. 'If we hadn't gone to the falls, if we hadn't ever come here—'

He took a deep, shuddering breath. 'Then Sally might have had a few more weeks. But that's all. She was on her way out, Lucie. Matt had already warned me. And she's had more fun with Dash and Keeley the last few weeks than she's had in the past couple of years.' He gave a sad laugh. 'She was like a puppy again. Like I remember her.'

'But now she's gone. She's gone, and there's no way to change that.' Lucie had her arms wrapped tight across her chest, her chin quivering as she fought her emotions.

'Luce, it's okay. Really,' he said gently, although a piece of his own heart had been torn out and he knew the wound would never heal. 'Nothing lasts forever. When it's time to go, there's no fighting it.'

She glanced up at him and her eyes widened in shock. 'Oh my god, Jack,' she whispered brokenly, her trembling fingers reaching to wipe the tears from his cheeks. 'I made you—I'm so sorry.' She shook her head, her dark eyes liquid. 'It's my fault, it's all my fault. I should have been looking after him, I should have taken responsibility.'

He knew that she wasn't speaking only about Dash. Impulsively, he pulled her to his chest, wrapping his arms around her, as though he could take away her pain, her grief, even as his own shredded him.

She pressed closer, her breath damp on his chest as she hid her face against him. The sobs that shook her seemed in danger of tearing her apart, her anguish so vast it diminished his own, at least temporarily.

'Ah, Lucie, it's okay,' he murmured, tucking her head under his chin, holding her tighter. He'd have to let her go in a moment or she might think he was taking advantage of her obvious distress. But until he was sure she could stand without his support, he'd relish the feel of her in his arms and the sharing of grief that seemed to slightly lessen the ache in his heart.

Eventually, Lucie stepped back, scrubbing at her face with both hands. She let out a shaky sigh. 'Sorry. I've kind of been bottling that up. But when I saw you . . .' She pointed at her own cheeks then mashed her lips together, as though uncertain whether to mention he'd been caught crying.

He shrugged. 'D-dad would have belted the hell out of me for that. But screw him. Sal deserves a river of tears.'

She fiddled with the yellow stone on her necklace. 'Does it help, do you think?' A jerky inhale interrupted her words as her chest spasmed. 'The crying, I mean.' A tiny frown furrowed between her dark eyes, so intent on him.

'You don't cry?' he asked softly.

She shook her head. 'I—well, as you just saw, yes. Sometimes. Snottily.' She half-laughed and gave a huge sniff. 'But I try to avoid it so I don't upset Keeley. Plus, I'm always afraid that if I give in, I won't know how to stop.'

'You'll stop when you're done,' he said. 'Besides, it's cathartic. Better than drinking your way through the pain.'

'How did you get to be so wise?' she said, and he understood she was actually asking about his experience with grief, looking for a commonality that would assure her that the loss of Gus would hurt less with time.

'Cried enough when I was a kid to find out, I guess. Probably lucky I was too young to drink back then.'

'You were—' She broke off as her phone blipped. She snatched it from the back pocket of her jeans, shooting him a distracted, apologetic smile. 'Sorry. Chloe and Lynn at the store are watching Keeley. I've never left her with anyone except Geoff before.' She quickly scanned the message then looked back at him. 'I mean, I'm not in the habit of trusting her to near strangers, but I wanted to get back here as quickly as—'

Something in his expression must have triggered her, because she froze, her expression horrified.

313

'Is there something wrong with Lynn? Or Chloe?'

'No. Not at all. I'd leave my own kid with either of them. If I had one,' he added, eager to avoid any misunderstanding. 'I'm just . . . confused. You left Keeley for the first time because you wanted to come here?'

She tucked the phone back into her pocket. 'I wanted to check you were all right, but I didn't think it was appropriate for Keeley to see. But maybe she should have. Am I being overprotective? Except I'm not protecting her, am I, because I just left her with strangers. Oh god!' She ran both hands through her hair, leaving it in wild disarray, and he immediately wanted to be the one messing up her curls. 'I'm sorry, it's just this parenting stuff is hard, you know?'

'Have you been doing it solo for long?' he managed to slip in.

'Forever. I mean, always. Since Keeley was born. Well, technically, anyway; though I couldn't have done it without Geoff.'

'Dad's not in the picture, then?'

'Dad's not ever going to be in the picture,' she said, suddenly fierce. 'He missed his opportunity and he needn't think he gets a second chance to screw up our lives.'

He needed time to unpack that. Though he was rapt that the guy was no longer involved, he also wasn't so thick that he didn't realise Lucie's anger meant baggage came with the package. Not that anyone had offered him a package.

Lucie waved a hand, as though dismissing her own emotion. 'I have to go. I mean, Chloe texted to say everything's fine, but still . . . Only, are you okay? I brought this with me.' She reached into the pocket of the zip-up wind-breaker she'd put over the top of the tight t-shirt he'd spent half the day admiring. Back at the waterfalls. With Sally. Sorrow punched at his gut again and he glanced at the cottage door. It was going to bloody hurt going in there, without Sal to greet him.

'Jack? Will you be okay?' Lucie repeated.

He nodded. 'Yeah. Just going to be quiet. You kind of get used to another heartbeat being around, you know?'

'Totally,' she said with a sympathetic grimace. 'I don't think I ever want to be alone again.'

Was he imagining meaning into her words? Obviously she would never be alone, she had Keeley. Yet it seemed she invested the words with more, that she was telling him she'd had enough of being single.

Damn, like Matt said, he needed to man up and just ask.

She pulled a paper bag from her pocket. 'Hawthorn tea. For heart healing.'

He reached for the bag, his fingers brushing hers. 'I'll probably poison myself trying to brew this. You might have to come back to do it for me.' He held his breath, could have sworn his heart stopped beating: everything depended on her answer.

Lucie didn't release the bag, her dark gaze direct as she paused for a long moment. Then the slight lifting of the corners of her lips—the lips he was thinking more and more about how much he wanted to kiss, how sweet she would taste, how soft her skin would be—let him know the pause wasn't because she was uncertain, but to add emphasis to her reply. 'Of course, Jack. Anytime.'

Her finger traced briefly—surely deliberately?—over his before she released the bag and took a step back. 'I really have to go.'

'I'll call you during the week.'

She nodded, again fiddling with her pendant. 'Okay.'

Should he hug her goodbye? Because he'd just had his arms around her, so now it wouldn't be odd. Would it?

Yeah, probably would, he decided reluctantly. They had met to trade his veg for her ointments for his grandparents, and to search for Mr Unicorn for Keeley, and to discuss the fact that The Twenty needed a new fence on the southern side, and for absolutely any other excuse he could concoct. But not once had they hugged. Not until today.

'I have to drop by some arthritis cream for Paul, anyway.'

Pops must be bathing in the stuff if he already needed more. 'Sure,' he said. 'And you'd be up for some milk soon, right?'

'I have enough to go into soap-making,' she admitted ruefully. 'But I'll chase up the information on home care if you think your grandparents would be interested?'

'You've no idea what a load off it'll be if we can work out something. I don't want just anyone out there with them, though. Bit like you with Keeley, you know?'

'Of course.' She waved her phone as though he'd reminded her of her reason for leaving. 'Anyway, you know where to find me. You know, if you want—' she lifted one shoulder uncertainly, as though not sure where to take the sentence '—me to make that tea. Or anything.'

'I do. I will.'

She nodded.

Damn, he should hug her. Kiss her. Do some bloody thing.

But no matter how he pretended otherwise, the property he loved was an insurmountable barrier. It was one thing to tell Matt the girl was more important than the land, but another to find a way to convince her of that. He couldn't make a move because—to hell with what the rest of the town would say—until Gus's last wishes were finalised, there was a risk Lucie would think he was out for what he could get.

Jack could only hope that Lucie was right, that her mother would inherit everything. Monica wouldn't hesitate to sell it from under him, but at least that would leave the way clear for him to tell Lucie how he felt about her.

'Okay,' Lucie said again. 'I've really got to make tracks.'

'Sure.'

She darted forward, quick as a swallow, and pressed a kiss to his cheek. 'Bye, Jack. Call me.'

34
Lucie

Lucie drove a couple of kilometres along the dirt track, crossing the small floodplain and winding up the hill opposite Jack's sheltered end of the riverside cove. Checking the mirror to make sure she wasn't being followed—or was she checking in hope that she was being followed?— she pulled the car onto the sandy verge. She blew out a long breath, her hands still gripping the steering wheel as though she needed an anchor.

Eventually, she pried one hand free and dialled Geoff from the console. He'd be at work, so she could only pray he would pick up. She needed to talk this through in an adult manner.

'Geoff Allen speaking.'

'I kissed him!' She rolled her eyes at herself in the rear-view mirror—so much for an adult manner.

'Wait a moment, I need to move to my office,' Geoff said. She heard the rustle of paperwork being shifted, then the tap of leather shoes. 'Okay, Tumbleweed, hit me with that again.'

'I kissed him, Geoff. And I'm not even sorry I did it.'

He chuckled. 'Thor? Is there a reason you should be sorry?'

'Well, there's that whole "I'm never going to trust a man again" thing. Along with "It's only me and Keeley forever".'

'And me,' he added, sounding a little hurt. 'I'm assuming from your tone that it was a good kiss, then?'

'Nope. It was a dumb kiss. I pecked him on the cheek. That's the only thing I *am* sorry about. But if he'd wrapped his arms around me again, taken advantage of the moment to turn it into something more, I wouldn't have fought him off.'

'Wait, wrapped his arms around you *again*? I'm checking my notes here and I don't seem to have a record of a previous occurrence. Thought you were supposed to be keeping me in the loop.'

'The *again* was the same time, really,' she said, squinting towards the river. Black kites soared high above the silver ribbon and she cracked the window to hear their hollow, haunting keen. 'We were talking. I was crying. He hugged me. I kissed him. There, you're all caught up.' Even mentioning the hug was enough to wrap her in it again. Jack had held her tight, her rock in a storm of grief.

'Whoa, back this right up, Tumbleweed. *You* were crying? In front of someone? Are you even the person I know? You'd better tell me this story from the top.'

Quickly recounting an abbreviated version of the day, she tried not to let sadness at the thought of Sally's death overwhelm her. She took a deep breath. 'Then, when he stood there with tears running down his face and he didn't give a damn that I saw him unashamedly showing how much he loved Sally, something inside me snapped. It was like everything that I've bottled up just poured out. All this time I've been trying to be mad at Dad because I figured that way losing him wouldn't hurt so much. I've been pretending I'm over here only to take care of business, not because I wanted to say goodbye to him. I need to come to terms with the fact that I'll never see his face again, never have him pass me a cup of coffee so dark and sweet it's like a dessert, never feel the scratchy roughness of his hands wrap around mine as he recites that stupid strawberry rhyme. But to do that I have to allow myself to feel the grief. And seeing Jack accept that Sally's gone, even though it's tearing him apart, helped me. I was in denial about Dad being d-dead.' She tripped over the word, but now that was okay. Even if she started crying while talking to Geoff, that was okay. Because if a guy like Jack could admit to his feelings, then she could find the courage to do the same. 'I wanted to pretend that I wasn't grieving, that Dad had left me a long time ago, and that it doesn't really hurt now. But none of that's true.'

'Great step, Luce,' Geoff said gently. 'I'm so pleased for you. Now you're allowing those feelings, do you think you're more open to others?'

'Other feelings? You mean like admitting I'm totally into Jack Schenscher?' she said with a grin, wishing she could see Geoff's shock. 'Yep, I might be persuaded to do that.'

'Awesome! I wish I was there, Tumbleweed. This is huge. What now? You said he didn't kiss you back.'

'No. But there's something between us, I know it. I just need to work out why he's playing it so careful. Except . . . I don't want to force the situation.' She felt the flush rise in her cheeks. 'Because that's kind of what happened with Jeremy. I wanted him, so I did everything I could to make him notice me, and to make myself available.'

'Your mum's right, then?'

'Let's not be too hasty there, okay?' she said begrudgingly. 'I was young and dumb is more the point.'

'Now you're so old and wise?'

'Now I'm determined not to screw this up. I'm not going to pretend that I don't feel anything for Jack, but I'm also not going to throw myself at him.' She tapped her cheek. 'Chaste kisses on the cheek only, unless he chooses to initiate something more.'

∾

Though determined she wouldn't push Jack, Lucie was disappointed he hadn't called by lunchtime the next day. Which was ridiculous: she knew how busy he was, running two properties, and she'd been flat out herself, sourcing the information for Evie and Paul. And today she was determined to get into Dad's paperwork, despite Mum's obvious but inexplicable roadblocks.

She slid the avocado tart onto the kitchen bench at Blue Flag. Mum would promptly relocate it somewhere tidier. 'I'm going over to the office, Mum. It's not safe for Keeley in the packing shed, so I want you to watch her here, please.' She had practised the words on the drive over—in between reminding Keeley to use her manners, reminding her that Nanna didn't like food to be dropped on the carpet, reminding her to take Dash out for a wee. By the time they arrived in Chesterton, she had been equal parts sick of the nagging sound of her own voice and tied up in knots at the thought of demanding Mum step up.

'Of course,' Mum said. 'It's a lovely day. Would you like to help me in the garden, Keeley? Perhaps you can pick your own bunch of flowers to arrange.'

Mum never picked flowers during the heat of the day: it caused them to wilt and drop their petals prematurely. Lucie stared at her mother suspiciously. 'What in particular did you want me to look at in the office?'

Mum flapped a disinterested hand. 'The accountant takes care of the pays and bills. Perhaps check through any other mail on your father's desk.'

Lucie pulled up short, as though she'd been struck. 'Accountant? You've hired someone?'

Mum picked up the tart and paused uncertainly between the fridge and the cupboard.

'Avocado, fresh coconut and limes on a flax meal base. The fridge,' Lucie snapped. 'This accountant? Did you have a recommendation?' Mum knew nothing about business— why on earth was she meddling now?

'I didn't *get* anyone,' Mum said, ignoring her direction and sliding the tart into a high cupboard. 'Dad has used him for years. Though goodness knows whether he's actually doing the job now. *Familiarity breeds apathy.* Bernbach.'

'But Dad always did the books.'

'Until shortly after you left. Then he couldn't manage anymore.' Her mother pressed her lips together, evidently holding in the sermon on how Lucie had failed the family.

'If he needed me that badly, why didn't he call? It was one thing when I believed we weren't speaking because he was disappointed in me, but that was never the case, was it? So why didn't he just call?'

Mum picked up the pruning shears that sat on the table near the back door. 'Needed you? Dad didn't need *you*, Lucie. There are plenty of people with your qualification.'

She shook her head in confusion. 'But he was adamant I study business management.'

Her mother scoffed. 'Dad didn't care what you studied, although he did eventually agree that it was important you pursue something sensible. Not your silly hobbies.'

'Like hell.' It was another of her mother's lies. It had to be. Because Dad's insistence on directing her future was why she had rebelled, why she had ended up in Jeremy's arms—ultimately why she had moved to Melbourne.

As Keeley skipped across the garden ahead of them, Lucie spoke fast and furious. 'Dad was always specific. He said I had to do the bachelor of business management every bloody time we argued.' The words choked in her throat. Dad had been stubbornly determined, parroting the name of the degree.

Almost as though he didn't realise there were other options, similar courses, giving comparable credentials.

As though he was merely repeating what he had been told would be best for her.

The shears made a decisive click as her mother snipped a deadhead from a daisy bush. 'A broad qualification like business management opens many doors, Lucie. You'll never need to rely on a man.'

Lucie stared at her mother. She had to be lying. Otherwise, the premise Lucie had built her adult life on, the story she told herself and everyone else, had suddenly been erased: she hadn't studied business because Dad needed her to but because her mother *wanted* her to. 'But Dad needed me at Blue Flag,' she pleaded.

Mum gesticulated with the shears. 'I'm not saying Dad wouldn't have appreciated your help, but he certainly wasn't dependent on it. That was all in your head, Lucie. You like to feel that you're indispensable, but there's no such thing. Georgius did not die because you weren't here to help him.'

'But you said—'

'I'm sure we've all said many things we don't really mean,' Mum said dismissively.

Holding her arms up like a ballerina, Keeley twirled towards them. 'Nanna, can us pick some flowers to go on Sally's grave?'

'Sally?' Mum said.

'Jack's dog. She saved Dash and she drownded,' Keeley said solemnly. 'Is sad. Isn't it, Mummy?'

'Very,' Lucie agreed, a wave of aching compassion for Jack washing through her.

'Jackson again?' Mum said. 'Very well. We shall pick flowers for Sally and for your grandfather's grave.'

Lucie stiffened. 'You had him cremated, remember?' she hissed, although Keeley wouldn't understand. 'No stone, no plaque.'

'Yes, but I created my own place to remember him.'

Lucie stared at her mother's retreating back. 'If Dad didn't need me, why am I even here?' she said tiredly, almost to herself.

Her mother turned, her hollow cheeks sucking in further with what looked like genuine confusion. 'Do you expect me to manage everything by myself?'

'Manage what, Mum? Alexis is in charge of the packers and pickers, Ken looks after the crop and apparently you already have an *accountant* to do the books.'

'I'm not talking about managing the business. I'm talking about selling it.'

'You can't sell,' Lucie gasped.

Mum looked at her levelly for the first time that day. 'Why not, Lucie? You know how to manage a business, thanks to your qualifications, but neither of us has any *interest* in Blue Flag.'

'It's Dad's legacy.'

'No, it's not. It's just a farm. A block of dirt and plants. You are your father's only legacy.'

∾

The sun was high, a burning fierceness that would last a few more hours yet. But it couldn't warm Lucie's chilled soul. Tangled in her guilt and grief, she hadn't wondered what her mother's plans were—but even if she had, it never would have occurred to her that her father was to be so thoroughly erased.

Leaning against the metal shed, desperate for the bite of its reflected heat, she pulled out her phone, meaning to call Geoff. Instead, her heart controlling her fingers, she dialled Jack. He had known Dad better than anyone.

'Lucie?' He picked up on the second ring. 'Everything okay?'

She closed her eyes and tipped her head back. The sweet scent of strawberries hung heavy in the air and, for the first time in four years, she wanted one. 'Yeah. Sort of.' A sob caught in her throat. Damn, when she'd decided it was okay to cry, she hadn't meant every time she spoke with Jack. 'I'm—I'm out at Mum's, and she just dropped a bit of a bombshell. She's rambling about going overseas. Plans to sell up everything.'

'Do you want me to come out there? You sound upset.'

She flicked her eyes open, frowning across the yard, towards the house, where she could see Keeley's golden hair catching the sun as she picked flowers in the back garden. 'Jack, did you hear me? Mum's selling everything. The farm, the equipment, the house. Jack, that means The Twenty—'

'Doesn't matter,' he interrupted firmly. 'As long as you and Keeley are okay, none of it matters.'

'Will you be able to buy out Dad's half?'

He gave a short laugh. 'Not a hope in hell.'

'But it's everything you've worked for,' she said.

'And it's nothing I can't afford to lose,' he said. 'Yeah, I'm going to be gutted. But it's just a place, Lucie. Somehow, I'll start again. Things can be replaced. People—and, damn it, dogs—can't.'

The rawness in his voice when he spoke of Sally spilled her tears, but she stared across the farmyard, letting them fall. Both he and Mum were right. This was just a place.

'Lucie? I'll leave now.'

'No.' She startled back to the present, realising she had the phone cupped in both hands, holding it to her ear instead of using the speaker, as though it would bring Jack closer. 'I'm fine. Really.'

'Lucie, in a way, this is good. I mean, I don't want to give up The Twenty, but this will s-straighten some other stuff out.' Jack sounded oddly hesitant.

'What stuff?'

'It'll just clear things up. Don't worry about it. When can I see you?'

It didn't matter how mysterious Jack's words were, his eager question was enough to wipe away her qualms. 'I'm going to have a look through Dad's office, then I'm heading to Adelaide to pick up some naturopathy supplies. I might throw myself into that stuff for a while.' The distraction would be grounding. 'Also, I spoke with a colleague in

Melbourne this morning. I have some leads on assistance for your grandparents, but I want to chase them up personally: sometimes providers say they're willing to travel for work, but they mean within the suburbs, not out into the *wilds*.' She intoned the last word dramatically. 'Anyway, that was a long-winded way of saying I'll have plenty of time to see you.' It was hard to control the lilt of excitement in her voice.

'If you can put off chasing up your supplies for a day, how about you and Keeley come out to dinner at Ma's tonight? I know Pops would like to meet you. And Ma will make sure he doesn't ask you to demonstrate how to apply the oil.'

She could picture the fine lines feathering around Jack's eyes as he spoke. 'I don't know—'

'Sam will bring the food,' he continued hurriedly. 'And I'll check the plates are clean myself.'

'It wasn't that,' she laughed. 'But I won't have time to get any kind of coherent presentation together to explain how the home care packages work.' She didn't much care why or where they met: she simply wanted to see Jack again. Where every interaction with her mother left her feeling heavy, confused, beaten, Jack was the opposite. He was a breath of light and sunshine, radiating the aura of pure quartz. 'Text me directions and the time. We'll be there.'

They talked for a few more minutes, deciding it would be easier for her to head out to The Twenty than find the farm. Neither of them seemed in a hurry to hang up, even though the chorus of bleating sheep in Jack's background meant he was working. Eventually, Lucie ended the call and pocketed her phone.

Her smile disappeared as she turned towards the small door into the shed. It was hard to find the enthusiasm to enter her father's office and tackle his paperwork—after all, what was the point when all that he had built would soon be gone?

Momentarily, she had a fear of walking in on the unknown accountant sitting behind Dad's desk, in Dad's grimy chair, but then she realised that the makeshift office in the packing shed wouldn't be good enough for anyone else. Even Jeremy had kept his visits infrequent, just enough to run over marketing plans with Dad, who had never been keen on using the computer or the phone, but had preferred to see everything on paper.

Although it was still a couple of weeks before the season would hit full swing, a few packers were at the far end of the shed, each seated behind their table as they sorted and graded the strawberries, dropping them into plastic tubs topped with Blue Flag stickers. The soundtrack of her youth was oddly comforting, with conversations pitched over the slightly off-tune radio, the banging of deliveries of trays of fresh-picked berries and beeping of the forklift as boxes of fruit for commercial sale were shifted into place.

Lucie sidestepped into Dad's office without making eye contact with anyone. Mum was right: she didn't know any-thing about the business, didn't even know the workers anymore.

She sank into Dad's chair, the scent of soil and berries and machine oil still strong, even after weeks of emptiness. Dad's smell. Her eyes closed and she imagined him there. Not so much as he had been in the last few years she was home, but before that. When he had plenty of time for her, when he'd lift her into his lap so she could draw on the blotter that covered half the desk, where he laboriously scrawled his figures, trying to make the maths work.

She shifted aside the piles of invoices and statements: sure enough, there was the blotter. Dad's handwriting wriggled across it, hieroglyphics squiggled in every direction, as though he'd moved around restlessly, longing to get outdoors while confined to the desk he loathed. Lucie traced a finger over the writing, a lump rising in her throat.

A coffee mug sat on the scratched wooden top, and she pulled it towards her. A forest bloomed in the bottom, and she gave a sad chuckle: Dad would have said the mould proved that coffee was healthy, a vital, living substance. Gingerly, she tugged open the top desk drawer: no bottle of whiskey. She opened the others. No alcohol of any kind. Perhaps, with the appointment of an accountant, Dad's stress had eased?

Not that it had ultimately done him any good.

She pressed the carnelian pendant against her chest as she surveyed the last markers of Dad's life. The warmth of the deep orange crystal chased away grief, but was also supposed to vibrate on a frequency that connected with the spirit world. Now, emotionally closer to Dad than she had been in years, she was surprised to find the discovery that

he hadn't needed her brought an odd mix of both disappointment and relief.

Still plugged into the charging cord that snaked across
the desk, the edge of the mobile phone Dad refused to
carry peeked from beneath a stack of *AgJournals*. Dad
rarely made calls, saying it was too hard to hear on the
phone. But he had mastered texting. Would his last texts
to her—from more than four years ago—look different
on his screen? Perhaps they would seem less prosaic, more
meaningful than the 'don't forget to check the tyre pressure'
messages that were the only memories in her phone. She
keyed in her name with one hand as she reached to pull the
nearest stack of sealed envelopes towards her. Despite her
belief that only Mum used snail-mail, it seemed popular
in the business world—and whoever the accountant was,
he certainly hadn't been checking in regularly at the office.

The messages scrolled up.

Screen after screen of lime squares, each with a red
exclamation mark and 'Not Delivered' printed below it.

Years' worth of messages she had never received.

Heart pounding erratically, she frantically scrolled back
until the screen would go no further, then clutched the
phone in both hands. Her lips moved soundlessly as she
read each message.

> Hey Luce, just checking in. Give me a call sometime.
> Love, Dad

> Mum said I missed your call again today. Can you
> ring after eight tonight? Love, Dad

Thought you'd like to know, I picked up a chough
fledgling today. Had to get a ladder up to the big gum
to put him back in the nest, the entire family were
going crazy. Love, Dad

Hi Lucie, I put the crystal you sent next to my side of
the bed. Reckon Mum will hope it helps with snoring
more than curing insomnia.

I was going to get a new phone today as this one's
glitching on your number. But Mum said it's just
an update problem or something techy and that
messages will still go through, so I'll stick with
texting. Maybe you could try ringing if you get a
chance, though. Love, Dad

Hi Lucie. Had the first strawberry of the season
today. They're coming in early, looks like being a
good one. Just thought you'd like to know, in case
you're heading home this Christmas. Love, Dad

Reaching Dad's last ever words to her, Lucie's tears came
hard and fast, great gasps of sorrow that stole her breath
and crushed her lungs. And she didn't give a damn that the
workers in the packing shed could hear. Dad's desertion
had existed only in her imagination and Mum's creation.
There wasn't a single word of rebuke or disappointment,
only ever concern. And love. He'd even tried ringing her,
despite his dislike of talking on the phone. And, though
he had rarely spoken the words, every message was signed
the same, making sure she would know: *Love, Dad.* She
clutched the device to her chest, holding Dad close. Eyes
shut, she finally allowed herself to remember . . . everything.

No censoring. All the memories, good and bad, that made a life. Dad's life.

As the tears gradually slowed and she managed to catch her breath, she clicked the information icon alongside her name, greedily hoping to find just one more hidden message. She was about to flick off the screen when something caught her eye. The number wasn't quite right, but it took her a second to realise why: the final three digits should be 713, but Dad had them as 731. He must have inadvertently changed the details; he'd never been much good with the phone, they liked him about as much as he liked them.

And such a tiny, innocent mistake had robbed them of the years.

She sucked in a ragged, aching breath and set the phone aside. Maybe by working through the messages on the answering machine she would find another connection to Dad. At the very least, she would be able to replay his recorded message, hear his voice one more time.

Pulling a notepad closer, she pressed the button alongside the steadily blinking red light.

Ten minutes later, the notepad forgotten, she stared in disbelief at the machine. 'What the hell, Mum?' she murmured. She toggled the machine back to the message she needed—one of six—then used Dad's phone to make a call. Then she sat staring at the hessian room divider as the familiar noises of the packing shed surrounded her.

Eventually, she shook her head, tidied the paperwork she hadn't made a start on and stood. Hesitating for a moment, Lucie stared at the desk. With a sweep of her arm, she shifted all the correspondence to one side, then tore the top sheet from the blotter, folded it small and tucked it in her jeans pocket.

Then she strode back to the farmhouse.

'Mum. we need to talk,' Lucie said as she pushed open the wire mesh gate into the back garden.

'Look, Mummy,' Keeley rushed up, clutching a huge bunch of flowers. Flowers that Lucie would never have been permitted to pick. 'For Sally and Grandad.'

'They're very pretty,' she forced herself to smile. 'We're going to Jack's tonight, so you can give them to Sally then. How about you take Dash and play chasey on the lawn? He needs to be tired out so that he's well behaved later on.' Not just Dash, either.

She turned to her mother. 'There were half-a-dozen messages from the solicitor on the machine. You inferred you had the probate stuff all worked out, that you changed your mind about needing my help on it, but the solicitor said he hasn't even been able to go to court to apply for a grant of probate because he's still waiting on an affidavit of assets and liabilities.'

'You could leave Keeley and the dog here,' her mother said, as though she hadn't spoken. 'It's not healthy for her to get attached to Jackson. You'll be going back to Geoff soon.'

'Geoff and I are just friends. Housemates. I've told you that before.'

'You also said you were only speaking with Jeremy for help with your studies,' Mum shot back. Then, oddly, her countenance seemed to relax. 'If Geoff means nothing, there's no need for you to go back to Melbourne.'

'I didn't say he means nothing,' Lucie frowned, trying to work out her mother's angle. 'The solicitor, Mum? He said there's no distribution of the will until we get a grant of probate. And there's no grant of probate without the assets register. We're right back at square one: it will take weeks to get a grant. Weeks from when you actually provide this documentation, that is.'

Her mother stripped ferny leaves from a bunch of blue and pink love-in-a-mist. 'I'm aware.'

'Aware? The solicitor said you're not even answering his calls.'

Her mother stared off across the lawn, where Dash and Keeley were rolling on the grass. 'I've just had that mowed. You'll have to give me Keeley's dress; I'll use Napisan to get the stains out.' Her oddly toneless voice didn't alter as she continued. 'Once the documents are lodged, probate will be granted and I'll be able to sell.'

'You literally told me only an hour ago that's your plan.' Lucie fought to keep her own tone even as frustration seethed through her.

'And you'll go back to Melbourne.'

'So?' Mum was being strange: distant, but not in her usual cold fashion, and concern prickled through Lucie. 'You said you're going overseas—even though you couldn't visit us in Melbourne because it was too far to drive and you don't like flying.' She winced, hating herself for clinging to the old hurts. 'Anyway, you'll be away, so it doesn't matter where I am.'

Mum sighed. 'I'm not going anywhere. Travelling is just an old dream. I have far too much to do here.'

'If you sell, there won't be a "here".'

Her mother's gaze roamed the garden, and she blinked repeatedly, as though trying to make sense of Lucie's words. 'No. But I still have the CWA, and the library committee. And we're considering creating a community garden next to the school. I must organise a new book club, too. I don't understand why no one can commit anymore: so rarely does anyone read the book I've selected, we're unable to have a proper discussion about it. And then they just stop coming altogether.'

Lucie had a fair idea why everyone bailed on the clubs Mum was in. 'You plan to sell the farm but stay in Chesterton?'

'Where else would I go?' Mum said. 'I gave up all my dreams to be with your father, to build this life. But what is it now?'

'Mum,' Lucie whispered, appalled at the sudden emptiness in her mother's tone, 'I thought you wanted to be alone? You made it sound as though you'd been waiting for the opportunity to move on.'

Tears glistened in her mother's blue eyes. 'I said I could carry on with my life, endure because I'd spent so long armouring myself against losing either of you. But apparently there's a vast difference between being *able* to be alone and *wanting* to be alone. I wish I'd ignored your father and kept my nursing registration up to date. At least

I'd have options now. That's why you had to have a quali-fication, Lucie: you mustn't let your life revolve around Keeley and Geoff.'

Lucie reached instinctively for her mother's arm. Mum had lied to her and sent her off to live alone: why should Lucie care about her loneliness?

But she did.

'Anyway,' Mum straightened her back, tone suddenly brisk, 'that's a problem for another day.' She shook off Lucie's hand and clapped her own sharply. 'Keeley, don't let Dash wee on the lawn, it will turn yellow. Take him over to the dirt near the back gate.'

35
Lucie

'Where Sally?' Keeley waved a fistful of wilting flowers at the dog bed that had appeared in Jack's kitchen.

Lucie shot Jack an apologetic glance. 'Sorry, she doesn't really understand,' she said quietly. She raised her voice. 'Sally isn't here anymore, remember?'

'But Dash wants to play,' Keeley pouted, clutching Purple Ted to her chest.

Jack gestured towards the wool-filled hessian sack Dash was sniffing. 'Couldn't bring myself to throw it out just yet. Moving it from the bedroom was bad enough.'

'Perhaps leave it here for when Dash visits?' Lucie suggested as the dachshund clambered up and curled himself in a tight ball.

Jack caught and held her gaze. 'As long as he visits often enough to make it worth me tripping over the bed on my way to the kettle each morning.'

Lucie's heart skipped like butterflies cartwheeling in the sun. 'I'm pretty sure the kitchen's big enough for you to manoeuvre around.' The River Gum Cottage was smaller than her rental in Settlers Bridge. Cosier. She had only seen the back room—which she noticed Jack had emptied of a mountain of dirty washing—the kitchen and the lounge directly across the hall, but the house had a homely, well-used, well-loved feel. Perhaps that was simply because she associated it with Jack. He exuded a sense of stability and earthiness, of being grounded.

And he made her heart soar as though she was anything but grounded.

Jack held the kettle up. 'Are you going to show me how to make that tea?'

'Do we have time?'

'Sure. It only takes ten minutes to get to Ma's. I know,' he shot her a shamefaced grin, 'ten minutes. You'd think I could find time to help them out more, right?' He leaned back against the laminate countertop, crossing his legs at the ankle. 'I've got to warn you again, it's going to be a tough sell to get Ma to let anyone in the house.'

'That's not unusual. But we'll see how we go.'

Jack looked dubious, and she patted his arm. Even though she totally didn't need to touch him.

He caught her hand, pressing it against his forearm. 'I'm glad you came, Lucie.'

She assessed him for a long moment, weighing up the risk of telling the truth. 'I didn't like thinking of you here alone.'

Jack's hand slid up to graze her shoulder, exposed by the broderie anglaise peasant top she wore with faded blue jeans. 'Didn't like thinking of me? A guy could take that to heart.'

'I'm pretty sure you know that's not what I meant.' She could swear electricity vibrated through his light touch, the air tight, crackling, ready to ignite.

'I know what I hope you meant,' he murmured, straightening so that he moved closer. The clean smell of sandalwood enveloped her.

Keeley said something loud but indistinguishable, and Lucie startled. Her daughter was curled on the dog bed with Dash, her thumb in her mouth and eyes closed. Lucie sighed. 'I'm sorry. She had a pretty full-on day with my mother.'

Jack stepped away from her, and she tried not to let her disappointment show as he left the room. He returned carrying a rug, which he placed lightly over Keeley and Dash. 'Let the poor kid have a nap. Dinnertime's fluid at Ma's, anyway. And it sounds like maybe you could do with a bit of a debrief.'

Lucie's throat closed. Here she was, wondering how to bring up the subject of Jack's home being sold from under him, yet his concern was for her?

'I'll put the kettle on,' he said. 'Take a seat. You can direct me from there.'

'Don't suppose there's any chance you have a teapot?' She sank into the chair.

Jack ferreted in a high cupboard and produced a brown ceramic teapot. He caught her look of surprise and chuckled 'Can't say I've ever used it, but Ma furnished the house from garage sales. I've more stuff in these cupboards than I'll ever know how to use.'

'Well, I'm sure you'll get the knack of this one. Just put a big spoonful of the herbs in the pot and cover with boiling water. Leave it to steep for a few minutes, like regular black tea.'

'Two-for-one lesson, huh?' Jack clicked his tongue. 'Now I know how to make black tea and this.' Haloed by the late afternoon sun streaming through the dusty kitchen window beneath daggy, sunflower-printed cafe curtains, he slid two mugs and the teapot onto the table. The rickety chair creaked as he dropped onto it, his knees brushing hers beneath the table. 'So, spill. What happened at your mum's?'

She lifted one shoulder. There was a fair chance she was going to cry again if she relived the tangled, emotional day. 'I told you, she plans to sell up.'

He nodded but stayed silent. Technique that would have impressed Geoff, she thought wryly.

'And it seems she's not so keen on travelling overseas after all.'

'Quick turnaround,' he remarked dryly.

'Yeah. Also, for all she tells me that I needed to learn to be able to be alone,' she rolled her eyes, 'it seems she's not so keen on it herself. She was . . . surprisingly human. I didn't honestly think she had emotions.'

'That's pretty harsh.'

'And past tense. It's just when I was really young, I always thought Dad and I were a team, that Mum was the awkward third. But apparently I was wrong about a whole lot of stuff.' It was hard to admit how very wrong she'd been. She pressed her fingertips into her eye sockets, trying to relieve the tension. 'I spent years resenting Dad for forcing me to study business instead of following my passion, but it turns out that was all Mum. Ironically, it's the one thing I never blamed her for.'

She spun the pot twice clockwise and once anti-clockwise, then poured the tea. Hands wrapped around her mug, she stared down into the steaming water. 'Thing is, knowing it wasn't Dad putting the pressure on should make me happy, because maybe it means that he wanted me to follow my own dreams. Instead, it just makes me think of how we wasted so much time because we didn't communicate.'

Jack's hands covered hers around the mug. 'Your dad might have chosen not to talk much, Lucie—trust me, I know what that's like.' An ironic smile lifted one corner of his mouth. 'But he had a different way of communicating. He had no reason to put money into a strawberry farm that was bound to fail, except that he wanted to create something that was a blend of the both of you.' He pointed towards the window. 'Strawberries for him, for your heritage. But sustainable practices for you, because he knew that was what you cared about.' His thumb brushed over her knuckles. 'He loved you. Don't ever doubt that.'

Lucie sucked in a shuddering breath. How was it that Jack viewed life with such clarity, a sense of purpose that gave him direction and motivation? While she was qualified in one area and passionate about another, she was employed in a third. Yet Jack . . . Jack channelled his enthusiasm to create the life he wanted.

She nodded. 'I found text messages from him. Messages I didn't get. And I can't decide whether I'd rather I had never seen them, because although it hurt thinking he didn't care, maybe it hurts even more knowing that he did.'

'Mummy, Dash needs wee,' Keeley said sleepily.

Jack's hand tightened on hers, as though he'd say something, but Lucie reluctantly stood. 'Okay, baby, I'm coming,' she called. 'Code,' she explained to Jack. 'We'll just use your bathroom, if that's okay.'

'What's mine is yours,' he said with a smile that seemed to invite her to read into the words well beyond the facts of the property ownership.

'I'll take advantage of that generosity,' she said, meeting his gaze. Then she hid her blush by hurrying Keeley to the bathroom.

∾

'Lucie, did you want some of this . . . what is it, Samantha?' Jack's grandmother called across the farmhouse kitchen to where Jack's sister stood at the sink.

'Lucie's the one who brought it, Ma,' Sam said.

'Oh yes, of course. I'm so used to you bringing all the desserts,' Evie replied. 'Lucie, what did you say it is?'

'Avocado lime tart,' Lucie replied. Jack's invitation had caught her short, so when Mum insisted on producing the standard two plain biscuits for afternoon tea, Lucie had liberated the unwanted tart to bring along. And tightly crossed her fingers it would be acceptable.

'Well, it's certainly interesting.' Evie cut another small slice and peered closely at it. 'Can't quite see it ever taking off at the CWA, but I like it. What do you think, Paul?'

'I think load me up with some more, whack some cream on top, and I'll give you my verdict,' Jack's grandfather said, rubbing his belly. 'Nothing like a woman who can cook, is there, Jack?'

'Ouch,' said Samantha. 'Pops is having a go at me because I buy in all the produce for the cafe,' she explained. 'Another failing in my wifely resume.'

'I meant no such thing, Samantha, and I'll thank you not to go putting words in my mouth,' Paul grumbled. 'You know I can't understand why you don't do your own baking; you were always a beaut little cook. But you do a fine job of operating a business and running after us, so don't you go thinking we don't appreciate it.'

'Okay, Pops,' Sam said, swivelling from the sink to drop a kiss on his bald head. 'I know. I was just being pissy at Grant. Ignore me.'

'Speaking of jobs,' Jack slid in smoothly, 'Lucie has an interesting one.'

Lucie cringed a little at having the attention switched back to her.

'Lynn at the IGA is telling anyone who will listen about all these creams and potions of yours,' Evie said. 'I never thought we'd have a naturist in Settlers Bridge.'

'Natural therapist,' she corrected.

'Shame,' Jack murmured with a grin, and heat sparkled through her like glitter.

His sister pointed a finger at him in a 'gotcha' motion. 'Heard that.'

'What's that all about?' Paul's hearing aid emitted a high-pitched squeal as he fiddled with it. 'Talk slower, you lot, I darn well missed it again.'

'Jack said he'd like to see Lucie n-u-d-e,' Sam said clearly, making huge eyes at Keeley, who was far more interested in her tart than the conversation.

'Jeez, Sam, take it easy,' Jack groaned.

Paul tilted his head to one side, assessing Lucie from below bushy eyebrows. He gave a shrug. 'Entirely understandable.'

'Okay,' she said, fanning her face with one hand, 'I'm a fully-dressed natural health therapist, folks, not a naturist.'

'In any case,' Jack said, flashing her a grimace of apology, 'that wasn't the job I was talking about. Lucie is also a home care assessment manager. You know those papers you got after Pops' stroke?'

'Government nosiness,' Evie said, in a reaction Lucie had heard many times. 'Pointless form-filling, as though I have time for that.'

'Hear me out,' Jack said. 'Lucie can cut to the chase and tell you what the forms mean. More importantly, she can arrange help for you.'

'I've told you, I'm not having strangers in my house, Jackson.'

Lucie knew the anger in Evie's tone came from fear, as reaching the point where she and her husband needed help more clearly defined their mortality.

'Ma,' Sam said, 'I know you want me to wash the windows before Christmas, like usual, but the cafe's flat out now I've got the zoo tour buses coming through. Perhaps Lucie could arrange for us to get just the outsides done, that way there'd be no strangers *in* the house.'

'You know how I feel about a job half done,' Evie snapped. 'If we have the outside washed, we have the inside done, so we can at least enjoy one day of clean glass before the dust storms come through.'

'I'm sure Lucie can organise that,' Sam said with a wink at her.

'We'll see,' Evie muttered.

'We can chat about it another time,' Lucie offered, knowing better than to force the issue.

'Played like a fiddle,' Jack said quietly to his sister. He raised his voice, 'Anyway, we're off.'

'But you haven't had a cup of tea,' Evie reproached.

'It's getting late for the little one.' Jack nodded towards Keeley. 'And I want to see Lucie into Settlers before I head home.'

'Niiice,' Sam drawled. 'You've never bothered seeing me home. Jack's bringing you to the fireworks on the weekend, Lucie?'

'I'm not twelve, I can organise my own social life,' Jack grumbled at his sister. 'Despite what half of Lynn's customers seem to think.'

'Can you though, Jack?' Paul put in. 'I mean, have you asked her?'

Jack pushed to his feet. 'Lucie, I was going to ask you later.' He shot an exasperated look around the table and she felt a little sorry for him. But at the same time, she was envious of his obviously close-knit family. 'But I'll put you on the spot now. Would you and Keeley like to come to the fireworks on Saturday?'

She chuckled. 'With all this input, I'm scared to say no.'

'I hope that's not your only reason for agreeing,' Jack murmured, covered by the noise of scraping chairs as the others got up.

Lucie met his gaze. 'It isn't.' Fireworks by the river on a balmy spring evening sounded impossibly romantic.

'I'll take care of the picnic,' Sam said, starting to pack the leftovers into the fridge. 'And I'll bring Ma and Pops. Jack's car's gonna be full,' she teased.

'Jack's car will be lucky to make it,' Ma added.

'The Holden gets everywhere she needs to be,' Jack said. 'Just loudly. And slowly.'

'Keeley's in a booster seat, so I need to take my car,' Lucie said. 'How about I meet you all there?' She wasn't entirely sure how what had momentarily sounded like a date had turned into a family outing. Yet being so easily absorbed into the group felt . . . comforting. 'Actually,' she said impulsively, 'would you mind if I invite my mum along? She could probably do with a change of scenery.'

She could kick herself. Mum made no effort to fit in and would be an embarrassment. But she couldn't erase from her mind the haunting loneliness in her mother's words.

In any case, Mum was guaranteed to reject the offer with an air of supercilious astonishment at having been invited to such an event.

36
Lucie

Her mother didn't refuse the invitation.

In fact, she responded with, 'Make sure you take a jacket for Keeley, it can get chilly down by the river at night.' And then she turned up carrying a huge wicker picnic basket.

Keeley squealed with delight, running into the front garden to greet her grandmother. 'Nanna, come see my fishes.'

'Have they changed since last time I saw them?' Mum asked, but she allowed Keeley to take her hand and pull her towards the side passage.

'I think they got biggerer,' Keeley said.

Feeling like something of an outsider, Lucie left the picnic basket near the front door and tagged along behind her daughter and mother.

'Shall we go in one car?' Mum said after making the appropriate interested noises over the goldfish.

It was only five minutes' drive to the area slightly south of the bridge that Jack had pointed out. She could tolerate Mum in close confines for that long. 'Sure.'

'You're not taking Dash, are you?' Mum asked.

Lucie sighed. Maybe five minutes was five minutes too long. 'I can't leave him home alone.' If the house was too large for her, it would seem enormous to the puppy.

'Do you have a tight-fitting jacket for him, then?'

'It's not that cold.' What was with Mum's obsession with extra clothing?

'It might help if he gets scared of the fireworks,' Mum said.

Guilt swept through Lucie. 'Oh. I hadn't even thought of that. Perhaps we'd best not go.'

'In my experience,' Mum said, 'puppies aren't as worried by fireworks as older dogs.'

'I don't recall having a puppy we took to fireworks,' Lucie said tightly. As Chesterton didn't run stock, they'd never needed a dog, and Mum had refused her childhood pleas.

'The dogs your grandparents had at the Siding got used to fireworks,' Mum said. 'Let's try Dash out. I can always bring him home early if he gets upset.'

'Okay,' Lucie said warily.

'If it runs too late, you may want me to bring Keeley home, anyway. I assume she has a regular bedtime. Routine is important,' Mum said in more typical style, edging unspoken judgment into her conversation.

'That won't be necessary,' Lucie started stiffly.

'Though I don't suppose the odd break in routine is a problem,' Mum continued as Keeley tugged on her hand, jumping up and down excitedly. 'According to the local Facebook page, the whole town is going.'

'Jack coming but not Sally. Cos Sally is dead,' Keeley said, pulling a mournful face. Then, with the resilience of childhood, she smiled brightly. 'But I telled Jack to bring Mr Unicorn in his poo, because Mr Unicorn wants to see fireworks.'

Lucie cringed, but Mum gave a snort of laughter. 'I shall be very interested to meet Mr Unicorn, then. Though I do hope he doesn't invite me into his house.'

'You silly, Nanna,' Keeley giggled. 'You don't fits in his house.'

'Well, that solves that problem. Are we ready to go? I read there's also a bouncy castle and some entertainment for the little ones, so perhaps we'd best make tracks.'

Lucie had intended to go late rather than wander around waiting for Jack and his family to arrive. But it was pointless arguing with her mother. 'Sure,' she muttered. 'Let me just go check my hair.' She needed to take a few deep breaths in private before she'd be ready.

'Your hair looks fine,' Mum said. 'Though those colours need redoing. I'll book you in with Leanne, she's quite good. Come on, Keeley, let's get you and Dash buckled in. Don't forget the jackets, Lucie.'

Lucie stared, her hand reflexively going to where the choppy chunks of colour she thought would annoy her mother hid among her natural chestnut. She needed to change her necklace to something that would help her process her mother's rapidly changing moods.

Though it only took minutes to reach the riverside grounds, parking required slightly longer. With the fences delineated by orange bunting that barely stirred in the balmy evening air, the short grass was almost obscured by vehicles already pulled up in neat ranks. Yellow-overalled members of the Country Fire Service directed Lucie to a vacant spot, and Mum dug in her purse and reached across Lucie to drop coins in their donation tin. 'I've always got time for the CFS,' she said. 'I recall a couple of the boys from a unit out here got in terrible strife last year. I wonder whatever happened to them?'

'No idea,' Lucie said absently, then connected the dots. 'Though the local doctor, Taylor, had me make burn cream for someone. I wonder if that's related?' Suddenly nervous, she found it hard to concentrate on her mother's meanderings. She fidgeted with the sweetheart neckline of her floral boho dress.

'You look lovely,' Mum said. 'Do stop fussing.'

The familiarity of Mum's one-two technique was almost comforting. Lucie threw a rug from the back of the RAV4 over her arm and reached to take the heavy picnic basket from Mum. 'Here, let me. Keeley, hold Nanna's hand. Really tight.' Mindful of their last outing, she added, 'And, Mum, can you take Dash's lead, please?'

They headed across the paddock, towards the sound of carnival music playing from a row of six small tents and a couple of amusement park trailers placed parallel to the river.

'I'm sure there are calories in that breeze,' Mum said as the sweet fragrance of fairy floss, hot donuts and toffee apples wafted over them.

'I'm hungry,' Keeley said as they neared the Lions barbecue tent, where a noisy, laughing crowd milled about, clutching napkins overloaded with white bread, sausages and onions dripping tomato sauce.

'I'll get you a sausage,' Mum offered, then glanced at Lucie. 'If it's okay with your mummy.' She lifted one shoulder. 'They won't have anything organic, but they'll be good country sausages.'

Lucie nodded. 'Go ahead. We have to live dangerously sometime.' The smell was making her stomach rumble, too, but she wasn't about to risk eating anything that might contain garlic. Because what if . . . ? Though, even if Jack considered tonight a date, they had an entire entourage escorting them.

'Lucie!' Roni trudged towards her, the twins in tow. She huffed as she plopped her esky on the grass. 'Matt's with the CFS crew—you probably saw him on the way in? Personally, I think the guys roster this stuff so they don't have to do the setting-up-camp bit. I should be like Taylor and join the CFS myself. Hours in the day, though,' she rolled her eyes. 'Never enough, right?'

Lucie angled her head to include her mother in the conversation. 'Roni, this is my mum, Monica.'

'Twins?' Mum asked, and Lucie's insides shrivelled. There would be a comment about them not getting adequate attention, or something similar.

Roni nodded. 'Three-year-old terrors.'

'I always loved the idea of having twins,' Mum said. 'Wasn't to be, though.'

Lucie stared. She had always assumed herself an only child by choice.

'I'm going to pick a spot, dump our gear, and then I've made a bouncy castle promise,' Roni said. 'Is Keeley allowed to come on?'

'Sure,' Lucie said. 'Though I guess we'd better take turns minding our stuff.'

Roni laughed. 'Wow, I thought I was the token city girl around here! It'll be fine—in five years, I've never known anything to go missing at an event.'

The comment took Lucie straight back to the security of her youth, a feeling of safety and community she'd lost in Melbourne.

Roni guided them past the row of tents towards a lawned area studded with enormous river redgums that had to be hundreds of years old. A barge bobbed gently on the river, a good distance from the Meccano-like structure of the rust-coloured bridge.

'Look, Keeley,' Mum said, pointing towards the open-fronted tents they passed. 'The laughing clowns. They were always your mum's favourite. Remember, Lucie?'

Nostalgia tickled the edge of Lucie's mind. 'The purple bear Dash and Keeley carry everywhere? I won that on the clowns when I went to the Royal Adelaide Show with Dad.' She indicated the row of heads turning in unison, their mouths gaping, waiting to be fed ping-pong balls.

'Perhaps Keeley can have a turn.' Mum smiled at her granddaughter, who skipped excitedly alongside her. 'And maybe you'll win something you can give to your mummy?'

Lucie sighed. It was no good, she was never going to understand her mother. She was far more complex, more layered, than Lucie had ever suspected.

As they crossed the lawn dotted with cheerful groups, colourful picnic rugs and loaded eskies, Lucie's excitement mounted. She hadn't seen Jack since Monday, and the five days since seemed an eternity. The stress of preparing the assets and liabilities register—which had been complicated by Mum deciding to randomly send documents to the solicitor—hadn't helped the time pass.

'This will do,' Roni said, piling her belongings on the red blossom carpet beneath a couple of huge gums.

Mum dug around in her knock-off Gucci. 'I promised Keeley a sausage. Would your twins like one, Roni?'

'That's lovely of you, Monica,' Roni said. 'But the kids are generally vegetarian, so we tend to steer away from sausages. Though they smell so good, I'm beginning to doubt my choices right now.'

Lucie cringed in anticipation of the lecture about food groups, the correct way to raise kids, and how ridiculous the current generation were with their soy lattes and alfalfa and chia seed.

'How about a toffee apple then? Or fairy floss?' Mum said, pulling out her purse.

'I'm sure they will *politely*,' Roni gave her kids a stern look, 'appreciate anything you offer them, thank you, Monica.'

As Mum walked away to investigate what was available, Roni added, 'Your mum seems really nice.'

'Today,' Lucie agreed warily.

'You're lucky to have her handy. Keeley obviously adores her.'

'Actually, Keeley barely knows her.' Lucie pulled her daughter onto her knees, pressing a kiss into her hair. 'But, yeah, they seem to get on like a house on fire.' She didn't care to untangle whether she was envious Keeley seemed to have found the relationship she had lost, or sad because she had to share her daughter.

Roni looked wistful. 'I have to admit, if I didn't have Tracey helping me out, I'd be totally jealous. It must be nice to have a mum who's into your kid.'

Lucie started unpacking the picnic basket, with the twins, Keeley and Dash hanging interestedly over it. 'Your mum's not nearby?'

Roni shook her head as Monica returned with bags of pink and blue spun sugar. 'Only when it suits her. She's a local. I'm the ring-in. If you hang around a couple more weeks, you're bound to hear all about it.'

'Really? Jack didn't—' She broke off because, as though the mention of his name had summoned him, Jack strode towards them.

And Geoff was right: he was every bit Thor.

The last rays of the sun, sinking behind the Mount Lofty Ranges, burnished the hair brushing the broad shoulders of the denim shirt he wore tucked into cream moleskins. He swept the Akubra from his head, his gaze locked to hers.

'Evening all,' he said without glancing around. 'You look amazing,' he added directly to Lucie.

'I'm sure we all do,' Roni teased. 'But on that note, I'm going to make myself and my crew scarce. Toffee apples and bouncy castle, here we come. Are you coming, Monica?'

Lucie's mother looked oddly hesitant, given her enthusiasm to treat the children only minutes earlier, but she gave a curt nod. 'Come on, Keeley. Leave the fairy floss and Dash here, give Mummy a kiss and we'll go and explore.'

Lucie wrapped her arms around Keeley, apparently holding her a little too long, as Mum tutted impatiently, 'She'll be fine. You can see us right there.' She gestured towards the row of tents only a few hundred metres away. 'And we can see you,' she added ominously.

'Be good,' Lucie cautioned Keeley, tying Dash's lead around the esky handle. Her daughter stomped off importantly in her wellingtons, one hand firmly clutched in her grandmother's, the other holding Purple Ted.

Lucie blew out a long breath.

Jack offered a hand to pull her to her feet. 'I mean it. You always look great, but tonight,' he shook his head, 'stunning.'

His compliment thrilled her. As did the touch of his warm hand, which he made no move to take from hers. 'Wow, you really are a smooth talker,' she laughed.

He grunted, though the side of his mouth curved up. 'Can't say I've ever been called that before.'

She tentatively touched her finger to the bow of his lips, completely aware of the intimacy of the move. 'You've always had a stammer?' His face hardened and she dropped her hand, resting it on his chest.

'No. Started when I was about six.' Jack glanced over the river as a kookaburra's chuckle echoed along the far bank, and she could feel his deep inhale, as though he was steeling himself. 'Caught my old man laying into my mum. So it's some sort of m-messed up psychological thing, I suppose. All I know is, it drove the bastard so nuts every time I stammered, he'd have to b-belt me. I guess it reminded him of his guilt.'

'He hit your mum?' Lucie gasped. 'And you?'

'Guy was a total waste of space,' Jack muttered. 'I don't want to talk about him. I want to talk about—' He broke off with a groan as Sam hollered from only a few metres away.

She arrived in a flurry, shooting an apologetic grin at Lucie. 'Sorry,' she whispered, sotto voce, 'but you guys were standing awfully close and Ma and Pops are coming along right behind me.'

Lucie dropped her hand but Jack slid his palm into the small of her back, drawing her closer to his side. 'As right behind you as a pair of octogenarians can be,' he said. 'Where's Grant?'

'Coming later . . . supposedly,' Sam said, the levity falling from her expression.

'Sam, what's going on with you guys?' Jack said. 'Is everything cool?'

'About as cool as Antarctica,' his sister mumbled. 'Let it go, Jack. Not tonight.'

Holding hands and each carrying a walking stick— although Paul wielded his like a sword, as though determined to prove he didn't need it—Jack's grandparents drew closer.

'What a lovely night for it,' Evie beamed as Sam spread their rugs on the ground, creating a large room anchored by the baskets and eskies.

Though reluctant to move away from Jack's hand, Lucie knelt to help lay out the new influx of Tupperware containers. 'I can guarantee Keeley isn't going to eat what I brought when she sees all this.' She indicated the tubs of sausage rolls, lamingtons, jam drops and quiches.

'Do you want us to put it away so she doesn't see?' Sam asked, her hand pausing on a container.

'Oh no! Mum's already given her fairy floss, and right now, she's off being stuffed with sausages and white bread. Any of this would be healthier.' She knew exactly where Keeley was, because she couldn't stop herself from looking over to check every few minutes.

'What did you bring?' Sam looked interestedly at Lucie's containers. 'I snuck the rest of your avocado tart home from Ma's. I might be a convert.'

'Raw coffee crème mousse with a chocolate pecan crust,' Lucie said. 'And an Oreo pie.'

Sam lifted her eyebrows at the layered chocolate creation. 'I thought you were into healthy stuff?'

Lucie grinned. 'The crust is nuts and dates, the cream is coconut and cashews, and the icing is avocado and cacao. But I probably shouldn't have told you that until you tasted it.'

'I'm still game,' Jack said. 'I'll try anything you put in front of me.'

'Yeah, right,' Sam chuckled. 'We got that.'

'Samantha,' Evie called sharply. 'Where's the chair for Pops?' Despite the order, it was Evie who leaned more heavily on her cane. Paul was brandishing his in animated conversation with a group of men.

'In the ute. I'll go grab them.' Jack dropped to his haunches on the pretext of handing Lucie a tub from Roni's stash. 'Think you can survive for five minutes?'

She laughed lightly. 'I'm tougher than I look.' Their faces were so close her heart fluttered wildly at the touch of his breath on her cheek.

He paused for a long moment. 'Okay. Better be going, then.'

'This week would be good, Jack,' Sam called.

Jack pushed back to his feet, scowling at his sister.

Samantha laughed it off and, as Jack strode away, Lucie inhaled deeply, preparing for the barrage of questions she could feel brewing in both Sam and Evie.

37
Jack

Jack practically ran to the ute and back. Not that Lucie
wasn't fine with his family, but Sam was in an odd mood.
Had been for weeks now. Though she usually reserved it
for family, she could turn bitchy when she wanted, and he
didn't want to leave Lucie dealing with that.

As he dumped the chairs on the picnic rug, Keeley
raced up, flinging her arms around Lucie's neck and nearly
knocking her from her knees. 'Mummy!' she squealed 'Look
what I gotted! I fed the clowns and I won like you did
when you was little.'

'Were little,' Lucie corrected, as though the lesson had
any chance of sinking in through the loud excitement. Lucie
unpeeled Keeley from her neck and turned to look at the
bright pink blob she held. 'Wow, what a gorgeous . . .' She sent
a questioning look at her mother, who had followed Keeley.

'Goat,' Monica supplied firmly.

Lucie lifted a doubtful eyebrow. 'Goat,' she agreed.

'Like Pamela, right, Mummy?' She turned to include everyone. 'Jack gets milk from Pamela for me to drink.' She held the toy above her head, tipping her face back as though she was drinking milk from it.

Roni's twins also raced up, both holding similar toys, and immediately imitated Keeley. Roni brought up the rear. 'Hello, hello,' she said, beaming at them all. 'Where's Grant?'

'No doubt saving the economy one beer at a time,' Sam said drily.

Roni squinted at Sam's arm. 'Ouch! What have you done there? That's a nice one.'

Sam pulled her sleeve back down to cover the bruise. 'I caught it on the stupid oven door.'

Jack's gut tensed. He'd heard that kind of excuse before. 'Sam—' he started.

She shot him her withering 'shut up' look.

Lucie reached to pull her beaded suede bag closer and rummaged in it. 'I have arnica in here somewhere. It'll take the bruise out,' she said. 'Keeley's at that age where she's always bumping herself.'

Sam took the tiny pot. 'Thanks.'

'I'll drop you off a bigger jar to keep in the fridge.' Lucie stood. 'Mum, I'm not sure you know everyone.' She gestured around the group. 'Roni, Sam, Jack—of course you know him.' She gave him a smile. 'And Evie and Paul—over there under the tree—are Jack and Sam's grandparents. My mum, Monica Tamberlani.'

Monica nodded pleasantly enough, though her presence made Jack wary. She moved over to talk to Ma, and he strained to hear the conversation over the kids squealing.

'—didn't realise Jackson had relatives still in the district,' Monica said.

He stiffened. Surely she wouldn't dredge up that old shit, not in front of his grandparents.

Ma waved Monica to a chair. 'Have a seat, love. Paul is fifth generation, so the kids have plenty of rellies around Settlers. And we practically raised Samantha and Jack.' The pride in her voice was unmistakable.

Jack clenched his fists. If Monica said anything to upset Ma, made any mention of—

'Come on, let's eat,' Ma said. 'I don't know what you all plan, but I want my hands free once it gets dark.' She raised her grey eyebrows towards Pops.

'Ma,' Sam groaned, 'when are you going to act your age?'

'Hopefully never,' Ma said. 'There's not a lot to be said in favour of growing older.'

'Except that it beats the alternative,' Pops added as he joined them. 'Anyway, what's on the menu?'

With the kids sprawled like puppies across the rugs, Jack sat close enough to Lucie that he could detect her faint fragrance of strawberries over the carnival smells. 'You also smell awesome,' he murmured.

She touched a hand to her throat. 'Thanks. I make the perfume, though I'd not done this one for years, and it still needs some time to mellow.' A shadow crossed her face and he wanted to caress her cheek, smooth away the sadness.

Keeley scrambled up and launched into his lap, wrapping her arms around his neck so she could stare into his eyes. She often did that, touching a finger to his lower eyelid, as though she was intrigued by the splash of blue across his dark iris. 'Did you bring Mr Unicorn?' she said in a loud whisper, like the bug was a secret.

'Sure did,' he said, reaching into his shirt pocket for the tin.

'I want to show Simon and Marian,' she confided as he prised the lid free. Instead of taking it to the twins, Keeley turned in his lap, using him as a chair as the other children crowded forward to look.

'Sorry,' Lucie mouthed, though her eyes sparkled as the solar lanterns hung in the gum trees came to life.

He wanted to kiss her. More than anything else at that precise moment, he wanted to kiss her.

And not just a peck on the cheek like she'd given him a week earlier.

Instead, Jack reached around Keeley to snag one of Ma's quiches. Stuffed it in his mouth, trying not to think about the state of the farm kitchen. If it hadn't killed him yet, it was unlikely to do so anytime soon.

Ma and Pops were talking with Monica, their chairs pulled close together, plates balanced on their knees. Lucie, Roni and Sam chatted, though Sam kept looking across to the parking paddock. No doubt waiting for Grant to show. The sullen sod was always late or a no-show, as though he didn't consider himself part of the community. Which he wasn't: he and Sam lived in Murray Bridge, where Grant had grown up and still worked. Yet Sam retained her roots in Settlers.

As giant sparklers burst into life along the riverbank, the children fell into awed silence. Although Roni's kids had been every year, he guessed twelve months was long enough for little kids to forget all kinds of things. Maybe even who their dad was: Lucie said she had nothing to do with Keeley's father, and he hoped like hell that was true. He didn't much like the idea of sharing either of them.

Monica scooped up the puppy, tucking him inside the light cardigan she wore, and Keeley scooted from his lap to her mother's, leaning back against Lucie as fountains of coloured sparks flamed into huge spires, reflected and multiplied on the still water.

As the first of the aerials shot up from the cannons on the barge near the bridge, Keeley pushed further back so she could follow the trajectory of the sparkling balls flung high into the sky before exploding into flowers. Lucie thrust a hand into the grass, awkwardly trying to counterbalance Keeley's position.

Jack stood, moved behind them, then sat again, stretching a leg either side of Lucie's. 'Lean on me,' he directed, wrapping one arm around both her and Keeley.

Lucie stiffened for a moment then melted against him, her gaze on the electric-coloured bursts over the river. 'Yes,' she whispered.

If he had a spare cent to his name, he'd donate it to the event fundraising committee, just so the ten-minute display could last all night. Hell, if he was going to lose his farm, just this one night, with Lucie's head tucked beneath his chin, her softness pressed against him, would be worth it.

Except he knew that was a stupid thought: he wanted far more than just this evening. If he had to build his dream over again, he wanted Lucie—and Keeley—to be a part of it.

As the fireworks reached a noisy, bright crescendo, Keeley leaped to her feet, clapping her hands. 'Mummy, did you see? Did you see the fireworks?'

'I did, baby—weren't they amazing?'

Keeley ploughed back into her mother's arms, and Lucie gave a soft 'oof' as her daughter landed knees first on her stomach. But she didn't move to extricate herself from his arms.

'We do clowns again now, Mummy?'

'Maybe a little later,' Lucie wheedled. 'How about you have something to eat first?'

'I had sausages with Nanna. They was yummy,' Keeley proclaimed. 'Wasn't they, Nanna? They was yummy and I ate it all, like you said.'

'They were indeed,' Monica said. 'And if you eat what your mummy tells you to, I'll take you to the clowns again. Perhaps Marian and Simon would like another turn on the bouncing castle, if you'd like to go on with them?'

'I'm sure they would,' Roni said, 'but at this rate I'll never dare bring them to the fireworks again. They're getting spoiled.'

'Then I'll just have to come each year,' Monica said, smiling a little rigidly, as though the movement didn't come naturally. 'Evie, why don't you come along with me? I could use someone to chat with while this lot burn off some energy.'

'Can you handle all three kids, Mum?' Lucie asked doubtfully, her hand stretching towards Keeley, who had abandoned her lap.

'Don't worry,' Roni said. 'Everyone will keep an eye on them. We're kind of into a "raised by the village" thing around here. But I'll go anyway. Hey, can Keeley swim?'

'Since she was tiny, but I wouldn't want to put the lessons to the test.' Lucie tilted her head towards the river.

'Once it warms up, bring her out to Justin's place. We have a regular barbie there, and the kids get first go at the pool. The adults generally need a bit more lubrication before they'll take the plunge. But it beats the muddy Murray.'

'I'll take you there,' Jack said into Lucie's hair. He'd promise to take her anywhere if it meant she would stay.

'Sounds like a plan,' Lucie agreed, as though she had no intention of leaving Settlers. 'Keeley, if you promise to eat some chickpea salad when you come back, then you can go with Nanna now. Leave Dash here, and hold Nanna's hand all the time, okay?'

'Nanna will come on jumping castle?' Keeley asked, staring at her hand, clearly trying to work out how to follow that particular instruction.

'No, I don't think—'

'Yes, Nanna will,' Monica said firmly. 'Nanna loves bouncy castles.'

Jack felt the disbelief stiffen Lucie's body. As Monica, Ma and Roni went off with three kids in tow, she shook her head. 'Can't say I saw that coming.'

'No?' he murmured. Lucie hadn't moved. She was still in his arms.

She relaxed against him, twisting slightly so she could look up. 'I'm pretty sure that's not my mother. But I'm one hundred percent down for the swap.'

'Well, I'm off to do some yarn-spinning,' his grandfather announced. Jack knew that meant he was going to disappear behind the stand of large gums to the south and knock back some port with his mates.

'And that leaves me floating around like an unwanted turd in a pool,' Sam said a little sulkily as Pops wandered off.

'As opposed to the wanted turd?' Jack asked.

'Whatever, smartarse,' Sam said, clambering to her feet. 'Be good, kids. Don't do anything I wouldn't.'

'Sam was never the wildest kid around,' he said to Lucie, 'but I think that gives us reasonable licence.'

'Except for the fact that there are about two hundred people down here with us,' she giggled.

He trailed his fingers from her wrist to her shoulder and back again, her skin softer than lamb's ears beneath his touch.

She shivered, and he couldn't help noticing her nipples punch against the fabric of her dress. The temperature was steadily dropping, but it wasn't yet that cold.

He dragged his gaze away, looking over the river. He was oddly torn: he wanted to make a move, yet he had never been as content as he was in that moment.

'What will you do?' she murmured, and he startled, thinking she had read his mind. 'About The Twenty?'

'I'll start over. I was thinking I might get some land towards Pallamana. It's drier there, goes for about four thousand a hectare. When something comes on the market, I'll get a diviner in, see if there's any water. And I'll move back in with Ma and Pops, that'll help sort them, too. It'll all work out.'

'But the cove makes the perfect microclimate, and the soil is so good on The Twenty.'

'Yep. But no point wishing for what I can't have.' Instead, he was focusing all of his energy on wishing for something that, with Lucie in his arms, for the first time seemed possible. 'Hopefully it'll take a while to sell The Twenty, though. I'm in no hurry to leave Sal.'

Lucie nodded, her fingers idly playing with Dash's ears. The pup had curled contentedly in her lap and fallen asleep. 'Jack, you said you had the impression Dad was leaving The Twenty to me?'

He gave a half shrug. 'Can't say anything about *leaving* it, because he intended to be here and give it to you.'

Lucie sighed. 'It's horrible to want to claim an inheritance because that means ... well, it's obvious what it means. But if Dad has left me his half of The Twenty, everything would be so easy. I'm still searching through files, but I haven't even found the title yet.'

His heart leaped—not at her inference that there was a chance of keeping The Twenty, but because she seemed to consider them a team. 'Doesn't matter, it wouldn't be worth it. Not if there's any risk of it causing a misunderstanding between us.'

'How would it?' Her brow furrowed, and he couldn't help but love the nature that prevented her from seeing the obvious issue.

'I own barely an inch of the property freehold, Lucie. It's either your father's, or my share is a loan from your father. So, technically, also your father's. If you inherited, it would then become all yours. I wouldn't want you to think that I'm just here for that. I'd rather lose the property than lose you.'

She nodded, falling silent, though she still toyed with his fingers, stroking the back of his hand.

He had never met anyone he could sit in complete, connected stillness with before, their gazes on the moon and stars floating in the silky river.

38
Jack

By the time their group returned from the carnival tents, which Jack knew from years of experience contained a mishmash of home-baked goods, gumnut crafts and artisan bits and pieces like tooled belts, dog collars and knitted baby clothes, it was getting cold. Yet neither he nor Lucie had moved.

Monica appraised him, her gaze hostile. 'I was thinking, Lucie, you might like me to take Keeley back to Chesterton tonight? She could have a sleepover. It seems that might be best for her.'

'Could be a lovely night for it,' Ma chuckled.

Lucie bolted upright. 'No!' she gasped, then moderated her tone. 'No. That's fine, Mum. Maybe another time.'

Monica nodded, buttoning her cardigan. 'Well, it's time for me to make tracks. If you like, I'll take Keeley to yours, put her to bed. I'm sure you can get a ride back a little later.'

There was no mistaking her insinuation. And, for the first time, Jack actually kind of liked her.

Lucie stood, hobbling a little, her legs obviously numb. 'No, you're right, it is bedtime. There's plenty of room if you want to stay over, though, Mum.'

That was one way to put paid to her mother's suspicions. Also totally killed the night for him, though, he realised bleakly.

'Should I?' Her mother observed her for a long moment. 'Another time. Perhaps we could meet Marian and Simon for a playdate?'

'Brilliant,' Roni said. 'Sam keeps a corner aside in Ploughs and Pies for the kids so we could all meet there. Maybe next weekend?'

'Sounds great,' Lucie replied.

Rain started to mist in, so light it was hard to pick from a damp cloud. As they all rushed to fold up rugs, laughingly fighting about who owned which container, Lucie rubbed her arms briskly and moved closer to him. 'If you'd like to come over for a drink, just give me half an hour for Mum to leave and to get Keeley to bed,' she murmured. Then, without waiting for the reply he was completely incapable of making, she turned, calling goodbye to the others and walking away with her mum, dog and daughter in tow.

Thirty minutes had never before stretched so long. Although he wasn't in uniform, Jack lent the CFS crew a hand making sure the fireworks were fully damped down and that none of the candles the kids had used for toasting marshmallows still burned. The Lions Club would take care of the bulk of the clean-up when they came to pack up their barbecue and the tents in the morning.

When the designated time was up, he added a couple of minutes to make sure he looked chill—then practically bolted for the ute.

The car rattled into gear and he pulled in behind the tail-lights of the last of the vehicles, easing through the rutted paddock then heading into town.

By the time he got to Lucie's, there was no sign of Monica's car. The verandah light painted the front garden in ghostly shades of white, but he wasn't wasting time smelling the roses. He took the steps up to the porch at a leap, then hesitated. He could be reading Lucie's signals all wrong.

'It's open,' Lucie called softly as he raised a hand to rap on the screen door.

She was illuminated from behind by the hall light, the rainbows in her hair sparkling with the remnants of the misting rain. Although it wasn't warm, she had taken off her jumper. And the top buttons of her thin dress were undone. A lot of buttons. Far more than would be a casual look.

Maybe he hadn't misread her signals.

As he stepped inside, she wrinkled her nose. 'I feel guilty. I invited you for a drink under false pretences—I don't actually have anything. Well, not unless you fancy a turmeric soy latte or a Dutch organic cocoa.'

She was beyond adorable. 'I'd settle for a glass of river water if it meant I get to spend an extra five minutes with you.'

Lucie fisted her hands on her hips and looked at him intently. 'I like you, Jack. A lot.'

Thank god for that inherited directness. Lucie never seemed to bother with small talk, but when she had something to say, she came out with it. Instead of letting him suffer the torture of wondering whether she was interested when he couldn't command words to persuade her, she was a no-bullshit girl.

He grinned. 'I like you, Lucie. More than a lot.'

She blew out a sharp breath, and he could almost feel her relief. The screen door banged behind him and she flinched, casting a quick glance towards what he assumed was Keeley's room. But then she was in his arms, her soft body pressed close, her cold hands wrapped around the back of his neck. 'Show me how much.'

His lips found hers with none of the awkward fumbling, nose mashing, trying to work out when to take a breath business. She was made to fit him, her height, her size, her softness, her willingness. Everything married up perfectly. He could lose himself in the feel and taste of her, and he needed nothing but for this moment to last forever, for Lucie to be in his arms, where she belonged.

Eventually, short of breath, he forced himself to pull back. 'Lucie, I have to warn you. I'm not a casual kind of guy. I'm not into one-night stands.'

She pressed her reddened lips together, observing him with the slightly unnerving silence she often adopted as she processed her thoughts. 'Good.'

That was it, apparently. No further discussion. He wet his lips and tried again. 'Thing is, I want to take this further. Now.'

She didn't pause this time but shot him a cheeky grin. 'Also good.'

'Not so good.' He shook his head, the embarrassment clawing at his gut. 'I kind of didn't come p-prepared. You know, because I don't regularly do this kind of thing.'

She blinked, then frowned. 'You mean you don't have any condoms?'

He grimaced. 'Not s-something I keep in stock. And not something I can pick up around here or the whole town will know. I'm kind of hoping that you've got something or are . . . y-you know, taken care of?' He could discuss breeding animals till the cows came home, but verbalising this was one hell of an ask. His old man would have laughed himself sick.

'The pill?' Lucie shook her head. 'Nope. Synthetic hormones, y'know? Plus, speaking of unprepared and irregular, this isn't something I generally do. In fact, not for about five years.'

'What?' He regretted the blurted word instantly, but was she seriously trying to tell him there had been no one for five years?

'Not since Keeley. Which is a whole other discussion.' She fiddled with the stone on the leather strap around her neck. He needed to kiss the hollow of her throat. He had somehow missed that spot. 'You know I have a kid . . . so I also have . . . a mum bod.' She gestured deprecatingly with one hand down her front.

Her sudden uncertainty freed him. He didn't need to impress her or prove anything: they were on this adventure together. 'Seeing as we're about as prepared as sixteen-year-olds, I reckon we're going to have to be inventive and get to know each other a whole lot better.'

'Oh.' The disappointment in her face was comical. 'I can put the kettle on?' She waved one hand behind her, towards where the kitchen must be.

'Not at all what I meant,' he murmured, drawing her back into his arms. 'We're a couple of intelligent adults. I'm sure we can come up with a mutually satisfying solution.' His fingers ran down the open neckline of her dress. 'I suspect there's a very sexy mum bod hiding under here, and you know I'm always keen to explore alternatives to the mainstream.'

She smiled slowly, her eyes dancing and cheek dimpling as she understood his intention. 'And I'm always keen to expand my knowledge. Teach me.'

39
Lucie

Lucie stretched languorously. For the first time in as long as she could remember, she woke totally at peace with her world, every part of her soft, stretched, supple, as though she had followed a yoga class with an aromatherapy massage. A delicious lassitude that came from being physically loved stirred a glow inside her. It had taken all her courage last night to cast aside her self-doubt, her mistrust of her own judgment, and make it clear to Jack that she wanted him.

But it had been absolutely worth the risk.

The hard length of Jack's body pressed against her side, so she turned over, lazily tracing the gold dusting of hair on his chest, barely visible as the fingers of dawn clutched the edge of the curtain.

Jack caught her hand and brought it to his lips, kissing each of her fingertips. Then he sat up, swinging his legs out of the bed in a single, fluid movement. He reached for the shirt he'd tossed to the bedroom floor only a few hours earlier and pulled it over his head. Unperturbed by his semi-nakedness, he stood, searching for his jeans among the tangle of clothing and bedding.

The sheet clutched to her chest, Lucie's stomach hollowed with disappointment. But she had promised herself she would take this relationship however it came, listen to what Jack wanted, instead of imagining their plans matched. Just because she longed to spend every minute with him didn't mean he felt the same. Perhaps she had learned something from Mum's lectures: she would never again beg for any man's affection.

She shoved up onto her elbows. 'You'd better go before—' She choked on the words. If she'd been smart, she would have faked sleep and let Jack make his escape. Then, if he'd decided he wanted nothing more from her, they could both act like the night had never happened.

The mattress sagged as Jack placed one knee on the bed, leaning across to find her lips for a long, gentle kiss.

He didn't kiss as though he wanted nothing from her. Goosebumps of relief rippled across her skin and, tangling a hand in his hair, she pulled him closer, hungrily searching his mouth. Arousal chased away every other emotion, and she struggled to her knees so she could press closer to him.

His hands slipped around her waist, then down over her hips, his fingers exploring. Then he pulled away with a short laugh, shaking his head. 'You're determined to distract me, aren't you?'

'You have to work today?' She made a disappointed face, but at least asking a question wasn't begging him to stay.

'Always. But it can wait a little while. Lynn opens up around five-thirty. I'll catch her while she's unlocking.'

'Lynn?' Her brain definitely wasn't in the same place as his.

'IGA.'

'Yeah, I got that, but . . . ? I have oats soaking for bircher, and plenty of fair-trade coffee. Keeley will be asleep for a while yet, but I can put on breakfast for you now.' As they'd been awake much of the night talking—among other things, her pulse quickening at the memory—Jack could have worked up an appetite. But such urgency?

He grinned, then kissed the tip of her nose. 'You might have plenty of food, but you don't have condoms.'

'Oh!' She blew out an unsteady breath. 'I thought you said no local shopping for that kind of stuff. Because . . . talk?'

Jack framed her face with his hands. 'If anyone wants to talk about how damn lucky I am to find you, they're welcome. Heck, I'm thinking about hiring a skywriter to share it with the world. But that'll have to wait because right now I want to make love to you.'

She stared at him without answering.

'I m-mean, if that's okay with you?' he added, dropping his hands. 'We did both say that we don't do casual, but maybe I'm still jumping the gun.' His gaze locked to hers, intense and questioning, demanding her response. 'Lucie, I'm laying it out straight: this is probably gonna get hellishly messy because everyone in this town talks. Some will say I'm into you because I want to grab any chance to keep The Twenty. They'll say you're stupid for giving me an in. But it doesn't matter what anyone says, only what we know. If you trust me, I'm here for the long haul.'

She had been concerned Jack would leave her guessing about where he stood as they eased into a relationship, yet now she was shocked at his directness, the way he viewed the world with a black-and-white clarity that left him certain of his path. Yet didn't that innate surety mirror his acceptance of losing Sally and The Twenty? He saw the roadblock, acknowledged the inevitability and moved on, accepting what he couldn't change. 'That's like . . . some statement,' she said slowly. 'Aren't you worried that you don't really know me?'

He shrugged. 'How can you ever really know someone? People change.'

Lucie sat back, pulling up the bed cover as she tried to contain the surge of longing that rushed through her. Jack understood. They were waves on a beach, continually in motion, perpetually evolving.

'You know my life is complicated, right?' she warned. 'For starters, I'm a package deal.'

'I'm here for complicated. And I'm here for Keeley.' Jack's face tightened as though he clenched his teeth for a moment. 'I understand that you've got to have reservations about letting me into her life.' He ran a hand through his hair, forcing it off his face, his jaw hard. 'You get that my d-dad wasn't such a great role m-model, right?'

God, every time he stammered, she ached to take the pain of that memory from him. Anger curled her hands into fists on the bedsheets: what sort of person could hurt a child, scar him in such a fashion?

Jack mistook her reaction for fear and dropped to his haunches alongside the bed, covering her white knuckles with his hands. 'B-but you have to believe that I'm not like him, Lucie. He taught me plenty: mostly, how to be better than he was.'

'I know you're not like him. I've finally realised that the whole nature versus nurture argument is crap because we are everything: we're a product of genetics, upbringing, our desires, what we make of ourselves *and* the path we choose.'

Jack looked relieved. 'Right now I'd say pretty much anything to get you to let me be part of your life, but I'm not going to lie—I won't pretend I know a thing about kids. Well, except for how to keep their bugs safe. But I can learn. I'll never do or say anything to hurt Keeley. And I'll never let anyone else hurt her.' He let go of Lucie's hands, as though allowing her space, intent on not forcing her to agree. 'I get that she is always going to be your number-one priority, that you're a pair and I'm the outsider. That's exactly how it should be. Hell, I can only imagine what it would be like to have a parent like that. But I'd love to be around as a backup. No kid can have too much protection, or too much love.'

Stubble rasped beneath Lucie's touch as she ran her fingertips along Jack's jaw. Joy—no, something deeper, a sense of *rightness*, as though finally the time, the place, the person had all come together—welled inside her. 'I know I should say that you're crazy, that this is too quick, that we've only known each other a few weeks. I should run a mile—one of us should run a mile!' She shifted her hand to cup his cheek, looking deep into his beautiful eyes. 'But you make absolute sense. We don't know each other, yet we're in sync. We share the same values and beliefs.'

Lucie took a deep breath, filled with both adrenaline and fear, as though she was about to leap from a cliff. 'And maybe the same dreams.' She had hidden from life for long enough: now it was time to take a chance, to trust her instincts. 'The rest of it, the risk, that's all part of the adventure, isn't it?'

Jack turned his head to kiss her palm. 'So you're in?'

She nodded, then burst into incredulous laughter. 'This is so nuts. But, heck, yes, I'm in. Boots, kid, dog and all.'

40
Jack

Jack looked across the paddock towards the strawberry plot as Keeley and Lucie's laughter pealed over The Twenty, competing with the plaintive call of the plover who still searched for her mate near the dam. He was putting in new fencing to try to contain the guineas to a smaller section, so they'd stop teasing the goats. He knew he was in denial, making improvements as though oblivious to how tenuous his ownership was. But farming was in his blood; he had no off switch.

Dropping the shovel, he leaned on the fence post, watching Lucie chase Keeley and Dash along the rows of deep green plants, her bare arms golden in the sun. Keeley squealed and Dash barked as Lucie grabbed her daughter, tackled her to the ground and tickled her.

Eventually, Lucie stood, dusted herself off and bent to speak to Keeley. Then she wandered through the patch, the orchard, then the chook yard towards him. The sun caught the colours in her hair and glinted from the tiny purple stud in her nose. Hell, he could lose an entire day just watching the woman—she was a walking rainbow and he wanted nothing more than to catch her.

'Man working hard?' she said with a grin.

'Man is hard,' he said, cocking an eyebrow. Their moments together were stolen; he'd never before given a thought to the boundaries imposed by parenting. He didn't resent Keeley, the kid was hilarious and was marching her way straight into his heart, but he also made sure not to miss an opportunity to let Lucie know how he felt about her. How he desired her.

Lucie chuckled—a deep, throaty, joyous noise that lifted his heart every time. Taking a strawberry from the bowl she had formed by pulling her t-shirt away from her midriff, she placed it between her teeth and leaned towards him.

He kissed her, stealing the berry and the sweetness that had nothing to do with the fruit.

Lucie ran her tongue over her lips. 'Definitely not commercial grade, but I think these are the best strawberries I've ever tasted.'

'They do have an extra something.'

'I has some?' Keeley said as she and Dash joined them.

Jack chose the largest berry from Lucie's stash, carefully rubbing it with his thumb to remove any dirt. 'You about

384

ready for that milking lesson, missy?' he asked Keeley as Marilyn gave an extended bleat.

'Yes,' Keeley agreed solemnly. 'We take some milk to Nanna's?'

'You're off out there again?' he asked Lucie, his stomach sinking.

'In the morning. I know you'll be busy hay cutting, so we'll try to stay out of your way for a few days.'

He shook his head. 'I'll start really early—'

Lucie pressed a finger across his lips, grinning as he flicked his tongue over it. Her pupils dilated but she continued. 'You get your work done. I have to spend time at Mum's anyway. You know, building bridges and all that. Besides, I've got an idea about your issue with Ma and Pops.'

'Which is?' He needed a solution, but more than that, he just wanted Lucie to continue talking. He'd grab any excuse to keep her there.

'You were right about it being difficult to get services here—'

'Man's favourite way to hear a sentence started. Well, I can think of a few others,' he said with a tilt of his head at Keeley, signifying he wasn't going to spell them out.

Lucie giggled. 'Behave. Anyway, you're right about the lack of service providers, and now I've quit the Melbourne office, I'm limited on how much chasing I can do. But I was thinking about Mum. She mentioned a couple of times that she doesn't know what she's going to do with herself going forward. Said that she regrets giving up her nursing quals and, while it's not nursing, I had a talk with her about how much your grandparents—and no doubt other people in the district—could use help that's kind of a bridge between professional health services and domestic help.' Lucie scrunched her nose. 'Mind you, "domestic help" probably wasn't the best choice of phrase—Mum nearly combusted. But I think she's clicked that there is potentially a valuable service she could be providing, a bit of a niche market that she could entirely own. And she does love to be in control of things,' Lucie added with a roll of her eyes. 'Anyway, I want to chat to her some more about it.'

Jack had steered clear of Monica since the fireworks—not that it had taken any effort. With forty kilometres and numerous small towns between Chesterton and Settlers Bridge, their paths had only previously crossed when he'd been out to Blue Flag. Though arguably Monica had seemed to thaw a minute amount towards him at the fireworks, maybe realising that despite what she thought she knew, it wasn't his entire history, he wasn't about to push the relationship. 'Okay, missy. Let's go and get some milk for your nanna.'

∽

As he walked in through the boot room, Jack clicked his fingers for Sally a fraction of a second before memory hit him. He cursed softly. How long would it be before the rawness of that wound healed? He could barely look at the working dogs up on the farm, convinced that giving them anything more than terse approval would be a betrayal of Sal's memory.

He crossed to the bathroom, his mood lifting as he noticed a couple of Keeley's brightly coloured hair elastics on the basin. When the girls had last been there a few days earlier, Keeley had asked to braid his hair. Fortunately, she was impatient, showing the same fieriness he'd noticed in Lucie, and he'd only had to suffer her yanking for ten minutes—but it had then taken him twenty minutes to untangle her handiwork and free the bands.

When the cottage was filled with life, noise and mess, he didn't have space in his head to miss Sally. Yet Lucie and Keeley's occasional presence made their absence worse: he would listen to the silence at night, imagining the familiar sighs and groans of the old dog chasing rabbits in her sleep.

He splashed his face with cold water. He'd already put in several hours at Pops' after feeding the animals on The Twenty. He would grab some of the raw nut slice Lucie had left in the fridge for him, then get back to the farm and the hay cutting.

The vibration of an approaching vehicle ran through the floorboards, and he gave his face a rub with a rough towel and headed back outside, fighting the urge to call Sally.

The sight of Lucie's RAV4 brought a ridiculous surge of happiness and an immediate grin to his face, and he strode to where she pulled up behind his ute in the shade of the magnificent river gum.

As Lucie turned off the ignition he opened her door, and she laughingly tumbled into his arms, pressing herself against him.

'Hey,' he murmured as his lips travelled up her neck. 'Didn't think I was seeing you until tomorrow.'

She twisted to find his mouth, her breath sweet and minty, her perfume strawberries and soap, and he lost himself for long minutes.

Eventually she murmured, 'I hope you realise the car is roasting my back.'

Guiltily, he pulled her away from the hot metal. 'Sorry. Better get Keeley and Dash out, too.'

Lucie's eyes danced. 'Mum's babysitting. I needed some time to produce a new anti-inflammatory Taylor wants to try.'

'Produce?' he said, gesturing at the garden. Although Lucie harvested herbs and other plants from The Twenty, she did her production in the clean kitchen in Settlers Bridge.

Lucie grinned. 'Done and dusted. Or bottled, or whatever. Point is, I seem to have a little time on my hands. Alone.'

His breath caught and desire leaped. Their time together, in anything but a platonic sense, had been found only in stolen, whispered, rushed moments when Keeley was asleep. 'You mean?' He tilted his head towards the cottage.

'I mean,' Lucie nodded, her hands going to his belt. 'If you can find time for me, that is.'

'I'll find time all right,' he growled into her ear, pulling her fiercely against him.

She hooked a leg around the back of his thigh, her arms around his neck, her voice lilting with excitement. 'I feel like we're making out behind the bike shed and my mum's about to catch us.'

'Can't say I've ever done that.' Nor did he want to know about her bike shed history. 'But I reckon we can adult it at next level.' He scooped her into his arms and strode towards the cottage. Parenting meant that their time alone together was always going to be limited, and he planned to make the most of whatever they had right now.

41
Lucie

Lucie stared at the email on Dad's computer screen.

Though she longed to be with Jack out at The Twenty, she was trying not to crowd him: she had learned firsthand how the addition of a child changed life. So over the last few weeks she had spent time building her naturopathy practice or at Blue Flag, eventually finding the documents the solicitor needed buried in random places in the filing cabinet, almost as though they had been hidden.

Mum was little help, at least with the paperwork. Instead, she invested her time in Keeley. Last week Lucie found them lying on the lawn beside the chamomile border. Even Dash was settled and calm, chin on his paws, as Mum taught Keeley to wait for the bees to move on before picking the apple-and-honey fragranced blooms for Lucie to make into a bedtime tea.

Yesterday the trio were in the greenhouse, Mum instructing Keeley how to snip a single leaf from the centre of an African violet, dip it in rooting powder, then plant the cutting in a miniature ceramic pot. Oblivious to her grandmother's occasional snappiness, Keeley excitedly informed Lucie that they were growing a forest of flowers for the fairies to use as umbrellas.

Lucie wished she was able to pretend her mother's admission of loneliness and change in attitude towards Keeley swept away the years of mistrust and hurt. But forgiveness was going to take time. And a whole lot of encouragement from Geoff.

Trying to calm herself, she ran her hands over Dad's blotter, pressing down to feel the imprint of his writing, although she'd stashed away the top page in her drawer, alongside her crystals. She took a deep breath and reread the email from the lawyer.

MTamberlani@BlueFlagStrawberries.com
LucieTam@hotmail.com
JSMackereth@gmail.com

As discussed by telephone, your attendance is requested at our offices at 3pm on the 27th of November to finalise the estate of Georgius Nikolas Tamberlani.

Her stomach cramping, Lucie hunched over the desk.

She hadn't misread, hadn't imagined the email address. He was back.

Seeing Jeremy's name in print after so long was an almost physical blow. And it had nothing to do with the memories, or the feelings of desertion or loss; she was well beyond that. It had to do with fear. This man could steal Keeley.

Her email address as visible to Jeremy as his was to her, Lucie pressed her hand against her chest, constricted too tightly around a heart pounding with dread as she warily refreshed her email screen for the fourth time. But there was nothing: Jeremy hadn't contacted her, hadn't asked to meet his daughter. Her fingers froze: she still had a tiny window where she could remove all possibility of that happening. Run back to Melbourne, change her email address. As Jeremy hadn't bothered with them in four years, there was little chance he would put effort into finding them now.

The second it formed, she rejected the idea. She wasn't running and she wasn't leaving Jack. Whether she inherited The Twenty or not, the three of them would build a future together. And, of course, there was Mum to consider. Their relationship was becoming . . . well, it was becoming something. Not comfortable, it would never be that; they weren't exactly sharing confidences. But even without the forgiveness she was still working on, it was perhaps more accepting, more honest—except that she never mentioned Jack and downplayed Keeley's chatter about him. She wasn't going to risk having Mum interfere in their relationship.

Like Geoff had been telling her for weeks, she and Mum needed to focus on their commonality instead of their differences. And Keeley was their commonality, Lucie thought, as her daughter exploded into the office, Mum and Dash trailing behind her like tethered satellites.

Mum unnecessarily rapped her knuckles on the office partition, her gaze roaming the shelves behind Lucie, as though she didn't want to look at Dad's desk, his chair.

Lucie got that: each time she walked into this section of the packing shed, she still half-expected to see Dad, his shoulders too broad for the chair, his jeans dirty from the paddock. His unwillingness to be tied to the paperwork and longing to instead get outdoors had been an almost physical presence.

'The solicitor rang and confirmed for this afternoon,' Mum said, holding her mobile up to prove she was finally taking the calls she had avoided for weeks.

'He emailed you, too.' Lucie pointed at the screen. 'Did he tell you who else he contacted?'

Mum shook her head.

'Jeremy.'

Mum's eyebrows raised. 'What on earth for?'

'Check your email,' Lucie snapped, then relented: this wasn't Mum's fault. 'The solicitor didn't mention it last week—probably some kind of privacy requirement—but I guess Jeremy is named in the will. He said that he's legally obliged to share the contents with every person named, regardless of whether they're a beneficiary. I figured that was only going to be us, but apparently not.'

Mum bent to scoop up Keeley, settling the child on her hip. Keeley wrapped her arms around her grandmother's neck, nestling close.

Although her daughter was baby-chubby, and her mother bordering on anorexic, Lucie was struck anew at how

393

similar they looked in their blue-eyed blondeness. And, for the first time, she didn't resent the fact.

'What possible reason could Georgius have for including *him*?' Mum said.

Lucie shrugged. 'All I know is that I never want to see him again.' She clamped her lips tight as a fresh wave of dread rippled through her. She had spent so many desperate months hoping every knock at the door, every telephone call, would be from the man she thought she loved. Now, nothing would make her happier than to hear there was no risk of him ever reappearing. Yet, with the meeting set for that afternoon, Jeremy was only minutes, metres, heartbeats away from her.

'Lucie, just close that chapter,' Mum said firmly. 'Put it behind you. What is it Einstein said?' She managed to make it sound as though the physicist was a personal friend she'd chatted with recently. '*Learn from yesterday, live for today, hope for tomorrow.* We've all had to do it. Forget about Jeremy, forget what you thought you had. It was never there.'

Overwhelming despair suddenly weighed Lucie down, and she clutched at her necklace. She had outgrown blaming Jeremy for her own choices, but the realisation that he was always going to be a part of her life was . . . suffocating. 'It's not that simple. I can't close the chapter.' She lifted her chin at Keeley. 'It's a work in progress.'

'No,' Mum snapped. 'Keeley is the epilogue. The story is finished. Jeremy can't just reappear, expecting you to act as though he's forgiven.'

Mum's vehemency startled Lucie, given that a few weeks earlier she'd seemed to advocate for Jeremy's rights. 'I'm not worried about him wanting back into *my* life, Mum, that window is locked tight. I'm worried about him claiming his rights.'

'No!' Mum gasped, her hand sweeping up to cover the back of Keeley's head, pressing the child closer to her chest. 'No. He's not doing that. He wouldn't dare. He doesn't have any damn rights, he's forfeited them. No third chances.'

'Third?' Lucie frowned. 'I wish I had your confidence, but I'm certain that legally he does have rights.'

'Then we'll fight him,' Mum said fiercely. 'I don't need the money from selling Blue Flag, the lawyers can have it all. I'll call them back right now.' She brandished the phone as though it was a weapon.

'I don't think they're the right kind of lawyers, Mum,' Lucie said, touched and surprised by her mother's reaction. 'In any case, I have to face up to Jeremy. I can't hide away, constantly dreading his reappearance. I need to deal with him, see if he has any intention of being part of Keeley's life. He said years ago that he wasn't father material: let's just hope he still feels the same way.'

Keeley wriggled and Mum set her down, blowing out a long breath. 'You're so like your dad, Lucie,' she said, with what could almost be admiration in her tone. 'You both tackle things head-on. Of course,' she added wryly, 'Dad did break his nose several times.'

Lately, many of Mum's comments seemed less barbed, more cynical than hurtful. 'If Jeremy is back in town, I should tell Jack about him, shouldn't I?' Lucie said, suddenly greedy for her mother's rare support.

'Jack? Isn't that over yet?' Mum snapped.

'Why would you even say that?' Lucie gasped. 'I thought you kind of liked Jack.'

'Why on earth would I like him?'

'It was pretty obvious at the fireworks that you were offering to babysit so we could have time alone together.' Her face flamed, though whether it was embarrassment at talking with her mother about such private issues, or anger at Mum's habitual backflipping, she wasn't sure.

'For god's sake, I was giving you an opportunity to get him out of your system!' her mother hissed. 'I'm well aware that if I told you to stay away from him, I might as well push you together. But enough is enough.' She glanced at Keeley who, busy re-pinning pieces of paper on the hessian room divider, was oblivious to their conversation. Her mum's face contorted, and she whispered furiously. 'Keeley doesn't need to be caught up in your . . . your addiction to your father's business partners.'

The parallel, which she'd never given a thought, froze Lucie's words for a second. 'Jesus, Mum, it's not an addiction. It's a . . . a coincidence. And Jeremy was barely Dad's partner. He only has a two-percent interest in Blue Flag.'

Mum batted away the defence. 'Partner, marketing manager, employee—it's all just a play on words, Lucie. The facts stand.'

'And the fact is, Jack deserves to know everything. I don't want any misunderstandings.' Not this time.

Mum cupped both hands over her nose and mouth, breathing deeply as though she was having trouble containing her emotions. 'Lucie, I realise that you think you know best, you always have,' she said, her voice oddly hollow behind her hands. 'But just this once, please, please listen to me. Jack's not who you think he is. I was hoping you would discover that these last couple of weeks. He's not who you think, and you're going to get hurt. Again.'

'Jack isn't going to hurt me,' she snapped, all desire to have her mother's support evaporating.

'Not intentionally, that's not what I mean.' Mum sounded desperate. 'Look,' she reached an imploring hand towards Lucie. 'Can you just wait? Until after you've seen Jeremy. Don't involve Jack, keep your options open until then. For me?'

Lucie snorted. 'For you?' As though she owed Mum anything.

'For Keeley.'

'Now you sound like you want me to get back together with Jeremy. I'm not interested, Mum. He's not interested. What the hell game are you playing this time?'

Her mother glanced towards the packing shed, where all the chatter had suddenly stopped at Lucie's raised voice. 'It's not a game, Lucie. You cannot possibly understand how desperately I don't want you anywhere near that man. Either man. If you won't listen to me, at least wait until you have all the facts. Then you can do whatever you want.' She enunciated *whatever*, like she was giving Lucie free rein, yet Mum's hand strayed towards Keeley, as though keeping her close.

42
Jack

Running the two properties was always a balancing act, but Jack was even shorter of time than usual because travelling to the city for the meeting was going to chew into his day. But that was fine; the unexpected summons this morning meant he'd see Lucie earlier than if he'd had to wait for dinner at Ma and Pops. Three days without Lucie had felt like three weeks.

'Bro? You in?' Luke hollered from the back door.

'Come through,' he yelled. He raised an eyebrow as Luke wandered into the kitchen on bare feet.

'Thought you might be getting a bit houseproud, now you've got regular company,' Luke explained. 'Didn't want to track dirt in.'

'The news is out, huh?'

His cousin grinned. 'Dude, the news was out more than three weeks ago, right after the fireworks. But Taylor said I had to play nice and wouldn't let me come round to shit-stir you straight away. Said something about being sensitive and all that.' He threw a hand wide to encompass the paddocks they couldn't see. 'So what happens with this lot?'

'Bloody nothing,' Jack said tersely, then relented. 'Lucie wants to keep it. She keeps trying to bring up what could happen if Gus left her the block. Seems to think that would be a solution.'

'Seems to me she'd be right.' Luke helped himself to a piece of the slice Jack was cutting out of the tin for smoko. 'Not seeing the problem.'

'The problem is that Monica never wanted Gus to go into business with me. She'll lose it when she discovers he lent me the money for my share. And she'll have the right to call in that loan.'

Hand partway to his mouth, Luke paused. 'Why would she, if Lucie wants to keep the property?'

'We have history.'

'If you call three weeks history.'

Jack shook his head. 'Me and the widow.'

Luke blew out a low whistle. 'Are you kidding me, man? How did I not know about this?'

'Jeez, settle down, not that kind of history!' Jack exclaimed. 'Just . . . some shit.' Regardless of Monica's attitude at the fireworks, he knew she wasn't the type to forgive easily. Even something that hadn't been his fault. 'Trust me, she'll want her dollars *and* a pound of flesh. So Lucie inheriting a share of The Twenty is the worst-case scenario. I can't tell her there's bad blood between her mum and me, and I can't afford to buy her mum out.'

'Why not tell Lucie? Seems that secrets probably aren't the best way to head into a relationship.'

'Because it's not my secret to share.'

∾

'What are you doing here?' Lucie flung her arms around Jack's neck almost the second he stepped off the street and into the reception area of the solicitor's office. Kissing him full on the lips, she was either oblivious to or uncaring of her mother's presence.

Jack had intended to call to see if Lucie wanted to head into Adelaide together—providing she wasn't going with Monica, because being cooped in a car together wouldn't be good for either of them—but the tractor had blown a hydraulic hose, and he'd spent most of the day covered in grease trying to fix the damn thing. Running late, he'd grabbed the bike and headed over, hitting the back roads at speeds Taylor Hartmann wouldn't have approved of.

Monica lifted an eyebrow, keeping a tight hold of Keeley's hand, as though to stop the child running to him.

'Jack,' Keeley piped, tugging against the restraint. 'We don't got Dash. He being babysat by Chloe. I not babysat because I big.' She puffed out her chest, patting at it. 'I nearly four now.'

'In a few more days,' he agreed.

'Jack,' Lucie murmured against his chest, 'I'm so glad you're here.'

As his hands moved up her back, he was astonished to realise she was crying. 'Luce, are you okay?' Dumb question, he realised, as the words left his mouth.

She nodded and sniffled a little, though she didn't look up at him, her forehead against his chest. 'Sure. It's all just . . . very final, you know?'

'I know,' he murmured, pressing a kiss into her dark hair.

She pushed away from his chest, using both hands to scrub at her face before offering him a watery smile. 'I wasn't expecting you, but I'm so glad you're here. I tried to call you earlier. I need to tell you something.' She shot a belligerent look at her mother, as though daring her to interrupt.

Monica dared. 'For the love of god, just have a little patience for once in your life, Lucie,' she hissed.

Apparently, the bridge building wasn't going so well.

'What is it?' he asked, willing to brave Monica's wrath. Though Ma and Pops seemed to like her, and she'd visited them out at the farm the previous week, then gone to the Settlers Bridge CWA meeting as Ma's guest, he couldn't imagine the frost between him and Monica thawing anytime soon.

'Ah, excellent,' a voice broke in as an interior door opened. 'You're all here. What I'll have you do is pop into my office one at a time.' The rotund guy had to be the Tamberlani estate lawyer. 'It will only take a moment to share with you the personal messages Mr Tamberlani left, and I'll provide you each with a printed copy of the will to peruse at your leisure.'

Lucie stood nearest the door, and the solicitor gestured her forward. 'Miss Tamberlani, perhaps you'd like to come in first?'

'But we're not all here,' she said with a panicked glance towards the door.

'Go on in,' her mother commanded. 'Get this over with. I'll watch Keeley.'

Seeming confused, Lucie followed the solicitor, though she cast a pleading look at Jack.

As Jack took a half step towards the door closing on the pair, Monica whirled on him. 'What are you doing here, Jackson?'

He lifted a shoulder, striving to keep his tone even as Keeley finally managed to make a grab for his hand, linking the three of them. 'I got a call from the solicitor this morning.'

Monica frowned. 'You too? Lucie didn't mention that.' She flipped a dismissive hand. 'Jackson, you have to tell Lucie before this—' she looked him up and down disparagingly '—before this thing goes any further.'

'Why the hell would I do that?' he said, shocked. He had expected Monica to demand his silence, not his honesty.

'Because you're with her under false pretences.'

'How do you figure that, Monica?' he said, his tone suddenly ice. Of all the things he could be accused of, dishonesty was the one that cut deepest. Hell, he knew the town would gossip, suspect his motives for being with Lucie, but Monica was sure getting in early.

'Omission is just a clever form of lying,' she shot back.

'But it's not my—' He broke off as the door opened. The solicitor obviously wasn't on an hourly rate and intended to shuffle them through as fast as possible.

Lucie crossed to him, her eyes shining with both tears and excitement. With a lurch of his chest, he instantly knew what she wanted to tell him. As they'd half-expected, Gus had left her a share of The Twenty.

'Mrs Tamberlani?' the solicitor said courteously. 'Mr Mackereth, if you wouldn't mind waiting a few more minutes, this one will take a little longer.'

How the hell was he going to explain to Lucie why her mother would be hellbent on calling in his loan? As he started to respond, Lucie's head snapped towards the solicitor. Her hands fisted. 'Mackereth? He's not here yet.'

The solicitor lifted an open hand towards him. 'Jackson Schenscher-Mackereth?' he asked, sudden doubt in his tone.

'Yep,' Jack answered, his gaze on Lucie.

She took a swift step away from him. 'Wh-what?' she whispered. 'What did he call you?'

The blood drained from her face and he reached out to grab her shoulders. 'Jack. Jackson.'

She threw both hands up, fending him off. 'Not that. Your other name. Your whole name.'

'Jackson Schenscher-Mackereth. I know, it's a mouthful, right?' he said. Even worse with a stammer, which was partly why he generally dropped half of it.

Lucie shook her head, her dark eyes suddenly wild. 'Mackereth? Oh my god.' She staggered backward. 'You—you're—' She choked on the words.

'I warned you to tell her!' Monica shrilled. She scooped Keeley up, her hand covering the child's head, as though shielding her. 'Tell her everything, quickly.'

She had to be mad. What would telling Lucie achieve? 'B-b-but it's not my—'

'Just tell her!' Monica yelled as Lucie shrank against the wall, trembling hands folded across her mouth, the hollow of her throat pulsing.

'I don't know what to s-s-say!' he bellowed.

He reached for Lucie, but she jerked away, shaking her head violently. 'Don't touch me! Oh my god, don't you dare touch me!'

Why the hell was she acting this way? 'Lucie, it's not that b-b-big a deal. We c-c-can talk about the affair, if you want, but it's just not that important.' He groaned in frustration. Damn it, his words were letting him down and it had never been more important to get them right. To let Lucie know that nothing could come between them. 'The affair's over and d-d-done. History.'

43
Lucie

She was going to be sick. 'Mum. Get Keeley outside,' she gasped.

'No, Lucie, you need to know—'

'Now!' she yelled. Keeley didn't need to see her like this.

Jack—no, *Jackson Schenscher-Mackereth*—still stood over her, the lines of his face hard and tense.

The face she had kissed. The face she had come to love.

'Jesus,' she groaned. She had to have it wrong. Surely she had leaped to some ridiculous conclusion that would earn her a lecture from Geoff. 'You're not related to Jeremy Mackereth, are you?' she pleaded, praying harder than she ever had. Jack had to say no, that the name was just some weird coincidence. The universe toying with her.

Yet it made complete sense that her father would go into business with his partner's son.

'Dad? Guess you could say that,' Jack responded with a faint chuckle, as though relieved the secret was out. 'He—'

She shoved her hand up, palm out. 'Get away from me. Get the fuck away from me, you sick bastard.'

'Lucie, what the hell's wrong?'

How dare he say that? He'd just admitted to knowing about her affair with his father, and knowing about it, he'd *pursued* her. She pushed past him and staggered towards the door as the office rang with appalled silence.

How much more shocked would the staff be if they knew she'd fallen in love with the son of her baby's father?

Or that she hadn't only fallen in love with Jack. She'd made love with him.

Just like she had with his father.

She barely made it outside before the contents of her lunch came up, splashing the pavement and her shoes.

Mum was there immediately, her arm around Lucie's waist. 'Come on, baby. Keeley's in the car. Let's get you home.'

She shook her head. 'Jack . . . Jack is . . . Jeremy's . . .'

'I know,' Mum said, her voice hollow. 'Both Mackereth.'

'Why didn't you warn me?'

'Would you have listened? I haven't been able to tell you anything for years, Lucie.'

'This, oh god, *this*, surely you could have. I *needed* to know.'

'And I warned Jackson that he *needed* to tell you, but he refused,' Mum said defensively. 'Look, I know it's not ideal, and it's something of a shock, but it's simply not that bad.'

'Are you mad? Mum, we-we—' Bile flooded her mouth again as images of her and Jack, alone, together, filled her mind.

'Come on,' Mum said, her tone absurdly pragmatic. 'Let's get home. I'll make a cup of your special tea. You just tell me which one.'

∾

Lucie refused to go back to Chesterton: if there was a risk Dad would have been ashamed of her before, it was now a certainty. Instead, she insisted they go to her rental in Settlers Bridge.

For once, the large house didn't seem too large: she needed space, room to be away from everyone, even Keeley, while she tried to process what had happened.

Except there was nothing to process, because there was no way to justify what she had done.

She ripped her clothes off and showered in scalding water, scrubbing furiously as though she could remove the taint of her actions.

Wrapped in the tatty dressing gown that had travelled across the country with her, the threadbare fabric for the first time failing to provide any comfort, she cracked the bedroom door, making sure Keeley wasn't nearby. The silence throughout the house meant Mum, Keeley and Dash would be out in the garden, their favourite haunt.

She dropped onto the bed and, with shaking fingers, keyed her phone.

'Tumbleweed.' Geoff's familiar voice had lost the magic she needed. 'Can't talk right now, I'm headed into a late meeting. Everything okay?'

'No,' she said on a sob.

Geoff's quick intake of breath almost choked his question. 'Keeley?'

He couldn't hear her shake her head, the movement splashing tears down her face. 'She's fine. But I've screwed up, Geoff. I need you.'

'Give me two seconds,' Geoff said. His voice faded as he apparently turned away from the phone, directing someone to make his apologies at the meeting. 'Okay, Luce. I'm all yours. Shoot.'

Where did she start? 'Geoff,' she whispered, 'he's my soulmate. He's everything I could ever want.'

'Well, that's degrees of awesome. I take it we are talking about Thor the hot farmer?' Geoff said cautiously, evidently trying to pinpoint the issue.

She took a deep, ragged breath. 'Jack is Jeremy's son.'

Silence greeted her words. 'Geoff?'

'Sorry,' he said slowly. 'Just processing. You mean your Jeremy? And your Jack?' She nodded, and although he couldn't see her, he kept talking. 'Okay. So this isn't really a problem. Unusual, but not . . . a problem.' He sounded doubtful, even as he tried to reassure her.

'Not a problem? Geoff, Jack is Keeley's *brother*.'

'Yeah, okay. Though it'd be half-brother, right?'

'Because that's so much better,' she snarled. 'For fuck's sake, Geoff, I had sex with him.'

'Okay, you need to calm down, Lucie. Is there someone who can pick me up at the airport? I'll get the next flight over.'

'No,' she moaned. 'Don't. Don't even tell Finlay about this, okay? I'll work through it. It's just . . . how could Jack even do that? How could he let this happen?'

Geoff's tone was thoughtful. 'Does Jack know about Jeremy? You said he asked whether Keeley's dad was still in the picture and Jack's, what, around thirty? There's a chance he didn't know what his old man was up to five years ago.'

God, she wished she could seize that glimmer of hope, even though it didn't lessen the magnitude of what they'd done. Instead, she gripped the phone tighter. 'He knows, Geoff. That's the worst part. He even said the affair doesn't matter, that it's history.'

'Ah,' Geoff grunted. 'Okay, that is an issue.'

'He played me.' Even as she said the words, she frantically tried to think of ways to disprove them. What they'd had was so good, so perfect—

'Lucie.' Geoff's tone was uncertain, as though he was unsure whether to pursue his point. 'Jack stands to benefit financially regarding the property if he's with you, right?'

'No!' she exclaimed. 'He's adamant about not wanting anything to do with sharing the property, says it has the potential to mess up our relationship.'

The silence on the other end of the phone meant Geoff was waiting for her to reassess her words. The sob that welled deep within her tore painfully from her throat.

'Open, honest and trustworthy. The hallmarks of any good conman, right?'

'Well, let's not jump to conclusions,' Geoff said.

'Conclusions about how damned sick this is, you mean?' she fired back.

'I know its raw right now, Lucie, but you have to tackle him about this. I'd usually tell you to give it some space, but I think this time you need the protection of your fury.'

'Tackle him to do what? Rationalise? To find out what degree of depravity we're talking about? Why he intentionally slept with his . . . god, I don't even know what I am.' She dropped her head into her hand, tugging at her hair. 'There's no bloody way to rationalise this. What is the point of talking to him? What am I going to achieve?'

'Closure. Find out why he hid who he is, or whether this is just some monumental mistake.'

'Pretty damn sad when I'm hoping to discover my latest relationship is "just" a mistake, isn't it?' she said, the words trembling. 'I should never have come home.' She closed her eyes, letting the back of her head slam the bedhead. 'I can't talk to him, Geoff.' She didn't dare. She couldn't bear to discover that Jack was no better than his father, both of them out for what they could get. And she couldn't stomach seeing him, knowing what they'd done.

What they could never do again.

Geoff tapped his keyboard. 'I'm on the red-eye tomorrow. Don't worry about picking me up, I'll hire a car.'

'No,' she sobbed, 'don't, Geoff. I don't want anyone to see me. I just want t-to—' Curl up and die, that was what she wanted to do.

'Where's Keeley?' Geoff asked, always the balanced voice in her darkest moments.

She didn't have the luxury of shutting out the world, not this time. Lucie was a mother, and she had obligations. She had to make the world right for Keeley. Her lip wobbled and she clutched the robe to her aching chest: Keeley who adored Jack just as much as she did. 'With Mum. Out in the garden.'

'Okay, so she's safe?'

She nodded. For the first time ever, Lucie realised she could rely on her mother. 'She is.'

❧

She needed to sleep, needed to pretend her life had never happened. But Jack hammered on the front door, demanding to be let in, and eventually Mum had to threaten to call the police in from Murray Bridge to make him leave.

Lucie threw her phone into the hall, enjoying a grim sense of satisfaction as it smashed against the solid wall, as though simply turning it off wasn't enough to block his incessant calls.

In the few minutes she forced herself from the room to tuck Keeley into bed, she refused Mum's offer of a Valium dug from the bottom of her Gucci bag. But maybe she should have drugged herself, because a sleepless night punctuated by crying jags didn't leave her feeling any better the next morning.

She showered, cleaned her teeth and tried to push her hair into some semblance of normality, for Keeley's sake.

Not that anything would ever be normal again.

It was early; she could tell by the birds' ridiculous carolling in the back garden. She wanted to go out, clap her hands, chase them and all their sounds of happiness and joy away.

Instead, Lucie stumbled towards the kitchen. To hell with tea, she needed coffee.

Mum sat directly opposite the door, her hands wrapped around a mug. Alongside her sat Geoff.

She should feel relieved to see him. He always saved her. But Geoff would insist she confront Jack. 'I'm not doing it,' she blurted before he even had chance to speak. 'You shouldn't have come, Geoff. I'm not talking to him.'

'Monica tells me you refused to let him in the house last night, or to take his calls.'

Lucie laughed harshly. 'May as well give the neighbours something to gossip about with randoms belting on my door at all hours. God knows, they'll have enough to talk about when this gets around.'

Mum sighed as though she was the one who was exhausted. 'I was hoping you'd make more sense today, Lucie. You wouldn't listen to me last night but, really, I don't know why you're making this such a drama.'

Apparently, being able to rely on her mother to care for Keeley didn't mean Lucie could expect a sudden measure of compassion.

'I thought that becoming a parent had helped you grow up, become less self-centred,' her mother continued, twisting the knife.

'It's open.' Geoff headed off their argument as he called down the hall in response to a loud knock on the front door.

Lucie froze. 'You didn't?' she hissed. 'Jesus, Geoff, you don't get it. There's nothing he can say to make this okay.'

'But *he* would at least like t-to know what *this* is,' Jack said from the doorway behind her.

She whirled around, snatching one of the kitchen chairs to put between them, as though she needed physical protection. '*You'd* like to know? Seems to me you're the one who has all the facts, the one who's been hiding the truth. I'm warning you, just keep the hell away from me and my daughter. Y-you with all your talk of protecting Keeley, of understanding she's the most precious thing in my life. You're sick!' Why the hell was some part of her still registering how he looked, his face drawn and tormented, as though she wasn't the only one who hadn't slept?

Jack raked both hands through his long hair. 'Lucie, if you're not happy with the will, take it all, I don't give a damn. I told you all along I'll walk away from The Twenty. You're far more important to me than any land, any dream.'

'The will? Why the hell would I care about the will? It's about your lies, Jackson Schenscher-*Mackereth*!' The legs of the chair skittered then snatched at the lino as she thrust it towards him.

'What lies? I've never lied to you, Lucie, not about a bloody thing. If you want to call this—' he waved a hand between them '—off, that's f-fine.' His tone hardened, his jaw firm. 'But just don't give me this hot and cold bullshit act. I'm not into playing games. My father did that for years, pretending we were a happy family as though he wasn't laying into us the moment the door was closed. There's no room in my life for lies.'

Lucie stared at him in disbelief. 'So your father's a bastard. At least that's something we can agree on. But the lies? You clearly learned how to do that well enough.'

'What are you talking about?' he scowled, his voice low and angry. 'You don't know my father.'

She scoffed. 'Don't know him? Oh, I *know* Jeremy Mackereth in every sense of the word.'

'Jeremy? What does he have to do with my father?'

She hesitated. She'd expected Jack's anger, his embarrassment at being caught in his lie. But not bewilderment. 'You said he's your father.'

'Tell her, Jackson,' her mother harped. 'You should have told her in the first place, but now you're making it worse than it needs to be.'

'Jesus, how can he make it worse?' Lucie shouted. 'Tell me what? That you and your father are so very different? Oh, wait, you fed me that bullshit before, didn't you? How you'd learned not to be like him. Or are you going to say that I should trust you? Even though you barefaced lied to

414

me? Tell me what, Jack?' she shrieked, hysteria clawing up her throat as her world crumbled. 'I know, why don't you just bring your father in here to back you up? He's really good at lying, too!'

Geoff thrust to his feet, coming to stand behind her, gripping her upper arms. 'Jack. Your father—'

Jack held up a hand, cutting him off. 'Has been dead for fifteen years. And, while I'd like to politely pretend I'm sorry about that, he was nothing but an oxygen thief. So I'd appreciate if you would *never* compare me to him.' His tone hard, the words drove into Lucie like ice daggers.

She staggered, only Geoff's grip holding her up. 'But Jeremy—'

Jack lifted an eyebrow, his expression a mask of cold fury. 'Jeremy Mackereth is my stepdad. Or he was, for six years, back when I was a kid. Long enough for them buy a house here but dump Sam and me on our grandparents while they travelled the world. And long enough for my mother to decide Sam and I should take his name, before she got bored with the deal and buggered off again.'

She'd known Jeremy had a house in Settlers Bridge. But did Jack's story make sense? Or was there was a hole there, somewhere, something she couldn't put her finger on?

'Okay. Good, good, good,' Geoff breathed behind her, and she knew he also was frantically churning the information in his mind, trying to make sense of it. 'So you're not actually related to Jeremy Mackereth?'

'Not by blood. He blows in and out of my life every few years,' Jack said. 'Last time was when he put me in touch with Gus. He knew I'd had my eye on a river block for the past decade and he helped me persuade Gus to buy The Twenty by saying it'd be an investment in Lucie's interests.'

Jeremy had actually kept one of his promises and told Dad about her studies? Lucie could barely hear Jack over the beat of the blood pounding in her head. But she welcomed the refrain: Jack and Keeley weren't related. Maybe . . . maybe . . . maybe it would be okay. Her head spun, pulsing as though it would explode as she tried to put it all together. 'Why didn't you just tell me that you know Jeremy?' she asked, her tone plaintive. Jack hadn't meant to hurt her, but why the secrecy?

Jack lifted a questioning hand, his voice softer now that she wasn't so strident. 'You didn't mention that you know him either—it's not like we shared a list of mutuals.'

'The affair makes him a bit more than some random mutual, don't you think?' she flared.

Jack glanced from Lucie to her mother, his forehead creased. 'That's what I don't get,' he said to Monica. 'Why you were so keen to have me—'

'No!' Mum shrieked, the coffee mug flying from the table as she pushed to her feet.

'—out the affair,' Jack finished, looking bewildered.

'Not that!' Mum said wildly. 'I wanted you to tell Lucie who you are, that you're Jeremy's stepson, so she'd have all the facts before it was too late. Before she fell in love with you. Because it's not fair how you men do that, how you make us fall in love, then rip it away. I wanted you to tell Lucie so she would have a chance, a choice. Not be trapped by her feelings.'

Lucie's blood ran cold. Her mother had betrayed her again. 'Oh my god,' she said. 'You told Jack about the affair with Jeremy to break us up, instead of simply warning *me*? You wanted that desperately to hurt me?'

'How would the affair with Jeremy affect us?' Jack said, sounding puzzled.

'I didn't tell him a thing!' her mother shrieked.

Lucie rounded on Jack. '*She* told you everything. Why are you still pretending Jeremy is nothing more than a mutual acquaintance?'

'I don't know what else y-you want to call him,' Jack said desperately, dragging a hand through his hair as though he could untangle his thoughts. 'He and your mum were done and dusted decades ago.'

44
Jack

Even angry, Lucie was gorgeous. She spat fury like a cornered possum, her dark eyes ablaze, the colour high in her cheeks.

He wanted to feel hurt and misjudged by her reaction, yet all he could think about was how to make this right, how to explain that she was everything to him. He couldn't fathom why she was so upset about Jeremy, but if Monica thought that outing her thirty-year-old affair with his stepfather would help, he was in.

'Jeremy and . . . Mum?' Lucie gasped, as though the idea was inconceivable.

'Yeah. Good old Adelaide, right? Three degrees of separation and all that. Jeremy warned me that negotiations with Gus would be tricky because Monica held a grudge from back when they were teenagers and was always dead against anything he pushed for.' He shrugged. 'But I figured seeing as he'd worked with your dad for years, there'd be no drama. Guess I wasn't entirely right on that one.' He shot a dark look at Monica: unable to retaliate against Jeremy, she was going out of her way to screw up his life instead.

Monica gave a small sob, burying her face in her hands and Lucie swung towards her.

'*Jeremy*?' Lucie whispered, the colour draining from her face.

'Lucie, they were kids,' he said, surprised by her reaction. Obviously, she loved her dad, but he hadn't expected her to be so protective of him. He took her limp hand and guided her around the chair she had pushed between them. 'Sit down.' He dropped to his knees in front of her as she collapsed onto the seat, but her focus was on her mother.

'You and Jeremy?' she repeated. 'Mum? Tell me that's not true. Oh my god, that's why you were so angry with me, isn't it? Because Jeremy was your l-lover.' She folded both hands across her mouth, her eyes huge.

Monica snapped upright, her moment of weakness disappearing. 'No. He was never my lover. I loved him, he didn't love me.'

Lucie laughed mirthlessly. 'He definitely has a pattern, then, doesn't he? But why didn't you just tell—wait! To be clear, you and he never . . . ?'

Lucie's intense interest in the old affair was strange, but Jack guessed she saw it as a betrayal of her father.

'Never,' Monica said, and Lucie blew out a tremulous breath.

'What Jeremy and I had was so *special*.' Monica put a snide inflection on the word. 'We thought—or rather, apparently, *I* thought—we would wait until after we were engaged. But Mack called it off.'

'Mack?' Lucie said with a note of appeal, as though she hoped they were talking about different people.

'Mack. Mackereth. Using surnames was cool back then,' Monica said. 'Anyway, Mack—Jeremy—found someone else. Several times, apparently,' she added acerbically with a hard glance at Jack, as though he had something to do with his stepfather's choices from decades back. 'I never expected to have to see him again. But when he turned up at Blue Flag, all I could do was try to limit how much he was in our lives.'

'Limit?' Lucie exploded. 'I could never work out why it was that you posted your letters to me from Settlers Bridge, when it's so far from home. But it was because Jeremy lived here, wasn't it? You were keeping a connection with him. Limiting how much he was in *my* life, not yours.'

'He sold his house here years ago. As Jack would know,' Monica said, as though trying to shift the blame back to him.

'Why didn't you just tell me about him?' Lucie demanded of her mother. 'At least when I got older. Why keep it a secret?'

Geoff grunted, but Jack wasn't sure whether the sound signified agreement or disapproval at Lucie's odd fascination with her mother's affair.

'You mean when you decided to chase after him?' Monica snapped, her tone dripping with acid.

'What?' Jack's neck cracked as he jerked his head towards her.

Monica eyed him coldly, then turned back to Lucie, her narrow face settling into lines of offence and disapproval. 'I had no choice but keep it a secret. You were too young, too self-absorbed to notice, but the only thing your father loathed more than accounts was having to go out there and sell himself to market his products. He simply wanted to grow the strawberries. As much as I loathed it, having Jeremy with Blue Star eased that pressure for Dad. But I had made Georgius a promise, long ago, that I would never again see the man who broke my heart. So all I could do was pretend that the Mack I knew had ceased to exist. I owed your father that loyalty.' Monica spat the last word as though it was a challenge.

Lucie's fists clenched, the knuckles white against her tan skin. 'Is that your idea of loyalty? Lying by omission?'

Monica seemed to deflate, her sigh sorrowful. But maybe she was a bloody good actor. All Jack knew was that she was a good liar, trying to throw Lucie under the bus to hide her own near-infidelity. 'If I'd said anything, Georgius would have fired Jeremy on the spot—and probably had a heart attack a decade earlier, as a result. So I did what I had to do. I stayed away from the business, kept my secret and your father had the help he needed.'

'But why didn't you tell *me*?' Lucie ground out, punctuating each word with a balled fist slammed on her thigh.

Jack covered her hand with his, trying to ease her pain, although he couldn't understand it. He knew she'd been close to her dad, but still her reaction seemed over the top.

'Are you going to pretend that you wouldn't have seen Jeremy as a challenge, a chance to score on me?' Monica shot back.

'Oh my god,' Lucie muttered. 'You're still making this all my fault? Don't you think maybe I would have been revolted and run a million miles?'

Jack glanced at Geoff, as though the guy could help him make any sense of the conversation. Geoff gave a sharp shake of his head, but Jack wasn't sure whether he was indicating his own confusion or directing him to shut the hell up.

Monica sighed. 'You forget, I know what Jeremy is like. You wouldn't have run.' She gave a cynical laugh. 'It was hard enough to persuade you to move a few hundred kilometres.'

'Because I didn't bloody well know what I should be running from!' Lucie shouted. 'Because you didn't tell me. I'm not saying I'm blameless, I made my own choices. But, hell, it would have been nice to make them with all the facts!'

Choices?' Jack repeated. His heart suddenly seized, a hard lump of denial in his chest. What the hell—was there some truth in Monica's wild accusation? He tightened his grip on Lucie's hands, as though he could prevent her slipping away. 'You . . . and Jeremy?

Lucie shifted her gaze to him, her face crumpling with doubt and despair. 'It wasn't only because of Mum's history with Jeremy that she didn't want you in partnership with

Dad.' The base of her throat hollowed and flexed, her lips trembling, and she freed one hand to clutch the crystal on the leather thong around her neck. 'It's because Jeremy is Keeley's dad.'

Jack released her hand and straightened. Absorbing the news. Processing. Putting everyone in their place in his mind. Jeremy and Monica. Then Gus and Monica. Jeremy and Lucie. Then him and Lucie. 'Wow,' he exhaled heavily. 'I did not see that one coming.' He nodded thoughtfully. 'Keeley's dad? Huh, cool.' He hoped Lucie didn't catch his slightly doubtful tone.

'Cool?' she gasped. 'How are you not freaked out about this?'

It was almost a relief to find she didn't view the situation as entirely normal. It was going to take him a while to get his head fully round it. He lifted one shoulder. 'We all make mistakes.'

She shook her head slowly. 'I can't claim it was a mistake, Jack. Because it wasn't. I was young and stupid and infatuated and all of those things. But in the only way I knew how back then, I did love Jeremy. And I can't pretend it was otherwise. Not to make myself feel better, or to save your feelings.'

He dragged his fingers down his face, not letting his gaze drop from hers. He was going to need a bit of time to process her words, but he knew that he wasn't going to let his stepfather's past get in the way of his own future. And he couldn't ignore that Jeremy had been instrumental in that future, engineering the partnership with Gus that brought Lucie into his life. For that, although any kind of family Christmas dinner was going to be bizarre, Jack could find a whole lot of forgiveness in himself. More than anything, he admired that Lucie would stand her ground and tell the truth rather than lie to appease him.

He realised instinctively that everything hinged on his reaction. 'Considering his history,' he gestured at Monica to make his meaning clear, 'that sounds like more understanding than Jeremy deserves. I mean, he's always done right by me, and I liked the guy but . . .' But Jeremy had known who Lucie was, and still he'd pursued her.

Okay, on second thoughts, that Christmas dinner family reunion was totally off the table.

'Yeah, I know,' Lucie said with a watery smile. 'Big "but", huh?' She rubbed a hand tiredly across her forehead. If this revelation had floored him, god knows how she felt. She turned to Monica. 'I still don't understand why you sent me away. Jeremy had happened, we'd broken up. It was done.'

He liked the finality of those words, the way she sliced the air with her hand.

A frown creased Monica's brow and she answered too fast. 'I told you, Dad would have been devastated by your affair.'

'I'm not buying that,' Lucie said decisively. 'Dad liked Jeremy well enough to employ him.'

Monica flipped from beseeching to belligerent. 'There's a vast difference between giving a man a job and giving him your daughter. Particularly when he's old enough to be her father.'

Jack winced.

'Dad would have dealt with it,' Lucie said firmly. 'I realise that now, so surely you had to know it all along? This was always your issue, Mum, not Dad's. Wasn't it?'

Monica pressed her lips together, the thin line moving as she chewed on them before taking an uneven breath. She clutched a teaspoon between both hands so tightly, he thought the steel would bend. 'I couldn't cope with the fact that if you stayed here, you might have everything I'd ever wanted. You would effectively have stolen all of my dreams. Jeremy was the love of my life: I wanted to marry him, I wanted to have his children, I wanted to grow old with him. Now I get to grow old as . . . what? The grandmother of his daughter. That was so far from being my dream, it was a nightmare.'

'Jesus,' Geoff grunted.

Jack balled his fists, controlling his instinctive desire to protect Lucie. Monica might be late laying it all out there, but she wasn't pulling any punches now.

Monica dropped the teaspoon and reached across the table towards Lucie, as though she'd take her hand. 'More than anything, though, I was trying to save you.' Her voice softened. 'If you'd stayed, you would have persuaded Jeremy that you could work it out. But I've watched him for more than thirty years, Lucie. I know he is irredeemable.'

Jack winced, but the characterisation was fair. Jeremy was a smart guy, had been a decent mate. But he'd never been the kind of man to stick a relationship.

'Better it was a decisive, swift cut,' Monica continued.

'Shouldn't that have been my decision to make?' Lucie's anger brought colour back to her face. She swapped her gaze to Jack. 'Don't get me wrong, I don't want a damn thing to do with Jeremy,' she reassured, then jabbed a finger at her mother. 'But it should have been my choice.'

'Perhaps,' Monica said. 'But you couldn't see what would happen because you were too busy living your life. I'd already been there. I could step away, see both the past and the future. And, as you'll discover, it's hard to allow your daughter to make choices you know will hurt her.' She gave a brittle laugh. 'It's funny how dreams change. When we're young, we dream of being rescued. As we get older, we want to become the rescuer. I wanted to save you, Lucie. Save you from the hurt and pain I knew the relationship would bring.' Monica drew herself up straight, taking her elbows from the table and placing her hands neatly in her lap. 'In any case, I obviously made the right decision for you, as you never tried to come home. Not to your father or to Jeremy.'

'You can't blame someone for leaving if you've pushed them away, Monica,' Geoff cut in.

The guy had balls. Even somewhat chastened, Monica was scary as all get-out.

Monica lifted a hand and rapped her thin fingers on the table, ignoring Geoff. 'I gave you the chance to make a life for yourself.' Jack caught the tremor in her voice, the hint of uncertainty. 'Far more of a life than you would have had here.'

'You hurt all of us, you know.' Lucie's despairing tone was more heartrending than her fierce passion. 'Dad. Me. Keeley. Now she'll never get to know her grandfather.'

'Keeley,' Monica whispered. Her shoulders caved, as though she couldn't fight anymore. 'Mack—Jeremy—hurt me, caused pain you'll never be able to imagine.'

'You think?' Lucie said dryly.

Jack's teeth clenched. He didn't want Lucie to hurt. But even more, he didn't want anyone else to have the power to hurt her.

Monica shook her head, dismissing Lucie's interruption. 'So I knew I couldn't bear to have his child around, to live every day with the evidence of the end of my dreams. Yet now I realise I was wrong, so very wrong.' She gave a short, sad laugh. 'Which, if it makes you feel better, means I ended up hurting myself, too. I've missed out on four years of Keeley's life. I never got to hold her as a baby, watch her take her first steps, say her first words.'

'How is that supposed to make me feel better?' Lucie said defeatedly, obviously picking up that the half-arsed apology was actually Monica's lament for her own loss, rather than what had been stolen from Lucie and Keeley. 'I don't get any pleasure from your pain, Mum.'

'Geoff!' Keeley squealed from the doorway. 'You is here for my birthday?' She raced into the guy's embrace. 'Is Dash birthday, too. Jack making a party for us.'

Both of those facts were news to him, but he'd run with it. 'Sure am. And I bet Mr Unicorn will be there, too,' Jack said.

Geoff shot him a grin. 'I've heard about this character.'

Keeley leaned back against Geoff so she could look over the table. 'Nanna, I thinked and I want the princess cake, please.'

'Then that is what you shall have.' Monica's emotions were swiftly under control.

Geoff swung Keeley into the air, landing her on his shoulder. 'How about we leave your mum and Jack to sort out the party plans, princess? We'll go hunt down a treat breakfast somewhere.'

'You won't find anything other than the IGA open this early,' Monica said. 'I've promised to teach Keeley to make pikelets so we shall do that today. We'll need white flour, Lucie. I don't know how to make them with that substitute you use.'

Lucie nodded tiredly. 'A treat is fine. Take my car to the shop, Geoff. Lucie's seat is in there.'

'I do know how to drive responsibly,' Monica huffed, not missing the slight. 'In any case, I really would rather go home first and change out of yesterday's clothes. *If you want to have clean ideas, change them as often as your shirt.*'

Lucie shook her head in disbelief and gave her mother a long, level look. Then, hand on her necklace, she blew out a deliberate breath, as though doing away with all of her negative emotions. 'Maybe you should just leave spares here, Mum.'

'Very well,' Monica said with the faintest glimmer of a smile. 'This once we shall make do with yesterday's clothes. But I'll wash my face, at least. There are clean towels in the hall closet, I presume?' Not waiting for a reply, she swept from the room. 'And that was Picabia, in case you're wondering,' she called back.

'Totally wasn't.' Geoff rolled his eyes and set Keeley down. 'Princess, give your mum a hug and we'll go and get you dressed. Then maybe we'll take a slow walk to get breakfast provisions with . . . Nanna?' He lowered his voice, leaning closer to Lucie. 'Seriously, I'm low-key worried about poisoned apples.'

'Wicked witches does that, silly Geoff,' Keeley scoffed. She kissed Lucie then flung her arms around Jack, squeezing him tight.

He returned the hug, more than ever aware of how damn lucky he was that Lucie had allowed him in their lives. But was she letting him stay?

'You're right, princess,' Geoff said. 'Silly me. Okay, I think Mum and Jack have to do a lot of talking.' He raised a meaningful eyebrow at them both as he guided Keeley through the doorway.

Silence ruled the room, the tick of the clock above the stove thunderous as they waited long minutes for the house to empty. Lucie stood so that she was closer to him. Her eyes were fixed on his, direct and honest, as always, but she mashed her lips together.

His chest constricted.

The front door slammed.

'I don't know how to unpack this, Jack.' Lucie's quiet words trembled. 'I don't know where we go from here. I was so angry with you, and I had no right to be.'

'It's okay. I get that your whole focus is on protecting Keeley.' She seemed unsteady, exhausted and washed out, and he took her upper arms to stabilise her. God knows, he felt pretty crushed himself.

She leaned in closer but shook her head. 'Not my whole focus. It should be. But I was devastated because I thought you'd lied to me. It's just—I feel vulnerable. I don't love Jeremy.' Her gaze was earnest, as though making sure he understood. 'But I did. Yet he lied to me, never told me about Mum, and now . . . I feel like maybe nothing is safe anymore. Like I shouldn't risk anything, because ultimately it affects Keeley.'

His heart clenched tighter than a coil of barbed wire. 'I'm safe, Lucie. I promise, what you s-see is what you get.'

'Rationally, I get that. But emotionally . . . it hurt so much, Jack.'

'When Jeremy left, you mean?' He had never expected to hate his stepfather. No, not hate: the surge of acid emotion was jealousy.

Lucie shook her head. 'No, not that. I *thought* that hurt, but it was nothing compared to the pain of the last few hours. Thinking that you'd lied to me. That I'd lost you. I felt like . . . like I was going to break, Jack.' She thumped a hand on her chest. 'So now I realise that loving you is too dangerous. I can't take that kind of pain again.'

If there were a way, he would shoulder all her hurt. Instead, Jack could only share his own hard-learned lesson. 'Isn't pain how we know we're alive?'

A frown creased between her eyes. 'Is it?' she whispered. 'Do we always have to hurt to live?'

'To live and to love, I think. You're a mother, so you tell me. Did having Keeley hurt?'

She nodded, and his heart clenched in anguish for her.

'But was it worth it?'

'A thousand times over.' The beautiful angles of Lucie's face softened at the memory.

'So, out of that pain, love was born.' Jack touched a finger to the base of her throat. 'Snow quartz. Symbolises clarity and helps you recognise potential.' Lucie knew he wasn't really down with her fascination with crystals, it was a step too far for his practical nature. But he'd secretly studied them each night he was alone, so that he would better understand the woman he loved. Perhaps now those crystals would help him reach her, help him find the words to explain that he would always be there for her, for Keeley. That they could dream a life together and work to make it a reality. 'Maybe we have to accept that love hurts. But it can be worth it, if we open ourselves to its potential.'

Lucie closed her hand over his, fastening his fingers around the crystal, gripping with surprising, desperate strength. 'Clarity,' she whispered. Eyes closed, she nodded, then took a deep breath before looking up at him. 'Meeting you was fate—thanks to Dad. Becoming your friend was my choice. But just loving me isn't enough, Jack. I understand now that I need someone who is *in* love with me.'

'Someone?' he managed.

Lucie bit her lip, still clutching the crystal and his hand. Then she shook her head decisively. 'There have been enough half-truths and living in the shadows around here. No, not someone. Not anyone. I need *you* to be in love with me, Jackson Schenscher-Mackereth.'

Jack waited, knowing that her words would complete them.

Lucie's dark eyes held his gaze, a tiny smile curving her lips. 'Because I am totally and utterly in love with you.'

Epilogue
Monica

Monica glanced around the white-and-beige lounge room, bending to plump a cream cushion. She'd had Lynn take away some of the clutter so she could bring in her furniture from the farm, and Jack had eventually hung the teaspoon cabinets on the wall, repurposed to display knick-knacks Keeley made from gumnuts and paper straws and other odds and ends. The teaspoons were in the kitchen drawer, easily accessible for Keeley's tea parties, where she invariably served the pikelets she had mastered the previous year. She was a smart girl. Shades of her mother.

'Nanna!' Keeley called from her bedroom.

She'd kept the princess room just the way Keeley liked it. After all, her granddaughter spent so much time at the Settlers Bridge house, it made sense for her to have her own space there, as well as her bedroom at the River

Gum Cottage. Of course, Monica hadn't rented a house for decades, but in a way she quite enjoyed the circularity of life. It was almost as though she was young again. And, of course, the income no doubt helped Lynn out.

Dash skittered into the kitchen, somehow managing to sound as though he had at least eight legs. Monica scooped him up. 'You're going to need a jumper on today, young man. It's chilly out.'

Keeley stomped in behind him. 'I'm all ready, Nanna.'

'Do you have the card you made for Ma-Ma?' It had been a trial coming up with titles for Evie and Paul. As honorary great-grandparents, they obviously didn't hold the same status as her, and didn't rate the generally accepted names. But, with a little persuasion, Ma-Ma and Pa-Pa had appealed to Keeley.

Evie hadn't fought her for the title, though Monica suspected, from the wicked glint in the older woman's eye, she knew the root of the corruption. Evie's wit and somewhat cynical attitude made her a worthy friend. Well, *employer*, she supposed. But that was a technicality that only existed because Monica chose to assist the elderly couple by providing the daily care Lucie had organised.

Keeley looked stricken. 'I took the card home to show Jack.'

'Well, that's not a problem,' Monica said. 'Put your boots on, it's horribly muddy out. We'll go past The Twenty first and collect it.' She'd planned to drop by anyway. She wanted to pick up some of the lavender truffles Lucie had made and take them out to Evie. And she'd cut a large bunch of St John's wort for the thriving naturopathy business Lucie had established in the boot room at the back of the River Gum Cottage. Lucie said the produce needed to be fresh to maximise the potency of the healing oils, although whether Lucie could get to making her salve would depend on what she and Jack were up to on the property. Since Georgius had used his will to negate Jack's debt, leaving that portion of The Twenty to Jack and the other half to Lucie, the couple had made huge strides with their plans to live sustainably.

Which was all very well if you liked goat's milk and alfalfa sprouts, but she would far rather visit Samantha's cafe for a nice cup of coffee and a vanilla slice.

Keeley flung her arms around her waist. 'I love you, Nanna.'

She rested her hand on Keeley's curls. 'Love you too, Keels.' It was hard to remember the time when she had believed that holding herself back from loving was the way to avoid heartache. 'Shall we wear our blue lace agate necklaces today?' Not that she needed a ridiculous crystal to bring her peace of mind, but the matching stones Lucie had given them guaranteed that someone would remark on her and Keeley's eyes, on how much her granddaughter resembled her.

And that was always welcome.

Acknowledgements

My thanks to my publisher Annette Barlow at Allen & Unwin, for hanging onto her faith in me and keeping the contracts coming. And, as always, my endless gratitude to editor extraordinaire Courtney Lick, who curtails my rambling and manages to soothe my savage beast when I disagree (usually ill-advisedly) with some minor point. Thanks also to editors Christa Munns and Simone Ford for keeping me on the straight and narrow—and coping with my pretty awful punctuation (sorry, Simone!).

I appreciate the assistance of Kathy Prosser at Aussie Apricots, Mypolonga, who provided information on riverside block sizes, the history of soldier-settler allocations, past and current land usage trends, water licensing and irrigation facts—and the down-low on a juicy local scandal, which I'm dying to use! Not all of Kathy's information made it into the book, but it was all invaluable in helping me form Jack's story. As always, any departures from fact are either my mistake or a deliberate reframing for literary purposes.

Sandie Docker, author of much-loved women's fiction, dealt out some harsh love in the form of feedback on the original, somewhat convoluted draft of *The River Gum Cottage*. Thanks for making me pull my socks up, Sandie (I've finished sulking now).

And, last but most definitely not least, endless gratitude to the readers, interviewers, bloggers and reviewers who create the most fabulous ripple effect whenever they talk about a book they've enjoyed. Your support is what keeps the stories coming.